ABSOLUTE PROOF

Peter James is a UK number one bestselling author, best known for writing crime and thriller novels, and the creator of the much-loved Detective Superintendent Roy Grace series. Globally, his books have been translated into thirty-seven languages.

Synonymous with plot-twisting page-turners, Peter has garnered an army of loyal fans throughout his storytelling career – which also included stints writing for TV and producing films. He has won over forty awards for his work, including the WHSmith Best Crime Author of All Time Award, Crime Writers' Association Diamond Dagger and a BAFTA nomination for *The Merchant of Venice* starring Al Pacino and Jeremy Irons for which he was an Executive Producer. Many of Peter's novels have been adapted for film, TV and stage.

Visit his website at www.peterjames.com
Or follow him on Twitter @PeterJamesUK
Or facebook.com/peterjames.roygrace
Or Instagram @PeterJamesUK
Or youtube.com/peterjamesPJTV
www.peterjamesbrighton.com

By Peter James

The Detective Superintendent Roy Grace Series

DEAD SIMPLE   LOOKING GOOD DEAD
NOT DEAD ENOUGH   DEAD MAN'S FOOTSTEPS
DEAD TOMORROW   DEAD LIKE YOU
DEAD MAN'S GRIP   NOT DEAD YET
DEAD MAN'S TIME   WANT YOU DEAD
YOU ARE DEAD   LOVE YOU DEAD
NEED YOU DEAD   DEAD IF YOU DON'T
DEAD AT FIRST SIGHT

Other Novels

DEAD LETTER DROP   ATOM BOMB ANGEL
BILLIONAIRE   POSSESSION   DREAMER
SWEET HEART   TWILIGHT   PROPHECY
ALCHEMIST   HOST   THE TRUTH
DENIAL   FAITH   PERFECT PEOPLE
THE HOUSE ON COLD HILL   ABSOLUTE PROOF

Short Stories

A TWIST OF THE KNIFE

Children's Novel

GETTING WIRED!

Novella

THE PERFECT MURDER

Non-Fiction

DEATH COMES KNOCKING:
POLICING ROY GRACE'S BRIGHTON
(with Graham Bartlett)

ABSOLUTE PROOF

PETER JAMES

PAN BOOKS

First published 2018 by Macmillan
First published in paperback 2018 by Macmillan

This paperback edition first published 2019 by Pan Books
an imprint of Pan Macmillan
20 New Wharf Road, London N1 9RR
Associated companies throughout the world
www.panmacmillan.com

ISBN 978-1-4472-4096-9

1 3 5 7 9 8 6 4 2

A CIP catalogue record for this book is available from the British Library.

Typeset by Palimpsest Book Production Limited, Falkirk, Stirlingshire
Printed and bound by CPI Group (UK) Ltd, Croydon, CR0 4YY

TO THE LATE HARRY NIXON

A LETTER FROM THE AUTHOR

Dear Reader,

I want to personally introduce you to the novel you're about to read, as I am more excited about it than anything I've ever written. I've been researching and working on it for an almost unbelievable twenty-nine years!

Like my Roy Grace novels, the book is fast-paced and twisty, an international thriller that moves between the UK, America, Egypt and Greece. The central character, Ross Hunter, is an investigative journalist – a role very similar to that of a detective – and an early part of the book mirrors something very closely that happened to me in 1989, when I had a phone call one afternoon, out of the blue, from an elderly sounding gentleman.

He assured me he was not a crank; he had been a decorated pilot during the War and was a retired academic. He had been given absolute proof of God's existence and had been told by a representative of God that the author Peter James was the person to help him get taken seriously.

The notion of what it would take to conclusively prove the existence of God intrigued me and I went to see a modern-thinking Bishop friend. He told me that for most religious people of all denominations, proof is the enemy of faith and if someone credible claimed to have proof of God they would most likely be assassinated – because whose God would it be? There would be divisions within Anglican, Catholic, Judaic, Islamic and all other belief systems, and nations like China would not like a higher power usurping them.

That was my lightbulb moment! I knew then and there I had the potential with this story for a terrific thriller, one that people could enjoy purely as a white-knuckle ride, but also in which there would be opportunities to explore the biggest question for all mankind . . .

Absolute Proof has been published in hardback, paperback and ebook formats, and as an additional thrill for me the audiobook is read by the wonderful Hugh Bonneville.

ABSOLUTE PROOF

1

January 2005

The downtown LA bar was a dump, and that suited Mike Delaney's mood right now. There was one free stool, between a middle-aged couple playing tonsil-hockey on the right and a surly looking drunk in a lumberjack shirt, jeans and work boots, hunched over a tumbler of bourbon on the left.

Delaney perched on the cracked leather cushion, caught the bartender's eye and ordered a beer. On the wall above was a fuzzy television screen showing a football game, with the sound up loud and no one watching. The drunk peered at him with eyes like bloodshot molluscs.

'Know you, don't I?' he slurred. 'You're the guy from that show, right? Some while back? That's you, right?'

The bartender placed a beer in front of Delaney. 'Paying cash or opening a tab?'

'A tab please.'

'Got a credit card?'

It was that kind of a place.

He eased the AmEx from his fraying wallet and laid it on the bar. The bartender palmed it.

'Mickey Magic, right?' the drunk said. 'That was you, on television.'

'You remember the show?'

'Yeah. Yeah, I do. It sucked.'

'Thanks, pal.'

'No, I mean it. How many years back was it? Ten?'

'About that.'

'Yeah.' The man downed the remnants of his drink. 'You were crap. No surprise it got dropped, eh?'

Delaney took a long pull of his beer and ignored him. It wasn't just his show that had been dropped; his agent, an hour ago, had now dropped him, too.

'Know what, kiddo?' Al Siegel had said over the phone from his swanky office on Wilshire. 'You gotta realize you're a dinosaur. I was struggling to get you anything before you went and freaked out. Your career's over. Face it, you're pushing sixty. Go retire, move to Palm Springs, take up golf or some-thing, you know? I got another call coming in I have to take. Listen, I'm sorry, kiddo, but that's how it is – are we done?'

That's how it is. Boy, did Mike Delaney know that. You were over the hill at forty here in Tinsel Town. When he went to his old haunt, The Magic Castle, hardly any of the magicians there were over thirty. He'd screwed up the last engagement his agent had gotten him, doing close magic at a big movie star's party in Bel Air. Messed up a trick and then lost the plot and threatened to deck the arrogant guy at the table who'd laughed at him.

'Know what I'm saying?' the drunk persisted. 'You gotta admit, you were shit.' He peered at him again. 'And you know what, you look like shit.'

He felt like shit.

The drunk snapped a finger at the bartender. 'Another Jim Beam, double, on the rocks.' He turned back. 'Beer, huh? That's a wuss drink.'

'That so?'

The bartender laid down the tumbler, filled to the brim with whiskey and ice cubes, in front of the drunk.

The man raised his glass. 'You should be drinking proper liquor like this, Mr No-Damn-Good Magician. Cheers.'

He tipped in a mouthful, then, almost instantly, spat it out. 'Jesus!' he yelled at the bartender. 'What the hell have you given me? I ordered Jim Beam. This isn't whiskey, it's goddam beer!'

The bartender, a tall, sad-looking man in his seventies who had been there forever, shook his head. 'I'm sorry, mister, you're mistaken. Maybe you've had enough?'

'This is goddam beer, I'm telling you! You trying to poison me or something?'

The bartender produced the half-full whiskey bottle and showed it to him. 'I poured it from this.'

'Yeah? Well pour another.'

Irked, the bartender produced a fresh glass tumbler and poured from the Jim Beam bottle. To his astonishment, a beer froth rose in the tumbler all the way to the rim and above, then spilled down the sides.

Mike Delaney smiled to himself and said nothing.

2

April 2005

Ross Hunter's Friday morning started with the hangover he had promised himself he would not have. Just like he had promised the same thing last week, and the week before. And the one before that. It had been the same every Friday morning since he had joined the *Argus*, as a junior news reporter, eighteen months ago.

But he had no inkling of quite how different today was going to be.

Coming up to his twenty-third birthday, Ross was tall and fit, with close-cropped dark hair and a good-looking but serious face, as if he was forever analysing everything, which most of the time he was. Except now.

Feeling like he had an axe stuck in his skull, he could barely think straight. He climbed blearily out of bed, yawned and headed into the bathroom in search of para-cetamol, cursing that he had done this to himself yet again. Every Thursday evening he agreed to have just one quick drink with his colleagues, to be sociable. Every Thursday night he ended up staggering home, late, from the Coach House pub in central Brighton.

Part of the reason was one particular young crime reporter on the paper, Imogen Carter. He fancied her like crazy but she seemed a lot more interested in one of the subs. And she was able to hold her drink better than all the rest of them. But he did feel that, little by little, she was starting to take more notice of him and flirt just a bit more each time.

Thanks for another great hangover, Imo, and for letting me watch you wobble off towards the taxi rank arm-in-arm with sodding Kevin Fletcher.

Recently graduated from the School of Journalism at Goldsmiths and highly ambitious, Ross looked forward every morning to getting to work in the newsroom, where as a junior reporter he could be sent to cover just about anything. A traffic accident, a cot death, a fire, a court hearing, a charity presentation or something as dull to write about as a school open day. All grist for the mill, learning his trade, cutting his teeth on this good, respected local paper.

Hopefully a workout in the gym, then a long, uphill cycle ride to work would clear his head. He listened to the local Radio Sussex news on the clock radio as he wriggled into his tracksuit and pulled the laces tight on his trainers, hoping for a big breaking story, the kind of story where one day in the future he might make his name and fulfil his dream of a national paper front-page splash and byline.

Gulping down the capsules with some water, he went into the kitchenette of his draughty second-floor flat off Portland Road, the faint smells of last night's cooking from the Indian takeaway two floors below not helping the nausea that accompanied his splitting headache. A couple of mouthfuls of banana at the breakfast table made him feel a little better; washing them down with some apple juice, he stared at the Post-it note stuck to the surface with the reminder he had written: *Dad's birthday card.* He'd pick one up somewhere, later.

He went downstairs, walked past his padlocked bike in

the hall and let himself out into the darkness and falling drizzle.

After a brisk, ten-minute jog he arrived at the gym shortly after 7 a.m. Several people were already there, working out in the mirrored room with its faint smells of sweat and polish. Most were alone on the treadmills, cross trainers and spinners or doing weights and crunches, and a few were having personal trainer sessions. The pounding beat of Queen was too loud for Ross's head as he stepped onto a cross trainer to do a twenty-minute workout programme and cranked its display into life.

As he built up his pace, watching his heart rate rising – 110 . . . 120 . . . 130 – he was startled to suddenly hear his brother, Ricky, scream out his name. So loud, so close, it felt like he was standing right beside him.

Except that wasn't possible. Ricky lived in Manchester, 260 miles away, where he worked as a trainee hotel manager. They rarely spoke on the phone but Ricky had emailed him only yesterday afternoon to discuss what present to buy for their dad's sixtieth birthday next week.

An instant later it felt like electricity was shooting from the swinging handles of the cross trainer into his arms. He was unable to move. His feet stopped in the treads. His brain began to spin, like it was hurtling down a fairground helter-skelter. In a flash of panic he wondered if he was passing out from lack of sugar.

Or was he having a heart attack?

The room swayed, a sea of grey machines that were now blurs.

He was being sucked into a long, dark tunnel. His whole body was spinning wildly now and he clung desperately to the handles of the machine. Ahead, in the distance, he saw a light, growing brighter and more intense by the second.

Images flashed past. An embryo. A baby. His mother's face. His father's face. A ball being thrown. A whiteboard with a teacher holding a marker pen and shouting at him. His life, he realized. He was seeing his life flash by.

I'm dying.

Seconds later, the bright light at the end of the tunnel enveloped him. It was warm, dazzling, and he was floating on a lilo on a flat ocean. He saw his brother's face float right above his.

'It's OK, Ross, yep? We're cool?'

Ricky. Whom he had loathed for as long as he could remember. He disliked the way Ricky looked, the way he spoke, the way he laughed, the way he ate. And he knew the reason why: Ricky was his identical twin. It was like looking into a mirror every time he saw him.

There was meant to be love between twins. A special, inseparable bond. But he'd felt none of that over the years.

Instead, just intense dislike.

It was mainly because his parents had always favoured Ricky, yet Ricky couldn't ever see that.

As soon as he was old enough to leave home, he'd escaped, got as far away from Ricky as he could. A different college, in a different city. He had even, at one point, been tempted to change his name.

Now his brother was drifting away, steadily being absorbed into the white light, and turned towards him, arms outstretched, as if desperately trying to reach his hands, to grasp him. But he was moving away too fast for Ricky, like a swimmer being sucked backwards in a rip current.

Ricky called out, with almost desperation in his voice. 'We're cool, Ross? Yes?'

'We're cool,' he replied.

The light swallowed his brother. Then momentarily dazzled him.

Faces were peering down at him. The light had changed. He smelled sweat, carpet, unwashed hair. Could hear pounding music. His heart was thudding.

Someone was kneeling over him.

'You OK?'

Ross stared around, bewildered. With a stab of panic he wondered, had he died?

Helping hands picked him up, steered him over to a weights bench and propped him up while he sat down.

A muscular man, one of the gym's personal trainers, stood over him, holding a plastic beaker of water. 'Drink this.'

He shook his head, trying to clear it.

'Maybe you overdid it on the machine?' a voice said.

'No – no, I . . .' He fell silent. Confused.

'Shall I call a doctor?' someone else asked.

He shook his head again. 'No, I'm fine – honestly. I'm fine. Maybe I need some sugar or something.'

'Stay sitting here for a few more minutes, until you're sure you're OK.'

Someone held out a spoonful of honey and he put it in his mouth.

'Are you diabetic?' a voice asked – one of the staff, staring at him with concern.

'No, no, I'm not.'

It was ten minutes before he felt able to stand without holding on to anything. A short while later, after persuading them he was OK, he left the gym and walked home in a daze, oblivious to the rain, the cold, to everything. He let himself in through the front door and climbed the stairs, feeling exhausted. It felt like climbing a mountain.

He'd said he was fine to the people at the gym, but he didn't feel fine at all. He felt terrible. As he let himself into his flat he heard his phone ring and felt it vibrating in his pocket. He pulled it out and looked at the number on the display, which he didn't recognize.

'Hello?' he answered.

He heard a tearful woman's voice. 'Ross? Oh God, Ross?'

It was Sindy, Ricky's girlfriend.

'Hi,' he said, still very shaken. 'Sindy? What's – what's up?'

She burst into tears. He listened to her sobs for several seconds before she composed herself. 'Ricky.'

'What?'

'The police just came round. Ricky was out for his morning run, in the park. A tree fell on him. Half an hour ago. A tree. Crushed him. Oh God, Ross, oh God, he's dead!'

3

After years of constant bombardment and fighting in the city streets, there were no hotels standing intact in Lashkar Gah, and those staffing them had either been killed by the Taliban or fled, long ago. Because of security difficulties and many journalists being kidnapped, some executed, it was considered a no-go area. The members of the international press corps who did venture there were housed in a tent within the white-walled compound on the city's edge that was the coalition military base for Helmand Province.

All the journalists had been advised to blend in as much as possible. To grow beards, wear beige clothing, not to walk around alone, and specifically not to wear their press tabards if unescorted, as that would single them out as kidnap targets.

'Twinned with hell', Ross Hunter had texted his wife, soon after arriving here. Or rather, had attempted to text her. It had taken over a day of regularly trying for the text to finally send. Unlike the other seasoned reporters, this was his first experience in a war zone, and at this moment, constantly afraid, he very much intended it to be his last. For large parts of most days, the sun was obscured by dense smoke from artillery and burning buildings. The air was thick with the stench of decomposing bodies, drains and cordite, and the muezzins' five daily calls to prayer were mostly drowned out by the constant clatter of helicopters.

Ross sat on the dormitory bed he had been allocated, scratching his beard, which itched constantly, trying to file his latest piece for the *Sunday Times* on his laptop, connected online through his satellite phone. To add to his discomfort, he was feeling something of a fraud. A year earlier he had written a piece in praise of a former boy from his old school, who, he discovered, had lost both eyes and his right hand in battle several years ago, and had managed to rebuild his life, marry, father two children and go skiing. In the piece, he talked about the unseen bravery of our troops in battle.

The article had prompted an enthusiastic response from the Army brass, inviting him to see a war zone for himself and to meet the troops. But it had also prompted a flood of emails from serving soldiers across almost all ranks, some giving their actual names, but many anonymous, telling him horror stories about how the UK government was letting down the troops and causing many unnecessary deaths through shoddy equipment or the lack of it altogether – thanks to scrimping on budgets.

The *Sunday Times* had arranged the necessary documentation and paid for Ross to attend a mandatory three-day Hostile Environment Training Course, in Hertfordshire. He had been flown out here on a C-130 Hercules military transport plane, via a circuitous route. His one request to the newspaper was that they did not print anything derogatory until he was safely back in the UK. He wasn't too keen on the idea of antagonizing any of the people responsible for keeping him safe out here.

And he quickly found there was much to write about. A complete exposé on the treatment of British troops by their own government. The list included British soldiers being provided with guns that jammed, armoured cars inadequately plated to protect them from landmines and a total absence of battlefield beacons to prevent deaths from so-called friendly fire.

In his last dispatch Ross had quoted, anonymously at the man's request, a senior military commander likening the equipment supplied to being on par with long-out-of-date mobile phones. And to add insult, there was now little sympathy, support or aftercare for the terribly wounded and often permanently disabled troops after they were brought back home. As Ross focused, he tried to blot out the background noise of the distant – and sometimes, worryingly, not so distant – pounding of shells, bursts of gunfire and sporadic bomb blasts that continued into the night.

Most of the foreign correspondents seemed to know each other like old mates, including the photographer who had been assigned to him, making him feel a distinct outsider. Some of them were playing poker with a deck of cards that had seen better days, beneath a sluggish ceiling fan that performed the trick of moving the hot, humid air around the interior without either creating a draught or changing its temperature. Ross was perspiring, feeling clammy and sticky and in need of another cold shower, although he'd had one a few hours ago. During the past two weeks he had barely slept, and he felt permanently exhausted and nauseous with fear.

But overriding all that at this moment, as he typed, was his anger. Anger at the aftermath of the rape and massacre of women and children by the Taliban he had witnessed. Anger at what he had seen in the house he had entered with troops, yesterday, where an elderly man was hanging from a makeshift noose, with the naked body of a young woman on the floor beneath him, her throat cut. They'd heard a woman crying, and found the man's wife hiding in an upstairs cupboard. All she could say, repeatedly, was a single word. An Afghan soldier translated it for Ross.

Why?

Where was God, he wondered? Having fun watching this carnage?

It really felt, being here in Afghanistan, witnessing atrocity after atrocity every day, that God had a very sick mind. That He had created this entire world for His own warped pleasure. To see what new layers of humanity the people He had created would strip away next.

Lying on his bed in the small hours, never sure if a shell was going to land on the press tent and blow him and the rest of them to pieces, Ross had his headphones plugged in, listening to music to try to block out the sounds. Imogen, whom he had married two years ago, had made him up playlists for this trip from some of his favourites: Maroon 5, The Fray, Kaiser Chiefs and loads of his country and western favourites, David Allan Coe, Willie Nelson and Patsy Cline.

On the night before the attack, he had tried to text her, as he did every night.

> I love u so much babes. Don't wish u were here coz wouldn't wish here on anyone. Thinking of u gets me through every day & night. Tried to read book on War Poets u gave me, but too sad. Especially the one that goes, 'If I should die think only this of me'. Because then he did die. I dream of being back in your arms. Seen some terrible things. How can any human being do this?
> Love u XX

To his relief, and as rarely happened, the text went through on his first attempt.

The following morning was a date that would forever be imprinted in Ross's mind. Friday, 17 July. The coalition forces scented victory, finally. The Taliban were on the retreat. Two squads were being sent to secure an area in the city that the Taliban had been pushed out from yesterday. The reporters were told at the briefing there would be a good opportunity to see and photograph more Taliban atrocities but, they were warned, there was still danger from snipers.

Ross had discussed it with the photographer, Ben Haines, a wisecracking, indefatigable veteran of several previous war zones, and they'd decided that with twenty United Nations ISAF soldiers, as well as several local soldiers and guides to protect them and the other reporters from around the globe, it was a relatively small risk to take. It was all new to him and it would be good for his career to see live action – he would learn fast.

At 7 a.m. they set off through the ruined city, the rancid stench of decaying human flesh filling the humid morning air, and helicopters, like giant cockroaches, hovering low above them. Ross and Haines wore helmets, military fatigues and body armour beneath their tabards printed boldly front and rear, PRESS. All around them were bleached-out walls pockmarked by bullets, bombed or shelled ruins and angry graffiti.

It happened without warning as they walked out of the protection of a narrow alley into the central market square. A maelstrom of fire that seemed to come from every direction at once.

An ambush.

Ross stood, for some seconds, rooted to the spot, more curious for an instant than afraid. Then a rocket took off the top half of the head of a local man right in front of him, in a spray of brains and blood. A grenade exploded a short distance away. He felt the blast and saw soldiers, journalists and photographers thrown to the ground. It was closely followed by another blast and a decapitated head rolled along the dusty ground, mouth open, eyes open in disbelief.

Ben, crouched with his camera, filming away, suddenly screamed in agony and began rolling across the ground like some demented whirling dervish.

Crazed with fear, everywhere that Ross looked he saw spurts of fire. From the rooftops of the single-storey dwellings. From the windows. Directly to his left was a tall, badly bombed-out shell of a bank, its front doors missing. He raced towards the entrance, the air around him thick with vicious cracking noises and bullets kicking up dirt and stone splinters. He entered the bank's darkened interior, looking around in blind terror.

The gunfire continued behind him.

He stopped and looked back.

Straight into the eyes of Ben Haines, who was lying on the ground, a pool of blood flowing from his side, his camera a short distance in front of him. He was trying to move, to crawl, to reach his camera, but couldn't.

'Ross! Help me! Help me! Please help me! For God's sake help me!' he shouted in an agonized, desperate voice.

All around lay soldiers, reporters and photographers. Some were motionless, others writhing or crawling.

A massive volley of shots rang out. Several stopped moving.

'Ross!' Haines screamed. 'Oh God, help me!'

Ross ran back out and towards him, zigzagging as he had been briefed if under fire, oblivious to the danger, determined to do what he could for his friend, somehow drag him to safety. But when he was just a few yards from the photographer, he heard a burst of machine-gun fire. Haines shook like a rag doll. Rips appeared in his clothes. His helmet was hit by something that made it fly off. A split second later a small piece of the top of his scalp was blown away and his head collapsed forward into the dirt.

Ross turned in shock and terror and sprinted back towards the building's entrance. He heard more shots, more cracking sounds from bullets as a line of dirt kicked up in front of him. Something pinged off his helmet. He felt a sharp pain in his right foot, then, as he reached the entrance, his head felt like it had been struck by a hammer and he tumbled forward. The stone floor rushed up towards him. Punched him hard in the face.

Had to get up.

Had to.

Saw figures, wearing the headscarves of Taliban fighters, running towards him, clutching blazing AK47s.

Bullets cracked all around him.

He fled into the interior of the building, ducking and weaving, running for his life. Sprinting past desks, the computers all covered in dust and bits of rubble. He vaulted a cashier's desk and ducked down on the far side. Waiting. His right foot felt as if it had a metal spike driven through it and his head was throbbing. He had lost his helmet.

He heard another short, hard burst of gunfire, outside somewhere, followed by sudden, miraculous silence.

No footsteps approaching.

He felt giddy. He looked up. The ceiling seemed to be revolving above him. His body was swaying. It felt as if all the blood was draining from his head. The floor thumped him in the face again, but he did not notice. He lay still.

Sometime later, he didn't immediately know how long, a squeak woke him. Ross found himself staring, in near darkness, into the face of a whiskered rat the size of a rabbit.

'Fuck off!' he hissed at it.

The creature scurried away into the gloom.

In the far distance was a massive explosion.

Another car bomb?

His head pounding, his mouth and throat parched, desperate for a drink of water, he crawled onto his knees, listening. Remembering. The cashier's desk he had vaulted over. Complete silence now. He tried to stand and his right foot was agony. There was congealing blood around his boot. He put a hand up to push his hair back and felt something sticky. He looked at his hand and saw it was also covered in blood.

It was all coming back and he shivered.

I'm alive.

Slowly, cautiously, he stood up, peering over the top of the desk. In the distance he could hear the call to prayer. There was faint daylight ahead beyond the doorway he had come in through.

He looked at his watch. 7.30 p.m. Jesus, it had been a few minutes past 7 a.m. when – when –

He walked painfully towards the doorway and peered out. Bodies everywhere, some coalition soldiers, some press corps, wearing their tabards, and several Taliban fighters, all lying on the dusty ground. The person he focused on was the photographer who had been his mate during this past horrific month.

Ben Haines.

Flies were already swarming around the bodies.

He was about to step forward when he heard voices.

He froze.

Voices getting louder, approaching.

He ran back into the interior, past the empty workstations of the tellers towards the back. Pushed open a door and saw stone steps leading down. He heaved the door shut behind him and noticed steel bolts. Hurriedly, he slid them home and ran on down. One floor, then another. Down. The heat was less oppressive here. In front of him was a walk-in safe, the door, with huge rotating handles on it, slightly ajar.

It took him several seconds to heave the six-inch-thick steel door open enough to slip inside, then using the light of his phone, he looked for an interior handle, but there wasn't one. He just pulled it shut as far as he could.

Standing still, he switched his phone to silent as a precaution, although it was showing there was no signal.

His heart was beating inside his chest, so loudly it was the only sound he could hear. Leaning up close to the tiny crack between the door and the frame, he listened for any sounds of movement above him. For anyone hammering on the door, two floors up, that he had bolted.

He could hear nothing.

Shaking uncontrollably, he looked at his phone screen. Imogen hadn't replied to his last text. Had it not gone through?

The terrible sound of the photographer's voice screaming for help echoed in his mind. The pitiful sight of the man writhing. Trying to crawl. The top of his scalp flying off.

Ross struggled to stop himself vomiting. From revulsion and fear.

Then he sat down on the hard, bare floor in the empty safe. His head was throbbing. Pain was searing through his right foot. And he was desperately in need of water – he hadn't drunk anything since before they'd set off.

He eased off his boot and sock, pulled his foot up and inspected it with his phone's torchlight. There was a jagged, bloody hole in the top, a couple of inches behind his toes, and an even messier hole at the bottom, where a bullet must have passed through. He raised his hand to his head and felt a small indentation, like a groove, above his right temple.

Shot twice?

There must be toilets somewhere in the building, and a kitchen of some kind where he could find water and perhaps a first aid kit. He would look later, when he felt it would be safe to venture out of his hiding place.

He curled up on the floor and slept.

Ten minutes later he was woken by something crawling over his face.

4

July 2009

Am I going to die down here? Alone with the rats?

In his sleep he dreamed of water and food. Simple food. Boiled eggs; stewed apples; French fries; burgers with cheese, relish, tomato ketchup.

When he woke he was in darkness. His phone battery had died. All he had to give him his bearings now was his watch, with the dial that illuminated when he pressed a button on the side. He felt feverish.

He thought of his brother. Ricky. Thought about him constantly with pangs of guilt and regret. He'd bumped into an old school friend at a wedding, a short while after Ricky had died. Jim Banting. Jim told him that Ricky knew Ross didn't like him, but he'd never understood why.

Sitting in the darkness, among the rats, with nothing to do but think, he dwelt on Ricky, feeling full of remorse for how he had treated his brother. Thinking all the time about Ben Haines's body lying outside. Rotting in the searing heat. It could have been him. Or perhaps if he had done something different, he might have saved Ben, somehow.

Last night he had crept up the stairs, unbolted the door and heard voices above him in Arabic. He'd hurried back down in panic, forgetting to bolt the door shut again. So parched with thirst, his tongue felt like an alien object, his lips stuck, painfully, together. His head felt better now, but in the faint glow of the light from his watch he could see pus on his foot. It was going septic. If he didn't get it treated, it would turn to septicaemia and he would die down here, alone. He needed to go and try to find some first aid stuff, quickly.

Then he felt a sharp pain on his right hand. Opened his eyes. Saw red eyes in the darkness.

A rat had bitten him.

'Get off!' He swiped wildly at the creature and stood up, unsteadily, giddily.

His right foot felt like it was burning.

'Fuck you!' he shouted at the rat.

Above him he heard a noise.

Footsteps.

He froze.

Shit. He had shouted out and given himself away.

Footsteps coming closer. Down the stairs. Step by step. Shuffle. Shuffle.

Getting closer.

Shuffle. Shuffle.

Closer.

He flattened himself against the wall.

Closer.

Shuffle. Shuffle.

Thinking. He would surprise the bastard. Jump on him.

Closer.

He heard a little grunt. Someone tugging at the heavy door. Heard it moving. Opening.

He was shaking in fear.

Then the voice of a child, timid, foreign. 'Hello?'

Ross pressed the button on his watch again. And saw the small boy. Dark hair so coated in dust it looked grey, his clothes ripped into rags. He just stared at Ross, numbly.

'It's OK, kid,' Ross said.

'English?'

'Uh-huh.'

'Taliban gone. Gone,' the boy said. He turned and ran away.

Ross heard him hurrying up the stairs.

He waited some moments before following him, warily, unsure this wasn't a trap, but almost beyond caring. He needed water so desperately. Food. At the top it was daylight. He watched the boy run out through the doorway, his arms in the air. Hesitantly, keeping to the shadows, ducking around the furniture but clumsily bumping into some, Ross followed him, weakly. Then peered out into the square.

The bodies had all been removed. Bloodstains had baked in the sun. The city was almost silent, for the first time since he had come here. Moments later he heard the roar of an engine and a metallic rumble. A tank rolled into the square. He recognized it as a Challenger 2. One of the few decent pieces of kit the government had supplied to the troops.

Ross ran out, stumbling, waving his handkerchief in the air.

The tank stopped in front of him, the front hatch opened and a man's head appeared. 'Need a lift, mate?' the man asked in a cockney accent.

'Going anywhere near London?'

'Hop aboard. I'll put the meter on.'

Ross staggered towards the tank, but hadn't the strength to climb aboard. Two of the crew climbed out to help him.

'Press, are you?' the man asked. He had a shaven head and a tattoo on his right arm of a skull topped by a winged eagle.

'Uh-huh,' Ross gasped.

'Which paper?'

'The *Sunday Times*.'

'Gave up reading 'em a long time ago. All them rags. Always a crock of shit, don't you think?'

Ross smiled. He had no fight left in him.

'The editors, they ought to come out here, know what I'm saying? See all this shit for real.'

'Do you have any water?' Ross pleaded.

5

Ten days later, after spending four of them in a US military hospital in Afghanistan, then having to wait for a flight out, Ross finally arrived back in England on a troop transporter, landing at RAF Brize Norton in Oxfordshire. He'd been put on a plane a day earlier than he had originally been told, and decided to surprise Imogen, who was not expecting him until tomorrow.

Arriving early afternoon at Brighton station, in light rain, he took a taxi, ordering it first to stop at a florist where he bought a massive bouquet of flowers, then a wine merchant, where he bought a bottle of Imogen's favourite champagne, Veuve Clicquot.

Shortly after 3 p.m. the taxi pulled up outside the tall, slightly shabby semi-detached building close to the Seven Dials, where they had their top-floor apartment. He paid and tipped the driver, climbed out with his holdall, bottle and flowers, limped up to the front door and let himself into the communal hall, with its familiar smell of damp and an irritatingly loud beat of music coming through the door of the ground-floor flat.

It felt strange being home. Surreal, almost. As if the past few weeks had all just been a bad dream. Except that the scar on his head and his painful foot reminded him of the reality. As did the terrors that came to him every time he closed his eyes.

He glanced at his watch. Imogen, who ran the website for an online magazine in Brighton, wouldn't be home for a couple of hours yet. It would give him time to shower and shave, put the champagne on ice and the flowers in a vase. He was so much looking forward to seeing her. To holding her in his arms, to the comfort of normality again. To making love to her – God, it had been so long – and to just talking to her, telling her about the nightmares he had been through and how thinking of her had got him through it.

Maybe later they'd go out for a curry; they both loved Indian food, and he craved the normality of a restaurant.

He climbed the three flights of stairs to the top floor, slipped his key into the lock and opened the door. As he stepped into their book-lined hall he heard music, The Fray, one of his playlist groups, which surprised him. Was she home?

He entered the living room and saw on the coffee table an open bottle of wine, half drunk, and two partly empty glasses. And a large bomber jacket slung on the sofa.

He frowned.

The music was coming from further along the apartment.

'Imogen? Darling?' he called out, his voice catching in his throat, a sudden cold feeling in his stomach.

He put his bag, the bottle and the flowers down, then walked out of the living room and along the hall, the music getting louder as he approached the bedroom door. He heard another sound, too. A moaning sound. He hesitated outside for a moment before he pushed it wide open.

And saw his wife, stark naked, a look of ecstasy on her face, her hair thrown back, her small, round breasts wobbling, straddling a naked, bearded man.

Then Imogen saw him.

6

The old man was trembling as he made his way slowly up the steep Somerset hillside in the darkness, weighed down by the burden he carried in his heart. The weight of all human history. The eternal struggle of good versus evil. The love and wrath of God. The mockery of Satan.

Unaware of the night-vision binoculars trained on him, he trod carefully on the slippery grass, guided only by the weak beam of his small torch, the GPS coordinates on his phone and the sense of mission in his heart.

Destiny.

His feet were wet inside his sodden brogues and a bitter wind blew through his thin overcoat; a chill clung to his back like a compress of cold leaves. He carried a heavy spade and a metal detector.

It was 3 a.m.

A skein of clouds raced across the sky above him, pierced for fleeting moments by shafts of stone-cold light from the full moon. Whenever that happened he could see the dark shadow of the ruined tower on the hilltop, a short distance to his right. There was a preternatural feeling to the night. The clouds felt like the travelling matte in one of those old Hollywood films. Like a scene he remembered where Cary Grant and Grace Kelly were driving along in a

26

convertible, apparently at high speed, with the scenery passing behind them, but their hair remained immaculately in place.

But tonight, old movies should be a long way from his mind, and his thoughts on just one thing.

Destiny.

Tonight, here, was the start of the journey. He was frail and he did not know how much time he had left on this earth. He had been waiting for the Call for so long he had begun to doubt it would ever come. And when it finally did, it was in His mysterious way.

There was someone whom he had been told could help him, but he was not able to find this person, not yet. And because time was running out on him, he had decided to go it alone.

The air was alive, electric; he could feel the prickle on his skin, like goosebumps. The wind was full of whispers he could not decipher.

He smelled the sweet grass. Somewhere close by he heard a terrible squealing. A fox taking a rabbit, he thought. The squealing became increasingly pitiful and finally stopped.

He checked the constantly changing coordinates on his phone against the ones on the slip of paper he had in his breast pocket. Closer. Closer.

Nearly there.

He stopped, drawing breath, perspiring heavily despite the bitter cold. It had been a tiring two-and-a-half-hour drive to get here, followed by a long walk round the perimeter, in search of a place where he could scale the fence. He'd forgotten his gloves, but it was too long a walk back to the car to fetch them.

Pulling out the scrap of paper, he studied the coordinates in his meticulous handwriting once more.

51°08'40"N 2°41'55"W

He was close.

He felt a burst of energy. Took several paces to the left, then a few more, further up the hill.

Closer!

An instant later, the digits on his phone's compass app matched.

51°08'40"N 2°41'55"W

He was here. On the spot. And at that moment the clouds above him moved away from the moon and a beam of light shone down from above. Someone up there was showing him. This was the sign.

His destiny!

Feverishly he began to dig, gripping the spade as hard as he could with his frozen, arthritic fingers. He dashed it into the ground, stood on it and pushed it down, then levered up the first clump of earth. Several worms squirmed. He moved the spade back a short distance, and dashed it in again.

As he did so, a bright light from out of nowhere danced all around him. Not the moon, now, but the beam of a powerful torch. Two torches. And he heard a voice. An angry male voice.

'Hey! You!'

He turned round. For a moment he was dazzled by the beams directly in his face. Blinking hard, he directed his own more feeble torch beam back. The light fell first on a young, uniformed police officer and next on the middle-aged man, in a parka, standing beside him.

'It's here,' he replied. 'Right where I'm digging. It's right under my feet!'

'What do you think you're doing? Are you crazy?'

'I'm saving the world.'

ABSOLUTE PROOF

'You're defacing private property.'

'Listen, please listen.'

'No, you listen,' the man in the parka said. 'You are trespassing. Who the hell gave you permission to start digging up sacred ground in the middle of the night?'

The old man replied, simply, 'God.'

7

Thursday, 16 February

A Latin quotation was fixed to a wooden door in the cloisters of the St Hugh's Charterhouse monastery, in the heart of the Sussex countryside, fifteen miles north of Brighton.

Mihi enim vivere CHRISTUS est, et mori lucrum.

Its English translation was: *For to me to live is Christ, and to die is gain.*

Behind that door, in the privacy of his spartan cell, Brother Angus sat at his desk, immersed in reading. For many years he had lived a solitary existence, spending many hours a day, seven days a week, on his knees in his tiny prayer cubicle.

But increasingly frequently in recent months he had ventured out of his cell and along the cloistered walkway to the vast, oak-panelled, galleried library. On each visit, he systematically searched for relevant volumes through the thousands of leather-bound titles – many pre-dating the printing press – and brought as many as he could carry back to his cell.

Any monk here could, if he chose, remain inside his cell and never leave it. Food was placed every morning through the hatch beside his door by one of the brothers. Brother Angus was a deeply worried man. And he had no one with whom he could share his concerns for a couple more days, when he was next permitted to speak – for just one hour – on the Sunday walk.

He would be sixty-three years old next month and he did not know for how much longer he would be serving his Lord. Not long, of that he felt certain. Perhaps, because of his sickness, it was likely he might not even see another winter. Perhaps not even another summer. Until recently, he had been content with the life he had been given, although it had not always been thus. A child of the 1960s, he'd once lived the wild life to the full. A university drop-out, he'd been lead guitarist in a heavy metal band, Satan's Creed, and had for many years lived an alcohol- and drug-fuelled rock 'n' roll life touring, mostly in Germany, playing gigs in clubs and out in the open air, and having endless sex with groupies.

Until one day he'd seen the light.

Several lights in fact. Penlight torches of doctors peering into his pupils after he'd massively overdosed on a cocktail of stuff he couldn't even remember taking. Operating theatre lights. Then the brightest light of them all. The light calling him.

A Greek Orthodox nurse in the North London clinic that dried him out, and saved his life, told him about her brother who was a monk, living in a monastic commune on the holy peninsula of Mount Athos. Angus had always been drawn to Greece, and something about the spirituality of the Greek Orthodox religion appealed to him. He converted. Then, with the help of the nurse's brother, he was given a visa to visit.

He went there for five days and stayed for five years, finding deep spirituality in the harsh regime of prayer, work, silence and little sleep. Until one day God called him back to Horsham in Sussex, England. His ageing mother was ill and needed him.

He nursed her through Alzheimer's for the next seven years until she died. He was planning to return to Mount Athos when, one day shortly after her funeral, he happened by chance to drive past the St Hugh's Charterhouse monastery gates and saw the light again, brighter than ever this time. He turned the car round, drove in and gave the vehicle to the Prior to dispose of, telling him to put the proceeds towards the upkeep of the place.

He had been there ever since. And he would never leave now. This was his home – or at least his temporary home, until –

Until he was truly home.

Perhaps.

St Hugh's had been constructed during the order's wealthy days as a safe haven for French monks fleeing the Revolution. But few French monks had ever gone there. Like so many such places in recent centuries, whilst it had been built to house over two hundred monks, new brothers were scarce, and as the older ones died, it was increasingly hard to replace them. There were currently just twenty-three monks in residence, including the Prior and his deputy, and most of them came from elsewhere in the world. Silence wasn't just rigidly enforced, it was naturally enforced, too. Of those twenty-three monks, seventeen of them each spoke a different language. The monastery, like many in the world these days, short of monks, welcomed brothers from all orders.

Few who came stayed for long, finding the discipline and routine too hard. Recommended to be in bed by 8 p.m., they had to rise at 11.50 p.m. for the next prayer session, which they took part in either in the solitude of their private chapels or in the communal chapel, presided over by the Prior.

Brother Angus's cell was unusually spacious by monastic standards. It was on two floors, and he had a self-contained walled garden where he could grow his own vegetables. The downstairs comprised his private chapel, where a picture of Jesus hung on the wall above a statuette of the Virgin Mary, on a makeshift pedestal fashioned from a tree trunk. Along the short corridor was a space housing his workbench and the tools he needed to carry out the maintenance on his cell and garden.

His upstairs quarters, consisting of two small rooms, were furnished with his bunk, a wooden desk and chair, and the prayer cubicle. A turquoise hot-water bottle hung upside down from a hook beside his little washroom, and there was a small wood-burning stove, providing the only heat he had during the long winter months. He should light the stove now, he knew, as he shivered, his cowled habit affording him only meagre protection from the bitingly cold draughts. But he was too immersed in the ancient English of the book he was currently reading, which he was having to decipher as he went along.

Seated at his desk, with his stack of library volumes, Bible, prayer books and prayer timetable laid out in front of him, he had a view out of the window across his garden wall to the peaceful graveyard, surrounded by the monastery's Gothic Revival cloisters.

Rows of plain wooden crosses marking, anonymously, the burial plots of the brothers who had gone before him. And one day soon his earthly body would lie among them. But where would his spirit be?

That was a question that until recently had never been a problem. But he'd spoken about it to the Prior on several occasions, and each time he had been less and less convinced by the Prior's assurances. The more he read and analysed, the more his faith was being tested. What, he had started to think increasingly frequently, if there was nothing? Nothing at all?

What if he had spent all these years – wasted all these years – praying into thin air?

He was searching through the pages of this book now, hoping God would guide him to a passage, buried within it, that would give him answers. It was imperative. He didn't know the outside world any more. So much had changed since he'd first entered holy orders. Even though he'd stepped out of them to nurse his mother, he'd been wary of technology. The outside world had moved on so much in these past decades. He rarely used a phone, though he was becoming more proficient on the internet.

He had been afraid that soon he would become extinct, just rotting bones beneath an anonymous cross, like all the others who had once been here with him and before him.

Then, only a few months ago, he'd received a message. The potential consequences of it had made him even more afraid, because the message was so unclear.

Something was happening. There was religious turmoil in the world that was increasing and polarized in a manner that had not happened for centuries. God was giving him signs and messages every night when he slept. Giving him instructions about going online, moving forward. But instead of clarity, he was feeling increasingly confused.

There were days – weeks, sometimes – when all the messages and signs blurred together, and he had turned from seeking religious texts to scientific ones. Most of the monks here lived without modern technology, but Brother Angus now found himself studying some of its more lateral-thinking exponents. One in particular whom he read avidly was an American called Professor Danny Hillis, the creator of the parallel processor and co-founder of the company Thinking Machines Corporation. The company's motto was: *We're building a machine that will be proud of us.*

And some of the inventor's words struck a chord with him.

There was one particular passage from a talk Hillis had given back in the mid 1990s that had stuck with Brother Angus: 'In man's search for God, I'm not sure we're necessarily going to find Him in the vaults of a Gothic cathedral; I think it is more likely we'll find Him in cyberspace; technology might be the way to open that hailing frequency.'

Angus had risked the Prior's wrath – and possibly exclusion from St Hugh's – by trying to convince him to give each monk a computer with internet access, rather than just the dated and slow communal one in the library, but he would not hear of it. He had dismissed it by saying, 'God tells each of us all we need to know. The day we cease to trust that is the day we should cease to be a monk. Perhaps you are having a crisis of faith, Brother Angus? Just remember, everything that ever was, still is. It is there in God. Seek and you will find. Ask him and he will tell you.'

In his prayers, Brother Angus asked Him with more and more urgency every day. The message he got back was that something was going to be happening, and soon. Something as fundamental to the Christian world as the Coming of Christ.

A Second Coming?

Or a Great Imposter?

8

Thursday, 16 February

Ross Hunter nearly didn't answer the call. The display on his landline read NUMBER WITHHELD. Probably yet another of the automated nuisance calls that were one of the banes of everyone's lives these days. He was on a deadline with his editor, Natalie McCourt, at the *Sunday Times* Insight section, who needed his piece exposing six Premier League footballers involved in a film production tax-evasion scheme by 4 p.m. – exactly twenty minutes away.

Montmorency, their dark-grey labradoodle, lying on the floor close to his desk, seemed focused on two deadlines at this moment. Would he finish that bone, which he was crunching noisily and irritatingly, before his master took him out for a walk? And would they go out for a walk before it was dark?

In the days that followed Ross often wondered just what it was exactly that *had* made him pick up the phone. But he figured even if he hadn't, the caller would have almost certainly rung back. And then rung back again. Ross was pretty high profile these days, and knew better than to ever dismiss any call he received. His first big break, years ago as a fledgling reporter on Brighton's *Argus* newspaper, was just such a call out of the blue. That had led him to the story of a sex scandal, which had ended with a local MP having to resign his seat.

'Ross Hunter,' he said, staring down at the darkening Patcham street from his den in the former loft of the house he and his wife, Imogen, had moved into, trying to start over, soon after that terrible afternoon when he had arrived home from Afghanistan to find her in bed with another man.

She'd begged forgiveness. Told him she'd been dreading being informed by the Foreign Office that he was missing presumed dead, and that she'd sought comfort with an old friend. Desperate to regain normality back then, he'd accepted her explanation and forgiven her. Subsequently he discovered she had not told him the truth and the affair had been going on for far longer. Their relationship had never been quite the same again. It was like gluing together the pieces of a broken glass. It was intact but the joins were ever present. They'd tried to paper over the cracks by moving home. Now she was pregnant, but he still felt doubt.

He just could not trust her. Not totally. There were days when she arrived home late from work with excuses he wasn't sure he believed. Occasions when she awkwardly ended a phone call when he walked into the room. Always then the memory returned. Her naked body on top of the bearded man in their bed.

A delivery van, its lights on, was driving slowly past. He saw one of his neighbours arriving home from the school run in her people carrier. She opened the rear door and from the glow of the vehicle's interior light he could see her helping her small son, an irritating brat who always seemed to be shouting, out of his seat belt.

The voice at the other end of the line was that of a cultured-sounding elderly man. 'Is that Mr Hunter, the journalist?'

'Speaking – who is this?'

'Thank goodness I've got the right person. It's taken me a while to get your phone number – I've phoned every R. Hunter in the phone book in Sussex.'

'You could have contacted me on social media – I'm fairly active on Twitter and Facebook – or you could have just emailed me – my email is on all my bylines.' Ross sipped some tea from the mug on his desk.

'This is not a social media or an email matter, Mr Hunter. Email is not secure, I could not take that risk. I've read many of your pieces. I was very impressed with the article you wrote some years ago for the *Sunday Times* about the government failing our troops in Afghanistan.'

'You read that?'

'My son died in Helmand Province. Killed by *friendly fire*. Or *blue on blue* as they call it, I believe. If he'd been issued with a battlefield beacon, he might still be with us today.'

'I'm sorry.'

'It's not the reason I'm calling, but thank you. My late wife and I tried not to be bitter about it.'

Ross was starting to think this was going to be a waste of some of the very few precious minutes that he had left to finish and then proofread his article.

'I'd just like to assure you I'm not a nutcase, Mr Hunter.'

'Good to hear that,' he replied.

'My name is Dr Harry F. Cook. I'm a former RAF officer and a retired history of art professor at Birmingham University and I know this is going to sound strange, but I've recently been given absolute proof of God's existence – and I've been advised there is a writer, a respected journalist called Ross Hunter, who could help me to get taken seriously.'

'What?'

'I know it must sound strange. I appreciate that.'

'Well, yes, actually, it does.' Ross thought for an instant. 'Exactly which God is it you have proof of?'

'There is only one God, Mr Hunter. There are many prophets and many different faiths, but there is only one *God*.'

'May I ask who told you I'm the person who could help you?' Ross asked, watching his neighbour shepherd her son up to the front door of their bungalow.

'God Himself,' Harry F. Cook replied, simply. 'Could you indulge me for a couple of minutes?'

Ross glanced at his watch, at the precious minutes ticking away. 'I'm afraid you'll have to make it very quick, Dr Cook, I'm up against a deadline.'

'Well, I'll be as brief as I can – or would you prefer me to call you back in a while?'

'No, go ahead.' He picked up a pen and scribbled down the name, *Dr Harry F. Cook, ex-RAF* and *Birmingham University – Art History – retd*. Then he took another sip of his tea, which was turning increasingly tepid.

'Well, the thing is, Mr Hunter, I need to come and see you, and explain everything more fully. I can assure you that I won't be wasting your time. I don't doubt you get oddballs contacting you every day. Would you meet me for just half an hour? I'll travel to anywhere that's convenient for you. And I have something I really believe you might want to hear. I have a message for you.'

'You do? From whom?'

'From your brother, Ricky.'

For some moments Ross sat, numb. Wondering if he had heard right.

'You have a message from Ricky?'

'I do.'

'Can you tell me it?'

'Not over the telephone, Mr Hunter.'

Ross felt a cold wind blow through the room. The lights out in the darkening street seemed to flicker, like a thousand candles guttering in a blast of wind. He shivered, and scribbled down some more with a shaking hand. 'You really have a message from my brother?'

He saw the blue flashing lights of an emergency vehicle heading up the street, and heard the wail of a siren. For a moment, he wondered if he was dreaming this conversation. 'Who exactly are you, Dr Cook?'

An ambulance raced past.

'Please believe me, I'm just an ordinary man, doing what I've been told. Please, Mr Hunter, I urge you, can we meet?'

Ross had dealt with and dismissed many nutters over the years, claiming to have world-shattering stories for him. But something in this man's voice sounded sincere – and intrigued him.

'I'll give you half an hour, OK? I can meet for a cup of tea. If you're able to convince me when we meet that we need longer than that, we'll take it from there. All right?'

'That's very fair. Very good of you. As I said, I'm happy to travel to meet you anywhere convenient to you. If you just let me know when and where?'

9

Thursday, 16 February

Boris perched precariously on the desk inside his large cage, half on it, half off it, hammering clumsily away on the keyboard of the computer. The capuchin monkey, with his round, wizened face, cream mane and long brown tail, although smart by monkey standards, wasn't smart enough to keep a log of his keystrokes. He didn't take any notice of the gibberish that appeared in front of him; all he looked at, expectantly, was the chute from which the occasional treat, such as a peanut in its shell or a banana chip, would appear.

He was aware that if he stopped, the supply of treats stopped, too. He had figured out that if he just kept tap-tapping away on those keys, the treats would keep on coming. Another thing he had learned over the past three weeks was that peeing or shitting on the keyboard didn't work. All that happened then was that no food appeared for a long time.

Dr Ainsley Bloor, former professor of biology at the University of Brighton, who some years earlier had sold his soul to big pharma, was now CEO of one of the world's fastest-growing pharmaceutical giants, Kerr Kluge. The coincidence of the two initials being the same as the first two of the Ku Klux Klan had not escaped many of its vociferous critics. They joked – not entirely without foundation – that the only difference between the two organizations was that the pharmaceutical giant, through its genetics division, knew how to change people's skin colour.

But Boris was unaware of anything beyond his immediate habitat. He just hammered away and the treats kept on coming.

Ainsley Bloor had long been one of the UK's most high-profile militant atheists. A youthful fifty-five-year-old, with sleek silver hair, unfashionably long for a captain of industry, he had a sharp, hawk-like face with piercing grey eyes, and was an ardent disciple of the group known at the time as the Four Horsemen of the Non-Apocalypse – Richard Dawkins, Daniel Dennett, Christopher Hitchens and Sam Harris.

Several of his New Atheism predecessors had attempted to prove the monkey and typewriter theory, which they believed would play a key part in establishing how the world had come into existence by pure chance, rather than by any form of so-called Intelligent Design.

It was a simple, elegant theory: given infinity, a succession of monkeys – or an infinite number of monkeys – at a keyboard, typing randomly, would eventually type out the complete works of William Shakespeare.

So far everyone who had tried this experiment had given up. A colleague of one of the UK's most famous atheists, the late Professor Antony Flew, had tried it and concluded that the number of sub-atomic particles in the universe was many times smaller than the probability of a monkey even typing out one Shakespearean sonnet, of just fourteen lines. Flew's colleague's conclusions were partly responsible for him turning from atheism, to believing in God in terms of Intelligent Design.

In his twenties, Bloor had published three books in his determination to ridicule the notion of a Creator – *The Big*

Goddy, Who Was God's Father? and *Just do the God Math.* The argument – and the theorem it had espoused – was as old as the hills themselves. It could be traced back to Aristotle, through Blaise Pascal and Jonathan Swift to Emile Borel and Arthur Eddington, all of whom had attempted to explain the origins of life through mathematics and chance.

But in Bloor's opinion, the way Antony Flew – and all the others before him – had attempted, or extrapolated from, this experiment was fatally flawed.

They had missed one crucial element.

Sitting in his office, with the computer algorithm he had spent ten years perfecting drilling its way through the three weeks – so far – of the monkey at the keyboard, a pattern was beginning to emerge.

Early days. But progress. Yes, very definitely progress! Of the six monkeys in six cages in the orangery of the former stately home in which Bloor lived with his wife, Boris was emerging as the star.

The thousand-mile march, he thought. As Lao Tzu said, 'The journey of a thousand miles starts with the first step.'

Or maybe keystroke.

10

Monday, 20 February

At 3.50 p.m., ten minutes before Dr Harry F. Cook was due to arrive, Ross was staring out of the window of his second-floor den, thinking about a news story he was writing for the *Sunday Times*, which was going to make a certain National Health Trust executive squirm. He watched an immaculate white Nissan Micra pull up against the kerb in front of his house.

A text pinged.

Looking down at the phone, he saw it was from Imogen.

> Will be home late, around 7pm. Want me to
> pick up a takeaway? Fancy Thai? Beware of your
> nutter – don't want to find you in little bits in
> the fridge!
> Love you. XXXX

He texted back.

> Sure! Chicken satay & a green curry with fish,
> pls. Am armed to the teeth! Love you. XXX

He returned to his work and tried to focus, but he could not. Late home again, he fretted. Why? What was she up to?

He stared, distractedly, out of the window at the man in the little Nissan.

Moments later as he walked downstairs into the hall, the doorbell rang. On the nanosecond of 4 p.m. He opened the front door.

A tall, elderly man stood there, holding an enormous attaché case. He was in his mid seventies, Ross guessed, neatly dressed in a pin-striped suit with matching tie and pocket handkerchief.

'Mr Hunter?' He held out a hand.

'Dr Cook? You found us OK?'

'Oh I did, indeed, thanks to the wonders of satellite navigation.'

As they shook hands, Cook leaned forward and said, staring at him imploringly, with sad, rheumy eyes, 'It is very good of you to see me, Mr Hunter. You do understand that you and I have to save the world?'

Ross gave him a hesitant smile. 'Well, I'll do my best!' Seeing the man so smartly dressed, he wished for a moment he had on more than an old pair of jeans, a baggy jumper and broken-down slippers.

'Mr Hunter, I can't tell you how much this means to me – and to the human race.'

Ross smiled. 'Yep, well, let's see. Come in, can I get you something to drink?'

'A cup of tea would be most welcome.'

A loud barking came from the kitchen.

'Monty, quiet!' Ross called out.

The labradoodle ambled across the black-and-white chequered tiles of the hallway, his tail wagging clumsily.

Ross patted the dog, then turned to the man, who was peering apprehensively at the curly creature. 'He's a total softie – the loveliest nature. Are you OK with dogs?'

'Oh yes, absolutely fine. *Monty*, did you say?'

'Yes. Short for Montmorency.'

'I seem to remember Montmorency was the name of the dog in that wonderful book, *Three Men in a Boat*.'

'That's where we got it from – well, it was my wife's idea, she always loved it.'

It was one of the books that he and Imogen had taken to Italy on honeymoon, and both read – he for the first time and Imogen for at least the third – and laughed at a lot, particularly at the first chapter, when the character was bemoaning feeling too seasick to eat anything on a cruise. Ross and Imogen had been on a free cruise, for the travel section of the previous magazine she worked for, and they'd been flat on their backs, feeling like death, for the first two days crossing the Bay of Biscay in a storm.

'My wife and I were always more cat people,' Cook said.

'We had a cat, too – a rescue one. Cosmo. But he was very odd, used to disappear for days on end sometimes.'

'Very hard to know the mind of a cat.'

'Yep. One day he disappeared for good. Maybe he got a better offer.'

The old man chuckled. 'Maybe indeed.'

Ross guided him to the sofa in their modern, airy lounge, then went through to the high-tech kitchen, which Imogen had chosen, and which had cost more than the national debt of a small nation – far more than they could sensibly afford – and put the kettle on. He made the tea then delved into a cupboard and found a pack of chocolate digestive biscuits, which he ripped open and tipped out onto a plate. Then he placed everything on a tray and carried it through.

A few moments later, seated in an armchair opposite Cook, and with Monty at his side, beadily watching the stranger stirring his tea, Ross said, 'So, you said you had a message from my brother, Ricky?'

'Let me come on to that.' Cook took a sip of his tea, then nodded pensively, lost in his own world for some moments. 'Allow me to begin at the beginning.'

Ross nodded.

'Well, you see, my wife, Doreen, was also an academic, lecturing at the same university, in physics. Six months ago she passed away from cancer.'

'I'm sorry to hear that.'

'Thank you. The thing is, Mr Hunter, during her last days in a hospice she asked me to promise I would go to a medium after she died, to try to make contact with her. She was really insistent about this. Frankly, as a committed Christian, I've never been a subscriber to that kind of stuff, but she became increasingly anxious, so of course I promised I would. And naturally after she passed I had to fulfil my promise.'

'Of course.' Ross was wondering where this was going.

'I managed to find a very nice lady, who came well recommended, and I had a sitting with her about three weeks after my wife's funeral. But instead of any communication from Doreen, a man came through who claimed he had a direct message from God. He said that God was extremely concerned about the current state of the world, and felt that if mankind could have its faith in Him restored, it would help to bring us all back from the brink. As proof of his bona fides, he said God had told him to give me three pieces of information that no one on this planet knows, in the form of compass coordinates. And he said there was a respected journalist, called Ross Hunter, who could help me to get taken seriously.'

'Really? I had no idea I was so highly regarded.'

'This man said he had someone with him who had a message for you. He said he had your brother, Ricky. He asked me to tell you that Ricky knew you did not like him, although he never understood why. But he forgives you.'

Ross stared at him, mesmerized. 'Did he say anything else?'

'He said he wanted you to trust me. He said two names – I think it was Bubble and Squeak. He said remember Bubble and Squeak. Remember when Squeak bit you?'

Ross stared back at him, feeling numb. Bubble and Squeak were two gerbils their parents had given them on their ninth birthday. Squeak had bitten him on his index finger, really hard. How on earth could this man, Dr Cook, possibly know this?

The old man looked down at the attaché case on the floor beside him, and nodded at it. 'It's all in there, Mr Hunter.'

'Right.'

Cook opened the case and pulled out a massive bundle of A5 paper, held together by elastic bands. 'I think we should start with you reading this. This was channelled to me directly from God, over several days following my visit to this medium.' He handed it to Ross. 'I have of course inked those compass coordinates out, Mr Hunter, in case this fell into the wrong hands.'

It was heavy. The top page was creased and blank, with a dog-eared corner. The journalist took a quick look through. There were no chapters, it was just continuous writing on lined paper – slanted, tiny, scrupulously neat, in black ink, with little patches of Tippex here and there, and peppered with annotations of arrows and boxes. The pages were numbered at the bottom. The last page was 1,247. 'Right,' he said. 'Well – if you leave it with me, I'll take a look.'

The old man shook his head, regretfully. 'I'm afraid that's not possible. You see, this is the only copy in existence.'

'You haven't made a copy?'

Cook looked almost affronted. 'I couldn't possibly take the risk of a copy falling into the wrong hands. I need to be here while you read it.'

Inwardly, Ross groaned. As he had feared, this man was beginning to sound like a nutter. Yet he couldn't dismiss what he had said about Ricky. How could he possibly have known about the two gerbils? He'd never written about them and, so far as he could remember, he'd never talked about them. So how did Dr Cook know? How? He held the manuscript up, weighed it in his hands, then flicked through it. 'This would take me about four days to read!'

The old man raised a finger. 'That's about right.'

Ross shook his head and smiled, humouring him. 'You're going to sit there, on my sofa, for *four* days, while I sit here reading this?'

'I cannot let it out of my sight.'

Ross shook his head again. 'Dr Cook, it's not going to happen. I'm sorry, but quite apart from anything else, I don't have four days free. You're going to have to take a massive leap of faith – either you leave this with me and I'll read it when I can, in my own time, or you take it away with you. And before I even start, I need to know a lot more about what's in it. And about this *proof of God* you claim to have. What are these three pieces of information you say you have?'

'I have been given three sets of compass coordinates – the first is for the location of the Holy Grail.'

'The Holy Grail?'

'Correct.'

'That's a pretty big ticket,' Ross said, noting it down.

'Not as big as the next, Mr Hunter. The coordinates for the location of a significant item relating to our Lord, Jesus Christ.'

'Does it come with a certificate of origin?'

'Please, Mr Hunter, as I said to you, I'm not some kind of a crackpot. Please hear me out. The third set of coordinates is for something so important it will, I assure you, have a tumultuous impact – in a truly positive way – on the world.'

'Are you going to tell me what this is?'

'In due course but not now, not until I can be sure you are the right man for this. But let's say the third set relates to the Second Coming.'

'The Second Coming?'

'That is correct.'

Ross thought for a moment and doodled a halo. 'OK. Have you checked any or all of these out, Dr Cook?'

Cook took a sip of his tea, then nodded pensively, lost in his own world. 'Indeed, I have. I've checked out the co-ordinates for the Holy Grail. They give the location as Chalice Well in Glastonbury.'

'Really?'

'As you know, this has long been reputed to be the place where Joseph of Arimathea is buried. Chalice Well is one of Britain's most ancient wells, in the Vale of Avalon, between Glastonbury Tor and Chalice Hill.'

'I do happen to know quite a lot about that, actually. I wrote a large piece on the Glastonbury Festival and the myths surrounding Glastonbury Tor for the *Guardian* a few years ago. All the Arthurian legends about the Holy Grail stem from around there.'

'Good, then you will know what I am talking about. Of

course, there is disinformation put out by enemies of Our Lord. I suspect you are man enough, Mr Hunter, to see beyond that. It's probably one of the many reasons why your name was given to me as the man who could help me.'

'So, have you investigated this claim?'

'I've been there with dowsing rods and with a metal detector, in a wide arc around where the compass coordinates pinpoint, and there is something down there.' Cook's eyes lit up with an almost messianic zeal. 'Chalice Well is run by a group of trustees, whom I then approached, asking for permission to carry out an archaeological dig, but despite explaining why I wanted to do this, they refused.'

'Did they give you a reason?'

'I've done all I can to persuade them, but I just don't think they take me seriously. I believe it would be very different with you – with your reputation for integrity, they'd have to take you seriously.'

'That's very flattering.'

'True, Mr Hunter.'

'There is a very big problem,' Ross said. 'From what I remember from my own research, yes, it is possible that Joseph of Arimathea came to England after the crucifixion.'

'Absolutely,' Cook said. 'Quite likely sailing across the flood plains of the Somerset Levels, bringing with him the chalice that contained some of Jesus's blood from his crucifixion, and arriving at the legendary island of King Arthur's Avalon, a hill now known as Glastonbury Tor. For safekeeping he buried the chalice in a secret place. Seven centuries after the death of Jesus, Glastonbury Abbey was built. In 1191, monks at the abbey claimed to have found the graves of King Arthur and Queen Guinevere. I believe all records were lost during Henry VIII's Reformation – when the Protestant Church broke away from the rule of Rome, and most monasteries were razed to the ground with their relics and records destroyed or lost forever.'

Ross sipped some of his tea. 'Yes, but during research for my article I discovered that many of the medieval monks were pretty commercial animals, and income from tourists was as important for the monasteries as it is for many seaside resorts today. Quite a number of scholars have said the discovery of these graves was made up, aimed at getting religious tourism. How much do you know about this, Dr Cook?'

'I know all about it. As a shrine, the place would have been visited by thousands of pilgrims. There would have been all kinds of holy souvenirs, and charlatans selling supposedly magical relics. But that was the norm for many monasteries. You are quite right to question this, Mr Hunter. And with so much destroyed in the Reformation, it is impossible to establish the truth all these centuries later.'

'Quite. So, have you checked either of the other two coordinates yet?' Ross asked him.

'I have. But I'm afraid that until I have your absolute commitment to helping me, I cannot reveal them.'

Whatever his scepticism at this moment, Ross could not dismiss what Cook had told him about Ricky. And there was a sincerity about Cook that he found touching. Clearly, beyond any doubt, Cook believed in what he had been given.

And yet . . .

'Dr Cook, you said God felt that by having faith in Him reaffirmed, it would help steer the world back from the brink, right?'

'Absolutely, Mr Hunter.'

'But the world never has been on an even keel, has it? Go back over the past thousands of years, and for much of this time almost everyone in the world believed in a god –

or gods – of some denomination, and worshipped them. Throughout time people have done the same horrible things they still do around the world today. Even though they believed ardently in their deity.' He paused for a moment and looked at the old man, who was staring at him attentively.

'Surely, Dr Cook, if he truly is God, and wants to see us all back on an even keel – whatever He means by that – why can't He just do it?'

'Because God gave us all free will. He sent His Son to save us, and we ridiculed and murdered Him. We've been suffering the consequences since. Now we are being given a unique second chance.'

All Ross's instincts were telling him this was a hiding to nothing. A simple Google search would have told Cook all he needed to know about him having a twin who died in an accident.

But Bubble and Squeak?

He decided to play a bluff. He glanced at his watch. 'Well, I'm afraid that's all I have time for – so I don't really know where we go from here. I suggest you take your manuscript away, make a copy and send it to me, if you'd like any further input from me. Otherwise –' he stood up – 'it's been very nice to meet you.'

Cook did not move. 'All right,' he said, pursing his lips and nodding pensively. 'I trust you, Mr Hunter. I'll leave the manuscript with you if you give me your reassurance you will not make a copy of it.'

Ross nodded.

'If you could read it as quickly as you can, then we can meet again and develop our strategy for saving mankind.'

'It's a plan,' Ross said. 'On one condition.'

'Which is?'

'You give me all three sets of compass coordinates you have.'

Cook hesitated, his eyes narrowing with suspicion. 'Why do you need them?'

'You're asking me to take on a big commitment of time. I'd like to check them out for myself.'

'I'll give you the precise coordinates I have for Chalice Well as a token of good faith, Mr Hunter. It's not, of course, that I don't trust you, but I cannot risk them falling into the wrong hands.' He stared intently at Ross again. 'You do understand there are a lot of people who would want them? In the wrong hands they could be extremely dangerous.'

'What kind of danger?'

'Need I spell it out?'

Ross could now see the teacher in the man. The impatient lecturer trying not to talk down to an imbecilic student.

'Lucifer, Mr Hunter.' Cook gave him a reproachful look. 'Satan. Kicked out of Heaven, he vowed to return and is biding his time.'

'OK,' Ross said, trying not to look as though he was humouring the man.

'When I feel it is safe, I will let you have the remaining coordinates. And I will also need your word that you will not attempt to excavate at Chalice Well – or at any of the other locations – without my being present.'

'You have my word.'

With some reluctance, Cook opened his wallet, took out a tiny square of paper, no bigger than two inches by two inches, and handed it to Ross.

He could barely see the tiny handwritten numbers and letters. Squinting, he read the coordinates out aloud:

'51°08'40"N 2°41'55"W –'

Then he read the numbers that followed:

'14 9 14 5 13 5 20 18 5 19 19 20 12.'

He looked at Cook. 'What are those numbers? They're not compass coordinates.'

'No, indeed not.'

'Is it some code?'

'I honestly don't know. I had a good look around Chalice Well whilst I was there, seeing if I could spot any numbers corresponding, but no dice. But they are clearly there for a reason.'

A few minutes later they shook hands at the front door.

'You will be careful with the manuscript, won't you, Mr Hunter?'

'I'll guard it with my life.'

Ross stood there, watching Cook climb back into his car, switch on the lights and drive off. It was a few minutes to 6 p.m.

Then he closed the door, went upstairs to his den and began to read.

The man in the dark-grey Vauxhall saloon, parked a short distance along the road, lowered his night-vision binoculars, switched off the video record mode and made a few notes on his tablet, before starting the car and pulling away.

11

Everybody was happy, and Pastor Wesley Wenceslas liked that. He liked happiness! And nothing made the forty-six-year-old minister happier than to spread the word of the Lord – well, the word of the Lord interpreted by him. An interpretation that, clearly, resonated with many folk. The *happy* Word.

Congregations were growing, week on week, in each branch of the Wesley Wenceslas Ministries. His church in South Kensington had been at capacity – 1,700 – for every service for several years. But when Pastor Wesley himself was preaching, usually on a Sunday evening, there would be hundreds more standing watching on screens outside, in pretty much whatever the weather, all praying and loving together. It was exactly the same in his other three churches in England, in Manchester, Leeds and Leicester. In addition, he now had three firmly established in America and was planning many more there. When you had God behind you, truly the world was your oyster – or, he joked, since he preferred his cooked, Oyster Rockefeller!

The stats were steadily rising on his YouTube channel. He had currently 5.2 million views on his broadcasts, beating the crap out of many mainstream broadcasters, and that made his sponsors very happy. Which in turn made his bank manager very happy. As well as the proprietors of his favourite jewellery, shoe and dress stores in Westbourne Grove, in London, and on Rodeo Drive in Beverly Hills, where he liked to buy gifts to bring back to England for his wife, Marina, who spent most of her time with their three small children. They were being home-schooled for both religious and security reasons in Gethsemane Park, their country estate in Surrey, which was both their home and the headquarters of Wesley Wenceslas Ministries.

His English Rolls-Royce dealers, in Sussex, were happy, too. The sporty, two-door golden-sand-coloured Phantom coupé in which he was currently driving himself was just weeks out of the showroom, and he had another five Rollers, all less than two years old, in his ten-car garage. Jesus may have been poor, he reasoned, but that was then – this is now. The world has changed, aspirations have changed, Wesley Wenceslas wrote and preached. Who is better placed to reach out to those most in need of spiritual guidance? Some pious monk in Jesus sandals on a pushbike or someone in a nice suit and with smart wheels?

Christian churches throughout the Western world were losing their congregations and wondering why. Some figured it was because they didn't appeal to the younger generation, so they stuck in rocking vicars who played electric guitars, turning the singing of hymns into a poor man's U2 concert, but they still didn't get it, did they? They still didn't pack 'em in. Harry Cohn, that old Hollywood movie mogul, had it right when he said, 'Give the people what they want and they'll beat your door down for it.'

'Hey,' Wenceslas liked to joke. 'It was the Good Lord Himself who said that a great *profit* shall come unto the land!'

People wanted colour, light, laughter, beauty, and they loved drama, sensationalism and miracles, but they *needed one thing* above all: *money*. In a hot country you could be poor, and so long as you had something to eat you could wander around barefoot in rags and survive with no roof over your head. But in a cold, wet climate like this country, you needed a lot more. And that cost money. He believed in the Prosperity Gospel: the bigger your bank balance, the more blessed you were.

He knew. He'd been poor once – and not so long ago. It was a simple equation but just like so many of the traditional churches in the USA, the established churches of England had been missing the point for decades – or rather, centuries. Just looking at the size of his congregations showed that. Packed churches filled with worshippers, spreading the message, the love of God. The true interpretation of His Son's teachings.

COMPASSION. TOLERANCE. SUCCESS!

How many churches over the centuries had made that last word taboo for their flocks – whilst amassing vast wealth themselves? How convenient it was to ignore the simple truth that it was the rich men who were the doers, the achievers. It was the rich men who made medicines that actually worked; who made aeroplanes; cars; food; schools; libraries; hospitals; roads. If it truly was, as the Synoptic Gospels had recorded Jesus saying, easier for a camel to pass through the eye of a needle than for a rich man to enter the Kingdom of Heaven, then what kind of place was Heaven, in reality? Pastor Wesley Wenceslas had a pretty shrewd idea.

A Heaven full of nothing but poor people was going to be a pretty crappy place, some kind of massive dumping ground for losers – and who wanted to spend eternity stuck with a bunch of losers?

Besides, he'd always had a problem with that quote, because he knew from his studies of Jesus that the Lord was a fair man. It was both judgemental and inflammatory to imply all rich people were bad and all poor were good. Because the scriptures were subject to a lot of bad translation, he had delved into this in depth, as it defied so much of what he stood for. And he eventually got to the bottom of it, in George M. Lamsa's Syriac–Aramaic Peshitta translation. There he found the word *rope* substituted for *camel* in the main text, with a footnote on the original in Matthew 19:24, which states that the Aramaic word *gamla* means both rope and camel.

It was a eureka moment for Pastor Wesley Wenceslas. What Jesus was really saying was that a rich man needed to focus on the way he lived his life, as hard as he'd have to focus to thread a needle with rope, if he wanted to enter the Kingdom of Heaven.

Of course, it made total sense. The monotheistic religions – those which believed in one God – had achieved their power and status through being control systems. And money was a big part of that. The incalculable wealth of the Vatican had been amassed through just that control – and the guilt it had imbued in the wealthy for nearly two millennia – with that one sentence.

Based on a mistranslation.

A deliberate one?

As he sat cocooned in the comfort of his leather seat, steering with one finger on the wheel, he listened to his own voice booming out of the radio, which was tuned in to his own internet station, Wesley Wenceslas Radio.

'Matthew 5:5 reads, "Blessed are the meek for they shall inherit the earth." Well, OK, think about that carefully, everyone. Just what does that actually mean? That if you try to stand up for anything you're doomed?'

The wrought-iron entrance gates of Gethsemane Park swung open as the black Range Rover in front of him, carrying two of his security guards, approached in the darkness. As the Rolls followed it in through the gates, a second black Range Rover containing two more of his guards was right on his tail. More cameras clocked the convoy as it made its way up the long, tree-lined avenue.

Wenceslas smiled at the view to his right, the grounds illuminated by thousands of lamps. A view fit for the Lord. Acres of verdant green grass gently sloping down to the lake, with his own private sanctuary surrounded by fountains in the centre. That was the place where he regularly spent time alone in devotional prayer and meditating on the Holy Scriptures, whilst at the same time looking at his computer and casting an eye over his weekly finances, to check that his flock were still generously supporting his God-given calling.

The grass was green enough, the colour he liked, and after months of bounteous rainfall, so it should be. But sometimes in the summer months, when the rain dried up and the sprinkler system struggled to prevent it from browning, he would have the grass chemically treated green. Influential and important visitors came to this place and everything had to look perfect for them. And that meant verdant grass. He saw nothing wrong in doing that. All of us needed a little helping hand at times in life, even God Almighty Himself. Perhaps never more so than in these increasingly dark and turbulent years.

Particularly in view of the troubling news he had heard earlier today.

12

'It's on the table and getting cold!' Imogen called impatiently.

'Coming!' Ross replied.

'You said that five minutes ago!'

'Sorry! Coming!'

He carefully put down the thick stack of loose pages from the manuscript Harry Cook had entrusted to him. The only copy in existence. Luckily, he thought. Because that meant no other poor sod was having to lose hours of his life, which he was never going to get back, attempting to read it.

He quickly checked Facebook and Twitter on his computer, but there was nothing of particular interest, then hurried downstairs.

'So what do you think?' Imogen asked as he entered the kitchen, with its panoramic view across the lights of the built-up valley of Patcham.

'I'm sorry, I was just about to come when you called first, then I saw a bit that I thought looked interesting – but wasn't.'

He sat down at the small wooden table, where she had set out the chicken satay and green fish curry, and a tomato salad. 'Smells wonderful!' he said. 'And, boy, do I need a drink.' He opened the fridge and took out a lager.

'Wish I could join you in that!' She raised her glass of mineral water. Beside her on the table was a pile of bills.

'You can still have the occasional glass.'

'I'm being good – I'll make up for it after Caligula's born.'

He said nothing; he had no doubt about that whatsoever.

When her recent three-month scan had shown it was a boy, they'd jokingly nicknamed the baby after the cruel Roman emperor, after the hellish morning sickness Imogen had been through. And besides, Imogen had said, she was not – sooooo not – going to become one of those gooey mums that they both detested. So the name had stuck.

When they'd first got married, they'd both decided that they didn't want children, certainly not for a while anyway. Most of their close friends didn't want children either and, bar one couple, had still not had any. After his return from Afghanistan, Ross's views on having children had hardened. He was genuinely worried about the state of the world and unsure what future there might be for a child. Added to that was his growing realization that he wasn't sure he wanted to spend the rest of his life with Imogen. A woman he could never fully forgive or ever trust completely again. Having a child would bring a major complication.

Those first months after he had come home he'd needed Imogen and she had been terrific – probably through guilt. His nerves were in tatters from his experience in the war zone, he barely slept, and when he did he had constant nightmares. She took care of him, did everything she possibly could to make up for what she had done and to help him mend. But subsequently, in the past few years, he'd felt a void growing between them. Then she fell pregnant.

It was a sign of how little he trusted his wife that he found himself sceptical when she told him she hadn't forgotten to take the pill. He took the view that she'd done it deliberately, perhaps worrying about her biological clock ticking or perhaps in a last-ditch effort to save their marriage. Although they barely made love at all these days, maybe once a month, if that.

Imogen raised her mineral water. 'Cheers,' she said.

They clinked glasses, staring into each other's eyes – something Imogen always insisted on. Then raising her glass again, she said, 'And here's to saving the world!'

'I'm not entirely convinced that if God wanted to save mankind He'd have chosen an elderly, retired history of art professor to do it.'

'He chose a humble carpenter's son last time.'

Ross smiled.

'And this time He's also chosen you to help make it happen. You may not be a humble carpenter's son, but you seem to care as little about money as Jesus did.' She nodded at the bills.

'Some nasty ones?'

'Every month we get nasty bills, Ross. You seem to think I'm a magician at making them go away. I'm not, I'm just very good at juggling them all around with our credit cards. You need a couple of lucrative jobs – and we've got to build up a cash reserve for when I have to stop working to have the baby.'

'Yep, well I think this story has real possibilities.'

'Ross Hunter, the man who has to save the world!'

'It's a big ask.'

'But my husband is up to it?'

'Your husband is up to it.' He debated whether to tell her what Cook had told him about his brother. But he held back. He'd told her before about his strange experience at the moment of Ricky's death, and she had been quite sceptical about it, which had surprised him, considering the traditional religious upbringing she'd had. Or perhaps it was precisely because of that.

'And how is my husband getting on with the manuscript that will help him save the world by bringing it back from the brink?'

'I'm afraid he is fifty-three pages in, out of one thousand, two hundred and forty-seven, and losing the will to live.'

'Persevere, brave soldier!'

'Huh.' He drank some more of his beer. 'Perhaps you should read it – you're the one who calls yourself a Christian.'

'I'm hardly a great example of a believer. But if you knew your Bible at all, you'd know God's views on mediums. And about not trusting anything that comes via them.'

'And can you trust anything in the Bible?'

Imogen gave him a reproachful look.

'Sorry. I'm finding this whole thing very strange.'

'Is it opening up your mind or opening up old wounds?'

'Ricky?'

She nodded.

'I don't know. I don't know what to make of it. I – I have an open mind, you know that. The last few days I've been thinking a lot about God, religion, googling some stuff – I've watched a couple of debates between Dawkins and believers. I guess there's one thing that makes me feel sorry for God, if He is real.'

'Which is?'

'How can He ever win? You have the vicar praying to Him for sunshine so that the village fete won't be a wash-out. At the same time you have the farmer praying for rain so his crops don't die. How does God decide?'

'He has to make decisions based on the greater need.'

'Really? So an eight-year-old girl is dying from a brain tumour. Who has the greater need – the little girl who wants to stay alive? Her desperate parents who want her to stay alive? Or the tumour that wants to destroy her? Was the tumour put there by Satan for fun? Or by God for a purpose?'

'You can't look at it that way, darling.'

'I just did. It's the question everyone asks, that how come if God really exists, He allows suffering.'

'You want to get into a long theological debate?'

He grinned and shook his head. 'Nope, I've got a book to read. One so turgid it makes the instruction manual for my car read like a Jack Reacher thriller. The book that will save mankind or the manuscript from Hell?'

'If it was channelled through a medium, probably the latter. Are you still going to Bristol tomorrow for the radio interview?'

'Yes.'

'Why don't you go by train, instead of driving? It'll give you a few hours to read.'

'I want to swing by Chalice Well on the way back – I'll need the car for that.'

'Take a train there, which will give you some useful time, and rent a car to come back in. The paper's paying for your travel costs, isn't it?'

'Good thinking, I'll do that. Too bad God's man didn't give it to Harry Cook as an audio file – I could have listened to it in the car.'

She shook her head. 'Too dangerous. Sounds like it would send you to sleep at the wheel!'

He grinned. 'Yep.'

'I've had to turn down a dream assignment, thanks to Caligula,' she said.

'What was it?'

'A week's diving holiday in the Maldives for the two of us. I just had to write a piece for a new online travel magazine for it. Business Class flights, the lot.'

One of their mutual interests was scuba diving and they both held PADI certificates. They'd enjoyed several diving holidays abroad. There wouldn't be another for some while, he thought ruefully, thanks to the baby.

'Shame. We'll make sure the little bugger knows one day what he made us miss!'

She grinned and held up her phone. 'Look, one hundred and nine hits on Instagram.' She handed it to him and he could see the Instagram picture of Monty sitting beside him, with a resigned look on his face, whilst he sat in his chair, reading. The caption read: *Montmorency waits patiently for his master to finish reading the manuscript, so he can be taken for his walk.*

'Love it!' he replied.

After their meal, and after downing half a bottle of very acceptable and quite potent Australian Shiraz, on top of his beer, Ross went back up to his office, clutching the bottle and his glass. He sat down in his armchair, charged his glass and resumed reading. There was one Biblical passage after another.

> But the fearful, and unbelieving, and the abominable, and murderers, and whoremongers, and sorcerers, and idolaters, and all liars, shall have their part in the lake which burneth with fire and brimstone: which is the second death.

ABSOLUTE PROOF

After half an hour, Ross laid the manuscript on the floor, to have a break, the tiny writing and annotations doing his head in, went over to his desk and logged on to Twitter. He typed out:

> Anyone got views on what they think would constitute absolute proof of #GodsExistence #DoesGodExist

He sent the tweet, opened Facebook and repeated the message, posting that too. Then he returned to the manuscript and continued to plough on through it. He yawned, tired, finding it increasingly hard to concentrate. Then he yawned again. His eyes closed.

13

A loud thud woke Ross from a disturbing dream, in which demons in flowing white robes were hurtling like human jet planes towards him, yelling in fury. He sat up with a start, blinking, disorientated, momentarily unsure where he was. He saw the light of the anglepoise lamp beside him. Pages of Cook's manuscript strewn on the floor.

Shit. What time is it?

He looked at his watch and was horrified to see it was 2.20 a.m. He'd fallen asleep in his chair.

Shit, shit, shit!

He had an early start for Bristol this morning. He was doing a radio interview at midday on BBC Radio Bristol about the secret, iniquitous influence that political lobbyists had on many of the decisions made in Parliament. It followed an article he had written for the *Sunday Times* which had caused a lot of controversy – so much that the paper wanted a further piece. He was also contemplating writing a book on the subject, and this interview, by a respected radio presenter, could help him with the ammunition he needed to secure a publishing deal for it. He needed to be on top form. Bristol was nearly 170 miles away. He had to take a train to Victoria and then change. A good three hours of reading time. If he speed-read he might, with luck, get through a few hundred pages of Cook's manuscript. If he could bear it.

He was feeling less and less sure it was worth dedicating any more time to Dr Harry Cook.

Leaving everything as it was, he switched the light off, crept into the bedroom, undressed and brushed his teeth, and slipped into bed next to Imogen, who was fast asleep.

Some nights he took a pill to help him sleep, but it was too late for that; taking one now would leave him drowsy all morning. He lay back against the pillows, thinking back to his meeting earlier with the strange old man.

You and I have to save the world.

From what he had read of it so far, the manuscript was nothing more than the ramblings of a disturbed mind. Bible passages, interspersed with random jottings of thoughts and certain words and phrases underlined. Was he missing something crucial?

Ross had tried – and failed – to read the Bible all the way through in his early teens; religious studies at school had bored him senseless. But nothing, ever, had bored him as much as the manuscript he had spent the evening attempting to read. Eighty-five pages of over twelve hundred. Would it get any better? He doubted it. But he felt he needed to get to the end, however superficially he speed-read it.

Three hours on the train to Bristol. Three hours of reading.

Reading the manuscript from Hell.

The road to Hell paved with good intentions?

14

The orangery was far enough away from the house that Ainsley Bloor and his wife would not be disturbed by the noises of the six caged monkeys, nor their smell.

Inside every cage was a computer terminal connected to a continuous paper feed. The first thing Bloor did every evening when he arrived home and every morning before leaving for his office was to check on his experiment.

So far, after more than three weeks, five of them had not got the hang of this at all, despite the incentives of a treat, automatically dispensed, after a number of keystrokes. They tore up the paper, chewed it and spat it out, and used the keyboards either as toilets or a toy to be flung around the cage.

But one, Boris, in Cage 6, was his shining star. His great white hope!

The CEO of the pharmaceutical giant, Kerr Kluge, in his tracksuit and trainers, ran breathless through the darkness, clutching a sheet of paper. He passed the concrete landing pad and the shadowy hulk of his twin-engined Augusta helicopter, and crossed the croquet lawn. Entering through a side door, he raced along the hallway and upstairs to their bedroom.

'Look at this!' he said. 'Cilla, darling, look, look!'

Startled by his voice, Yeti, their white shih-tzu, jumped off the bed.

It was 6.45 a.m. Cilla had never been an early riser, and he knew that if disturbed before 8 a.m. she'd be in a grump for the rest of the day. But this was worth the grump.

Bloor switched on her bedside light and held a sheet of computer printout in front of her, waiting for her reaction with a triumphant smile.

She blinked then peered at the page. It was filled with rows of letters of the alphabet, interspersed with numbers and symbols.

'What am I meant to be looking at, exactly, my love?' she said in her usual sarcastic tone.

'This!' He tapped one letter, circled in red pen. 'I'.

She looked up at him with a frown. 'Am I missing something?'

'I.'

'Have you been drinking?'

'At this hour? I don't think so.'

'"I"? You've woken me to show me this?'

'You don't see it, darling, do you?' he said, impatiently.

'I see the letter "I". Sorry, am I being dumb?'

'You're not seeing the *letter* "I" – you're seeing the *word* "I".'

'The word?'

'There's a space either side and it's capitalized! Don't you see what that means?'

'You've lost me. Do you want to tell me in *English*?'

He balled his fists in the air. 'This is a breakthrough. This is momentous. This is the start of absolute proof that God does not exist!'

She peered at him through sleepy eyes. 'The letter "I"? Are you sure you haven't been on the bottle?'

'You don't get it, do you?'

'No, I don't get it, and would you mind not talking in riddles?'

'OK – Boris!'

'Your monkey?'

'Yes! Boris! Boris wrote it! Don't you see? Don't you get it?'

'No, I'm sorry, I'm afraid I don't get it. The letter "I" with a space either side. What exactly am I missing?'

'It's a word, darling. An intelligible word! It's taken him three weeks, but he's got there! A monkey has typed a word!'

She peered at the sheet again. 'Do you think he knows what it means?'

'Does that matter? I can't believe you are even asking that question! This is the most exciting thing – possibly – ever! A monkey typing a proper word! No one's ever achieved this before.'

'Once he's proved your point and typed the collected works of Shakespeare, in the right order, then I will be impressed.'

'You are totally missing the point!'

'Are you sure it's not you who is missing it?'

'A friend of the atheist Antony Flew did this same experiment with a monkey and a typewriter and a perpetual paper feed. In twenty-eight days, the monkey typed forty pages of gibberish. There wasn't one single intelligible word. Not even an "I" surrounded by a space. From doing the maths, he believed the earth would run out of resources before the monkey ever typed anything intelligible, and used this as evidence for the existence of God. He was wrong! Just mark this date down in your diary. The day God's existence began to be conclusively disproved.'

'The "I"s have it,' she said, dismissively, called out to the dog and appeared to be drifting back to sleep.

15

'Thank you, Ross Hunter,' the BBC presenter, Sally Hughes, said, then leaned in closer to the microphone in the small studio. 'If you want to read Ross Hunter's truly fascinating article on political lobbyists, you can find it on the *Sunday Times* website.' She read out the link, took a breath, then went straight on. 'You are tuned to BBC Radio Bristol. It's coming up to 1 p.m. and Rory Westerman is here with the latest travel news and weather. After the news, we'll have recipe time with *MasterChef* winner Charlie Bouvier. I'll be back at 2 p.m. talking to my next guest, the novelist Val McDermid.'

She reached forward, pressed a switch and the red ON AIR light went off. She smiled at Ross.

'Was that OK?' he asked.

'Great!' she said.

He sipped the last drop of cold coffee from the mug he'd been given before entering the studio, then picked up his rucksack containing Cook's manuscript.

'Are you doing any more interviews locally?' she asked.

'No – I've organized a rental car as I'm heading back to Sussex via Glastonbury,' he said. 'Something I need to check out whilst there's still daylight.'

'Glastonbury?'

'Yes.'

'Have you been there before?'

'A few years ago.'

'You should take a look at Chalice Well while you're there. Amazing place – it's very spiritual.'

'Did you say *Chalice Well*?'

'Yes.'

'That's so weird you should mention it,' he replied. 'It's actually where I'm going. What do you know about it?'

'Well, quite a bit, actually – my uncle's a trustee.'

He looked at her, astonished. 'Your uncle? A trustee of Chalice Well?'

'Yes, Julius Helmsley – he's married to my mother's sister. Why?'

'This is such a coincidence!'

'Coincidence?'

He looked at his watch, then at the clock on the studio wall. 'Do you have time for a quick bite? You're back on at 2 p.m.?'

'There's a cafe two minutes down the road. I need a sandwich or something.'

'Me too.'

Ten minutes later they sat at a table, Sally Hughes with a green tea and a tuna sandwich, Ross with a double espresso, a Diet Coke and a microwaved ham and cheese panini. In her thirties, with a mass of dark curls framing her face, she had a warmth about her that had instantly put him at ease in the radio station, and she had a gravelly voice he liked a lot. She wasn't beautiful in any conventional sense but she had an air of intelligence and a vibrancy that made her attractive.

She looked very much at ease now, in a roll-neck black pullover with a loose, gold-link chain, jeans and black boots, and wore several rings, but none on her wedding finger, he observed.

'So, what's this coincidence?'

He told her the entire story of his encounter with Harry Cook. When he had finished she sat in silence.

'What do you think?' he prompted, after some moments.

'What do *you* think?' she came right back at him.

'I think he's probably a nutter. At least I did until you mentioned Chalice Well!'

'Are you religious?' she asked.

'I guess I'm kind of an agnostic. I was veering towards atheism in my late teens, then, in my early twenties, something happened.'

'What was that?'

'It's a bit – well, embarrassing really – too personal to talk about.'

'A blinding light on the road to Damascus?'

'Along those lines. What about you? Are you religious?' he asked.

'I don't believe in the God of the Bible – but I think there's something. Some kind of higher intelligence. I guess my view is that it would be a pretty bleak day for mankind if it was ever conclusively proved God does not exist and there is no afterlife – and no reward or retribution. We'd be left with the sheer despair and pointlessness of existence, don't you think?'

'I don't know. I was OK as a non-believer until –'

'Until the thing that happened in your life?'

'Yes. And your uncle – what's his name again?'

'Julius Helmsley.' She shook her head. 'He's a director of a pharmaceutical company – he doesn't have any religious beliefs.'

'But he's a trustee of Chalice Well, a holy site?'

'That's because he has a weekend home in the area and

his company provide funding to help maintain Chalice Well – out of a kind of civic duty. They have an R&D plant in Somerset.'

'Do you think your uncle would talk to me?'

'About Dr Cook?'

'Yes, and Chalice Well in general.'

'I'll ask him what he knows about the guy and get back to you.' She gave him an enigmatic smile.

There was something very appealing about her. But he didn't want to give out any signals. With fatherhood approaching, whatever his feelings towards Imogen these days, he felt a sense of duty to her. He looked at his watch. 'What time do you need to be back in the studio?'

'Twenty minutes, before my producer starts fretting. What you haven't told me is your view on this manuscript Cook gave you.'

'So far, I'm struggling. I'm finding it complete tosh.'

'Except for the compass coordinates for Chalice Well?'

'Maybe.'

'And the other two sets of coordinates you don't yet have? Are you interested to get those?'

'I guess with my investigative journalist hat on, yes, I am.'

She smiled again. 'It's been good talking to you.'

'Likewise.'

'Let me know if you're coming down this way again.'

'For sure.'

'Do you have a card? I'll see if I can get my uncle to call or email you.'

Ross handed one to her. Then, after they'd finished their lunch, he gave her a clumsy cheek-to-cheek kiss. 'I'll keep you posted.'

'I'd like that. Maybe you can come and talk about Harry Cook on my show sometime?'

'The man who saved the world?'

'And the hot-shot reporter who helped him!'

Ross tapped his heavy rucksack on the floor beside him. 'Maybe it's all in here.'

'You look like you're wearing the responsibility well. No pun intended.'

As the presenter dashed off back to the studio, Ross walked up to the counter to pay, deep in thought. The co-incidence was strange. Weird. Very weird. Chalice Well coming up twice in two days. A sign? Could it be? Or just coincidence?

16

From his forty-fourth floor, glass-walled office at the top of the KK building – nicknamed the 'pill box' by its employees – Ainsley Bloor presided over the ever-expanding Kerr Kluge empire with a cold eye and even colder heart. Situated on the South Bank, it gave him a magnificent view across the Thames to the Gherkin, amongst the City's other monoliths.

KK's Research and Development plant, in rural Somerset, was located in a much less high-profile building. The secretive plant, spread across a vast campus, showed only three storeys above ground. It had a further seven storeys beneath, deep underground. Part of the work carried out there was research using animals, kept well away from prying eyes and animal rights activists. But the even larger part of their secretive work was gene sequencing, and from this bunker construction they operated the largest genetics facility in the United Kingdom.

Bloor and his board of directors believed the long-term strategy for their company should be patenting gene sequences for controlling chronic ailments like diabetes, psoriasis, arthritis and depression, and maintenance treatment for those with life-threatening conditions such as Parkinson's, dementia and cancer.

Until a few moments ago Bloor had been in a very good

mood. He'd just signed a deal with the largest supplier of pharmaceuticals into central Africa. The company would take off their hands all out-of-date drugs on their shelves, and in addition, had agreed to distribute in that continent one of their largest-selling and most lucrative products of recent years, an antihistamine which the FDA had recently banned after it was found to be linked to fatal effects on heart rhythms. A week ago it had looked as if this FDA ruling could seriously harm their bottom line. Now it was quite the reverse.

He had been looking forward to a good lunch with his close colleagues today, to celebrate the deal.

And on top of that he had his progress with Boris to celebrate, privately, too.

A young, recently graduated doctor who had just joined the firm would dine out for years on his interview with the CEO. 'Steven, you need to know one thing about Kerr Kluge and one thing only,' Bloor had told him, here in this office. 'We're in the business of making a profit and that's all that matters to us. If we happen, through our pharmaceuticals, to make life better for a few people, that's not my problem. Understand where I'm coming from?'

But at this moment the CEO had an altogether different problem.

He sat at his desk, phone to his ear, watching a tug towing a barge along the river below him. It was a fine day outside, the kind of sunny, winter morning when London looked its very best, when it was truly, in his opinion, the most beautiful city in the world.

A world that was filled with opportunities for his firm. As yet unconquered markets. New patents applied for. New patents that had been granted, with the drugs in final – years long – stages of testing.

Sometimes when he met people for the first time at drinks parties and they asked him what he did, he took perverse pleasure in telling them he was a drug dealer.

But he wasn't getting any pleasure from this phone call.

At its heart, the whole foundation of his company – and all of the other pharmaceutical companies, both giants and minnows – depended on one thing: that no one, ever, found an instant *magic bullet* cure for any of these conditions. Their profit centres lay in products that prolonged the lives of sufferers for as long as possible – managing their conditions. Not freeing them.

He barked an instruction into the phone.

17

Tuesday, 21 February

Navigating via the Google Maps app on his iPhone, Ross drove the small rental Toyota through the outskirts of Bristol. He negotiated a roundabout with signs to Bath, Shepton Mallet and Wells, and took the Wells exit, then followed the A37 as directed. The device showed he would arrive in fifty-four minutes.

The earlier heavy rain had cleared and patches of blue sky showed through the cloud; he was relieved that he wasn't going to have to traipse around getting soaked. But at the same time he had a strange feeling that he was missing something.

He leaned forward and fiddled with the radio until he found Heart, and heard a new Passenger song playing. It was a band he liked.

As he listened to the music, reflecting on his chat just now with the broadcaster Sally Hughes, the feeling he was missing something persisted. Like a shadow in the car with him.

Then he realized.

'Shit!' he said aloud. 'Oh shit, shit, shit!'

He'd left the rucksack, containing the pages of Harry Cook's manuscript, on the floor of the cafe.

How? How could he have done this? Because he was overtired, probably.

Frantically, he looked for somewhere to turn round. The road was busy, with cars behind him and a stream of oncoming vehicles. Coming up to his right he saw the entrance to a farm shop. His heart pounding, perspiring heavily, he indicated, waited for a gap in the traffic and turned into it, bringing the car to a sharp halt. Then, looking behind him, he waited for another gap, reversed out into the road, then accelerated across the path of a lorry, which blasted its horn at him, and drove as fast as he dared back towards Bristol.

Jesus. The only copy in existence. What if someone stole the rucksack, thinking it probably contained a laptop? How could he explain that to Cook?

Entrusted with saving mankind, he had fallen at the first hurdle.

Shit, shit, shit.

There was a tractor in front of him, driving at 15 mph. 'Come on, come on!' He pulled out to see past it, but there was a solid line of traffic then the brow of a hill.

His insides felt twisted up. How could he have been so dumb?

What if it had gone?

He had managed to skim-read the first thousand pages. Wherever he had stopped for a more in-depth read, he had found it consistently impenetrable. He could have happily mailed it back to Harry F. Cook at this moment, but he felt he owed it to the old man to read it all the way through. He owed it to the human race, didn't he? Maybe?

Although he wasn't convinced. Not remotely.

And yet the coincidence of Sally's uncle was not something he could dismiss.

Be there, please still be there. Please!

Twenty minutes later he pulled up on a double yellow

line outside the cafe and raced inside. It was almost empty. He ran past the counter to the rear where they had sat, and looked on the floor, under the table.

It was gone.

He felt hollowed out inside.

Then a voice called out to him and he turned. There was a young woman behind the counter, with bright red hair, the woman who had served them, he recognized.

'Can I help you?'

'Yes – I – I was here about forty minutes ago. I left a rucksack on the floor.'

'Ah, yes. You're lucky there are some honest people in the world. It was handed in by a gentleman.'

She ducked down and reappeared holding up a black nylon rucksack. 'This it?'

Relief flooded through him. 'You're a bloody angel!' he said. He nearly kissed her.

He unzipped it to check everything was there, then he hurried back out to his car.

The traffic was heavy all the way, and Ross reached Glastonbury just before 4 p.m., with thirty minutes to spare before closing time at Chalice Well. The road into the town was narrow, with a row of grimy houses on his left butting right up to it, and a hedge to his right which barely allowed room for two lorries to pass. The hedge ended at a lane going uphill. On the far side of the lane was a high grey wall with a green and white sign, and an arrow.

CHALICE WELL TRUST

Fifty yards further on was a much larger sign by an opening in the wall. He turned into it and found himself in a parking area, with two cars and a dozen or so empty spaces in front of a row of attractive cottages. In a different location, he thought, they could be village tearooms.

There were several signs.

WELCOME TO CHALICE WELL AND GARDENS

CHALICE WELL IS A SANCTUARY AND WORLD PEACE GARDEN

DISABLED PARKING ONLY

A smaller sign below that said there was a car park two hundred yards along the road.

He turned the car round, drove back onto the main road and almost immediately saw a sign for Chalice Well parking and for a factory shop. He drove down a recently resurfaced road and saw a modern, two-storey factory building with the name R. J. DRAPER & CO high up in large white letters. In front was a large, empty car park. A board indicated the parking was £2 and to pay inside the factory shop.

He removed his rucksack and pulled it on, not wanting to risk leaving it in the car. He paid, then hurried back along to Chalice Well on foot, entered the car park and looked around, getting his bearings. Then he followed a cobbled pathway up an incline, past the tearoom-like cottages and along a trellised walkway. There was an illustrated sign of a phone with a red cross over it and the wording MOBILE FREE ZONE.

Dutifully he turned his to silent as he walked on, past a small building, then reached a wooden ticket hut, with a sales window manned by a solitary woman. He paid the £4.20 admission fee, and the helpful woman handed him a leaflet containing a map and explained the layout.

'Does this path take me up to the Tor?' he asked.

'No.' She pointed across to her left. 'That's the other side of the lane – if you walk up it you'll see the signs.'

He thanked her and studied the map. It was all much more ordered and neatly laid out than he had imagined, with the feel of a well-kept city park. He headed on up the path; it was bounded by a low hedge to his right and flower beds to his left. Beyond that was a steep grass slope rising up the side of the hill, dotted irregularly with large bushes and trees. Down to his right, set in a beautiful part of the grounds, he saw a circular pool, with rusty-looking water flowing through a fountain and out into a narrow stream cut through the paving slabs, passing beneath a stone bridge. The Vesica Pool, the map said.

Ahead were two magnificent yew trees. Then a short distance further uphill was an ornate gateway topped by a small shield bearing the embossed words CHALICE WELL.

He took a photograph on his phone.

An elderly man in gardening clothes came down towards him, pushing a wheelbarrow, wished him a peaceful afternoon and carried on. After a few more paces, Ross saw another sign to the well. He looked, but at first all he could see were the low branches of huge trees, and a mass of surprisingly unkempt bushes and shrubbery, all badly in need of cutting back.

But then as he walked closer, towards a fence that he presumed marked the boundary, and where the lane ran up the far side, with the Tor beyond, he saw a sunken, circular wall, and two sets of steps built into it.

At the bottom of the steps lay the well itself.

As he looked down he felt a slight sense of anticlimax. It was smaller than he had imagined, no more than three and a half feet across. He had not known quite what to expect, but he thought it might be more dramatic-looking, in some way.

He descended the three large steps and stopped at the bottom, studying the well head. Uneven flat stones lay around the area and the well itself was gridded, to prevent anyone falling in. There was a raised cover, with ornate symbols on it, that rested against a stone support and was chained in place.

According to the guidebook, the reddish colour of the water, which had never dried out, represented the blood of Christ.

He took a series of photographs, then looked at the compass coordinates Cook had given him, which he had programmed into his phone. They showed he had some distance to go. He left the well area and followed the co-ordinates, which took him through the ornate gardens and out, to the left, onto the steep grass slope. About two hundred metres above the well, the coordinates showed he had reached the exact spot.

51°08'40"N 2°41'55"W

The place where Cook had told him he had been metal detecting, and had picked up something beneath him.

Someone had been digging here.

He stared down, feeling the hairs on his skin rising. They'd been digging very recently. It looked like they had dug a trench about four-foot long and two-foot wide, then filled it in again. They had replaced the soil and planted fresh grass seed, with just the faintest signs of shoots starting to appear.

Who?

Harry Cook. Had to be.

It was an eerie feeling. The low sun was in his face, and he could hear sheep bleating somewhere in the distance.

Eerie and yet . . .

There was a gift shop, the map showed. You could buy souvenirs. Had those medieval monks really created the myth that Joseph of Arimathea was buried here to increase tourism? A cynical theory?

The Holy Grail was supposedly, according to legends, either the cup – the chalice – that Jesus had drunk from at the Last Supper or the vessel that some of his blood was poured into whilst on the cross. Or both.

From what Ross had googled during the past few days, Joseph of Arimathea was a rich man, a bit keen on entering the Kingdom of Heaven. He had been a closet disciple of Jesus – as it wasn't too smart to be one openly – but later got Pilate's permission to take away Christ's body and put it in the grand tomb he'd originally planned for himself.

In one of the clearer passages of Cook's literary ramblings Ross had found, it said Joseph subsequently, for reasons unclear, had to make a fast exit from his country. He'd grabbed some souvenirs, one being the chalice, fled and arrived in England, where he founded the first Christian church – here at Glastonbury, according to some.

Ross stood still, thinking. *OK, so I'm Joseph. I've had to flee my homeland after putting the Son of God in the tomb I had prepared for myself. I've fetched up in this aggressive, pagan land, in this weird place, with its very strange hill and a deep well. I have a souvenir from my great nephew – the Son of God. It is the only evidence I carry that He ever existed. Not much. Just a cup He drank from or had His blood poured into. But it's a link. I need to protect and keep it safe for future generations to discover.*

So, I need to hide it in case the pagans discover it and destroy it.

Where?

Ross looked around him. *If it was me, would I dig a hole in this bit of hillside? I don't think so. I'd be a lot smarter than that.*

Cook might have detected something under the spot where he was standing at this moment. But it could be anything. There was no evidence that the vessel Christ drank from at the Last Supper, and into which some of His blood had been poured while He was on the cross, was metal at all. It might have been. Or it could have been wood. Less ornate and showy than metal for such a humble man. In which case it would not have been picked up by Cook's metal detector.

He looked down towards the well, the shrubbery making it invisible from here, thinking hard. Then around. At the trees, bushes. Pondering.

He tried to wind the clock back two thousand years. What was here then? What would have been the most obvious place?

18

Tuesday, 21 February

Ross walked back down through the gardens and went into the gift shop to see if he could get something for the baby's room. He glanced along the shelves of healing essences, replica chalices and candles but couldn't see anything that might appeal to a baby.

Disappointed, he bought a guide book and headed for the street. When he got there he walked the short distance to the lane that ran on the far side of the fence, and walked up it. He passed a very New Age-looking house with a huge floral mural painted on it. Then a stone temple, built over a spring. A short distance further up the hill, on his left, was the wooden fence he had seen from the other side, running up by the well. He must be about opposite the well itself now, he calculated. The fence was constructed on top of a stone wall, clearly to deter anyone from trying to enter without paying.

He saw a footpath sign a short way ahead to his right, to the tor, and a narrow lay-by where a few cars could pull in. He walked up the footpath towards the tor until it came into view after a few minutes. And took his breath away.

With its seven symmetrical ridges, Glastonbury Tor had mythological links to King Arthur and Avalon, and Ross could feel that sense of history, standing here now. It was a weird landscape, reminding him of hills he had seen some years back when he and Imogen had travelled around New Zealand.

He looked at the remains of St Michael's Tower, and then trudged up towards it. When he reached the summit, he walked around the ruin, then stared back down and across at the higgledy-piggledy buildings of Glastonbury town, and at the fields around. Some distance away he could see the sheep he had heard bleating. The sun was very low in the sky now, and the light was fading. He glanced at his watch. 5.10 p.m. He had a long drive home in his little rental car, a good three and a half hours. He'd seen enough and he was even more sure now.

There was a path that led straight down the front of the hill. Ross took it, and when he reached the bottom paused for a moment to text Imogen, to say he should be home before 9 p.m.

From the top of Glastonbury Tor, from far enough back in the darkness of the entrance to the ruin of St Michael's Tower so that there would be no tell-tale glint from the glass catching the late-afternoon sun, a pair of binoculars remained trained on him.

19

Ross Hunter had first met the Reverend Benedict Carmichael when the clergyman had held the post of Vicar of St Peter's, Brighton. With Carmichael's help, he had exposed a satanic coven involved in ritual child abuse in the countryside close to the city. It had given Ross one of his first national newspaper front-page splashes, and it had also resulted in an enduring friendship between himself and Carmichael. And he had been surprised to learn this seemingly devout man had doubts.

Over an off-the-record lunch with him one day in Lewes, during the trial of the principal members of the coven, Carmichael had opened up to him, telling him that he had a problem with the literalist interpretations of the Bible. He had strong faith, but at the same time was deeply uncertain about many of the teachings – and the literalist approach to the Scriptures.

Ross had been delighted for the clergyman when, just a few months later, Benedict Carmichael had been given the post of Bishop of Reading. And equally delighted when Carmichael, who was fluent in Welsh, had written to him a year ago telling him he had now been appointed Bishop of Monmouth.

As soon as he returned home from visiting Chalice Well, he phoned Carmichael, whom he had not seen for some years, asking if he could come and talk to him, quite urgently.

Two days later he drove his dark-grey Audi A4 into the cobbled car-parking space in front of an elegant stone mansion in the heart of Monmouth. He climbed out into bright sunshine, stretched after the long drive and entered the building. After only a few moments' wait, Carmichael's smiling middle-aged secretary led him upstairs, along a narrow corridor and into the Bishop's cosy, cluttered office.

Carmichael was wearing an open black jacket, revealing his purple dog-collared shirt; hanging from his neck on a golden chain was a huge, ornate cross. He had put on weight since Ross had last seen him, and his hair had thinned and greyed, but his face still looked youthful and his eyes sparkled with zeal.

They sat down in a pair of armchairs and chatted, catching up on each other's lives, until the secretary came in with a tray of coffee and biscuits.

'So, Ross, you said there was something urgent?' Carmichael said. He had a rich, friendly voice, the kind of voice that could engage an entire cathedral full of worshippers as easily as holding its own against a fierce Radio 4 *Today* programme interrogator.

Ross opened his rucksack and lifted out the pages of Cook's manuscript.

'You've written a book, Ross?'

'No – it seems that God has.' Ross smiled.

Carmichael gave him a quizzical look.

Ross told him the entire story, starting with Cook's phone call and ending with his lunch with Sally Hughes and his visit to Chalice Well.

When he had finished, the Bishop dunked a digestive biscuit reflectively into his coffee. 'Hmm,' he said after some moments. 'Knowing you, you've done some due diligence on Dr Cook?'

'I have, and he checks out. Ex-RAF, then lectured in art history at the University of Birmingham. His late wife, Doreen, was also an academic at the same uni. One child, a son in the army who was killed by friendly fire in Afghanistan. He has no criminal record – seems a pretty ordinary guy. Played amateur chess to a reasonable standard in his youth. He was quite a polymath, with an interest in anthropology and biology. Published a couple of academic papers some years back challenging established Darwinian theories and supporting Lamarck.'

'Lamarck? Jean-Baptiste Lamarck?'

'Yes.'

Carmichael looked down with a flash of irritation as the soggy part of the biscuit fell away and landed in his coffee. He dipped his spoon in to retrieve it, then laid the bits in his saucer.

'Interesting. Lamarck has always intrigued me. You probably know this, but whereas Darwin proposed that organisms evolved through natural selection, Lamarck believed they evolved through necessity. If you took a frog out of water, within a couple of generations it would lose its webbed feet and develop pads instead.'

'But that didn't make him any less of a deist than Darwin, did it, Benedict?'

'Well, I would argue that point. If Lamarck had known about genes, he might have said the frog's brain informed its genes to produce pads instead of webbed feet. What exactly informed the frog's brain? Or who? But that's not why you're here, is it?' He reached out, patted the manuscript pages and said, a little dubiously, 'Is this what you want me to read?'

Ross shook his head. And instantly saw the relief in the bishop's face. 'No. I want to know what you think about what I've told you – about what Dr Cook told me.'

'Truthfully?'

'Of course, that's why I'm here.'

'Well, this man is telling you God believes that if humankind could have proof of His existence reaffirmed, it would help steer the world back from the brink. So, he's offering three sets of compass coordinates as proof of God. The location of the Holy Grail, a significant object relating to Jesus Christ, and the real location of the Second Coming?'

'Yes.'

'OK, well that is contradicting the argument that proof is the enemy of faith. Or perhaps puts a different slant on it.'

'How do you mean, Benedict?'

The Bishop's eyes closed for some moments and then opened again. 'The thing is, I'd want more than three sets of compass coordinates to have proof of God. And frankly, if I were God wanting to give someone proof of My existence, I'd do better than just giving sets of compass coordinates. I'd personally want to see something far more convincing.'

'It's interesting,' Ross replied. 'I posted the question on social media a few days ago – what it would take for someone to have absolute proof of God's existence.'

'I imagine you got some interesting answers?' Benedict smiled, quizzically.

'I had a fair few replies telling me I faced eternal damnation for even asking the question. But I did get some responses I thought were quite smart.'

'Such as?'

'One said finding the DNA double helix engraved at the rear of Christ's tomb.' He looked at Carmichael, who seemed unimpressed.

'That could too easily be dismissed as a fake, Ross.'

'I suppose. Another which I quite like was the solving of one of the world's unsolved mathematical problems. The Yang–Mills Existence and Mass Gap problem, for example. Or perhaps all seven of them.'

'It's a nice idea, but sceptics would put it down to advanced computer algorithms.'

Ross smiled. 'OK, so what would convince you, Benedict? If you were God wanting to convince the world you really existed, what would you do?'

Ross ate his biscuit, the silence broken by the crunching sound.

The Bishop leaned back, interlocking his fingers. 'I'd need something that would convince a diehard atheist – something they could not just reject out of hand or explain away. Something that defies the laws of physics of the universe. In other words, a miracle. And a very big one.'

Ross reflected on this. 'You mean like the parting of an ocean?'

'We live in a much more sceptical world than in Jesus's time,' Carmichael said. 'Most of us have seen David Blaine, Dynamo, Derren Brown – and countless other magicians and illusionists. I think we'd need something pretty spectacular – something the whole world could see – and quite simply could not dismiss or explain away with science.'

'Like the sun rising from the west instead of the east?'

'It would need to be on that scale.'

'OK,' Ross said. 'And if someone could deliver that miracle – what then?'

Carmichael gave him a wry, sad smile. 'Do you know what I really, truthfully think, if someone credible claimed to have absolute proof of God's existence, Ross? I think that person would be killed.'

20

It might have been Ross's imagination, but it felt that the sky outside had darkened. The window was behind him and he didn't want to turn round. 'Killed?' he echoed. 'You mean assassinated? What makes you think that, Benedict?'

The Bishop raised his hands. 'I'm not at all convinced that absolute proof of God, if such a thing could be established, would put the world back onto an even keel. I think it would have the reverse effect to what your Dr Cook believes. Think of the ramifications. The upset it would cause among so many of the world's religions. It would throw them into chaos. Desperation. Everyone who for centuries has tried to lay claim to their own religion being the exclusive path to God. Fuel for the fanatics of every denomination. Panic to everyone with a vested commercial interest in a belief system. Where would all the Abrahamic religions stand? Is it the Catholic God? The Anglican God? The Judaic? Islamic? What about Hindus? Sikhs? There'd be fundamentalists who would be outraged, calling it blasphemy. It wouldn't make the Scientologists look too clever either, would it?'

Ross stared at him. Carmichael continued with a wry smile.

'There would be a lot of people extremely unhappy, Ross, because they'd be out of business.'

'Starting with the Vatican?'

'The Vatican would be extremely uncomfortable, yes. They consider themselves to be the one true Christian church – so they'd have to find ways urgently to reassert their primacy. But proving God's existence could legitimize the Jews' claim to the Promised Land – which would have huge implications for Palestine and Israel. For Putin, even though there is a grudging acceptance of religion in Russia, he would see it as a huge threat to his power if a degree of authority was given to the Church. Even more so in China. China is in a period of vying for world supremacy. Treading a fine balance between opening up to capitalism whilst wanting to keep autonomy. There is a significant underground church in China, although China is primarily an atheistic country. If God were shown to be true, it would undermine authority in China if people owed allegiance to a superior being.'

Ross was silent. He tried to keep calm, but inside he was boiling with excitement at the potential reach of this story, if there was any substance to what Cook claimed.

Or perhaps even if there was not.

'None of this occurred to me, Benedict. But it's making sense.'

Carmichael gave him an unreadable smile. Then his face became serious again. 'Many of the world's religions are as much about business as they are a belief system, Ross. I can see absolute proof putting them all out of business. A lot of people are not going to want that. And there's something else to consider. Something very important indeed.' Looking troubled, he paused.

Ross waited patiently.

'It worries me that some of this information has come via a spiritualist – a medium. These are dangerous people.

What if this is the work of the Antichrist? The Bible talks about the Devil being cunning, a master of disguise. I think you'd find a lot of people taking that view – and in a very dangerous way.'

'Dangerous?' Ross stared at him, trying to absorb all of this. 'So what you are saying, Benedict, is that Cook is wrong? His message is not from God but from the Antichrist?'

'Well, of course, there is an incident in Scripture where God does seem to have allowed, in exceptional circumstances, a dead person to speak to a living one. It was when King Saul consulted a medium at Endor. The prophet Samuel turned up, and told Saul he was about to die. Such a dramatic situation as you say we are facing might have meant that God has made another exception.' He smiled, then went on.

'I'm trying to steer you through all the different perspectives on this, and the ramifications. The kind of proof of God's existence you are talking about would not unite the world. It wouldn't save mankind, in my opinion. It would cause even bigger divisions around the globe than there are already. My advice to you as an old friend is to take this manuscript back to your Mr Cook and tell him you're sorry, but you are not his man.'

'Is that what God's telling you? What about everything in the New Testament about the Second Coming?'

'In the Gospels, Jesus says that before His Second Coming there will be false prophets, catastrophic events, wars, famines, earthquakes and disasters and fierce persecution. The apostle John goes even further and writes about an Antichrist appearing before Jesus's return.'

'I don't remember the Bible that well. I thought the Second Coming was meant to be a momentous occasion when Jesus would return to judge the living and the dead, to save the world from extinction and to establish a new heaven and a new earth?'

'Yes, that is what most Christians believe. A Second Coming of varying sorts is what all the Christian and Islamic faiths believe.'

'But not the Jews?'

'The Orthodox Jews believe in the coming of the Messiah.'

'He's not Jesus?'

'No, they believe Jesus is a false Messiah. But the Second Coming is not just going to happen out of the blue. There are a lot of references in the Bible to there being a forerunner, as John the Baptist was. The Jews believe Elijah will appear before the Messiah to announce the Kingdom. Jesus certainly suggested there would be a future appearance of Elijah on earth.'

Ross frowned. 'It's all very complicated – and convoluted.'

'It is – but it would also be a pretty significant event.'

'So what's your own personal view on the Second Coming, Benedict?'

Carmichael answered with another smile that Ross found impossible to read. After a pause he said, 'Ross, this is me speaking to you as a friend who cares about you. You're treading on very dangerous terrain and you're out of your depth. Not just you – anyone in your position would be. It's not only the complexities of the world's belief systems or about fanatics laying claim to different faiths or factions of these faiths, there's a ruthless commercial world out there, both within and outside the religious embrace, with enormous vested interests that could be seriously harmed. For example, how do you think a snake oil salesman would feel about the possibility of a miracle cure that was a lot better than his potions – and which he couldn't own?'

'Wouldn't the genuine return of Jesus Christ provide an incontrovertible answer?'

'When you and I first met, you told me you had been a non-believer, but after the death of your twin brother, you said your mind had been opened – a little. Yes?'

'Yes.'

'So, you are prepared to accept that Jesus existed?'

'Possibly,' Ross replied. 'Whether he was genuinely the Son of God or just an ordinary human being is something my personal jury is still out on.'

'He was put to death when he came, over two thousand years ago. Do you think it would be any different today?'

'Harry Cook does.'

'The return of Jesus today would need to be accompanied by something extraordinary, Ross, both a miracle and a sign of some kind – something universal, that united everyone.'

'Such as?'

'I don't know. Something that no one has ever seen or perhaps even been able to imagine. But I don't know what.' The Bishop smiled again. Once more that same, unreadable smile.

21

Pastor Wesley Wenceslas made a point of spending two nights of every week at home in his private wing at Gethse-mane Park. He helped Marina bath and put to bed their three children, Matthew, Mark and Ruth, aged eight, six and four respectively, and he would read them each a short passage from the New Testament. Then he would kneel and say prayers with them, asking God to help them be good, follow in the Lord's ways and to bless them abundantly.

Afterwards he would dine with his wife on food pre-pared by his chef-in-residence and served by his butler. They would start with a glass of Krug, followed by fine white or red wine from his extensive cellar, depending on whether they were eating fish or meat. Afterwards he would retire to his study to check the daily Excel reports showing the tak-ings at each church, the sales of his books and merchandise, his online and telephone dial-a-prayer services, and all his other revenue streams.

When he was away from home, on the other five nights of the week, either at one of his churches in the UK or in the US, he carried out the same scrutiny of the day's takings.

He was terrified of ever being poor again.

His mum, abandoned when pregnant by his dad whom he had never met, worked nights cleaning offices to put food on the table and fund her bingo which she played obsessively in the daytime. She was deeply religious and would take him to a High Anglican church twice most Sundays, being dismissive of the happy-clappy evangelicals – although they looked more fun, to the small boy. She refused to have a television in the house and the only books she would allow were the Bible and Bible commentaries. Left home alone most nights when he was old enough to read, he read through the Bible several times. The stories intrigued him – and appalled him.

What he mostly took away from the Good Book was just how ruthless the Old Testament God was. He seemed to the small boy like a power-crazed egomaniac. You worshipped Him or you died; or saw someone you loved sacrificed; or had some other hardship dumped on you – or, in Job's case, you had the whole lot dumped on you.

Well OK, he thought, if God created the world then He was entitled to do what He wanted – and to get angry if He didn't feel appreciated.

He had no way of knowing, back then, that his intimate knowledge of the Holy Bible would serve him well one day.

The only things that interested him as a child, aside from the Bible, were cars and music – especially reggae. And the band that he connected with most was Bob Marley and the Wailers. But with no radio at home, the only opportunity he had to hear them was on a friend's Walkman at school.

Cars were easier to access. They lived in a first-floor flat at the Southwick end of one of the main roads into Brighton, Old Shoreham Road. The flat was crammed with religious artefacts and an Angelus bell, which struck three times during the day, at 6 a.m., 12 p.m. and 6 p.m. He would stare out of the window at the passing vehicles and dream.

Dream of the time that he would be driving a Porsche, Lamborghini, Ferrari or an Aston Martin.

He knew how much each of them cost, what their 0–60 mph time was, their top speed, the size of their engines and their power output.

When he was fourteen his mother had a big win at bingo – a very big win. She'd arrived home with her eyes glazed, pulling five-pound notes from her handbag and throwing them around the living room like confetti.

God had told her in a dream how to win it because, she said, He wanted her to give her special boy a special treat, to make up for all the lousy Christmases he'd had because she couldn't afford nice presents. God had told her in that same dream to use the winnings to take her boy to Disney World. At first she had been unsure, as Disney World went against all her beliefs, but in two further dreams God had been adamant she should give the boy this special treat because he was a good child.

At the end of the summer school term, they flew to Orlando. After take-off they were showing movies on screens, but his mother wouldn't let him watch any of those. Instead she gave him a Bible to read, out of respect for the Lord's gift. And the Holy Virgin on whose wings they flew. He tried to read, but his attention wandered. He was excited about the trip. Even more than the Disney World rides, he was looking forward to seeing lots of American cars. And he was also distracted by the movie on the screen in front of the man sitting to his right, in the aisle seat. The man was wearing headphones, so he couldn't hear what they were saying on the screen, but he was mesmerized by a woman with enormous breasts who kept appearing, sometimes in underwear or a bikini. Watching her was making him feel increasingly aroused. He knew it was disrespectful, but he was grateful to the Bible on his lap for concealing the bulge.

In the taxi from the airport his eyes were out on stalks, watching all the shiny American cars and trucks. He especially looked out for the muscle cars, new and old, Camaros, Corvettes, Mustangs and Firebirds, as well as the massive trucks, particularly the Macks. It was the first time he'd ever seen a Mack truck for real, and he loved looking at the adornments the drivers had added, like the huge horns and the mascots.

When they arrived at their hotel he stood by his mother at the reception desk, waiting patiently whilst she handed over her passport, then signed her name, Marigold Smith, and his, Thomas Smith – which was his real name back then. He watched a uniformed bellhop push an ornate, gleaming brass luggage cart, stacked with suitcases, across the lobby. He hoped a bellhop would come and take their luggage on a cart like that, too.

But instead his mother told the man at the check-in desk they did not need a hand with their luggage, thank you, and whispered to Thomas, as they traipsed across to the concierge desk, towing their wheeled bags, 'We'd have had to give a *tip*.'

She made the word *tip* sound like it was a bribe to Satan himself.

Now they were here and he had seen some cars, he was excited to get to the theme park tomorrow and to go on the rides some of his schoolmates had told him about. But his mother had other plans. Church had to come first, where they would ask for forgiveness for visiting the pleasure park.

'Can you tell us appropriate places to worship? Are there any convenient High Anglican churches?' she questioned the man at the concierge desk.

'Well,' said the tall, beaming man in a dark suit, 'you've arrived at a very good time if you'd like something really *special*. Tomorrow in the Orlando Stadium we are blessed to be visited by Pastor Drew Duane!'

'Drew Duane?' His mother frowned.

'He's pretty special, I'll tell you, oh yes. If you've not seen him, you shouldn't miss this chance.'

'He's High Anglican?'

'I don't know, ma'am, but he's *special*. He's the best preacher I ever heard. He'll be preaching to an eighteen thousand sell-out capacity. But I may be lucky and get you some tickets – know what I'm saying?'

His mother hesitated, not entirely sure. 'Well, I guess we are on holiday.' She turned to her son. 'What do you say? Try something American while we're here?'

The boy nodded, dubiously.

'I suppose the Lord will forgive us for trying a different kind of church – as a one-off holiday experience.'

'He will indeed! You won't regret it. I'll be there myself.'

She opened her purse and pushed across the counter a ten-dollar bill. 'Praise the Lord!' she said.

'Thank you kindly, ma'am.' He slipped the note into his pocket. 'I'll send a confirmation up to your room. Praise the Lord indeed!'

The following day they did actually get to go on some rides, after lengthy queues, and Thomas got to talk to Donald Duck, Mickey Mouse and Pluto as they walked around. Then at 2 p.m., after a hamburger lunch, they left in a taxi for the stadium. Pastor Drew Duane was not due there until 6 p.m., but as his mother said, it was important to get there early to ensure they got close to the great evangelist.

Otherwise he might not see them, and if he did not see them, then surely God would not either.

Their seats were ten rows from the front. But it wasn't until near 7 p.m. that Pastor Drew Duane finally arrived at the venue. Thomas Smith watched one of the huge screens to the side of the stadium in awe as a white Rolls-Royce pulled up, greeted by fifty baton-swinging cheerleaders singing the hymn 'Tell Me the Old, Old Story!'

But it was the car that young Thomas noticed the most. He watched the evangelist climb out of the rear door, and heard the screams of adulation from the vast crowd.

Want that car, he thought. *Want it so bad.*

22

Thursday, 23 February

Ross had a gruelling drive home from Benedict Carmichael's residence, the last two hours of it battling through
rush-hour traffic in pelting rain and darkness. The journey
had given him plenty of time to reflect on his meeting with
the bishop, and although he was tired, his brain was buzz-
ing with thoughts.

Imogen was lying on a sofa in front of the television,
digging a spoon into a large tub of butterscotch ice cream
– her current craving; Monty sat beside her, tongue out,
looking at her expectantly and salivating. He barely gave his
master a glance.

Ross kissed her. 'How was your day?'

She grabbed the remote and pressed the pause button,
then screwed up her face. 'A bit sort of – meh! After you left
this morning, I felt too sick to go into the office, so I've
been working from home. Feeling better now. So how did
it go?'

'Really interesting!'

'Lucky you. As I've been at home I've cooked some
dinner – do you want to eat soon?'

'Can you give me half an hour? I just need to look something up whilst it's still fresh in my mind, then I'll tell you
all about it.' He peered at the frozen television screen.
'What are you watching?'

'An old episode of *Frasier*. There's quite a funny bit with his brother.'

He went through to the kitchen, made himself a quick espresso and carried it upstairs.

There were the usual dozens and dozens of emails. He ran his eyes down them, but saw nothing that couldn't wait. He sipped his coffee and thought back to earlier today, to what the Bishop had said.

I'd want more than three sets of compass coordinates . . . Something that defies the laws of physics of the universe. In other words, a miracle.

OK, fair play.

Proof is the enemy of faith.

It wasn't a new expression. He'd heard that said before, and this was something that bugged him, because he could not understand the logic. Sure, that was probably a good argument for all churches, of whatever denomination, to use on doubters: *Believe in me, o ye of little faith.* But *little faith* was precisely why, according to Cook, God had communicated to him. It was the reason why he had sent him so-called proof.

He googled the words 'proof is the enemy of faith'.

The first thing that came up was a quote from Thomas Jefferson that lost him. Next was a quote from Anaïs Nin: 'When we blindly adopt a religion, a political system, a literary dogma, we become automatons. We cease to grow.'

He tried another search and found an eighteenth-century quote from Henry Adams: 'Even theologians – even the great theologians of the thirteenth century – even Saint Thomas Aquinas himself – did not trust to faith alone, or assume the existence of God.'

Thomas Aquinas was a theologian and philosopher who died in 1274. He wrote: 'To one who has faith, no explanation is necessary. To one without faith, no explanation is possible.'

Ross was familiar with Aquinas, and had come across his teachings in the months following his brother's death, when he desperately sought explanations for what had happened that morning in the gym.

Aquinas argued that everything – sensory organs, the food chain, what we know today as the nitrogen cycle and so on – works towards an end. He argued that the order of the universe cannot be explained by chance but only by design and purpose. That design and purpose is a product of intelligence. Therefore, nature is directed by a Divine Intelligence or a Great Designer.

Ross was interrupted by his mobile phone ringing. He looked at the display and it was a number – from another mobile – he didn't recognize. He hesitated for a moment, wondering if it was a sales call, then answered.

'Ross Hunter.'

'Hi, Ross, it's Sally – BBC Bristol?'

'Hey!' he said, instantly cheered by her voice. 'Good to hear from you – how are you doing? I really enjoyed meeting you.' In truth, he was surprised to hear from her, assuming she had probably forgotten all about him after doing another twenty or so interviews since.

'Me too,' she said. 'How was Glastonbury? You got there OK?'

'Yes, it was interesting.'

'I said I'd speak to my uncle – the one who's the trustee of Chalice Well? Julius Helmsley?'

'Yes – you did?'

'I asked him about your *friend* – Dr Harry Cook.'

'Thank you, that's really kind of you.'

She sounded hesitant as she replied. 'Well, I'm afraid I

don't have particularly good news for you. My uncle knows all about this man and says he's a nutter. Apparently he was found in the middle of the night some weeks ago, at Chalice Well, digging with a garden spade – and sent packing by the police. Then, somehow, he's got hold of my uncle's – and all the other trustees' – home phone numbers and he calls them up in the middle of the night, shouting abuse at them, telling them they should be helping him to save the world – not putting obstacles in his way. Apparently about a week ago he actually told my uncle Julius he was the Antichrist!'

'You're kidding?'

'No, I'm not. He's seriously deranged. I don't think the elevator goes to the top floor, if you understand.'

'I understand.' Ross was feeling deflated.

'If I were you, I'd really forget about him. I think he's just trouble.'

Ross thanked her and ended the call, after promising to let her know next time he was going to be in the Bristol area.

Imogen called out that supper was ready.

He did not hear her.

He stared at the manuscript on his desk, beside his keyboard. On the top was Harry F. Cook's address and phone number.

'Ross!' Imogen called out again. 'Supper's ready, come on, I'm starving!'

'Give me two minutes, Imo,' he said. Then he picked up his phone and dialled Cook's number.

After several rings he heard the old man's voice.

'Mr Hunter?'

'You didn't tell me you'd been digging at Chalice Well, Dr Cook. And that you'd nearly been arrested. And that you'd been abusive to several of the trustees,' he said.

'Well,' Cook said, sounding deeply apologetic. 'It was

very foolish. I – I was desperate to find some evidence, so I thought I would do a dig – but I never got very far. Just one spadeful before I was found and stopped.'

'Just one? You didn't dig more?'

'No,' he said, agitatedly, 'I never got the opportunity – there was a police officer and another man, I think one of the trustees – he was pretty mad at me – threatening me with criminal damage proceedings.'

'Are you telling me the truth?'

Ross was thinking about the four-foot trench that someone had clearly dug, recently.

'I am telling you the truth. I accept I was stupid – I lost my temper. These people, for whatever reason, just don't seem to accept, or perhaps don't want to know, what they are sitting on. Please believe me, I'm not the nutcase they'd have you think. You *must* believe me, Mr Hunter. They want to block me for some reason.'

'Dr Cook, I was just at Chalice Well. Someone has been digging in exactly the spot your compass coordinates took me to.'

'What?' He sounded genuinely shocked. 'Digging – in what way exactly?'

'It looked like a trench – the kind archaeologists dig. It had been dug and then filled in again.'

'This is terrible news.'

'If it wasn't you who was digging there, who else did you give the coordinates to?'

'You must believe me, Mr Hunter. No one. Absolutely no one. You are the only person in the entire world.'

'It's not possible other people have been given the same message?'

Cook was silent for some moments. 'I think I would have been told, if that was the case.'

'Well, clearly someone else knows,' Ross said. 'Any ideas?'

'I've never revealed the coordinates to another living soul, you have my word, Mr Hunter.' He sounded sincere.

'But you said you were found by a police officer and someone from the trust, you thought. They knew where you were digging.'

'I've never given the trustees the coordinates.'

'You wouldn't have needed to, if they'd found you at the spot.'

Was it someone from the trust or was Cook lying about no one else having the coordinates, Ross wondered? Or were they not quite so secret or special as he imagined? It was open knowledge that Joseph of Arimathea supposedly visited the place, and that he might have had the chalice – the Holy Grail – with him.

'It is unbearable to think it – that the Holy Grail might have fallen into the wrong hands, Mr Hunter,' Cook said. 'Is this why you are phoning? To tell me about the dig?'

'No, I'm really calling to tell you I honestly don't think I'm your man.'

Cook replied instantly and assertively. 'Mr Hunter, you are, I assure you. Look, since we spoke, I've found something that I think will change your mind. Please don't dismiss me as a harmless old loony. Give me the chance to explain what I've found.'

'OK, I'm listening.'

'I don't want to tell you over the phone, it's too dangerous – and it's too important. We need to meet. Please, I'm imploring you, give me the chance to do that. If you hear me out, what I've calculated about these coordinates and number sequences – I think you'll understand. It does have something to do with what you found – the digging . . . just do me that favour.'

There was something in his voice that cut through Ross's scepticism. It didn't convince him, but it made him hesitate. All his journalistic instincts were telling him there was a story here. Probably not the one Cook had in mind, but maybe it was worth seeing him again. The kind of story that perhaps the *Mail* would buy to run on a quiet news day. *The man who was so convinced he could save the world he got arrested digging up Chalice Well.*

He pulled up his diary for tomorrow on his computer. Friday. A clear day. Maybe it would be interesting to meet the man in his home. Take a few pictures of him. 'OK,' he said. 'How about I drive up to meet you at your house tomorrow? I could get to you late morning.'

'You won't regret it, Mr Hunter, I assure you. You'll bring the manuscript with you?'

'I'll do that.'

23

Friday, 24 February

Shortly after 11 a.m., following the satnav directions for Harry Cook's postcode, Ross drove along the high street of a small, pretty village, about ten miles to the west of Birmingham. At dinner last night, when he had told Imogen about his meeting with the Bishop of Monmouth, the subsequent phone call from Sally Hughes and then his conversation with Cook, she had bluntly told him to forget it, the man was clearly a fruit loop and he should not waste any more time on him.

The satnav told him to turn right in one and a half miles.

He passed a country pub, a petrol station, followed by an ugly little industrial estate. Then a couple of minutes later he saw a road sign, partly concealed by shrubbery. He turned right onto a single-track lane, drove over a hump-backed bridge across a narrow river, past a car-repair yard, a farm shop advertising fresh eggs and home-made cheeses, then down a long, wooded gradient. A countdown to his destination began on the satnav. It was followed by a chequered flag, and the almost triumphant female voice, 'You have arrived!'

To his right, up a short drive, was a neat bungalow, with an integral garage and an immaculate front lawn, the grass looking as if it belonged on a bowling green. Parked in front of the garage, dead centre in the driveway, was the white Nissan Micra he recognized from when Cook had visited him earlier in the week. It looked showroom clean.

He turned into the drive, parked his Audi behind the Micra and climbed out. He'd done a lot of driving the past few days, he thought. It was bitterly cold and there was a sweet smell of woodsmoke from nearby. A sparrow was washing itself in a birdbath. Glad of his fleece-lined parka and warm boots, he locked the car and walked up to the front door, carrying his heavy rucksack by one of the straps, and rang the bell. There was a faint two-tone chime. But no response.

After some moments he rang again, and once more heard the chimes.

Again, no response.

He tried again and this time also rapped hard with his knuckles.

A vehicle was approaching down the road. He heard a distinct diesel rattle. A muddy Land Rover Defender, towing a horsebox, passed by.

He pushed open the letter box and peered through. He could see a narrow, empty hallway. He knocked again.

Cook knew he was coming, and had his number. Surely he would have rung if he was going out?

He pulled out his phone, dialled Cook's mobile number and waited. He heard the sound of a ring tone somewhere in the house.

It rang on. After ten rings, he heard the old man's very precise voice.

'Hello, this is Harry Cook. I'm afraid I am not able to take your call at this moment. Please leave a message and your telephone number and I will call you back as soon as possible. Thank you so much.'

Ross ended the call without leaving a message, anxious. Cook's car was here.

He pushed open the letter box and shouted, loudly, 'Dr Cook? Hello!'

There was no response.

He decided to walk round to the rear of the house. Stepping over a low lavender hedge, he passed a side window and stopped to peer in. And froze.

It was a sitting room, with an old-fashioned television, a three-piece suite, pictures on a mantelpiece above an electric fire and a walnut cabinet filled with Capodimonte ornaments. But it looked like a bomb had hit it. All the seat cushions were strewn on the floor and ripped open, as were the sides and backs of the chairs and sofas. The cabinet doors were open and several of the ornaments lay broken on the carpeted floor. There was a small wooden bureau on the far side, all its drawers pulled out, the contents scattered.

The old man had been burgled, and this must have happened very recently, he guessed. This morning, even. But where was Cook?

The icy thought occurred that the burglar – or burglars – might still be here.

Should he call the police?

But if he did so he would have to explain why he was here. And that might compromise whatever it was the old man had wanted to tell or show him.

Gripping the heavy rucksack more firmly, as a makeshift weapon, he hurried past a trio of wheelie bins, each with a different coloured lid, and reached the back of the house. There was a square conservatory extension to the kitchen, with patio doors, and the rear garden looked as well-tended as the front, with beds planted with shrubs running down each side of a long lawn, an ornamental pond and a wooden summer house at the far end.

He walked up to the rear entrance and rapped loudly on the patio doors, braced again with the rucksack. After some moments, he tried the door. It was unlocked and slid open. Almost instantly there was a streak of ginger racing towards him and a cat shot past and out into the garden, as if fired from a cannon.

He stepped into the conservatory. There were two wicker chairs and an assortment of gardening magazines fanned out perfectly on a glass-topped wicker table.

'Hello, Dr Cook. Hello!' he called.

He heard a clock tick, loudly. Then a moment later two chimes made him jump. It was 11.30 a.m.

He called out once more, again ready with the rucksack if anyone came at him.

But just silence, broken only by the ticking of the clock.

He stepped forward, walking hesitantly through into the kitchen, and there was more clear evidence of the break-in here. Every cupboard door and drawer was open. Cups, bowls, vases lay scattered around on the linoleum floor. The contents of jars of tea, coffee, sugar and flour had been tipped out.

He hesitated.

A partially eaten breakfast was laid out on the kitchen table. In the centre was a copy of today's *Daily Telegraph*, resting against a reading rack. A packet of cornflakes, a jug of milk and a cereal bowl, a spoon lying in it, with remnants of milk and cornflake fragments around the side. Two boiled eggs, their tops sliced off but their contents untouched, sat in eggcups on a plate, a neat pile of salt and pepper on one side and a clean spoon on the table. There was also a teacup, filled to the brim. The wooden chair was pushed back at an angle, as though Cook had risen in a hurry from a meal he had not returned to. It looked like there should have been a second chair, opposite.

Feeling very nervous now, he looked about for a better weapon than his rucksack, and saw a brass doorstop on the floor. He picked the heavy object up, then stood, ready to swing it, listening. He stepped through the debris and reached the table; he dipped a finger in the tea and it was stone cold. He also touched the side of one egg and that was cold, too. For the tea to be that cold, Cook must have stood up from this table well over an hour ago, he estimated. Maybe two or three hours ago, or even more.

He walked through into the hall he had seen through the letter box, and called out again, more loudly still. 'Hello! Dr Cook?'

There was a grandfather clock, and its loud tick was the only sound that came back. Hanging on the wall opposite was an embroidered quote, in a frame.

Be still, and know that I am God – Psalm 46:10

The place had a slightly musty, old-people-and-cats smell that reminded him of his grandparents' house.

There were three doors leading off. The first opened on to a bedroom with a double bed. All the bedding had been pulled away and the mattress slit open in several places. Clothes had been pulled out of the fitted wardrobes and lay on the floor. The drawers in both bedside tables were open.

The next door opened on to a small den, with a desk and chair, and a power cable for a Mac – although there was no computer – lying under the desk, along with a plugged-in Wi-Fi router and a wastepaper bin. There were three metal filing cabinets. All the drawers were open and files were scattered across the floor, their contents spilled out.

On the desk was a mouse and an assortment of pens

and pencils in a circular holder. He saw a pad of notepaper, a couple of inches square – the same pad, he presumed, that Cook had written the Chalice Well coordinates on for him. There was a faint indent on the top sheet of the notepad, a long line curved to the left at the bottom, the shape of a hockey stick, and what looked like numbers. He knelt and looked in the bin. There was just one item, a crumpled scrap of paper. Listening and glancing around again for a moment, he then unfolded the paper. It must have been the top sheet from the pad, he realized. There was a black roller-ball line, curved left at the bottom, which matched the indent. Beside it were the numbers that looked like the ones that had accompanied the compass coordinates, although he couldn't be sure.

14 9 14 5 13 5 20 18 5 19 19 20 12

It seemed a strange doodle, and it made him curious. He folded it, tucked it into his wallet and took another careful look around the study. Then he went out into the hall, walked past the clock and approached the final door, on the right. It opened on to a sparsely furnished dining room, with a four-seater table and one solitary print on the wall beside an oak dresser, a picture of the Doge's Palace in Venice. The drawer in the centre of the dresser had been pulled open as well as each of the two doors, where glasses were stacked on one side, and place mats and napkins on the other.

Sensing a shadow move behind him, he spun round, gripping the doorstop. But there was nothing. He went out, crossed the hallway and peered into the ransacked living room. On the mantelpiece, above a fake coal electric fire, was a framed black-and-white wedding photograph of a much younger Harry Cook in a dark suit, holding hands with a sweet, rather prim-looking woman with dark wavy hair.

He returned to the kitchen, his heart thudding, and looked around. And then he saw it. A closed door he had somehow missed earlier.

He turned the handle and opened it towards him. Beyond was a wooden staircase descending into a basement or a cellar of some kind. He called down. 'Dr Cook? Hello? Anyone there?'

His voice sounded strangely high-pitched. Tight with anxiety.

There was a switch and he pressed it. A light, from a single bulb hanging from a brown cord, threw stark shadows and another appeared to come on at the bottom of the stairs. He would take a look down here and if there was still no sign of the old man, then he would call the police, he decided.

He began to descend the steps, one at a time, his grip on his makeshift weapon even tighter. As he approached the bare concrete floor at the bottom he saw it was some kind of a junk depository. Contents of files were scattered all around. A couple of old suitcases lay on their sides, opened.

Then, *Oh Jesus.*

Oh shit.

No.

No.

He understood now why there was no second chair at the kitchen table. It was down here. Harry Cook's bony, naked body was secured to it with grey gaffer tape, and there was more tape across his mouth. His arms were stretched out, his hands nailed to the wall.

Ross shot another nervous glance behind him, then walked over to the body. Cook's eyes were open, sightless, with an expression of terror. His face and body were marked with what looked like cigarette burns. And his throat had been gashed open. A pool of congealed blood lay on his chest.

Ross turned and fled up the stairs, through the house and out through the rear door. He vomited onto the lawn. Then, pulling out his phone and with shaking fingers, stabbed out 999, getting the numbers wrong three times before he finally, to his relief, heard the ringing tone. Followed by the voice of the emergency operator.

24

'Have you all decided?' The smiling waiter stood in front of them in the packed, buzzy Curry Leaf restaurant in Brighton's Lanes.

After a moment, Imogen said, 'We can never decide here – why don't you just bring us a selection of starters and then mains – whatever you think.' She looked at the other three at the table. Her friends nodded but Ross appeared lost in his own world.

'Ross?' she said.

He looked up with a start. 'Sorry – I was – I was just thinking about yesterday – I –'

'I'm ordering a selection of starters, OK with you?'

'Good idea,' he said.

'Excellent!' said the waiter. 'Now, do any of you have any allergies, anything you do not eat?' He looked at Ross, Imogen and their two closest friends, Hodge and Helen.

'Small babies,' said Helen, a chiropractor with a very quirky sense of humour.

'That's all?'

'Anything healthy,' said Hodge, who was Finance Director for an international outlet store. 'Nothing healthy, please.'

The waiter pressed his hands together. 'That is good! I

122

can promise you no small babies and nothing *too* healthy on the menu tonight – only just a little bit good for you.'

As the waiter departed, Hodge raised his Cobra beer. 'Cheers.'

The four of them clinked glasses.

'So,' Helen said to Ross. 'You had a pretty traumatic day yesterday?'

'You could say that. Yes.'

'You're looking pale.'

'I didn't sleep too well.'

'I'm not surprised, mate,' Hodge said. 'I'm amazed you even came out tonight.'

'Yup, well, it's nice to have some normality after what I saw and then what I had to go through with the police and all their questions.'

'Was it like bodies you saw in Afghanistan?' Helen hesitated. 'Sorry, that was pretty insensitive.'

'No, it's OK. I thought that nothing would ever shock me again after my time out there. But I was wrong. I've never seen a murder victim here in the UK in situ before.'

'How did it make you feel?' asked Helen, looking very interested.

'Actually, a bit shit.' He drained his beer and looked around for a waiter to order another. 'Even more shit when I got taken to the police station and interviewed for three hours like I was a potential suspect.' He shrugged. 'But all grist to the mill for my story.'

'Which is?' Hodge asked.

'The quest for proof of God's existence. Or rather a man who believed he had the proof.'

Hodge, who had spiky hair and a trim beard, replied, 'And you have it?'

'Not yet – not that I'm convinced of.'

Hodge gave him a sardonic smile. 'The Bible was basically written under the supervision of God, right? It is, to many believers, the undisputed word of God?'

'As I remember from RE classes – which I never paid much attention to,' Ross replied.

'I read it all the way through once, Old and New Testaments. I vaguely remember that the earth was described as flat and sitting on a pedestal – and in Revelation it has four corners. "I saw four angels standing at the four corners of the earth, holding back the four winds of the world."' Hodge raised his eyebrows. 'If God created the world, didn't he know that it was round – and not mounted on a pedestal? Seems like we have quite a lot to teach him.'

Ross smiled. 'I guess there's a lot of metaphor in the Bible.'

'There's a lot of metaphor in many fairy tales,' Hodge replied.

'Did this Dr Cook have children, Ross?' Helen asked.

'Yes, a son who was killed by friendly fire in Helmand Province. I guess that was one of the things that I connected with.'

More beers arrived.

'What about a motive?' Hodge asked. 'Did the police say anything about that?'

Ross shook his head. 'No.'

'Sounds like a burglary that went wrong,' Helen said.

'Early morning?' Imogen queried and looked at Ross. 'You said it looked like he was in the middle of his breakfast. Seems an odd time for a burglary.'

'It's actually quite a common time,' Ross replied. 'The police told me. Someone driving around in a van late at night looks suspicious. But no one pays any attention to one in the morning.'

'What did they take?' Helen asked.

'Well, that's what I hope to find out.' He drained his glass again. He was still feeling shaken.

'If you want to forget golf tomorrow, mate, don't worry about it,' Hodge said.

'No, I think a few hours out in the fresh air is what I need. And the forecast's good.'

'If you're sure?'

'I'm looking for a major win!'

'In your dreams.'

Ross grinned. Hodge beat him consistently.

'Ten o'clock tee-off OK with you?'

Ross nodded.

'It will do you good,' Imogen encouraged.

Ross looked at her and nodded. But his suspicions about her returned. Even though she was three months pregnant, they just wouldn't go away. Four or five hours without him around. Was she being altruistic, a good and caring wife? Or did she have another motive?

'This all started when this man, Dr Cook, contacted you out of the blue with his weird message?' Helen went on. 'And you didn't hang up on him?'

'I'm a journalist, always looking for an angle.'

'Aren't you worried after what's happened to him?'

'I am,' Imogen said. 'I've told Ross to forget it. When you start messing with religion, you don't know what kind of nutters or fanatics you're going to attract.'

'As Helen said, it could just have been a burglary that went wrong,' Hodge tried to reassure her.

'Oh sure. He was a retired university lecturer – not a drug dealer,' Imogen retorted. 'They tortured him. They were after something they wanted very badly.'

'The manuscript?' Hodge suggested.

'Not necessarily,' Ross replied. 'You do get sadistic burg-lars – they're rare, fortunately, but it happens. Here they had an old man living alone in a secluded property. Maybe they were convinced he had a safe hidden somewhere.'

'I dread to think if they'd been there when you arrived.' Imogen picked up her wine glass, started to reach across for the bottle, then stopped. Hodge lifted it out of the cooler and held it towards her. 'I can't,' she said. 'One glass is my limit at the moment – although I could do with a whole bottle. I can't believe that this poor man, Harry Cook, was in our house on Monday – and now he's dead. Tortured and murdered. I just think this is too coincidental to be any-thing other than connected to the manuscript. The one dictated by God, that you said is total rubbish.'

'It is,' Ross said.

'If that's what they were after, then perhaps someone else doesn't consider it to be rubbish, you know?' Imogen said.

'Did you tell the police about the manuscript?' Hodge asked.

'No.'

Imogen turned to him. 'What? You withheld informa-tion? Isn't that a criminal offence?'

'I figured if I told them about it they'd want it as evi-dence.'

'And what's your problem with that?' said Imogen.

'What did you do with it?' Hodge asked.

Ross hesitated.

'Don't tell me you still have it?' Imogen said.

'I didn't want to part with it – not until I've had a chance to copy it, Imo.'

'So where is it now?' she said.

'Safe.'

'Safe where?' she demanded.

'It's in the garage, OK? I'm going to take it to our solicitor's on Monday and get it put in their vaults.'

'Jesus! You told me it was utter rubbish. Why do you want the bloody thing? Who's going to want it?'

'The people who tortured and murdered Harry Cook?' suggested Hodge, helpfully.

'That might not be the reason he was killed. No one knew about this manuscript,' Ross replied. 'So far as I'm aware. Other than a BBC presenter I talked to in Bristol and I don't think she is a killer.'

'Sure,' Imogen said. 'Maybe that's what Cook told you, that no one else knew about it. Maybe that's what he wanted you to believe.'

'I'll tell you what I really believe.' Ross glanced at their friends. 'I believe Cook was probably a deluded, well-meaning nutter. But – and this is a very big but – what if he wasn't? What if he was right?'

'And you're willing to risk your life for that?' Imogen queried.

Ross had no immediate answer. Maybe the beer was giving him courage. Maybe it was his sense of obligation to Cook. All he knew was that he wasn't ready to let this go. 'Imo, you know my job. I'm constantly digging deep and writing stuff that upsets people. You know I've had threats. The game changer would be the moment I felt that your life and our baby's life was in danger, that's when I'd forget about it.'

'Let's hope the money's worth it,' his wife replied tartly.

25

Sunday, 26 February

Pastor Wesley Wenceslas delivered two sermons most Sundays, one at Arise, Shine and the other at the evening Praise! Each was in a different church, whether he was in the UK or the US. He moved around the seven he shepherded in steady rotation, ferried by either the Wesley Wenceslas Ministries helicopter or Boeing 737 jet, both in the WWM livery of white, adorned with the distinct and elegant ministry logo of a winged fish entwined round a cross.

Of all the things he liked doing most, preaching, spreading the words of the Lord to his adoring flocks, feeling their love – and hearing their love – these gave him the most joy. Well, almost as much as entering the garages on his English and American estates and looking at his fleet of gleaming supercars. Almost even as much as selecting the Angelhelper – and often Angelhelpers – who would share his bed for the night.

But this morning, despite the stunning blue sky beyond the helicopter's window and the crystal-clear view of the Thames, the pastor wasn't feeling the usual joy in his heart.

Instead he had a deep sense of foreboding. And growing, dark anger.

There was a threat – only small at this stage, but small could do a lot of damage, small could turn big mightily fast.

In one of the sermons he liked to preach from time to time was a quote from the Dalai Lama: 'If you ever thought you were too small to make a difference, you never shared a bed with a mosquito.'

The bite could give you a small itch. Or it could give you malaria, dengue or zika virus. Any of those could kill you. That was why when you saw a mosquito you didn't take the chance. You snuffed it out, fast.

And there was a human mosquito out there now.

The world had always been a dangerous place, balanced constantly between good and evil. His mother had been taken from him because he hadn't been there to protect her, to hold her hand as she crossed the street. It was his fault. He should have been there. He was never ever again going to let something be taken from him. Never ever again let something happen which he could have prevented.

God had sought him out and given him this mission in life, made him His foot soldier, and he had risen to become His general. But now there was a threat and he needed to deal with it the same way all generals deal with threats.

A sudden jolt shook him and gave him a moment of panic. He liked the convenience of his helicopter, and the grand entrance he made wherever he landed, with the second matching helicopter a few minutes behind carrying lesser members of his entourage – his hairdresser, make-up artist, personal chef and four bodyguards. He received regular death threats from religious fanatics of different faiths who did not subscribe to his teachings. They scared him to the point of paranoia. Almost as much as flying in helicopters scared him. Even though the Lord should be protecting him. Though he wasn't too sure about that – wasn't too sure the Lord approved of his lifestyle.

They were rapidly losing height, sinking down to the London Heliport in Battersea. A number of helicopters sat on the ground, and from up here they looked like hunched, angry insects.

He was angry and hunched, too. In today's sermon was his message for his faithful: 'Focus on the positives. There are so many negatives in life. Negatives drag you under, positives raise you up. Just like the Lord was raised from the dead, by all the positives that surrounded him.'

'Smilealot', as he called the Managing Director of his empire, was strapped in the cream leather seat opposite, a short, dapper man with neat dark hair. He was dressed in one of his trademark grey chalk-striped three-piece suits, pink tie and immaculately buffed black Gucci loafers. It was Smilealot who had alerted him to the new threat, after being contacted by a police officer in Somerset who was a member of their congregation.

Smilealot was at this moment reading the sermon, frowning and tut-tutting as he made each annotation with an ornate Montegrappa pen poised daintily between his manicured fingers. His real name was Lancelot Pope, and when Wenceslas had first met the man, he'd said, 'I've got to have you – I've got to be able to tell folk I have the Pope working for me!'

'I'm not sure about this bit, boss,' he said, sharply.

'Which bit?'

Pope read aloud: 'I'm telling you that Satan is all around us. He's not a fiery man with a tail and a pitchfork. He's in the aisle of every supermarket tempting you with sugary confections. Eat rubbish and you are being duped by Satan. He's poisoning you by stealth.'

'What's your problem with that? It's an important message.'

'I'm thinking about our YouTube sponsors.'

'And I'm thinking about our moral obligations. This is on-message. This is the message of today.'

'I'm not comfortable with it.'

Pope rarely smiled and when he did it was thin and colourless, like a ray of sunlight failing to quite penetrate a bleak, wintry sky. And hey, praise the Lord, Wenceslas didn't pay the man to smile. He paid him to run his business with an iron rod. To keep an eye on every detail, down to fine-tuning every sermon. To deal with problems.

Smilealot did just that. A pernickety, highly efficient control freak, utterly ruthless, he was the only employee of the Wesley Wenceslas corporation who dared to answer his boss back or criticize him. Partly because he knew too much about the pastor.

Both men were aware that Lancelot Pope could bring the entire empire crumbling down with a single press statement. Equally, both of them knew he would never do that, because of the stake Wenceslas had given him. He would never destroy the golden goose that had already made him a millionaire and would, if things continued the way they were headed, one day make him far, far more money. Riches beyond his dreams.

Wenceslas knew that God had sent this man to take care of him and all he stood for.

Because for a long time in his early life, he'd had no one to take care of him. The day after he and his mother had returned to England from Disney World, probably confused because of suffering from jet lag, the coroner had said at her inquest, she had looked the wrong way whilst crossing Old Shoreham Road and gone under a bus.

From that moment, he had lost all faith in God, and turned into a rebel at school. He started stealing and found he had an ability to persuade others to do things for him. Anything. Within a year he had a network of five pupils distributing drugs around the school for him.

When, inevitably, he was caught, he was hauled before the headmaster. Mr Collins spoke to him calmly, telling him he felt sympathy for him since the terrible tragedy of his mother. But he had no other option than to expel him. 'You know, Thomas, you have so much charm, and I think beneath all of this you are a decent young man who has lost his way. You are good with people. I could see you in sales one day or in public relations. Don't destroy your future by getting a criminal record. Given the chance, what would you like to do in life?'

'I want to make a lot of money, Mr Collins,' he had replied. 'And have a Roller with a chauffeur.'

'You do?'

'Yes.'

'Anything is possible, Thomas, if you believe in yourself and work hard. It's what I try to teach everyone here. You don't have to go down a criminal path to make money, you just have to make the right choices.'

'And what would they be? What are the right choices to make a lot of money?'

'I'll tell you what I would do if I wanted to become rich. I think I'd become a property developer or a banker. Or –' he hesitated and smiled – 'I might start a religion!'

26

It was one of those cold but almost impossibly beautiful February mornings, where a sparkling cobweb dew lay across the grass either side of the fairway of the first hole at the Dyke Golf Club.

Exercise had always been Ross's way of dealing with stress, and despite all his turmoil over Harry Cook, he decided to play today. Also, it would help his appalling hangover, he hoped. But his mind was clouded with deep dismay over what had happened to Cook, and about the two sets of compass coordinates he would now never have. Coordinates someone had wanted badly enough to kill the old man?

Coordinates that he needed to progress any story he could write about him.

He tugged his driver out of his flashy new bag – a Christmas present from Imogen – rummaged inside for a ball and laid his bag on the ground. He held the ball up and read the markings. 'Titleist 4,' he announced to his partner. Then, for a moment, he took in the spectacular view across acres of farmland, down to the single chimney of Shoreham power station and the English Channel beyond. But his mind was somewhere way beyond that.

Hodge, who had won the toss, went first. He planted his red tee into the soft, moist soil, placed his ball on top, then lumbered into position, bending his knees and arching his back. He had a couple of swings, then took a step forward, tapped the grass behind his ball a couple of times with the club head and gave a mighty swipe.

There was just a faint, sweet click. Ross watched the ball rise dead straight into the air, losing sight of it for an instant against the bright sky, then saw it land a good two hundred and fifty yards dead ahead, in the centre of the fairway, and roll.

'Brilliant!' he said. 'Great shot.'

Hodge pursed his lips and nodded, looking very smug. 'Not shit!'

Ross pushed his own tee into the ground and placed his ball on it. The ball fell off. He tried again and it fell off again. He felt like a hot wire was sawing through his brain. The third time, the ball stayed on.

He took his stance, made a practice swing, then stepped up to the ball and swung his club.

And totally missed the ball, doing an air shot.

'Three off the tee,' Hodge said, reproachfully, and looking even more smug. He pulled out a small cigar and lit it.

Ross took a couple more practice swings then stepped up to the ball again and swung his club. It struck the ground about a foot in front of the ball, sending a massive divot flying up into the air and landing a few feet away.

'Shit!' he said. 'Shit!'

He replaced the divot and noticed the next group to play, a four-ball, were standing right beside them, watching, their patience being tested.

On his third attempt he managed a respectable shot, but it fell well short of his friend's, lagging up behind a bush.

Ross's performance wasn't much better over the next

two holes. He was totally distracted by his thoughts about Cook.

As they waited for a four-ball ahead of them to tee off at the sixth, Hodge relit his cigar and said, 'What's Imogen doing this morning?'

'She was talking about going to Matins – she tries to go once a month or so.'

'Do you ever go with her?'

'Occasionally – mostly when it's pissing with rain and golf isn't an option.' Ross grinned.

'So where do you sit on religion these days? You've never really told me,' Hodge asked. 'Apart from trashing charlatan preachers.'

Ross smiled. Hodge was referring to a large piece he had written for the *Sunday Times*, about five years ago, on the world's richest evangelists. The Wesley Wenceslas Ministries in the UK had threatened to sue the newspaper for what he had written about Wesley Wenceslas. The lawyers had only dropped the allegations after the paper threatened to publish the pastor's former criminal record.

'We were brought up by not particularly religious Christian parents. Then when I was fourteen my mum, who my brother and I adored, got sick with cancer. I prayed every night for her and she still died, three months later. I stopped praying after that – just lost all my faith. Our dad brought us up on his own. Then something very strange happened some years ago that I just can't explain.'

'What was that?'

'Haven't I told you about it? Ricky, my identical twin brother?'

'No.'

'He died in a freak accident. He was a couple of hundred miles away but I felt an incredibly strong connection with him, for – I don't know – at least a minute or two – which I found out later was at the exact time he died.'

'I've read about identical twins having some kind of telepathy. Maybe that's what happened to you?'

Ross shook his head. 'No, it was way more than that – I had a distinct mystical experience. It's hard to explain without sounding crazy, so I don't tend to talk about it.'

'And that's turned you into a believer?'

'Not in God – but in the sense that there might be a bigger picture.'

Hodge puffed on his cigar. 'This guy, Dr Cook, right?'

'Yes?'

'Which God is he talking about? Anglican, Catholic, Judaic, Islamic? Hindu? Sikh? Rastafarian?'

'I'm not sure.' Ross gave his friend a quizzical look. 'You're a pretty hard-core atheist, right?'

Hodge nodded as he watched, through a wisp of smoke, the incredibly slow four-ball ahead finally move off the tee. 'Yep, I have a big problem. Stephen Fry was talking about it a while ago and summed it up beautifully. He was saying if God really did create us, what kind of a sick mind did he have to create a parasite that only thrives inside the eye of a child, that burrows from the inside of the eyeball outwards, and the sole purpose for its existence is to blind children?'

'Some religions would have an explanation for that.'

'All religions have some kind of lame explanation for suffering. But look at all these different monotheistic religions – and the divisions within each of them – Anglican, Catholic, Sunni, Shi'ite, Sephardic, Hassidic – and when you drill right down, what's the difference between them all? What are all their arguments about? I'll tell you. They're about whose imaginary friend is the best.'

Ross smiled. 'I guess of all the faiths that believe in a single God, I understand Christianity the best. With a few exceptions in Bible-belt areas in the States, it has morphed over the centuries from something very tyrannical – think about the Inquisition, where if you weren't the right kind of Catholic you could be put to death – into more of a benign social structure.'

They watched one of the four players ahead of them, whose ball had landed barely fifty yards in front of the tee. The doddery octogenarian stood, lining up his next shot, for what seemed like an eternity.

'Christianity, the absolute tenet of which is belief in the Resurrection,' Hodge replied. 'Two thousand years of belief based on a conjuring trick with bones.' He took a puff of his cigar. 'Or did your Harry Cook have anything better to offer? It must be great to believe in God. You can hand over all responsibility – and blame him for any crap that happens. Come on, Ross, you're a smart reporter. Get real!'

'Can you explain why we are here, Hodge? How we came to exist? Did you read Stephen Hawking and claim to understand what he wrote? Can you explain human exist-ence?'

'Do I need to, in order to enjoy my life? In order to love my wife? To enjoy my game of golf here on this beautiful morning? What's God got to do with any of it?'

'Apart from maybe creating all this?'

'OK, so who created God? Can you answer that? Should I be worshipping him in the fairy-tale hope that he'll give me a seat at a decent dinner table in the afterlife? Does God have some machine that monitors each of our lives and gives us a credit every time we pat a dog or drop a coin in a busker's hat or a homeless person's hand?'

'Don't you ever question existence, Hodge? Isn't that

what we should be doing with our so-called intelligence? Didn't Socrates have a point when he wrote, "The unexamined life is not worth living"?'

'Are you saying if I don't challenge existence my life is not worth living?'

'No, not at all. What I'm saying – I guess – is that . . .' He fell silent.

'Go on.'

Ross remained silent for some moments. Just what did Harry Cook have in mind? Was his death part of a bigger picture? Was this journey he had embarked on going to give him anything beyond a few column inches in one of the papers?

'OK, Hodge, let me ask you a question. What would it take for you, as an atheist, to be convinced of God? Or, at least, the existence of a Creator of the Universe – an Intelligent Designer?'

Hodge pulled his driver out of his bag and walked up onto the raised tee. 'That's a pretty big ask for a Sunday morning.'

'I need to know, I value your opinion. What would it take?'

'I guess I'd need to see something for which I couldn't give you any explanation. Something I couldn't explain myself. Something that could not be dismissed as a conjuring trick.'

'Such as?'

'I don't know. Maybe the tide not going out when it should – although that could be connected to an eclipse or something.'

'So, if the sun rose from the west, you'd then believe in God?'

'I'm not sure. My first reaction would be that the

physicists – or astronomers – had screwed up on their calculations. That maybe it's something that happens every
few millennia.' He shrugged.

'So, go on, what would it take?'

'I guess something in the realm of physics that we know
to be impossible. Maybe then.'

'And if that happened?'

He bent down and planted his tee. 'Ross, my friend, get
real. It isn't going to happen.'

He struck the ball, which shanked off right, landing in a
dense thicket.

'See?' Ross said. 'God didn't like that!'

27

It isn't going to happen.

The expression had become a mantra for Pete Stellos. He had said it to his mother when she asked him when he was going to meet a nice girl and settle down – and produce grandchildren for her. He wasn't interested in girls, or boys, and he had none of the sexual desires that he'd read he was supposed to have.

There was something about people, generally, that he just did not connect with – or even like, really – which had caused him difficulties in his past. It was why he'd spent the first part of his working life doing solitary, lonely jobs. First, working the night shift in a McDonald's in Des Moines, Iowa. Then, after feeling he should see more of the world – or at least his own country – he got his licence and became a long-distance truck driver, hauling auto spares one way across America and grain the other.

As a child, he had been brought up in the Greek Orthodox tradition, although subsequently he'd had no interest at all in religion. But at a funeral – of a great-aunt – he'd met for the first time a cousin, Angus, who told him he was a monk and had, for some years, lived a monastic life on Mount Athos, in Greece. The conversation reignited Pete's interest in the Greek Orthodox religion. Angus felt Mount Athos was a place that might be of interest. But, he cautioned him, it wasn't a simple case of turning up. There was a lengthy application process. And a lonely existence if he was admitted.

Pete asked him to tell him more.

28

Sunday, 26 February

In the weeks following his premature departure from Blatchington Mill School, six months shy of his sixteenth birthday, Thomas Smith, in his urgent quest to make money, ignored all of his former headmaster's advice. He became a runner for the drug dealer who had supplied him with the cannabis, Ecstasy and other assorted drugs that he had been distributing at school.

For the following six months, he made good and easy money, delivering heroin, mostly, to users around the city of Brighton and Hove. Until he got arrested with three thousand pounds' worth, street value, in his pockets.

He spent two years in a Young Offender Institution. He found it helpful in there, building up a great network of future dealers for the drugs empire he had begun planning. By the age of nineteen he had a cool apartment on the seafront, with a view over the Channel. With the steep monthly rent he had to find, he had not yet amassed enough money for the car he currently hankered after, but he had stashed fifty thousand pounds towards it – in what he jokingly called his 'Ferrari Fund'. In the meantime, he drove around in a nice black ten-year-old Porsche with a personalized plate.

Then, a few days before his twentieth birthday, at 5 a.m., his front door caved in, and with it his world. Six coppers yelling 'POLICE! POLICE!' piled into his flat.

They found twenty thousand pounds' worth of crack cocaine, heroin and other bits and pieces. He was pretty sure he'd been informed on by a rival dealer. He got a harsh eight-year sentence and, almost as bad, the Porsche and his cash were all seized under a confiscation order.

It was God who saved him. He found God in prison – or rather, as Thomas liked to tell people, God found him. His reading of the Bible as a child, and then as a teenager, served him well. He could remember large tracts of it and he found he had a natural ability to preach – and quote at length – from the Good Book.

Thanks to the support of the enlightened governor of Highdown Prison, where he was sent to spend the majority of the four years he would serve, he was allowed to hold his own 'church' every Sunday in the recreation area. Within a year he had over one hundred regular worshippers. By the end of the second year he had over two hundred. He was so popular, he began holding daily Revival Meetings after breakfast in the prison dining room.

Then one night in his cell, God spoke to him directly. God told him to mend his ways, to forget drugs when he came out. To take a new path, His path. And to take a new name, a name that had charisma, for a new beginning. And a whole new identity.

One of the inmates who had become a dedicated follower had a friend who was a clergyman in Tooting Bec, who had an unused church hall.

Within three months of his release, Pastor Wesley Wenceslas began preaching the Word of the Lord in what was little more than a large, rusting, corrugated-iron shed, filled with rickety folding wooden chairs.

The rest, as he was proud to tell anyone who asked him, was – Praise the Lord! – history.

The helicopter lurched then dropped sharply for a moment. Then it jolted, several times.

Wenceslas felt a moment of fear. He closed his eyes and prayed, silently.

Oh Lord, make us safe.

He opened his eyes again and looked out of the window. The helipad was looming. He could see the markings, clearly.

'Bumpy!' Pope said. 'Bumpy ride we're having.'

Wenceslas stared at him. 'God takes care of us, remember?'

The ground came up towards them, swiftly. At the last moment, the helicopter hovered on a cushion of air.

Then Wenceslas felt, beneath him, the reassurance of terra firma.

Above him the rotors continued their *flacker-flacker-flacker* sound.

He removed his headset, and Pope did the same, then tidied his hair with his fingertips and checked his small white Hublot. 'On time!' he announced.

'Praise the Lord!' said his boss.

29

Sunday, 26 February

When Ross arrived home from golf, shortly after 2 p.m., Imogen's car was gone. There was a note from her saying that she had taken Monty out for a walk with a girlfriend and her dog, and would be back at three – and reminding him that it was his turn to do the Sunday roast.

He wondered which *girlfriend* it was. But it suited him well that she was out. He'd done most of the preparations for the meal yesterday afternoon. He switched on the oven, put the chicken and potatoes in, set the timer on his watch, then hurried upstairs. Fifteen minutes later, showered and changed, he went to his office, logged on and opened Google Earth. Then he entered the compass coordinates Cook had given him. The position where he had stood on Tuesday afternoon.

51°08'40"N 2°41'55"W

The place where Cook was convinced the Holy Grail was buried.

In the middle of a lawn – although back then, two thousand years ago, it would have been an open field.

I don't want to tell you over the phone, it's too dangerous – and it's too important. We need to meet. Please, I'm imploring you, give me the chance to do that. If you hear me out, what I've calculated . . .

What was it the old man wanted to tell him – but was scared to do so over the phone?

The meaning of those numbers that followed the coordinates?

He pulled the piece of paper he had found in Harry Cook's waste bin, unfolded it and looked at the strange hockey-stick shape and the numbers written neatly beside it.

14 9 14 5 13 5 20 18 5 19 19 20 12

Was the shape connected to these numbers? Were they some kind of code? Computer code?

He typed them into an email and sent them to his IT guru, Chris Diplock, asking him if he could shed any light on them. As usual, even though it was a Sunday afternoon, a reply pinged back from the man almost instantly.

> These look like some kind of code, Ross. No idea what, I'm afraid. I'm guessing the gaps between are significant, and the repetition of some is also significant. There are a stack of code-breaking websites and forums on the net. Attaching some that might be of interest.

Diplock had put a long list of links underneath.

Ross toyed with the idea of posting messages on Twitter and Facebook asking if anyone knew what these numbers might mean. But then decided against it as he didn't know who might answer and what questions they'd start to ask back. Instead, he had another idea. Some years ago, he'd written a story on computer hackers and had met an oddball character in the Computer Science Department at Brighton University whom he had found engaging, if unpredictable. His name was Zack Boxx.

A nocturnal creature, with few social graces, Zack's sole interests appeared to be computers and craft beers. Ross had spent two hours with the geek one evening at the university, during which Boxx had shown him how to hack into a whole range of top-secret government departments, not only in the UK but the US and other countries, and military installations as well, including a US drone operation in Iran, whilst leaving, he assured Ross, untraceable footprints. They'd spent the following day getting totally wrecked at a craft beer festival in a hall in Horsham.

To Ross's amazement, Zack had never been arrested, and now worked freelance, advising companies on cyber security. Ross had kept in touch and because Zack always had stories to tell, had joined him at the occasional beer festival around the county, partly because he liked the guy and the beers, and partly because, after a few pints, Zack was likely to let slip the occasional nugget.

Knowing that the geek would probably still be asleep at this hour, he emailed him, asking if he had any idea what these numbers might mean. And suggesting it was time for a catch-up over a beer somewhere.

And he felt in need of a beer right now. Despite his relaxing time this morning, and Hodge's company, which he always enjoyed, the events of Friday were still hitting him hard. He went down into the kitchen, pulled a Peroni out of the fridge, fumbled around in a drawer for the bottle opener, popped the cap off, then carried the cold bottle back upstairs, swigging some as he went. Sitting back at his desk, he stared at his computer screen, his mind elsewhere.

On the image of Harry Cook, bound, in his chair.

Shit.

If Harry Cook's torture and murder was connected with all of this, should he let it go? Walk away?

Imogen was scared by what he had told her. Was he out of his depth as Benedict Carmichael had suggested? Was anything worth risking their lives for? He tried to recall Cook's words as he had relayed the message for Ross received via the medium.

This man said he had someone with him who had a message for you. He said he had your brother, Ricky . . . Ricky said he wanted you to trust me. He said two names, I think it was Bubble and Squeak.

How could Cook possibly have known about his brother? By reading about the accident in the papers, perhaps – but that was years ago. The internet? But no way could he have known about the gerbils.

Just what had Cook's killers been after? The manuscript? The coordinates they thought it contained? Or was that all a total red herring and they were just chancers after an old man's hidden money?

What was it Cook reckoned he had calculated, that he had been so excited about on the phone?

The only obvious item that had been taken was Cook's laptop. His wife's wedding ring was on the floor in its original box, one of the detectives had told him. There was also two thousand pounds in cash in one of the opened drawers in the bedroom. The fact that so much cash and so many valuables had been left untouched pointed to something else that Cook had, which his assailant – or assailants – were after. Information on someone – or something?

Ross came back to the manuscript again.

Whatever the truth, he didn't like the idea of keeping it in the house. Tomorrow, as he had told Imogen, he would take it to his solicitor. Or maybe it would be better to take it to a storage depot near Shoreham Harbour, where he and Imogen had once rented a unit for some of their furniture between moving from the flat to their current house.

He googled Glastonbury Tor. According to the details

that came up, a wooden church had been built on the top in the tenth century and destroyed sometime later. The current structure, the ruin of the Church of St Michael, was built in the 1200s. If Joseph of Arimathea had come to England, bringing with him the Holy Grail, that would have been nearly one thousand years before the first church had been built.

He did some further internet searching. The only thing that would have been there, for certain, when Joseph visited, was the well itself.

If I had wanted to hide the chalice, he thought further, would I have dug a hole halfway up the hill – or used a more convenient hiding place?

Yet the compass coordinates indicated halfway up the hill.

What were the other coordinates that Cook had kept to himself? Gone. For good?

He couldn't get out of his mind the thought that Harry Cook's death might have been some kind of bizarre modern version of a crucifixion. Or some hideous take on it.

He tried a different train of thought. OK, I'm God, and I want to reveal to Cook where the chalice is. Do I give him the exact coordinates or ones close? I would know where it is, wouldn't I?

Apparently, the wily, often bolshy Old Testament God set people tasks and challenges. He never made anything easy, from what he remembered of his scant reading of the scriptures as a child. Might God have set Cook a challenge, too?

Was that what Cook had wanted to tell him?

After the glorious start to the day, the sky was dark and droplets of rain were running down the window. He thought about the thick sheaf of papers of the manuscript, held untidily in place by two elastic bands, and suddenly felt afraid.

Should he just burn the damned thing?

And lose his story?

He had already, Holy Grail or no Holy Grail, the bones of a sensational article. One of the tabloids would buy it for sure. But there was one more piece he needed to put in place. A very big piece. It could be everything – or nothing.

An email appeared. It was from Zack Boxx.

He opened it.

> There's a beer festival at Yapton, near Bognor, next Saturday. Might go along. Some good Sussex versions of German weissbeers there. 14 9 14 5 13 5 20 18 5 19 19 20 12. Could be a numerical letter code. Each represents a letter of the alphabet. It spells out, Nine Metres S (south?) T (turn?) L (left?) Helpful?

Then a possibility occurred to Ross. Excitedly he returned to Google Earth, pulled up Chalice Well and looked at the hockey-stick shape.

It fitted!

He grabbed his wallet, logged out of Google Earth and began a shopping spree on the internet.

Just as he clicked the final 'Confirm Purchase' button, he heard Monty bark downstairs. It was followed by Imogen's voice calling out.

'Ross, I'm home!'

'Great, I'm starving,' he shouted back. 'The chicken should be ready in ten minutes.'

'How was your golf? Did you win?'

'No, but I came second!'

Monty bounded into the room, soaking wet, shook himself, spattering water everywhere, then trotted over to him, sat on his haunches and raised his front paws.

'Hey, wet boy, had a good walk?'

He tickled the dog's tummy.

Normality.

Something that was badly missing from his life.

But he felt incredibly excited – and more than a little scared.

He emailed Zack Boxx back.

> You're a genius!

Boxx replied seconds later.

> I know. Ok if I go back to bed now? It's still pretty early for me.

30

Monday, 27 February

Monaco worked well for his purposes. The rocky principality, the second smallest country in the world, about two square kilometres. Bordered on three sides by France and on the fourth by the Mediterranean, much of it is jam-packed with shoulder-to-shoulder high-rise apartment blocks. There are no beggars and no homeless people, just conspicuous wealth managing to be quite inconspicuous, wherever you looked.

The country's fame as a glamorous tax haven, the sunny climate and the short hop to the international airport of Nice were all attractions to him, but not the main reason he was here. It was the anonymity this place afforded – and which the residents could afford – that suited him most of all.

Here in Monaco, at the deli counter in a supermarket you could find yourself standing next to an F1 driver or a Russian investment banker or a Brexit exile – or Big Tony. Who was actually small.

Although you didn't really want to be standing next to Big Tony if you could help it. Not that he smelled bad or anything. It was just his aura. He wore it like a black cloak.

Big Tony had a quite unremarkable physical presence and his complexion was pallid. He didn't go out much, except to ride one of his powerful motorbikes fast around the corniches – the twisting mountainous roads between here and Nice. He'd got used to being indoors, felt more comfortable there. But he liked knowing that these days he at least had a choice – unlike half of his adult years, which he had spent in a supermax prison in Colorado. If he had been small and hunched when he went in aged twenty-six, now at sixty-three he was even smaller, thinner, with a nervous demeanour and bird-of-prey eyes. He had good reason to be nervous; there were a few people with scores to settle, in particular a couple of mobsters in prison who had boasted to him, and then he'd ratted on them, in exchange for a cut in his sentence. He'd be looking over his shoulder – and underneath his car – for the rest of his life.

Big Tony had carried out seventeen successful hits by the time he was twenty-five. The eighteenth was an expensive screw-up – not for his paymasters, who got their two hundred thousand dollars' worth of dead shitbag. But for him. Sheer bad luck. A tyre blew out on the 401 in North Toronto in his rental Durango, on the way to the airport. As he'd pulled over to the hard shoulder he'd been side-swiped by a truck driver who'd been playing a game on his cell phone, he learned later. While he was recovering from his injuries in hospital over the next three months, the RCMP had a field day with the gun in the trunk of the car and his laptop data, and some months later he was extradited to face trial in the USA.

Now twelve years on from his release he was back on his feet, big time. No more random assignments for him, from now on he would pick and choose carefully. And only the richest of pickings. He remembered the words of the US army general, Patton, in a movie he had seen years back: 'No bastard ever won a war by dying for his country. He won it by making some other poor dumb bastard die for his country.'

These days he was, mostly, Mr Fixit. He got things back for people. And just occasionally, plain simple, got things for people that they wanted.

And the arrogant shit of a man with stupid red glasses, wearing a neat suit and carrying a briefcase full of what British criminals like to call *folding*, who had just entered his twelfth-floor apartment, was someone who needed his services. He had it written all over his face, however hard he was trying to mask it.

They sat in the bay window with its southern view overlooking the heliport and the Mediterranean beyond, and a small park to the east, where a woman was walking a dog. The Englishman held a large tumbler of twenty-five-year-old Glenfiddich in his hand. Big Tony, who never drank whilst doing business, held a Virgin Mary. It turned out to be an appropriate drink, from what he was about to hear.

'We have a problem,' the Englishman said. 'I've been told you are the man who could solve it for me.'

'In that case,' Big Tony said, with his slow Mississippi drawl, in a voice that was much deeper and stronger than his appearance hinted, 'guess you're the one got the problem, mister.'

The Englishman frowned. 'Me?'

'I don't solve problems, mister, I just do things for people.'

'Then we're on the same page.'

'Depends what you got inside that bag of yours.'

The Englishman opened it and showed the contents. Bundles of banded five-hundred-dollar notes. 'Two million, you asked?'

'And the same again on delivery.'

'You're expensive.'

'I'm expensive?'

'Yes. Very.'

'Close the bag.'

'Close it?' the Englishman queried.

'Uh-huh.'

'Why do you want me to do that?'

'Because you're gonna pick it up and carry it back outta here. I'm not your man.'

'What do you mean?'

'What part of that did you not understand?'

The Englishman looked awkward. He took a long pull on his drink. 'OK, look, I think we just got off on the wrong foot. I'm cool with your price.'

'I'm not. It just went up.'

'Hey, I'm sorry. I'm happy to pay your price.'

'Fine. It's now eight million.'

'What?'

'You heard.'

'It's doubled.'

'I know who you work for. Money's no object. Come back with the right amount and we'll talk again.'

The Englishman looked like he was chewing a wasp. 'Look – please – let's—'

'Let's what?' he interrupted. 'Look, mister, two things you'd better know about me if you want to do business. First is I don't negotiate. Second is I'm not a good person to have not liking you. Understand what I'm saying?'

'I understand.' The Englishman looked at his watch. 'I could come back tomorrow.'

'After eleven. I have my Pilates trainer here first thing.'

'OK – but in the meantime you may want to take a look at this.' The Englishman handed Big Tony a USB stick.

'I'll take a look when I see the colour of your money. And no negotiation.'

'No more negotiation. As you say, my boss has very deep pockets.'

'Likes playing pocket billiards, does he?'

The Englishman chewed another wasp. Then he said, 'You come very highly recommended.'

'I don't go for bullshit. Come back tomorrow or go find someone else. You ain't gonna change my life either which way.'

'I'll be back tomorrow, after eleven, with the money.'

'Yeah, you will.'

31

Monday, 27 February

Ross had spent the first years of his journalism career as a reporter on the *Argus* newspaper in Brighton, then had moved to the City desk at the *Daily Mail*. After a spell there, he'd joined the *Sunday Times* Insight team, where he had really cut his teeth in investigative journalism, and found that was what he loved doing best. Then three years ago, feeling he'd made enough contacts with major newspaper editorial teams, he made the decision, supported by Imogen, to go it alone.

He'd never regretted that, although there were days when he missed the camaraderie – and the buzz – of daily office life.

It had taken Ross a long time to get used to working from home. He enjoyed the luxury of being as scruffy as he liked, and the freedom to pursue any stories he fancied, but there were plenty of days when time dragged and ended being broken down into little highlights.

One was when the newspapers arrived. Another was the morning post. Another was the sporadic delivery of Amazon and other online orders. And he always made time to take Monty for a long walk in the early afternoon.

The post used to arrive at 10 a.m. promptly, but recently the postman had retired and his replacement was erratic, with no post arriving some days until well past midday.

Today was one of those. But he'd been kept busy most of the morning with three separate Amazon deliveries from orders he had placed yesterday – two of them very bulky packages.

He'd opened them and stashed their contents at the back of the integral garage, part of which they used as storage, not wanting to have to explain them to Imogen.

As he sat back at his desk, responding to a suggestion from an editor that he might like to take a look into the personal wealth and tax affairs of a recently knighted retail tycoon, he heard a clatter from downstairs, accompanied by several loud barks from Monty.

The signal that the post had finally arrived. He glanced at his watch – it was 12.35 p.m. – and went downstairs. The post had indeed arrived, a thin stack bound by an elastic band, lying on the doormat.

He carried it through to the kitchen and flicked through it. A large envelope from his accountant (probably not going to make good reading, he thought), a typed envelope addressed to Imogen, a buff envelope from HMRC that looked suspiciously like a tax demand and, at the bottom, a small, handwritten envelope addressed to him, with a Birmingham postmark.

The writing was old-fashioned and he recognized it at once.

Putting Imogen's post on the hall table, he went back upstairs with the rest of his, sat down and opened the handwritten envelope.

Inside was a letter.

Dear Mr Hunter
   I am worried about what I have been told – and passed on to you. As a safeguard, because it is so

*important, if anything should happen to me, I have
entrusted the two remaining sets of coordinates to
the care of my solicitor, Mr Robert Anholt-Sperry at
Anholt-Sperry Brine, in Birmingham, who has them
safe. He is instructed to hand them to you, alone, on
proof of identity and no one else – should the first
set, at Chalice Well, convince you, which I sincerely
hope it will, of my bona fides. In the event anything
should happen to me, sole responsibility for saving
the world will rest with you.*

   Yours most sincerely,
  Dr Harry F. Cook

Ross read the letter through again. 'Well, that's a big
ticket, Harry!' he said aloud. He smiled, but inside he was
shaking. Then he jumped as the doorbell rang.

Peering out of the window, he saw a UPS van. He hurried downstairs and opened the front door.

It was another delivery of stuff he had ordered yesterday.

He signed for it, then took Monty for a long walk. He
crossed the footbridge over the A27 carriageway, and then
on up the sloping, open fields towards the Chattri, the
beautiful temple-like memorial built on the site where Sikh
soldiers, who had died in Brighton from injuries they had
sustained in the First World War, had been cremated.

It was an area where Monty loved to roam off his lead
and where Ross could do his best thinking.

And, despite being filled with misgivings about the
strange old man, he had one overriding thought.

What if, just what if – however improbably – Harry Cook
was for real?

Nine metres south turn left.

He was going to give the man one last shot, he felt he owed him that. If that came to nothing then *finito*. End of.

Tomorrow night, Tuesday, was Imogen's book club night. A good time to be out, too. Maybe if it all went well, he'd be home before her. Although in his heart he doubted that. He was nervous at the thought of what lay ahead. But he knew that unless he went through with it he would forever be wondering – for the rest of his life.

But the disturbed earth on the Chalice Well hillside bothered him. If Cook had been telling him the truth, had someone else attempted to excavate in the same spot? Someone ahead of the game?

Had they found the Holy Grail already?

He didn't think so. And if they hadn't, then they would still be looking, too.

Was it possible they could be watching him? Waiting for him to lead them to it?

As soon as he got home he picked up his wallet and keys, went out to his car and drove the ten miles to the county town of Lewes. The Lewes Flea Market, sited in a historic building, was partly supplied by house-clearance companies. The two hundred stalls-within-a-shop contained everything from old furniture and paintings to pre- and post-war artefacts and bric-a-brac, much of little value, but too collectable to be considered junk.

Ross found what he needed there after only a few minutes.

32

Monday, 27 February

The tall, forty-eight-year-old American was perspiring in his heavy, hooded black habit as he lugged an armful of fresh bedding up the stone steps from the monastery's basement laundry. The knuckles of his right hand were raw, the skin scraped off, and hurting. He was feeling terrible today, but he was trying to carry on as normal, as if nothing had happened.

After morning prayers, Brother Pete had stripped the beds of the overnight guests, then washed their towels, sheets and pillowcases and hung them out to dry. Here at Simonopetra, perched high up on a rock promontory overlooking the Aegean, the monastic tradition of food and overnight accommodation to visitors was upheld rigorously. But guests were only permitted to stay for one night, before moving on to another monastery, several kilometres' hike away.

He made his way along the network of dark passageways, towards the guest dormitory, and entered the room. It had an austere, prison-like feel, with rows of metal bunk beds, bare walls and a view from the tiny casement windows of the blue sea, several hundred metres below. Water that, on stifling Greek summer days, he sometimes longed – sinfully – to jump into, but swimming was considered pleasure, and all pleasures were forbidden here in this ascetic community that was his home, and which he could never see himself leaving.

There was limited electricity. Radios and televisions were forbidden and communication with the outside world was severely restricted. A monk, once admitted to permanent residence, could never leave without the consent of the Abbot.

Only one woman had set foot here in Mount Athos since 800 AD, when the first of the twenty monasteries on this long, narrow and mountainous peninsula in Northern Greece was founded. The Autonomous Monastic State of the Holy Mountain, ruled by the Ecumenical Patriarch of Constantinople, had been Christian Orthodox for eighteen hundred years. Seventeen of the monasteries were Greek Orthodox, one was Russian Orthodox, one Serbian Orthodox and one Albanian Orthodox. None of the monks spoke to each other, except when it was vital, and then only with the consent of their Abbot.

Sealed off from the mainland by an impenetrable mountainous barrier, there was no road in. The only way to reach Mount Athos was by ferry from Thessaloniki, where access was permitted to only twelve non-Greek Orthodox males at any one time, and all visitors had to present themselves to the Monk Bureau in Thessaloniki to be inspected to ensure they were not females in disguise. Boats carrying females were not permitted closer than one kilometre to the shores, and the highest female life forms allowed on the peninsula were hens. Not even female dogs or cats were permitted.

All of this suited Brother Pete fine. The tall, gangly, heavily bearded and shaven-headed monk had spent many peaceful years as the Guest Master in this monastery. But when he had first arrived, the dwindling population had been a worry to all the monks here, as well as to all the other monasteries.

When the previous Abbot had died, a few years before Pete's arrival, there had been too few monks in residence to carry his coffin. Fortunately God had intervened, and during the past decade the numbers here in this monastery had increased from two to twenty-five – people like him escaping for whatever reason from the wider, materialistic world to devote their lives to serving God. And the numbers had similarly increased throughout the peninsula.

Mount Athos had no means to recruit monks. To replace those who died, the community relied entirely on visitors deciding to stay. Just as he had done himself. Pete Stellos had visited at the suggestion of his cousin, and understood the Lord's calling when he arrived.

His days were filled peacefully with work and prayer, and his devotion enabled him to ignore the privations – which included the sticky heat of the summer and the freezing cold of the winters. His routine was to rise at 2 a.m., enter the chapel and pray until 6.30 a.m. when the morning meal was served, six days a week. The seventh day was fasting. The meal, of cheese, salad, fish and white wine, was eaten rapidly, in silence, whilst the Abbot or a deputy intoned the day's reading from the lectern in the refectory.

After the meal he would pray again until 9 a.m., and then he would make the beds in the visitors' dormitory, do the laundry and afterwards pray again until the evening meal of salad, cheese and white wine once more. After that he would pray until 10 p.m. when he would retire to bed.

If any visitors wanted to talk to him, they had to request consent from the Abbot, and usually would be granted this for fifteen minutes after the evening meal. Brother Pete pre-ferred not to have to speak to anyone, but he knew that these rare occasions when an audience with him was requested was an opportunity to perhaps convince someone to consider a calling here. Most of those who visited were devout men of faith paying respects or those desperately seeking God's help in curing a dying loved one, or the recently bereaved seeking understanding and solace, or those seeking restoration.

But last night one visitor who had requested to speak to him had caused him consternation, and left him deeply troubled, praying all night for forgiveness. It was an aggressive and sceptical American journalist who had been granted a five-day entry permit to the peninsula. Calculating that Brother Pete spent sixteen hours a day in prayer, he asked him if he ever got bored with praying.

'Sure,' he had replied. 'But, you know, all jobs have boring bits.'

'Praying is a job?' the journalist asked, his condescending voice laden with scepticism that bordered on pity.

'Uh-huh.'

'So what do you pray for?'

'I pray to God to intervene in the world's problems. To bring peace to Syria, Iran, to help stop the persecution of kids in Nigeria by Boko Haram, to help the earthquake victims in Japan or Italy or wherever these disasters happen, and for all those persecuted for their faith around the globe.'

'But you have no radio, no television and no newspapers. How can you know what's going on in the outside world?' the journalist had queried.

'God tells us,' Brother Pete replied, simply.

'That's what you believe?'

'Absolutely. To be a monk, you have to *believe*.'

'And you never have doubts?'

'Why would I? When you give yourself to serving God, He takes care of your doubts.'

'OK. And if it turns out there is no God, you've wasted your life, right?'

Pete looked at his watch. The Abbot had granted fifteen minutes for this interview. To his relief the time was almost up. 'I'm going to have to wrap up now,' he said.

'One last question. What do you miss most about your life before here?'

'Miss?'

'Yes, you know – movies, freedom, burgers, the internet – anything that you had to leave behind?'

'Nothing. God provides everything I need.'

'And you plan to stay here for the rest of your life?'

Brother Pete opened his arms and walked across to the window, which had no glass. Way below lay the deep blue of the ocean. 'You have a view like this from your office window?'

'This is your *office*?'

'I guess.'

'And where do you go next, up the monk corporate ladder? To the penthouse suite?'

Ignoring the jibe, he replied, simply, 'Why would I want to be any place else? I'll be here until God calls me.' He shrugged. 'Then I'll go on to wherever He needs me.'

'One question again, Brother Pete, do you really never have any doubts at all? Don't you ever feel sometimes that maybe you are in the attic apartment of a house, where there's a great party going on downstairs that you haven't been invited to?'

The monk gave him a look of pity. 'Never had a moment's doubt since I set foot here. No, sir. In God I trust. And I'll tell you something. I'm sensing that feeling's mutual – but you just don't want to admit it.'

'You're wrong. I respect your views, but I'm not some kind of a closet Christian. I have an open mind and that's why I'm here.'

'You're planning to go home to America and write a piece for the *New Yorker* about the loony monks of Mount Athos?'

'I'll write that I pity you, and all of your fellow deluded assholes.'

Pete stepped forward and punched the journalist as hard as he could in the face, busting his nose.

33

Tuesday, 28 February

At 5 p.m., an hour before Imogen was due to arrive home from work, Ross loaded up the boot of his car with all the equipment he reckoned he would need, much of which had been delivered yesterday and stored in the garage. He was glad of the pelting rain and dark skies to give him extra cover – and hoped the weather would remain bad, as forecast.

He left her a note on the kitchen table.

> *Gone out on a work assignment, might be late.*
> *Monty fed. Have a fun book club nite! X*

Then he headed off on the long, crawling drive through the afternoon rush hour, with Glastonbury programmed into his satnav. He was so focused on his task ahead that for some while he did not notice in the fading light the dark saloon, staying a steady two or three cars behind him all the way along the A23, the M25 and then the M3 motorways passing Basingstoke, then Salisbury, then almost three hours into his journey, passing Stonehenge on the A303.

That was when he first became aware that someone might be following him. Just after the car right behind him had turned left, off the road, and the lights of the vehicle behind seemed familiar. Most lights, apart from those of recent model Audis and some other high-end cars, which had distinctive LEDs, were the same. Moments later, in a blare of blue-tinted light, something came up close in his mirrors then shot past him with a roar. The tail of a Porsche 911.

There were no longer any lights behind him.

Whoever it was must have turned off, he thought to his relief. But he remained wary and vigilant. And his nerves were jangling about the task ahead of him.

It was shortly after 8.30 p.m. when he finally arrived in Glastonbury. The weather was on his side – it was still pelting with rain.

Perfect. He could not have hoped for better cover.

Then, with a twinge of unease, he thought he saw something in his mirror. He slowed right down, repeatedly checking as he passed beneath street lights. Nothing.

Just his imagination. He was being jumpy.

Jumpy as hell.

He pulled into the deserted car park, in the forecourt of the factory outlet where he had been previously, turned off the lights and sat, looking around, but there was still no sign of another vehicle. It was raining too hard for anyone, except the most diehard of dog walkers, to be out on this foul night.

Then his phone pinged, startling him.

It was a text from Imogen.

Hope you're OK. Big argument about this book going on! X

They had been reading *Shantaram*. He texted back.

Tell them you think it's the new *Fifty Shades of Grey*!

He started the engine and drove back out of the car park, looking for any vehicle that hadn't been there when he had driven past a few minutes earlier, but still could see nothing.

He turned left, into the lane between Chalice Well and Glastonbury Tor, which he had walked up on his visit here last week, and drove on, then swung into the lay-by where the footpath to the tor began. There was ample room for his car. It was perfect. No one around at all.

He opened the boot and lifted out the three waterproof holdalls into which he had packed all the kit he thought he would need. Then he lugged the heavy bags the short distance back down the lane, ready to dive into the shadows and freeze if any car came by. He pulled on a head torch with a red filter – a low-level light, he had researched, could not be seen from any distance – and hoisted each bag over the fence, letting them drop down the other side, then clumsily scrambled over.

He stared around at the darkness, trying to accustom his eyes.

Could he really go through with this?

His phone pinged loudly again.

He tugged it out and glanced at the display. It was another text from Imogen.

Ha! XX

He smiled, uncomfortably, feeling bad that he'd had to avoid telling her the truth about what he was doing tonight. But he hadn't wanted to scare her. He turned the phone to silent.

A tiny speck of light flared in the darkness, then died, on the far side of the fence. He switched off his head torch, his heart thudding, breaking into a cold sweat, and stood still, staring.

Nothing.

After waiting for a couple of minutes, with the rain continuing to pelt relentlessly down, he turned away, switched the torch back on, picked up the bags and trudged towards the well. Carefully descending the treacherously slippery steps, he stopped in front of the wellhead, with its raised circular lid.

This is crazy.

Go home.

He was soaking wet, cold, apprehensive and feeling increasingly scared about just what he was getting into.

You idiot, he thought to himself. *Forget it.* Images of Harry Cook's horrific death flooded through his mind. Were the old man's torturers and killers waiting out in the darkness, here for him?

He shivered.

Forget it, his brain screamed at him. *Go home, find another way to save the world.*

But he had come this far.

He put down the bags, walked to the edge of the narrow well and peered through the metal grid down at the inky water below. A smell of moss and weed rose from it. He was thinking about that crumpled page he had recovered from Cook's waste bin. The compass coordinates and the email Boxx had sent him deciphering the numbers.

> Nine Metres S (south?) T (turn?) L (left?)
> Helpful?

If you paced *nine metres south and turned left*, from the exact spot those coordinates indicated, you were at the wellhead.

He bent down, unzipped one bag and pulled out an adjustable spanner. For several minutes, he struggled to undo each of the nuts and bolts that held the grid secure. None of them, probably, had been moved in years – or even decades. By the time he had undone the last one, he was sweating from the exertion. Then just as he kneeled down to try to lift the grid, hoping it wasn't going to be impossibly heavy, he heard the sound of a car.

It was driving slowly up the lane, on the other side of the fence. He held his breath. If it was local police would they wonder what his car was doing there – or just assume he was a night walker gone for a stroll around the sacred hill?

He could see the glow of the headlights on the over-hanging branches. Moving past. The sound of the engine faded and he resumed his task. Gripping his hands around two of the black metal cross-bars of the cover, he pulled sharply upwards.

Nothing happened.

Shit.

He tried again. Then again.

Until he saw the problem. He'd only removed five bolts. There were six holding the grid in place, and the sixth one was by his left hand. He had missed it.

His nerves, he realized. He wasn't thinking clearly.

He removed the final nut and bolt, bent down and gripped the bars again. The grid came away easily; it was lighter than he had expected.

Breathing deeply with relief, he laid it down carefully to the side of the well, then delved into another bag and pulled out the improvised piece of kit he had rigged earlier today. It was his GoPro camera in the waterproof casing he used on scuba diving holidays, attached to a metal wrench for weight, and with a waterproof LED torch secured to it, along with a polypropylene rope.

He switched on the torch and the camera, set it to video, then lowered the contraption into the water, paying out the cord as it went down, keeping a rough count. Ten feet. Twenty feet. Thirty. Forty. Fifty.

The guidebook said it was eighty foot deep.

Sixty. Seventy. Eighty.

The cord went slack.

He pulled it taut, then slowly twisted it round for several revolutions, before, slowly and steadily, hauling it back up. Every few moments he paused to look around him in the darkness, his phone torch casting a red glow along the circular stone wall beyond the wellhead.

Then he thought he heard a footstep.

He stopped. Turned the torch off. Sat very still, listening. The rain pattered down. He hauled the camera up further, then stopped and listened again.

The only sound was the rain.

Shivering from the cold, he switched the torch back on. The camera surfaced with a tiny plop.

He lifted it up, popped open the casing and removed the camera itself, then sheltering it as best he could from the rain inside his parka, he pressed the replay button.

For a minute, maybe longer, he watched as the video played, the grainy image showing bare wall, some with moss and tendrils of weed, as the camera descended. Then the image jigged, unsteadily. The camera must have reached the bottom.

It began to rotate. He could see what looked like a

number of coins. The camera completed what seemed like a full rotation, stirring up silt. Nothing.

Shit, shit, shit.

But at least now he knew. Harry Cook had been—

Then he froze as the camera rotated again, and he noticed something in the murk.

He stabbed the pause button.

There was something that was not part of the bottom of the well, nor the wall. A dark shape. It lay on the bottom. He replayed it. And he could see it slightly more clearly now as his eyes were adjusting to the gloom down there.

It felt like a bolt of electricity had shot through him.

What was it?

He replayed the image a third time. There it was, nestling in the silt. Impossible to figure exactly what it was. Maybe it was just a large stone.

Next, he pulled out the sections of flexible wire caving ladder he had bought on the internet, along with Maillon Rapide section joints, and began assembling it with shaking hands.

When he had finished creating it, he used a tow strap to anchor the rope-like ladder to a tree at the edge of the fence, then lowered it into the well, paying it out until he reached the end.

From the third and heaviest bag, he removed his scuba equipment. Then he stood still. Staring at the darkness all around him. Shivering. This was madness. Forget it. Go home. The well was barely wide enough for him to fit into.

He asked me to tell you that Ricky said you should trust me. He said to mention Bubble and Squeak.

Harry Cook's voice was echoing all around him.

He'd come this far. He would bloody well see it through. He stripped off his clothing and, shivering from the cold, wormed into the wetsuit. He tugged on rubber shoes and gloves, secured the air tank to his buoyancy jacket and then fixed the regulator in place. He turned on his air and checked the tank capacity. He only had half a tank left. He cursed himself for not having checked it, but was sure it would be more than enough for the depth he was likely to be descending to, especially as he would not be contending with any current – unlike his last and rather hairy dive last summer, with Imogen, on the Elphinstone reef in the Red Sea. He fastened his weight belt, strapped his diving knife holster and powerful underwater torch to his legs, donned his jacket, head torch and dive computer, grabbed his mask and then scooped up the first bag. He climbed over the rim of the wellhead and, gripping the sides of the ladder, handles of the smallest holdall over his arm, began to descend.

The man who had followed him all the way down here from Patcham, concealed nearby, watched him through night-vision binoculars with a built-in video. A hazy green image. Shortly after Ross had disappeared from view, he zoomed in.

34

Ross climbed down the swaying, unsteady ladder, increasingly nervous with every step, until after only a short distance from the wellhead he reached the surface of the water. He hesitated. All his instincts were screaming at him to pack up, forget all about this, go home. But after some moments he finally plucked up courage, grabbed the mouthpiece of his regulator, adjusted his mask and gently let himself down.

Instantly, as his head went below the surface, he felt its icy chill.

Tendrils of weed touched his face and he shuddered. A short distance down he stopped and attached the holdall he was carrying, with its contents, to a rung.

Then he continued his descent into the eerie darkness that was only faintly illuminated by his head torch. He could hear the steady roar of his breathing, the popping of bubbles and the *thud-thud-thud* of his heartbeat. He was shivering with cold despite the protection of his diving kit.

It seemed he was going down for an eternity.

And he felt very scared.

He stopped, wondering whether to abort. The cold was getting worse and he wasn't even halfway to the bottom.

Probably just a damned bit of rubbish down there.

The sound of his breathing was getting louder, echoing.

More weed growing off the wall brushed his face like a cobweb. His feet found the next rung. And the next. That was the final rung. Twenty feet down from the top now. He released his grip and sank, steadily and rapidly.

It felt like he was gaining speed.

Thirty feet. Forty. Fifty.

He'd dived inside sunken wrecks off Barbados, in caves in the Red Sea, down deep shelves off the Maldives, and he'd never been scared before. But now he was terrified. Sinking deeper and deeper down this narrow, inky shaft.

Sixty feet.

He thought about their unborn baby. Then Imogen. Diving solo, anywhere, was a no-no. Diving solo into a confined space – an unknown one at that – was insane. If he got into trouble of any kind, no one was going to be coming to rescue him. He'd never see his child born.

Seventy feet.

In his nervous and fearful state, he made the cardinal mistake of not checking his buoyancy and, like a rank novice, squelched down heavily on the soft, muddy floor at the bottom of the well shaft.

Furious at his own incompetence, there was nothing he could do as the mud rose like fog around him, and he could only wait for it to settle. Checking the pressure gauge on his regulator, he saw that his air supply would only allow him another fifteen minutes or so. His panic had caused him to use far more air than he would do normally.

Stupid to panic, he knew. That was what killed divers. He had to calm down. Somehow. But his thoughts were ragged with anxiety.

It had taken him seven minutes to descend and he needed to allow all of that and more to ascend. But the water was still too cloudy to see anything.

Slowly it began to clear.

Eleven minutes left.

Ten.

He could see a few coins, what looked like a KitKat wrapper, a partially disintegrated takeaway carton, then a large, old-fashioned Nokia mobile phone. *Can't have been the object that the camera saw? It was bigger. Much bigger.*

He turned, and more mud rose, obscuring everything. He knelt and groped around in the deep mud and slime with his gloved hands, stirring it up even more, and feeling repulsed. What was down here? What disgusting things? What dead animals – or live bottom feeders? He touched something that felt like a dead frog and shuddered. Then a solid object. Covered in slime.

The shape he had viewed on his GoPro?

He lifted it up, bringing it close to his face, and could just see, in the faint glow of his head torch, strands of slime and weed hanging from it.

He wiped them away, and finally saw, to his disappointment, that it was a child's red wellington boot, filled with silt.

After making sure there was nothing else he was missing down here, he at last began his ascent.

Eight minutes left.

He rose as fast as his bleeper would allow, pausing briefly at the rung, some way below the surface, where he had attached the holdall on his way down. He unzipped the bag a little, to let water in, and zipped it again. He carried on up and broke the surface, pulled out his mouthpiece and with relief gulped down the fresh night air. He slung the bag over the top of the wellhead onto the ground.

And froze.

A shadowy figure was standing in front of him.

Something hard slammed into his face, knocking him off the ladder. He began plunging feet-first back down the well, dazed, scrabbling feebly with his hands for the ladder and swallowing water.

Finally getting a purchase on the ladder, and holding his breath, he scrambled as fast as he could back up. As his head broke the surface he coughed, spitting out water and looking up, and pulled his diving knife out of its sheath, gripping it tightly with his right hand. He continued climbing. In the darkness, it was hard to see how far he was from the top, so he slowed now, ascending one rung at a time, stopping after each and waiting.

Suddenly, he heard the roar of an engine firing up, the squeal of tyres, then the sound of a car heading away, fast.

Bastard.

He scrambled up the remaining rungs to the top, then stopped, in shock.

The metal grid had been put back into place above him.

His nose hurt, but he barely noticed as he peered, tentatively, through the grille. His plan had worked.

The two large holdalls were still visible, but whoever his assailant was had taken with him the smaller bag and its contents that he had put up there moments earlier. The contents which he had bought yesterday in the flea market. A rusty 1930s biscuit tin and a silver-plated christening mug which he had wrapped in cloth and placed inside it.

He waited, listening carefully for any sound of movement, but could hear nothing.

Finally, he pushed hard against the grille, but it would not budge.

He was entombed.

35

Ross pushed the metal grid as hard as he could, again. Then he removed a glove and ran his fingers to one side. And felt the nut and bolt. The nut was tight, impossible to budge with his cold fingers. Working his way round, he found three more of the original six, bolted tight. Far too tight.

Bastards!

For some moments, he was gripped with blind panic. Would he have to stay here all night, gripping the ladder? Would someone hear him shout in the morning?

Could he hold on that long?

Removing his weighted belt, he secured it to the ladder, followed by his jacket and air tank, feeling freer without the encumbrances and able to think more clearly. He focused, determined to keep calm. There was nothing at the bottom of the well. But if, as he had surmised, Joseph of Arimathea had wanted a hiding place for the Holy Grail, and had chosen Chalice Well, what would he have done with it? And who named the well?

Joseph wouldn't have had diving equipment, so short of dropping the chalice down the well, he'd have to have put it above the surface of the water, surely?

He looked at his watch. 9.07 p.m. Around twelve hours, probably, before workers would be arriving here. He'd worry about his story then. But in the meantime, he had almost twelve hours to explore the surface area of the well. He'd think about something to say to Imogen later.

He decided on a methodical approach. He pushed up his mask and, starting at the top, right below the metal grid, pushed every stone lining the round wall, prodding at the edges with his knife, then steadily working his way downwards.

As he was on the verge of giving up, a large piece of stone, just above the surface of the water, felt loose.

He worked his knife into the gap between it and the next stone for several minutes, feeling it getting steadily looser and looser, pushing at it constantly. It was coming away. Finally, to his surprise, it tumbled inwards, exposing a hole.

Heart thudding, he peered into the darkness, unsheathed his waterproof torch and shone the beam in. It lit up a sizeable cavity that appeared to stretch away some distance. There was a blast of cold air on his face.

He began to work on another slab of stone until that came loose too, and he was able to push it through. Then another, until that fell through into the cavity as well. Now there was enough room to get his head and shoulders inside. He could feel the blast of cold air much more strongly.

What was at the far end of this opening? Some way out?

Worming his way in, he felt a cobweb against his face and brushed it away, squirming with revulsion, then saw two tiny red dots in the distance. An instant later they vanished. A rat. He'd hated them since his time in Afghanistan.

There was a dank smell, but the walls looked dry. Rough stone. Was it a natural cave or something man-made, he wondered as he hauled himself in. Even with his head torch and the one in his hand, it was hard to see more than a few yards ahead.

There was barely enough height, inside, to kneel, and the curved ceiling was uneven and covered in small stalactites. Holding his torch in one hand, he crawled along for several yards, then, ahead of him, it narrowed and the roof lowered. There was just a tiny opening.

Shit!

He was never comfortable in confined spaces. He didn't even like sitting in the rear of a two-door car. To get through he would have to flatten himself on his stomach and crawl.

He pushed the torch through in front of him. Another pair of tiny red eyes gleamed in the darkness. *Sod off.* He heard a squeak. A scratching, echoing sound of scampering feet. Silence.

He took a deep breath, flattened himself on the ground and worked his way forward, feeling his head brush against the roof of the cave. The cold air blowing on his face increasingly strongly. Giving him hope that there might be an opening at the end.

In the beam of the torch he could see the tunnel narrowing further. A few yards on, his head was rubbing against the roof and his chin against the ground.

He was breathing harder and harder.

Was he going to be able to go any further? He was starting to panic, to hyperventilate.

Calm down. Deep breath. Steady. Deep breath.

The roof and sides of the cave were pressing in on him. Like being in a coffin.

I've come this far. Keep going. Keep going.

He could hear his breaths echoing around him. And the scraping sounds his body made with every push forward.

What if I get stuck?

He put the thought out of his mind.

Squirmed on forward.

Then, twenty yards or so along, it all appeared to open up. It gave him a spurt of energy and he wriggled onwards. A minute later he was in a cavern, with a ceiling high enough to enable him to stand up, then narrowing into another tunnel at the far end.

He clambered to his feet, unsteadily, with a surge of relief. Picking the torch up off the floor, he shone it around the bare walls, the bare floor, and saw a tiny recess over to his right.

Dust-covered stone chippings on the floor beneath it indicated that this was not a natural hole in the wall. Someone had chipped it out. Curious, he stumbled over to it and shone the torch in.

And saw an object inside, right at the back.

He reached in and lifted it out.

It was wooden, unevenly shaped, the size of a rugby ball, coated in dust, and appeared to be made of two halves which were fused together by a bonding as hard as rock.

The hairs on the back of his neck rose.

This was man-made.

36

Ross stood there, mesmerized by the object. He could think of nothing else. All his fear was, for the moment, gone.

Was this what Harry Cook had been looking for?

Had died for?

What was inside it?

He was tempted to try to prise it open right here, with his knife. But his priority was to protect it and to get out of here without running into his assailant again. At some point, whoever it was who had kicked him in the face and run off with his bag would discover its real contents, and might return.

Maybe the tunnel that continued on from the cave would take him somewhere he could escape from.

He had no choice but to try it.

He carried his find over to the far side of the cave, crouched, knelt, then had to flatten himself once more, pushing the torch and the wooden object in front of him.

He crawled on through another long tunnel, barely wide or high enough to fit through. But all the time the air blowing on his face was getting stronger, colder and fresher. After twenty minutes he saw the end. A wall of stone ahead of him with crude steps carved in it and another cavity high enough to stand up in.

Holding the torch in one hand and the object in the

other, he climbed up about twenty feet, to his relief the cold air getting fresher with every step. Above him he saw another circular, rusted metal grid. With darkness beyond.

He reached it, having no idea where he was, and gave it a push.

It did not budge.

Fighting panic, he jabbed his knife hard, upwards, around the edge. And felt it cut through something soft. Earth fell onto his face and into his eyes, momentarily blinding him.

He blinked hard, wiping his eyes, then pulled his goggles on. He continued working his knife round the circumference for some minutes.

Then he pushed again.

And felt the grid move, a fraction.

Using all his strength, he pushed again. The grid moved further, several inches.

He pushed once more. And on his next attempt, with a sucking sound, as if the earth gave it up reluctantly, the grid rose upwards and fell away.

He scrambled up the final two steps, clambered through the opening he had made and shone his torch beam around.

He was inside dense undergrowth. He worked his way through it until finally emerging onto a grassy hillside. And then he realized exactly where he was.

A hundred yards or so above him stood the ruins of Glastonbury Tor. Where he had been last week. To his left, from where he had just emerged, was a huge, impenetrable-looking hawthorn thicket, with a number of trees rising from it.

He stood in the rain, staring into the night, back towards Chalice Well.

37

Ross made his way back to the well where he had started, checking carefully that his attacker was no longer around. His remaining two bags were still there. He carefully wrapped his find inside a towel and placed it in a holdall on its own. When he had finished, he set about concealing his tracks.

He unbolted the grid that had imprisoned him, hauled up the ladder with his weights and air tank, and repacked everything. Then he closed and re-bolted the grille, not worrying about replacing the stones concealing the opening he had made below. Finally, he tugged off his wetsuit and put his clothes back on. When he was ready he lowered the holdalls over the fence and clambered over himself, listening hard for the sound of any approaching footsteps or a vehicle.

He left Glastonbury and drove several miles towards Brighton before spotting a secluded lay-by. He pulled off into it and stopped the car out of sight of the road, behind a closed catering trailer. Locking the doors, he switched on the interior light, unzipped the sodden bag on the passenger seat beside him with shaking hands and peered at the strange, dusty, oval-shaped object inside the towel.

He lifted and jiggled it and felt something move, very slightly, inside. Glancing around again, checking no one was approaching, and breathing fast, he carefully scraped away, with his fingers, the heavy coat of dust from a tiny section, exposing the wood beneath. Then he held it to his ear and tapped it. It sounded hollow.

Trembling with anticipation, he tried to pull the two halves apart but could not do it. He'd have to leave it until he got home.

He wondered just what might be inside. Was this what Cook had predicted – could it possibly be?

Or could it be nothing, a massive anticlimax?

He hardly dared to hope it might be real. The chalice. Someone, whether it was Joseph of Arimathea or not, had sure gone to a lot of trouble to hide it for it not to be discovered all of these years.

Glancing in the mirror, he saw a trail of dried blood from his nostrils and down the front of his mouth, as well as scratches on his forehead and cheek. He wet his handkerchief and cleaned up his face as best he could, his nose painful to touch. It might have been the shadows in the poor light, but it looked like he had dark rings round his eyes. A sign his nose was busted.

He arrived home shortly after 2 a.m., adrenalin pumping, and pulled up in front of the garage, alongside Imogen's Prius. They only used the garage for storage and as a workshop, and never bothered putting either car in there.

He looked all around him in the darkness, checking as best he could before getting out of the car and stepping up to the garage. He unlocked and opened the up-and-over door as quietly as he could, switched on the interior light, unloaded the bags, pulled the door shut behind him and checked it was locked.

Hurriedly hanging up his scuba gear above his road bike and his folded Brompton, he unlocked the integral door and carried the damp bag containing the curio into the house, past Monty who was asleep in his basket, and laid it on the draining board. The dog opened one eye and closed it again as Ross tiptoed out and up to the bedroom.

His press release to Imogen on his busted nose and scratches would be that he got punched by an angry City hedge-fund manager whom he door-stepped, following up his story on film tax evaders.

She was sound asleep, and had left his bedside lamp on for him.

Good.

He was about to tiptoe out again when she murmured, 'How was your evening?'

'Pretty uneventful.'

'Good.'

'Yours?'

'Not everyone liked the book. Some thought it was too long, but I disagreed.'

He walked over and kissed her. 'Sleep tight.'

'Love you.'

'Love you too.'

He tried to make it sound like he meant it, but he found it hard to say those words.

Closing the bedroom door as quietly as he could, he went back downstairs and into the kitchen, pulled a bottle of Craigellachie whisky out of the cupboard and necked some down straight from the bottle to try to calm himself. Then he pulled on a pair of rubber gloves, carefully lifted the object from the bag, laid it in the sink, on a dry tea towel, and took a photograph with his phone.

Next, he steadily and delicately wiped the dust away

with a cloth, not wanting to risk using a brush in case there was any wording or anything painted or written on the surface that he might damage. The object was definitely wooden and he guessed it was oak. It seemed it might be a container of some kind, fashioned from two halves of a narrow tree trunk which had been cut open and then stuck back together.

The object felt very old and the wood was dark. Like something he might see in a display case in a museum. He kept staring at it and wondering.

Wondering.

Dr Cook, is this what you were looking for? Is this what God had wanted you to find? The first of three items he'd given you compass coordinates for?

The light dimmed just a fraction. It flickered. Then it brightened again. He shivered. Looked up at the downlighters. Heard his heart thudding. He listened carefully for any sounds of Imogen getting out of bed. But apart from Monty lapping away at his water bowl, all was quiet.

Should he not touch this at all, not attempt to open it and damage it, but take it to an expert – perhaps the British Museum?

But then he would have to explain how it came into his possession. And be obligated to share the knowledge of whatever it might contain. At this point he wanted to keep the information to himself.

He took more photographs of it. Then he selected a large, heavy knife from the wooden block by the sink and set to work on the seal. But it was more than rock hard, it was diamond hard. Try as he might, careful not to let the blade slip, he could not penetrate between the two halves. Tired and frustrated, he carried the object through into the garage, placed it in the jaws of his vice on his workbench –

which he had bought in the as yet unfulfilled hope of improving his DIY skills – and wound the handle, clamping it as hard as he dared without risking cracking it. Then he picked up a hammer and chisel.

Placing the blade of the chisel against the seal, he tapped it with the hammer. Nothing happened. He tapped again harder, then harder still. Finally, it broke through.

Fifteen minutes later he had chipped away enough of the seal. He unwound the vice, pushed the chisel in again and twisted the handle.

The top half opened up like a clamshell, with a loud, cracking sound. Cradled inside the bottom section was a bundle of dark-brown cloth of some kind, wrapped around an object and bound with coarse strands of what looked to him like raffia.

He laid both sections carefully down on a cloth he had placed on the workbench, then lifted the object out. It was light and felt hard. He began to unwind the cloth wrapped around it. The material was old and some of it crumbled into dust in his hands. Then finally, after unwinding several layers, he saw what the object inside was.

And felt a strange prickle tugging at his skin. As if every hair on his body was being stretched tight.

It looked like a hand-carved wooden drinking vessel. A chalice.

He took several photographs, then lifted it up. It was uneven, but it was beautiful. Quite delicate, with an elliptical bowl and a small, flat, round base.

In the bottom of the bowl was a dark crust.

He wondered what he was really looking at.

An elaborate prank? Or something Christianity had been trying to find for the past two thousand years?

Was it possible?

The garage door suddenly shook as if someone was trying to open it. He froze. Then calmed down. It was just the wind. He looked back at the vessel. Could it be the Holy Grail? Was it possible he had found it?

Whoever had followed him to Chalice Well, and subsequently kicked him in the face and run off with a bag of car-boot-sale tat, clearly believed it was.

He stared down again at the vessel. The roughly hewn cup.

The chalice that Jesus had drunk from? That some of his blood had been poured into, according to legend, while he was on the cross?

That Joseph of Arimathea had brought here and protected by hiding it in a cavern, with concealed entrances, near the well?

He wondered how long it would be before his assailant realized that he had been stiffed. And come looking for the real thing.

The same person – or persons – who had tortured and killed Cook?

He needed to hide it.

He stared around the garage, his brain racing. Where would someone not think of looking?

He still had his old golf bag, empty, in a corner of the garage. He pushed the wooden container into the side pocket and zipped it up. Then he wrapped the vessel in his waterproof golfing jacket, put his head torch back on and carried the vessel out into the back garden. He walked down to the shed at the far end and took out a spade.

There was a space a couple of feet wide behind the shed where he had his compost heap. He moved some aside, dug a deep hole in the earth, laid the wrapped cup at the bottom, filled the hole back in and smoothed the earth over, then shovelled the compost back on top.

When he had finished he went back into the house, removed his muddy shoes and, feeling drained, climbed upstairs to the bathroom. His head was pounding from the blow to his nose. He took out a couple of paracetamol from the cabinet and swallowed them with a glass of water, cursorily brushed his teeth, removed his clothes, had a very quick shower and climbed into bed.

The clock said 2.49 a.m.

He was exhausted. But he was far, far too wired to sleep.

He lay thinking. Listening. Fearful of every sound he heard.

What danger had he put himself and Imogen in?

What should he do next?

First thing in the morning, he planned, he would call an alarm company, get them to come over and secure the house as much as they could and install panic buttons.

Then he lay there, images of Harry Cook's tortured body burning in his mind. Thinking about earlier. Whoever had kicked him in the face, taken the bag and tried to trap him inside the well was not going to go away. Especially not when they opened the bag.

Not much had made him smile recently, but that thought did. Very fleetingly, before the fear flooded back.

38

Wednesday, 1 March

The refectory of Simonopetra was a vast, high-ceilinged, austere room, amply capable of accommodating the three hundred monks for whom the monastery had originally been constructed.

Square, white, ten-seater tables, fashioned from marble quarried on the peninsula, were ranked along its length. The monks sat at three tables, eating their morning meal in silence whilst the Abbot stood, reciting from the scriptures at a lectern in the centre of the hall in his monotone voice.

Separated from the rest of his brothers, Brother Pete sat at a corner table; it was the monastery's 'naughty step'. Where monks who transgressed were sent to eat on their own, to atone.

He would be denied the wine that the others were drinking for this month. Instead he had to make do with the tepid fish, the feta cheese, tomatoes, lettuce and bread, eaten alone with his thoughts and his raw, painful knuckles, still hurting from the punch he had delivered to the journalist.

He had been summoned to the Abbot's chamber a few hours after and chastised. Told solemnly that he had brought the monastery into disrepute.

'You realize that without funding, in particular from the EU, this monastery – and this entire commune at Mount Athos – could not survive, Brother Pete?'

'I do, Father.'

'Perhaps you are too steeped in your American ways of violence to fit in with us? You confessed to me, when you first came here, that you had spent two years in prison for assaulting a man who was rude to you in the hamburger restaurant where you worked. Perhaps you still carry that same violence in your heart?'

'No, I care deeply about all we do and stand for here, Father. This was different, this newspaper reporter wanted to make us look bad. I was worried it would affect the grants from the European Union on which we depend. I felt I had to take a stance and defend us.'

'Violence is not our way.'

'I apologize. I've been unsettled by visions recently – I feel that our Lord might be communing with me, giving me specific words of guidance.'

'You do?' The Abbot half closed his eyes and stared directly at the monk. 'What makes you think that?'

'It's hard to say, but I feel it so deeply within.'

'What has He been telling you?'

'That our Lord Jesus might be back on earth, and no one realizes. He has come to save the world. But He needs our help.'

'This is quite an assertion, my son. And if you are wrong, it could get you in serious trouble. Tell me, why would our Lord talk with you when violence is not his way? Violence is not the way to help.'

Pete looked at the floor. 'I sinned, and I'm sorry, but I feel this so strongly.'

'We all know our Lord is coming back. His messages have always been of love and forgiveness. We have to spread His word. What do you think that striking an influential newspaper reporter will achieve?'

Pete had the grace to blush.

But now, as he sat alone with his thoughts, half-heartedly forking his breakfast into his mouth, he wished desperately that his cousin, Angus, had remained here. He felt he could talk to him in a way that he could talk to no other human.

He wondered increasingly if his cousin felt the same thing he felt.

The sense that something momentous was happening. That our Lord was preparing to return to save us and no one realized.

39

The sign outside the shopfront, in Brighton's Lanes, proclaimed DEREK BELVOIR ANTIQUES AND RESTORATION. Ross Hunter, in the private office at the rear of the tiny, cluttered premises, removed the sunglasses hiding his black eyes. 'So what do you think?' he asked Belvoir.

Ross had met the old rogue almost a decade earlier, when he had been writing an article on the history of Brighton's infamous 'knocker boys' – the crooks who, in the heyday of the city's notoriously bent antiques trade, used every trick in the book to con old people out of their most valuable antique possessions.

Derek Belvoir had talked to him then, openly and shamelessly. Perhaps bragging, he'd told him in detail how, for instance, you could make a fake Georgian chest or dining table. Or how, if you had a couple of chairs missing from a genuine antique dining table set, you could make them up out of modern materials in a way that would be almost undetectable.

The antique dealer sat behind his desk, his silver hair groomed with élan, wearing a tweed suit and sporting a yellow cravat. Through the jeweller's loupe, screwed into his right eye socket, he was examining first the two halves of the wooden container Ross had brought him. Out of respect, Belvoir had put on a pair of white cotton gloves and placed a black velvet cloth on his desk beneath them.

His small, reedy, cockney voice betrayed his carefully conceived aristocratic appearance – as did his cheap grey loafers and his single gold earring. But one thing Ross respected about Belvoir was that he did know his stuff. So much so that, for a short time, he had appeared on the hit television show *Antiques Roadshow*, before receiving a three-year prison sentence for handling forged antiques.

The last time Ross had seen him, Belvoir's emporium had occupied a vast, two-storey premises in a prominent position in the Lanes. But in recent years, the domestic and international trade in so-called 'brown furniture' had pretty much collapsed. Most of the respectable Brighton antique dealers had moved into antique jewellery or Oriental an-tiquities. Some of the dodgier ones had moved into drugs.

'Blimey, Ross, where'd you get this from?' He gave him a quizzical look.

'What can you tell me about it?'

'It's oak. I don't think I could put a date on it, but there's a clue in the sealant used.'

'Sealant?'

'The bonding – glue – between the two halves of the outer shell?'

Ross nodded.

'I'd struggle to replicate this – not that I'm into any kind of repro any more, you understand? I don't do that no more, I gone straight, legit.'

'I understand, Derek, I'm not trying to catch you out. I just need to know the provenance.'

Derek looked up at Ross, at his black eyes. 'Nice shiners!' Then down at the goblet. 'Did someone fight you for this?'

'Very funny.'

Belvoir focused again on his task. 'This is not something I've ever seen before.' He lifted it and held it close to his face. He turned it over, slowly and carefully, several times. 'Made with a lot of skill, a proper carpenter, but before the lathe was invented. It's very old. Yeah? Like, I could not put a date to it. There's some crusted gunk at the bottom – maybe what its owner had been drinking? The petrified glue – sealant – used to stick the two halves together is really interesting. A lab could tell you for sure about the outer casing and the cup. The glue's possibly tar or, more likely, tree sap.'

'How long ago was that used, Derek?'

'First used a thousand years ago, if not more – maybe a lot more.'

Ross tried not to let anything show on his face. 'Is that so?'

Belvoir laid it down gently on the cloth, and removed his eyepiece. After some moments he looked up, beadily. 'Mind if I ask you where this came from?'

'Picked it up in a car boot sale.'

'What did you pay for it – a couple of quid?'

Ross held up a single finger.

'One pound?'

'Yep.'

'Well, you've got the bargain of the century! Not sure I could put a value on it, because it's so unique. These two outer bits are obviously a container of some kind. I'll hazard a guess that this had some use on a ship – oak is one of the most water-resistant of woods – some types of it. This is one. It's very old, for sure.'

'You say tree sap as glue was used over a thousand years ago? So might that make this over a thousand years old?'

'I couldn't tell you. You could get it carbon dated by a

lab. How accurate you could get on its age would depend on where it's been stored. Are you looking for a value?'

'Not so much, more its provenance.'

'I'll give you five hundred for it – if you throw in the goblet.'

'That's all?'

'Too bad you don't have more info. It could be priceless. Could be the Holy Grail itself!' He grinned.

'Yep, who knows?'

Belvoir stared hard. 'It's unique, Ross, but that's its problem – there's nothing to compare it with.' He looked up. 'I don't suppose there are any more where this came from?'

'Oh sure, my local supermarket is stacked full of them.'

40

Thursday, 2 March

Ross took a jam-packed early morning train to London Victoria, checking out all the people on the platform and the fellow travellers in his carriage for anyone who might be following him. Although, he was uncomfortably aware that members of a good surveillance team were likely to be all but invisible.

After the tube across London to Euston Station, he settled into a seat on an Intercity train to Birmingham. Imogen had taken the morning off work to be there for the alarm company who were going to install motion sensors, panic buttons downstairs and in their bedroom, and window locks. To allay her worry about the costs, he told her a white lie that the *Sunday Times* had given him a cash float for expenses.

He opened his laptop and first checked his social media. Responses were still coming in from his post last week, asking what people would consider to be proof of God's existence. Mostly they were from committed Christians, quoting Bible passages, and one was from a Muslim, quoting from the Qur'an. One told him to go out on a summer evening and look at the sunset. And one told him if he even had to ask the question, he would rot in Hell for eternity.

He began to make notes, inspired by his meeting with

Benedict Carmichael, of what might constitute absolute proof – and the consequences that could result.

In a largely secular Western world, what difference would it make to have God's existence conclusively proven? he typed.

As the train pulled out of the station, a stream of people who had just boarded walked past him. A woman stopped to consider the empty seat beside him on which his laptop bag sat. She caught his eye, giving him a hostile glare, but he really didn't want someone next to him reading his screen, so he faced her down. Then his face twitched, involuntarily. She moved on hastily, to his relief. God made that happen! He grinned at the thought. Then focused back on his work.

The buffet trolley came by. Ross bought a coffee, a bottle of water and an egg sandwich, which he ate ravenously before returning to his work.

He flipped through the notes he had taken at his meeting with Carmichael and then wrote, *Proof is the enemy of faith?*

Through the window he saw a landscape of grim buildings and fat, squat chimneys belching smoke out into the grey sky. Heading north made him think of Ricky. And the guilt that always came with that.

Ricky had always tried to be friendly and he had pushed him away, more and more. Ricky had never understood why. He'd constantly tried to reach out to Ross, unable to grasp why his brother was so cold towards him. Ricky had been dead for well over a decade. And yet that moment of his death was as vivid now as it ever had been. As was his guilt.

He closed his eyes, his heart feeling heavy. Thinking about how mean he must have seemed to his twin. His dislike of his brother had increased as he had grown older, and eventually he shunned him almost completely. He'd barely seen him in the few years before his death.

Had Ricky's dying moments been his one last attempt to draw them together, to bond? To give him a message?

Should he, like Harry Cook, go to a medium and try to make contact with him?

He didn't like the idea, and yet he couldn't quite dismiss it.

He lapsed into a troubled doze and was woken some while later by the loud, droning announcement over the intercom.

'We will shortly be arriving at Birmingham New Street. This train terminates here. Please ensure you take all your belongings with you.'

41

Thursday, 2 March

As Ross sat in the back of the taxi, focusing on the purpose of his visit, he reflected on the tumultuous past week. He thought of Harry Cook's denial that he had been digging at Chalice Well. So, if he had been telling him the truth, that he had been stopped within moments of beginning, some-one else had been digging there after him. Cook had assured him he'd not given the coordinates to anyone else. Yet someone had carried out a thorough – albeit narrow – dig on the exact spot.

Who?

And why?

The person – or persons – who had attacked him, taken the bag and entombed him in the well?

Cook had approached and upset the trustees of Chalice Well. They weren't a secretive bunch, Ross had googled them and seen all their photographs. Their aims were listed on the website. They were primarily to preserve Chalice Well and the gardens in perpetuity.

Had these trustees carried out a dig, Ross wondered, after being alerted by the retired professor? Had Cook given them more information than he had let on to Ross?

Had they subsequently dug in the place where they'd caught Cook digging, in order to satisfy themselves that he was indeed deluded?

Or . . . ?

He peered out through the taxi's window. They were driving down a main thoroughfare with dilapidated semi-detached four-storey red-brick houses on either side. They pulled up outside one.

'Number thirty-three?' the driver checked.

'That's it.' Ross glanced at his watch. 11.50 a.m. Perfect timing for his midday appointment.

He paid the driver, gave him a decent tip and walked up the steps to the entrance porch. The brass plate, in need of a polish, read: ANHOLT-SPERRY BRINE, SOLICITORS.

He pressed the bell and there was a click of the door lock. He entered a reception area that was as old-fashioned and decrepit as the exterior. A woman, with grey hair pulled into a severe bun, peered at him from behind a tall wooden counter. 'May I help you?' she said in a voice laced with suspicion.

'I have an appointment with Robert Anholt-Sperry.'

'And you are?'

He gave his name and was told to take a seat.

Five minutes later a much more pleasant younger woman escorted him up three flights of narrow stairs, opened a door and ushered him into a cluttered office, with stacks of files covering the desk and most of the floor space. A man, of similar vintage to Cook, lumbered to his feet to greet him. He had a heavily jowled face, with pronounced moles on his chin and on each cheek, and a threadbare comb-over. The frayed collar of his checked shirt was rucked by his badly knotted Old Harrovian tie. He had a world-weariness about him, moving slowly, a man aware time was running out on him, so why hurry any of it along?

'Mr Hunter?' His voice was deep and resonant, and as posh as his name. He held out a liver-spotted hand.

Ross shook it firmly.

'Do sit down.' He indicated the solitary, worn leather chair in front of his desk. 'Coffee or tea?'

'Coffee please.'

'Two coffees, Sandra, thank you,' he said to his secretary.

The walls were bare, apart from a few rows of bookshelves, untidily stacked with legal tomes, and an ancient framed Admission Certificate from the Law Society. The grimy window looked out across the busy street.

The solicitor peered hard at his face and Ross was aware he was looking at his eyes. The dark rings were less livid today, but still very noticeable.

'Been through the wars, have you?' he asked.

'I walked into a door,' Ross replied.

'Of course – dangerous things, doors.'

Both men smiled, aware the truth was different.

'Terrible thing that happened to dear Harry,' the solicitor said, changing the subject after settling into his chair. 'I understand it was you who found him?'

'I did.'

'You hadn't known him long?'

'Just a few days,' Ross replied. 'Were you good friends?'

'For over fifty years. I was godfather to his son – who was sadly killed in Afghanistan. I believe Harry told you?'

'Yes, he said by friendly fire.'

'He was very impressed with the piece you wrote in the *Sunday Times* about the lack of equipment supplied to our troops out there.'

'He told me.'

Anholt-Sperry gave him a wistful smile. 'You need to know that Harry was a decent man. Genuinely concerned for the world.'

'I got that impression.'

'He spoke to me after meeting you, and he told me that he trusted you.' He gave him that wistful smile again. 'Was he right to trust you, Mr Hunter?'

'I had been planning to tell him that I felt I wasn't his man, if you want to know the truth. But he said something over the phone that intrigued me enough to give him another chance. That's why I went to see him. Have you had any information from the police about who might have killed him?'

'Not so far, other than that the preliminary postmortem report is that he died of heart failure – perhaps from the shock of being tortured. I have a contact in that force who's promised to update me when they know any more. At the moment one of their lines of enquiry is that it's a sadistic burglary – the intruders were obviously after something. Apparently, there's been a bit of a spate in his area of this particularly nasty style of burglary, targeting vulnerable elderly people in rural dwellings, but that's all I know for the moment. What my chum in the police did tell me was they haven't ruled you out yet as a suspect.' He gave Ross a sudden, hard stare.

Ross felt a moment of unease. His fingerprints would have been in the house. He had a story that he had given the police. But what motive did they think he might have? He shook his head. 'You can't seriously think I would have done that? Why would I? He approached me out of the blue, eager for me to help him.'

'So what was it he said to you over the phone that intrigued you enough to give him a second chance, Mr Hunter, and pay him a visit?'

'He said that since we had spoken, when he first came down to see me at my home, he had found something he thought would change my mind about not helping him. He

implored me not to dismiss him as a harmless old loony –
his words – and to give him a chance to explain what he had
found. I asked him what it was, but he said it was too dangerous – whatever he meant by that – to tell me over the
phone.'

'So you never found out?'

'When I arrived at his house, I could see it had been
ransacked. I probably shouldn't have gone in – I know that.'

'So, why did you?'

'The police asked me the same question – why didn't I call
them immediately? The thing was, I didn't know if he was
inside or not. I was concerned he might be in there somewhere, lying injured. I know that my local force don't respond
at all to some burglaries – and it's a crime that's low down on
their priority for a response. I thought it would be better to
have a look first, myself.'

The solicitor nodded. 'Did you find anything of interest,
before you discovered Harry?'

'Actually, I did. I found something in a wastepaper
basket in a room I presume was his office. I don't know if it's
what his assailants were looking for – but I just have a feeling it might have been.'

'What was it?'

'When Dr Cook came to see me he gave me the compass coordinates he had been given for Chalice Well. In
addition there was a series of numbers following these
coordinates. I asked him what they meant and he said he
had no idea.'

'And these were?'

Ross pulled out his iPhone, opened the Notes app and
read out the numbers.

Anholt-Sperry frowned. 'How very interesting,' he said
after some moments. 'Most interesting.'

'I think he had finally worked out the meaning – and that's what he wanted to tell me.'

'And what was it you found in the wastepaper basket?'

'A diagram, crudely drawn.' Ross retrieved the crumpled square of paper from his wallet and laid it on the desk.

The solicitor peered at it intently. 'Looks like a hockey stick.'

'It does.'

'And do you have any idea what the numbers mean?'

Ross pulled up the photographs of the oak container and the vessel it had contained on his iPhone, and passed it across to the old man.

Anholt-Sperry pulled on a pair of half-frames and studied the screen, flicking through the images. 'You found these where Harry said you would?'

'It took a little deciphering. They're in a code based on the numbers of letters of the alphabet. *Nine Metres South Turn Left*. The well itself lies nine metres south and immediately to the left of the spot indicated by the coordinates. Harry, and whoever had dug there subsequently, had been looking in the wrong place,' Ross said. 'The cup was in a recess of the well, sealed in a container made of oak. I'm told by an antiques expert that, in his opinion, it could have survived in this container for a thousand years or more. Maybe much more.'

'Good Lord. You are aware what this vessel is – or might be?'

'I am. So is someone else, who tried to kill me.'

'Who closed a door in your face?'

'You could say that.'

'But you are a resourceful young man.' The old man's demeanour had totally changed. 'This is incredible. Quite incredible. Do you understand the significance of this find? For the world?'

'I do.'

He thought, for a moment, that Anholt-Sperry was going to come round the table and hug him. The solicitor looked almost delirious with happiness. 'You have it in a secure place – away from our enemies?'

'The chalice and the container are in a secure storage unit in Shoreham. The manuscript that Dr Cook gave me is in my solicitor's vaults in Brighton.'

'He was right to trust a young man. I'm old, you see.' He patted his chest. 'Ticker problems, like Harry. I'm fine for now. But you never know, do you? And should, God forbid, anything happen to you?'

'I've instructed my solicitor to give my wife the code to the storage unit and to tell her where the key is located.'

The secretary brought in their coffees on a tray. Ross took his cup gratefully, blew on it and drank.

'What I don't understand, Mr Hunter, is why the compass coordinates only gave the approximate location, and it required the deciphering of the numerical code to find the exact spot. Do you have any thoughts?'

'I've been thinking about it a lot. The best answer I can come up with is that if the location of the Holy Grail was indeed given to him from God as he claimed, perhaps the numerical code was put in as an added level of security.' He raised his hands in the air.

The solicitor nodded approvingly. 'I think Harry was right to trust you, Mr Hunter.'

'Thank you.'

'And are you willing to investigate further, based on this?'

'I was followed by someone to Chalice Well. And attacked in the process. Dr Cook has been tortured and murdered. If the two are connected, it's a pretty daunting situation. My wife is pregnant and I have to consider her and my unborn child.'

'You'd put them ahead of saving the world?'

Ross stared at the old man. He saw the same sincerity, the same zealousness in his eyes as he had seen in Harry Cook's the first moment they had met.

It is very good of you to see me, Mr Hunter. You do understand that you and I have to save the world?

'I wouldn't be here if I did,' he replied.

Anholt-Sperry smiled his sad, wintry smile. 'That's why you were chosen.' He reached across his desk and handed him a small square of paper, of similar size to the one that Cook had given him previously, with the compass coordinates for Chalice Well.

Ross looked down at the numbers.

25°44'47.1264"N and 32°36'19.1124"E.

The coordinates were followed by a word. *Hatem.*

'Have you checked out where these coordinates are for?' he asked.

'I have, Mr Hunter. The Valley of the Kings, in Egypt. Queen Hatshepsut's Temple.'

'And the word, Hatem?'

'You're the cipher breaker, Mr Hunter. I'm sure it must be significant, but I've no idea who or what Hatem is.'

'I used to play a little chess at school, but I've always been a bit rubbish at puzzles – especially cryptic ones,' Ross replied. 'Though I know someone who might be able to help.'

Robert Anholt-Sperry gave him the beatific smile of a true believer. Of someone utterly convinced that, no matter their earthly foibles, their seat at Heaven's top table was reserved. 'Clearly you have been sent to save us, Mr Hunter. What you have revealed to me on your phone is the first sign. Just believe in yourself, because surely our Lord believes in you, that's why He has chosen you.'

Ross was startled by the man's sudden clear and unexpected show of devoutness. He found himself envying him his conviction. How simple it would be to embrace God, he thought. To hand over absolute responsibility for all your actions to some higher power. *I'm so sorry I shouted at my neighbour's cat, but he did keep shitting in my garden. I apologize for calling that man in the station ticket office a total moron. In future, I will spread your message of love.*

'I'm honestly not sure I'm your man,' he replied. 'I was pretty much a non-believer for a long time.'

'Until your brother, Ricky, spoke to you.'

'Is that what Harry Cook told you?'

'It's not important who told me. What matters, Mr Hunter, is that *you know*. Don't you? In your heart, deep down. You have the choice. You can walk out of here and get on the train and go home and forget this mad old man and his ramblings, just like you were on the verge of dismissing Harry's ramblings, too. But you aren't going to, are you? One way or another, as a journalist you have a story. At worst you could cobble together something that will give you a page, maybe a two-page spread in one of the tabloid rags. At best?' He let the words hang in the air before continuing. 'Think about that. Are you going to be able to live with the knowledge that you once walked away from the chance of bringing mankind back from the brink?'

Ross shrugged.

The solicitor opened a drawer in his desk, pulled out a fat envelope and handed it to Ross. 'Harry instructed me to give you this if anything happened to him before he could give it to you himself.'

'What is it?'

'Expenses. Ten thousand pounds in cash.'

'What?'

'Take it with you. If you decide not to proceed, then return it to me.'

'I can't take this.'

'Yes, you can,' Anholt-Sperry said, assuredly. 'If you decide to walk away, just return it to me, but I don't think you will walk away. Come back to me once you have found what awaits you at the second set of coordinates. Then you will know for sure. Once you have proved yourself – and proved *to* yourself – I am authorized by Harry Cook to give you the third set of coordinates. With the third, you will find the location for the Second Coming of Christ Himself. You can either believe me or just walk out of here. The choice, Mr Hunter, is yours.'

42

Thursday, 2 March

The mock-Tudor semi-detached house at the end of a close in Walthamstow, East London, looked unloved. Thick blackout curtains for privacy had been drawn shut across all of its windows, both upstairs and downstairs, for as long as many of the neighbours could remember. The brown pebble-dash rendering was missing chunks in several places, and the window frames, badly in need of putty and a coat of paint, were rotting. The front garden was a riot of weeds.

The only clues that the house was occupied were occasional deliveries from Ocado, the online grocery service, a weekly delivery of Arabic newspapers by a local newsagent and the occasional visitors, most of them in the traditional robes of Muslim clerics. None of the neighbours could remember the last time they had seen its male occupant emerge.

In the gloom of the upstairs back room sat a blind man of fifty-six, with a shaven head and a long, greying beard. His name was Hussam Udin. Fifteen years ago, wrongly identified, convicted and imprisoned for being the leader of an al-Qaeda cell, he had been blinded and badly disfigured in an attack in HMP Belmarsh, first having had battery acid squirted in his face, followed by a poultice of scalding wet sugar.

His 'crime' for which he had been punished by Muslim inmates was that, although born a Muslim, he had declared himself to be concerned about Islam, both because of the violence of some of its factions and because few imams within the faith were prepared to stand up, publicly, against the violence.

His name meant, literally, 'Sword of Faith'. Notwithstanding that, and despite his tribulations, Udin believed in tolerance, and in the years since his release he had followed a spiritual path, using all the strength and wisdom he had been given to spread messages of peace.

Seven years ago, after being freed from prison on the basis of wrongful conviction, through the dogged work of an Amnesty International lawyer, he had retreated to his home, which he and his wife had turned into a fortress, and where he remained in constant fear for his life. He spent his days drilling through the braille texts of the Qur'an, trying, through a series of papers he published, to demonstrate that, unlike the claims of groups such as ISIS, and their interpretations of the Holy book, Islam was a deeply misunderstood religion that in truth promoted peace and tolerance. The tolerance, when necessary, to accept non-believers.

The *Sunday Times* had sent Ross Hunter to interview Hussam Udin shortly after his release, and Ross had really liked the wise and witty man. He admired him for the fact that he held no grudge against his assailants and for his determination to spend however much time it took – the rest of his life if necessary – to correct the Western myths about the religion he had turned his back on, but still respected.

'You have to understand, Mr Hunter,' Udin had said at that first meeting, 'that in Christianity, and Judaism, if you have doubts you are free to choose that path. That it might take a lot for a non-believer to become a believer. In my religion it is different, there is a different question you have to ask, because from the time we are born, belief is instilled in us. The question you need to ask a Muslim is not what it would take for him – or her – to believe in God. Rather you should ask, what would it take for a Muslim to *not* believe in God?'

On his way back down from his meeting with the strange, but sincere, Birmingham solicitor, Ross decided to call in on this man. Greeted like an old friend, he now sat with Hussam Udin in his office, surrounded by piles of audio tapes, cassettes and memory sticks, sipping the strong, sweet coffee and gratefully eating the biscuits that Udin's wife, Amira, had brought him.

Udin, dressed in a brown robe and wearing dark glasses, smoked a cigarette. There was an old Cinzano ashtray on the coffee table in front of them, and he seemed to know its approximate position. After every few drags he leaned forward and flicked the filter tip. Sometimes the ash landed in the right place, other times it sprinkled on the table. A dozen butts lay stubbed out in the ashtray. They chatted for a while, catching up, before coming to the point.

'You were very generous to me, in your piece in the newspaper, Mr Hunter. I have always felt I owed you something for the way you portrayed me.'

'That's very kind of you, thank you.'

'So to what do I owe the pleasure of such a distinguished journalist giving up his valuable time to visit me?'

'I need your help.'

'Oh? What help do you seek?'

'You told me when we last met that you were born and raised in Egypt. In Cairo?'

'Indeed I was.'

'Are you still in contact with people there – friends or family?'

'With some – not just in Cairo, but in other places of my birth country, too.'

'That's what I was hoping.'

'I'm sensing you need something? Urgently and importantly?'

'Do you have any contacts in Luxor?'

'Luxor?'

'Yes. I need someone in Luxor with a car, whom I can trust.'

Udin raised his head, holding like a dart his third cigarette since Ross had arrived, and drew on it again. Ash tumbled down his front. Oblivious to it, Udin said, 'I have a cousin there who could help you. Would you like me to speak with him and vouch for you, my friend?'

'I'd appreciate that, very much.' Ross sipped some more of his coffee.

'He will keep you safe. I'm sensing you need someone to protect you. Am I correct?'

'You are very perceptive, Hussam.'

'Ever since I lost my sight, I've devoured audio books. I like the works of William Shakespeare. King Lear, who was blinded, has always interested me. Such a great play. Such wisdom. "Your eyes are in a heavy case, your purse in a light. Yet you see how this world goes."'

'You seem to be coping well with your handicap.'

'Do I have an option? I cannot hop along to Specsavers and buy a new pair of eyes. They don't keep any in stock – and someone might try to kill me on the way. Don't worry – you have nothing to fear when you leave here, no one will kill a non-Muslim who doesn't believe. It's just me they are after, and always will be. I'm fine with that, you know. I'm OK. I see how this world goes and that sustains me. If I can help you in some way, that would make me happy. I will call my cousin. I don't know why you are going there, and I don't want to ask. I sense it is important. I hear it in your voice, Ross. You're a man on a mission. My cousin will take care of you. I will let him know you are going to contact him. Just tell him the day and the time and he will be there.'

He gave Ross the man's email address and phone number.

Then Ross asked, 'I have one more question – does the word "Hatem" mean anything?'

'Hatem?'

'Yes.' He spelled it out for him.

'No, it does not. But it is not an uncommon name for a man in Egypt.'

43

It was after 9 p.m. that evening when Ross arrived home. He had concealed the envelope of cash that Robert Anholt-Sperry had given him down behind the rear seat of the car. For the moment, he decided to say nothing to Imogen about it.

He unlocked the front door and went inside. Monty padded towards him, barking excitedly, tail wagging, followed by Imogen, in loose jumper, jeans and slip-on shoes, who was white as a sheet.

Her appearance alarmed him.

'Are you OK?'

'No,' she said. 'You'd better come and take a look at this.'

He gave the dog a quick pat and followed her through into the kitchen. She flipped open the lid of her laptop on the kitchen table. A jar of pickled onions with a spoon sticking out of it sat next to it – another craving. She hit a sequence of keys. Moments later an image appeared. A five-pointed star. He recognized it as an inverted pentagram.

Beneath it was a message.

YOUR HUSBAND IS WORKING FOR SATAN.
YOU MUST STOP HIM. FOR BOTH YOUR SAKES AND
FOR YOUR UNBORN BABY'S. YOU ARE WARNED.

Imogen was staring at him.

'Where's this from?' he asked.

'It came in this afternoon – when I was in the office. One of the guys tried to trace the address for me but it's anonymous, probably run deliberately through a series of servers around the world.'

Ross leaned down and clicked on the sender. It was a Hotmail address that was just series of numbers, which included '666'. It sent a chill through him. He looked at it carefully, then attempted for some minutes, without success, to find the source himself. 'It's just some nutter – probably responding to my Twitter post last week.'

'The same religious nutter – or nutters – who killed Harry Cook?'

'Harry Cook wasn't killed by anyone, he died of heart failure according to the postmortem.'

'Someone dying whilst they're being tortured doesn't count as murder? Hello?' she retorted.

'The police are saying there's been a spate of copycat robberies in the area – old people living alone being targeted and tortured.' He was aware he sounded more convincing than he felt.

'You have a list of dozens of stories to investigate. Do you really need to pursue this one? Religion breeds fanatics, Ross, we really need to be careful. Let it go. You've already been told Cook was deranged – why can't you see it?'

'What do you mean by that?'

'You're obsessed with this story, you're prepared to put it before me and our child. But that's how it is with you, Ross. You first. Always. I never wanted you to go to Afghanistan. I sat at home in terror, waiting for a knock on the door to tell me you were dead.'

'And shagging yourself senseless in the process.'

Instantly, he regretted saying it. The words just came out. It was like they had been piling up, steadily, for years, an avalanche waiting for the right temperature.

'I'm sorry,' he said, immediately. 'I didn't mean that.'

'You did.'

It was the elephant in the room. It had been there ever since that day he came home from Afghanistan. They'd cleared the air in the days that followed, and he'd forgiven her. But the elephant never went away. It was never going to.

He sat down opposite her and put his hand out. But she pulled hers away. 'Imo, if I felt there really was a risk, I would drop it, immediately. But . . .'

'But?'

'This could be the biggest story I've ever had. I just have a feeling about it.'

'So, you're willing to ignore my feelings?'

He reached out again to take her hand, but she withdrew it again.

'Imogen, come on!'

'I'm getting scared, Ross. OK? Can't you understand that?'

'I do understand. There's all kinds of fanatics who come out of the woodwork when you write about anything to do with religion. I was trolled on Twitter and had death threats after I wrote that piece on the charismatic evangelists a few years back, remember? But I just have a gut feeling about this, I really do. There's a big piece here, whichever way it pans out. Look, I think it would be smart to get a locksmith to fit a safety chain on the front door and a spyhole to add to the other security we've put in. Would that make you feel better?'

'It would make me feel better if you considered dropping this story.'

'Graham Greene once wrote that every writer needs to carry a splinter of ice in his – or her – heart.'

'And that's what you have – regardless of the threat to your family? That splinter of ice? Are you cold-hearted enough to ignore my feelings? All because a nutter came to see you with – what you said yourself – was a crazy notion?'

'Imo, listen. I do love you. If I ever felt for one moment that you or I were in real life-threatening danger over a story I was working on, I'd drop it in a flash. OK? But please understand something. If you'd felt what I felt that morning Ricky died, you'd have to pursue this too. Just to see if there is anything at all in it. It's not an option for me, I *have* to do this. It doesn't mean I don't love you. But please understand I have to do this, please stay with me on it – I will protect us and our baby, I promise.'

'You've just said yourself that religious subjects bring out all the fanatics.'

'Yes, but ultimately they're harmless – mostly.'

She gave him a dubious look. 'Two years ago, when you were investigating that crook who'd killed a policeman and had gone into hiding in Spain, you had death threats. The police warned you that you could be taking a risk writing about it. But it didn't stop you. You went ahead and published the piece. Just as you did accusing Putin of being behind that Russian's murder – Litvinenko – in London.'

'It's what I do – it's what I've always done. I expose people who do bad things.'

'Dr Cook didn't do anything bad, Ross. He believed he could save the world. Perhaps he died because he stirred up the hornets' nest of religious beliefs.'

'Imo, I've just said, there's no evidence he was killed by fanatics.'

She tapped the screen, pointing at the pentagram. 'There. That's your sodding evidence. It's a pretty clear message.'

'I think Satan will be a lot happier with me when I publish my piece debunking Cook and the whole myth of proof of God.'

'That's what you're planning?'

'I spoke to my editor at the *Sunday Times* on the way down this evening, and she likes the story. I've started working on it. She's willing to fund my research – she's offered to pay my air ticket to Egypt to investigate the second set of coordinates.'

'What?'

'I got them today from Cook's lawyer in Birmingham – another nutter.'

'You're going to Egypt?'

'Listen, I had an idea. Why don't you come with me? I thought we could make a short holiday out of it – we could go back to Sharm El Sheikh and go on to do the pyramids – we still have our visas. What do you think?'

'You know what I think? You've lost your marbles.'

44

Two years ago, when Ross had been working on an article about illusionist Derren Brown who had vehemently debunked psychics, he had gone to Southampton to interview a celebrated medium, Christopher Lewis, and his medium wife, Gill, and their protégé, Dean Hartley.

Intending originally to trash them, he had been impressed with their sincerity – so much so that he'd ended up writing favourably about them. After the piece had been published they had written to him to thank him, and offered him, free of charge, a reading with Hartley any time he would like.

He had decided to cash in on this offer.

Now, in the downstairs room of the mediums' home, he sat, still a little cynical. Dean Hartley, who was in his mid twenties, with shoulder-length blond hair Rastafarian-style, like strands of rope, and every inch of his slender body that was visible covered in weird tattoos, switched on a recorder which was perched on a table covered with a pink-and-black patterned cloth.

A black Buddha sat on the floor in one corner, a small white filing cabinet in another, and a white desk with a mirrored top, on which were a glass of water and a box of tissues, was against the wall beside him.

The medium, gentle and polite, checked that Ross was

comfortable, then closed his eyes and sat in silence for some moments.

'I'm hearing the name *Pip*,' he said. 'He was born *Philip*, but all his friends called him Pip. Does that mean anything?'

'No,' Ross said. 'Well, in a way it does, because that's my father's name, but as of this morning, he is still very much alive.'

The medium was completely still, with his eyes closed, for another long moment. 'I'm getting Richard.'

'Richard?'

'Rick? Ricky?'

Ross stared at him.

'Ricky's telling me something – that your wife is pregnant. Imogen, I think, is that her name?'

The name was something the medium could have found out easily. But not that she was pregnant.

'Do you know the sex of the baby?' Ross asked him.

'He says she is carrying a boy.'

Ross hesitated before replying. How on earth did Hartley know this? They had told very few people that she was pregnant, feeling it might be a jinx to do so, and certainly no one that it was a boy. There was no way the medium could know this. On the other hand, he reasoned, the medium could see his wedding ring and could figure out from his approximate age that he might be in the process of having children. And to guess the sex was simply fifty-fifty odds.

'What can you tell me about my son?'

The medium closed his eyes for a moment, then frowned, screwing up his forehead. 'I'm being distracted,' he said. 'Someone very agitated who needs to communicate with you. I'm getting a name. *Cook*. I think a man called Cook who has recently passed into spirit. He is coming through and I'm sensing urgency. He wants me to give you a message. Do you know this person?' Dean Hartley kept his eyes closed.

'I know him,' Ross replied, trying to give nothing away.

'He wants me to tell you that he is aware you think he is a bit crazy. He says he wasn't ready to pass and had important unfinished business. He needs you to carry it on for him; he is depending on you.' He frowned again. 'He's telling me about the Valley of the Kings in Luxor, Egypt. You are thinking about going there. He tells you you must, it will unlock everything. He's giving me a name. Bolt. Kerry. No, something similar. Anbolt? Skerrit?'

Ross waited, and did not reply.

'Anholt-Skerry?'

Shit, Ross thought, feeling a chill and a frisson of excitement.

'Anholt-Sperry,' Hartley repeated. 'Does this name mean something?'

'It does.'

'I'm being told you must trust this man. Does that make sense?'

'Yes.'

Still without opening his eyes, Hartley said, 'I'm getting another name. Egyptian. I think it is Hatem. Does that mean anything?'

'*Hatem?*' Ross replied, astonished, and spelled it out to be sure. The medium confirmed.

How? How, Ross wondered, could he possibly know this name? He felt goosebumps. 'It does.'

'I'm being told Hatem will be waiting for you when you go there.'

'Go where?'

The medium closed his eyes again. 'I'm being given numbers. A list of numbers and letters. They feel like compass coordinates.'

As he read them out, Ross wrote them down. He was trying to remain neutral, neither believing the medium nor completely disbelieving him either, but he was deeply confused. Was Dean Hartley pulling a fast one on him? Was the gender of their child simply a lucky guess? Ricky, he could have found out about easily. But Hatem? Anholt-Sperry? The Valley of the Kings? Were Anholt-Sperry and Dean Hartley in cahoots to convince him? Ridiculous. That was even more preposterous than –

Than what?

Than believing what Hartley was telling him was real?

45

Monday, 6 March

From the window of the aeroplane, Ross watched the lush green vegetation either side of the deep blue Nile give way to a desert landscape of sand and mountainous topography.

Every few minutes he looked down at the notes he had made in his meeting with Robert Anholt-Sperry. And in particular at the compass coordinates he had been given by the solicitor.

25°44'47.1264"N and 32°36'19.1124"E

And then at the numbers and letters that Dean Hartley had given him, along with the word, Hatem. The same.

25°44'47.1264"N and 32°36'19.1124"E

The coordinates for Queen Hatshepsut's Temple.

Would the mysterious Hatem be there? And how would he find him?

He was filled with guilt and misgivings about the trip. Imogen was not happy, hoping that it would turn out to be the ultimate wild goose chase, and that afterwards he would come to his senses, write a disparaging piece and then drop the whole thing.

He was uncomfortable that he had still not told her the truth about his visit to Chalice Well and what he had found there. Nor had he told her about his sitting with Dean

Hartley, but he felt, for her peace of mind, it was better she did not know. He had also kept quiet about the £10,000 from Anholt-Sperry.

As the plane taxied along the runway, he texted Imogen.

Landed. X

She texted back.

We all missing you. Monty has rolled in something horrible, he stinks. Had to shower him, which he hated. Be safe. XX

Thirty minutes later, with his overnight bag slung over his shoulder, he emerged into the clammy heat and total chaos of the arrivals hall. A barrage of names being displayed on paper, boards and iPhones greeted him. Among them was his own.

He made his way over to the smiling, happy-looking moustached Egyptian who was holding his name. In his early forties, short but exuding energy, the man was dressed in a beige djellaba and sandals, with a traditional red and white keffiyeh held in place with a black band round his forehead. He held out his hand.

'Ross Hunter? I'm Medhat El-Hadidy. You call me Hadidy, please.'

'Good to meet you, Hadidy!' he replied, shaking his hand firmly. He liked the man instantly.

'Welcome to my country. I will be your guide here. I will look after you, yes?'

He insisted on taking Ross's bag.

They walked outside, crossed over into the covered car park and headed over to a black, recent model Toyota Land Cruiser. Hadidy opened the rear door for him.

Ross sat in the leather air-conditioned interior, shielded from the outside world by tinted privacy glass. As Hadidy started the engine, Egyptian music played, a tad too loudly, on the car's radio.

Hadidy pushed a ticket into the machine at the exit and the barrier rose. As he did he turned his head. 'You are friend of my cousin, Hussam Udin, yes?'

'He's a good man.'

'He is,' Hadidy echoed. 'A good man in a crazy world, yes?'

'You can say that all right.'

'I'll keep you safe.'

'Thank you.'

'No, thank *you*, Mr Ross. Good to do business with you!'

'You must tell me how much you charge – you have a daily rate?'

'Mr Ross, you are my cousin's good friend. It is an honour to have you in my country. I do not charge you one Egyptian pound for as long as you are here. Please. No more talk about money.'

'You are very kind. But I insist on paying you. I can charge all my expenses back to my newspaper.'

'I am happy you are here! No payment. No argument!'

They headed out of the airport along a dual carriageway. Soon they were entering a conurbation, with angular beige and white buildings of varying sizes and heights all around. Ross felt secure, cocooned in this strong vehicle.

'Hussam Udin speaks to many people, and some, they don't like what he tells them,' Hadidy said.

'That's right.'

'You know, here in Egypt, we all get along. You want to believe in one God? Or many gods? Or no god? My people used to be fine with that. You know? Believe what you want.'

He pointed upwards. 'He doesn't mind! But now Christians are dying, many killings. Why?'

'In many other countries, too, Hadidy.'

He drove in silence for some minutes, then he said, 'Now I take you to hotel. Tomorrow we go to the Valley of the Kings. The funerary site of the pharaohs. To visit Queen Hatshepsut's Temple, that is correct?'

'Correct.'

'I will be at your service. So long as you remain in my country, you are my guest. Tonight you rest. Tomorrow we begin your purpose. That is good?'

'Sounds like a plan.'

46

Tuesday, 7 March

Ross had checked in to the Steigenberger Hotel. After a largely sleepless night, and with Egypt being two hours ahead of the UK, he struggled with his body clock to get up after the alarm woke him at 6.30 a.m. It was only 4.30 a.m. UK time.

When he opened the blinds, he had a view across the almost magically blue water of the Nile, to the far bank and hilly desert beyond. The whole landscape seemed washed in a different, much more intense light than England's. It reminded him of the hues of a Hockney painting. He took a photograph on his phone and texted it to Imogen, know-ing she'd probably be up, because she wasn't sleeping well.

The view from my hotel window! X

He ate a room-service breakfast, then dressed in light-weight summer trousers, a white T-shirt, linen jacket and trainers, with his sunglasses in his pocket, packed his few things into his overnight bag, and met the ever-smiling Hadidy downstairs, as arranged.

A text pinged back from Imogen.

Lucky you. Pissing with rain here. Take care. X

Ross checked out and paid the bill. He had a seat booked on the late-afternoon flight back to London, although he was unsure what the day might bring.

As they drove away from the hotel in the constant blare of horns, he yawned, feeling sleepy. He watched a man in white robes astride a donkey, with panniers on both sides laden with long-stalked green vegetables. He receded into the distance as they drove along a modern road busy with cars, buses, motorbikes, mopeds – many with two people on them – and bicycles. They passed a line of horse-drawn calèches with black canopies, headed along a winding road past the port and negotiated a hectic roundabout with a fountain in the middle.

'You know the history of Queen Hatshepsut?' Hadidy said above the din of the music in the car.

'Only a little.' Ross yawned again.

'She was debatably our first woman pharaoh. She is come to the throne in 1478 BC – and ruled with Thutmose III. She was a good pharaoh, she did much building throughout Egypt. She was the fifth pharaoh of the Eighteenth Dynasty of Egypt!'

'OK.'

'You have a special interest in her, Mr Ross?'

They were heading through the outskirts of the town now. The traffic was thinning. To his right, he saw a decrepit row of single-storey shops that were little more than covered market stalls. Two men in dark robes sat on the crumbling sidewalk drinking what looked like coffee. A motorcycle swerved dangerously past, pulling in front of their car, causing Hadidy to brake sharply. He shouted angrily at it, through the windscreen, then raised both hands off the steering wheel in a gesture of despair.

'Crazy drivers here!' he said.

'We have them in England, too.' Ross, with the window lowered, was busy taking photographs of his journey.

'Why the hurry, you know? You are where you are! Enjoy!'

'My sentiments exactly,' Ross said, glad that Hadidy seemed a far more sensible driver than most of the others here. He could see the Nile. He closed the window and sat back.

After a short while the comfortable rear seat and the motion of the car was making him feel very sleepy.

Just as he lapsed into a doze, he was woken by a ping from his phone.

It was another text from Imogen.

Say hi to your dead pharaoh buddies! XX

He sent her back a smiley.

They were on a bridge, crossing the Nile.

Ahead of him was starkly barren, mountainous terrain, with steep escarpments.

'The pharaohs,' Hadidy said, giving him an unprompted history lesson. 'They wanted to be buried with all their wealth and jewels, food and weapons for their journey through to the underworld. But because they were worried about grave robbers, they created this valley, here on the west bank of the Nile, away from Thebes – Luxor – where their tombs could be guarded.'

'Very smart of them. I'd be pretty upset if someone robbed me after I was dead,' Ross replied.

'That's why some tombs are still hidden today. So many centuries later. Maybe forever.'

'We have an expression in my country, Hadidy. That you can't take it with you when you die.'

Hadidy lifted his hands off the steering wheel. 'Maybe not. But if you can, think of the party you could have!'

Ross smiled, unsure of his driver's beliefs and not wanting to risk offending him. Then he stared in awe at the sight of the elevated, colonnaded building ahead of them. Three storeys high, with sharp angles, tall, thin windows all evenly spaced, and a wide ramp rising up to the second storey. It looked like something that had been designed by one of the great modern architects, Frank Lloyd Wright, Frank Gehry or Le Corbusier. Behind it was a backdrop of dramatic cliffs.

'Is that it, Hadidy?' he asked.

'That,' Hadidy said, his voice filled with pride, 'is Queen Hatshepsut's Temple!'

Around the bottom of the ramp dozens of tourists milled about, some in groups with guides, some solo, almost all of them snapping away.

Hadidy drove into a car park, passing several tourist buses, and pulled into a bay. 'We have to walk from here. You like me to come with you and negotiate a good deal for a guide? It's better. Many are no good. I know the best ones, they are all my friends.'

'I'd like you to come with me, Hadidy. I have to meet someone. Can you come and make sure no one pesters me?'

'Sure. OK. But you want a tour, yes?'

'Maybe. It depends.'

As they left the car, he stopped and took another photograph, then put on his sunglasses. Walking towards the bottom of the ramp, they were besieged by men and women, some in traditional dress and some in suits, all holding up tourist tat. Plastic models of the temple, of the pyramids, and jewellery bearing Egyptian symbols.

Ross was glad about his decision to ask Hadidy to accompany him, because the Egyptian did a sterling job of keeping the hawkers at bay, speaking to some politely and to many others quite ferociously in their native tongue.

They walked past a group of Japanese tourists, all circled around a guide with a loudhailer, then another group around a man in a djellaba who was standing on a box, and arrived at the foot of the ramp.

A robed man, arms laden with scarves, spotting his chance, hurried towards them. Hadidy brushed him away.

Feeling very self-conscious, and ignoring whatever Hadidy might think of him, Ross stood still, staring around.

Hadidy looked at him strangely. 'We go inside?'

'No.'

The group of Japanese tourists filed past him, following their guide.

He continued to stand still, mindful that it was right here, in 1997, that fifty-eight tourists and four locals were massacred by an Islamic organization.

Then a wiry, elderly man in white robes and a red-and-white cotton headscarf, similar to Hadidy's, appeared out of the mêlée heading towards him. He had a wrinkled, dark-skinned face and just two crooked teeth in his mouth, like tombstones in a forgotten graveyard. He spoke in broken English and looked very nervous.

'Excuse me. You Mr Ross Hunter, yes?'

Ross looked at him warily. 'I am – who are you?'

'Hatem Rasul.' His nut-brown eyes darted everywhere. 'I have been waiting for you for a long time.'

Hadidy stepped forward and spoke to the man for a couple of minutes in Arabic, before turning to Ross.

'This is the man you are here to meet, Mr Hunter. He says he will take us to his sister. He wishes us to follow him into the mountains. It will be a long journey. Two hours, perhaps. You are OK with this?'

Ross frowned. 'Did he say who asked him to meet me, Hadidy?'

'He said it is your friend in England. Mr Dr Harry. Yes?'

'Dr Cook?'

'Dr Harry Cook, yes.'

47

In a daze, Ross followed the two men back up to the car park. Despite his apparent age, Hatem Rasul strode energetically and purposefully.

Harry Cook.

His insides were jangling. Was any of this real? Where were they going to be taken? He looked at the barren, sandy, mountainous terrain beyond them.

How did this strange old man know Harry Cook?

As they reached the car park, Rasul headed over to an ancient khaki-coloured motorcycle, climbed astride and kick-started it into life. For a moment, Ross was reminded of the movie *Lawrence of Arabia*.

Hadidy opened the rear door of the Land Cruiser and ushered Ross to climb in.

He did so, as if in a dream.

As they followed the motorcycle out of the car park Ross leaned forward and asked, 'What else did he say to you, Hadidy?'

'He's OK,' he replied, reassuringly. 'We can trust him. He has been sent here to guide us by your friend. Mr Dr Harry Cook.'

Ross thought before replying. 'Is that what he said?'

'He said that God will protect us on our journey.'

'Good to know that.'

'God has His purpose, Mr Ross.'

'Let's hope so.'

'It is written.'

Soon after leaving the car park, the motorcycle turned off the main road onto a track, kicking up a trail of sand behind it. They followed, climbing a winding, unmade and barren mountain pass, heading deeper into the hills. After half an hour they drove through a village with a row of open-fronted shops, and swerved past a man, in the middle of the road, tugging a goat on a tether.

They climbed higher, Ross taking pictures constantly. And wondering. He was feeling nervous and curious in equal proportions.

Then they descended a tortuous track down into a valley. Once they reached the bottom, they began to climb again. They passed a farmer, or a shepherd, with a flock of around sixty sheep, then abruptly turned off the track into pure desert. Through the windscreen Ross watched the agile old man ahead, sliding his motorcycle up a dune and down the far side, and they followed.

They climbed an escarpment that seemed almost impossibly steep, between two tall, rock promontories.

'Did you come alone to Egypt, Mr Ross?' Hadidy asked anxiously, concentrating hard on his driving to keep the car pointing forward and maintaining traction on the loose sand.

'Yes.'

'Someone is following us.'

Ross turned and looked through the rear windscreen. And saw a plume of sand.

A slick of fear slid through him.

'There's a wadi in a few kilometres. Maybe supplies being delivered. Maybe is nothing.'

'You've been here before?'

'No, never. But it shows on the map.'

Ross felt relieved. 'OK, good.' He turned and peered through the rear window. At the cloud of sand from a vehicle some way behind them.

They descended into another valley, where he could see the wadi, a mile or so to his left. A bunch of tents and several camels around a watering hole. They began to climb again. Ross pulled up the compass app on his iPhone. Saw the tiny blue dot moving through a wilderness. They were heading north-east. The landscape, beautiful and desolate though it was, became monotonous. Climb and descend. Climb and descend. He really had no idea, now, where they were. Nor what they would find at their destination.

He looked behind him again. To his relief, there was nothing. No longer any plume of sand.

As bidden by Hadidy, he helped himself to first one bottle of mineral water from a compartment beneath the armrest, then a second.

Almost exactly two hours after they had left the temple car park, they passed an ancient, faded Coca-Cola sign. He saw an elderly man in Arab robes ahead of them, seated on the side of the track, engaged in conversation with another man, with a camel standing close by. A small strip of ramshackle, open-fronted shops. A kid ran out in front of them, excitedly. An almost biblical scene of a man walking a donkey on which sat a woman cradling a baby. Then, ahead, the motorcycle came to a halt outside a primitive-looking shack. Their guide dismounted and went inside.

He came back out, a few minutes later, accompanied by an elderly looking woman in black garb and sandals, with a grey headscarf. With some difficulty, Hatem Rasul helped her onto the motorcycle's pillion, remounted himself, started the machine and rode on.

'Any idea who she is, Hadidy? His sister that he spoke of?'

'Perhaps. I think she must be important lady.'

'Important?'

They followed the motorcycle up an increasingly steep track, negotiating the mountain. After some minutes, as the track levelled out, the motorcycle halted and the pair dismounted. Rasul kicked down the stand as Hadidy pulled up the Land Cruiser beside them. They climbed out into the searing, dry, midday heat, then Ross ducked back in, took out another small bottle of water – the last in the rear compartment – and jammed it in his jacket pocket.

'Mr Hunter,' Hatem Rasul said. 'This is my sister, Sitra.'

Close up he could see just how ancient and wizened she looked. She gave Ross a toothless smile and nodded, ignoring his proffered hand. Then she beckoned with a gnarled finger for him to follow.

They walked up a steep, narrow goat track, under a cloudless sky. The old woman was driven by an energy that Ross lacked, and the higher they climbed, the less he looked down at the sheer drop beneath them. If he stumbled and fell, it would be instant death. High above, Ross could see a row of caves.

He tried to blank the precipice from his mind and kept focus on the path in front of him. He was perspiring heavily, his jacket slung over his shoulder now, wishing he had left it in the car. He was grateful for his water, which he rationed carefully, taking just small sips every few minutes. His lips felt parched, the sun burning his face. He wished he'd thought to bring sun cream.

Slowly, as they climbed, the caves above loomed nearer.

Finally the old woman, followed by Rasul then Hadidy, turned right across the mouths of the caves. She walked past the first three, gave an instruction to Rasul and made a left turn into the fourth. The three men waited outside.

Several minutes later the old woman reappeared, cradling a bundle of cream-coloured cloth in her hands, which she held out to Ross. She nodded, encouragingly.

Smiling a thank you, he took it from her.

It was almost weightless.

Rasul said something to Hadidy, and his guardian turned to him.

'You may open it, Mr Ross, with care.'

It took him some moments, unfurling one layer of cloth after another, the bundle getting increasingly smaller, before he reached the contents, visible inside a tiny muslin bag.

An ochre-coloured, enamelled object.

All three of them were staring at him.

'A tooth?' he queried. 'Is this a tooth? Where's it from?'

Rasul spoke in Arabic to Hadidy, who then turned to him.

'Sitra says, Mr Ross, this is indeed a tooth. A very special tooth. When Jesus Christ was being taken to the cross on Calvary, along with the criminals, local people lined the road and threw insults and hard objects, including many stones, at them. One stone hit Jesus in the mouth and knocked out one of his teeth. This is that tooth.'

Ross stared down at it, then looked at Hadidy. 'How do they know this, for sure?'

Holding the almost transparent bag in one hand, he photographed it with his phone camera.

Hadidy continued. 'Hatem Rasul said that one of the disciples stepped forward and picked it up. Knowing it was a dangerous thing to possess he decided to take it out of Judea and hide it. He brought it here, to Egypt, and asked a family he trusted – who lived in a remote, rural community – to hide it. It has remained in this cave ever since. For generations this family has been in charge of guarding it. For two thousand years they have been awaiting for the chosen person to collect it. Sitra says that her brother tells her you are that chosen one.'

Ross looked down at it, staring hard, and shivered. Could this be real? Could this tiny, almost weightless object really be Christ's tooth?

And if it was?

He trembled at the thought. The possibility. He looked back at the three of them. All were studying him, intently.

Rasul stepped over to Hadidy and spoke to him in Arabic again.

When he had finished Hadidy turned back to Ross. 'Hatem Rasul says Dr Harry Cook has a message for you. Dr Cook says this tooth is real. Take it back to England, to his friend in Birmingham. Mr – this is a strange name – Mr Ano-Spiry. You know this man?'

Ross was transfixed by the tooth. 'I know him,' he said, his voice sounding distant, as though it was someone else speaking.

'Mr Hunter,' Hadidy said. 'Hatem Rasul is telling me. When you see Mr Ano-Spiry again, you will receive the final proof. It awaits you. The absolute proof!'

A sound in the sky made all four of them look upwards. High above them was the tiny speck of a helicopter. It was too high and too far away to identify. It flew overhead and, within moments, the sound had faded away.

Ross turned to Hadidy and gave him a quizzical look.

Hadidy shrugged. 'Tourists.'

Ross looked back up at the sky. First a car had followed them. Now this helicopter had appeared.

It made him deeply uncomfortable.

'Sightseeing,' Hadidy went on. 'You can take a heli tour over the Valley of the Kings.'

Ross nodded, still feeling very uneasy. They were a long way from the Valley of the Kings. Even for a helicopter.

Sitra remained at the cave, saying she would make her way home later, whilst the rest of them retraced their steps to where they had left their vehicles, Ross walking as fast as he could. He sensed the nervousness in the other two, also.

48

Back in the car, they began to head down the steep track, with the sheer drop to one side; it was even scarier going downhill. Ross tried to blank it out. While Hadidy wrestled the wheel, Ross focused on the small, enamel-like object with its tiny brown root.

Was there any possibility this could be real? One of Jesus of Nazareth's teeth?

In a cave in Egypt?

It was almost impossible to believe and yet . . .

His knowledge of the scriptures, and of Egypt, was scant. He knew about the Old Testament Exodus. How the Jews fled Egypt.

Could someone really have returned with a tooth and hidden it in a remote cave in this country, with local peasants as its guardians?

As the serpentine dirt track ahead unwound through the front windscreen, at times so steep he was almost hanging forward against his seat belt, he watched Hatem Rasul leading the way, skilfully piloting his ancient motorcycle around the bends with the agility of someone half his age and the skill of an autocross racer. At times the machine seemed to slide away from him and he only remained upright by his feet skidding along the ground.

Then, above the sound of the vehicles' engines, came the thrashing of a helicopter.

Hadidy let out what sounded like an oath. He was looking in his rear-view mirror.

Ross turned round, peering anxiously through the rear window. And saw the black underside of a helicopter, so low he could see the skids, swooping towards them.

His first thought was that it might be police or military. Were they in some illegal zone here?

He hurriedly wrapped the tooth back in the cloth and pushed it into the inside pocket of his jacket.

A shadow passed over them. As it did so he saw Hatem Rasul spin his motorbike round, 180 degrees, and race off back the way they had come.

Then the helicopter appeared through the front windscreen, a few hundred yards in front of them. The door was open and there was a man leaning out. There was no mistaking what was pointing at them. The long, black muzzle of a gun. He was aiming straight at them.

Hadidy screamed in fear.

Ross, terrified, snapped open his seat-belt buckle and threw himself down into the gap between the seats. He felt the car braking hard, its wheels locking up, sliding along on the sand.

He heard Hadidy cry out in terror as the Land Cruiser slewed violently.

Ross felt the car plunging.

The car pitched forward steeply – so steeply for a moment Ross thought it was going to roll, end over end. He could feel it picking up pace.

'Hadidy!' he yelled.

They were going faster.

Faster.

It felt like he was hurtling downhill in a roller coaster.

'Hadidy!' he yelled.

There was no reaction.

He cautiously raised himself. The driver's door was open. Hadidy had bailed out. Ross looked behind him and glimpsed, way up on the ridge, his driver running away, fast.

The car was careering down a steep slope. Somehow, miraculously, still pointing forward.

Lurching, bumping, flying through the air. Crashing back down.

Ross reached over the seat in front of him, stretching round the headrest, and lunged at the steering wheel.

The car was heading straight for a rock.

He turned the wheel to the right and missed the boulder by inches. A drop was looming now. He turned the wheel to the left and the car went up a sandy embankment, almost tipping over onto its side. Then swinging right, back down towards the valley, the vehicle began to slide.

Heading sideways towards a rock face.

Somehow, the car missed it, and hurtled down a steep gully.

Then another. Zigzagging through an obstacle course of boulders.

He held on to the wheel, totally gripped by terror.

Moments later the car was heading up an incline towards a drift, and came to a jarring halt, planted in deep sand.

Jesus, no.

He scrambled out of the rear door and looked up. The helicopter was descending rapidly. He dived into the driver's seat and looked down at the controls. He found the one for locking the differentials and accelerated hard. As the helicopter blotted out the sun, to his relief the vehicle moved forward, slowly, gaining traction. Up the sandy incline. Towards what looked like a precipice.

Shit. Shit.

He lifted his foot off the accelerator. As he did so the helicopter appeared right in front of him. He could see the man with the gun, door still open, aiming straight at him.

As he dived down below the dash and floored the accelerator, he heard a sound he had last heard in Afghanistan. A burst of gunfire.

The car lurched forward. Forward.

Towards the precipice.

If he stopped he was dead.

All the terror of Afghanistan came flooding back.

If he kept going he was probably dead, too.

He made the split-second decision to keep going. There was another burst of gunfire.

Then the car lurched crazily forward.

Falling.

He was catapulted upwards, against the steering wheel, his head striking the roof of the car painfully. Saw rock. Sky. Rock. Sky.

He hurtled down, striking his head against the steering wheel. Then, somehow, incredibly, he was back in the driving seat and the Land Cruiser, now the right way up, was hurtling down a steep, but no longer vertical, incline.

He gripped the jigging wheel. They were travelling at a crazy speed. More rocks and boulders ahead which he somehow avoided. The engine was screaming. Somehow, he did not know from where it came, he had the presence of mind to shift out of the diff lock position.

The engine note instantly changed.

The incline was becoming less steep and the valley was now just a short distance ahead.

So was the helicopter. He ducked below the dash as he saw flames from the muzzle of the gun and heard the crack and ping of bullets striking the ground in front of the car. Sitting up again, he understood what was happening. The man was trying to shoot his tyres out, to stop him.

He reached the valley and there was just one narrow route in front of him, through a gulley, bounded on either side by vertical cliffs. The helicopter dropped down and landed dead ahead. Again Ross ducked as flames spurted from the gun's muzzle and he heard more bullets strike the rocks around the vehicle.

Suddenly, the man inside the open rear door stopped firing. He began tugging at the weapon, looking panicky. Either it had jammed or needed a magazine change. He yelled something at the pilot.

Ross saw his chance. He floored the accelerator pedal, feeling the car surge forward, getting full traction on the solid surface. The helicopter loomed closer. Closer. Closer.

The man in black was still struggling frantically with the gun and yelling at the pilot.

As he raced towards it, Ross saw a fog of sand rise up all around the helicopter. The pilot was trying to lift off.

No, no, no you don't, you bastards!

The gap was closing. One hundred metres. Fifty. Twenty-five.

Ross could see air between the skids and the sand below.

Not enough. Oh no.

T-boning it full on would probably make it blow up, killing them all. At the last moment, seeing the look of terror in the gunman's face, he jerked the wheel right and, gripping it tightly, threw himself down below the dash.

An instant later there was a jarring crash, glass was flying everywhere and he felt the blast of hot air.

He sat up and looked through what little remained of the windscreen, feeling hot, sandy air on his face, at a vast desert landscape. In his mirror, he saw the main section of the helicopter lying on its side. Its jagged tail end and rotor lay several yards away. Someone was struggling to get out.

He kept on going, traversing the dunes, until they were no more than a speck in his mirror. Then, on the crest of a particularly high one, he stopped, shaking.

He heard a ping.

A text. With trembling hands he pulled his phone out of his trouser pocket.

It was from Imogen.

How's your day going? XX

49

Somehow, despite all the damage it had suffered from gun-fire and rolling, the Toyota was still running. Ross could barely think straight. He just knew he had to get out of here, and away from Luxor.

He stared ahead, through where the windscreen had been shortly before, at the arid, desert landscape, with a ridge of hills in the hazy distance. There was what looked like a track a short distance to his right. He tried to figure out the satnav, which came up on the screen in Arabic, but his hands were shaking so much that his fingers kept miss-ing the button that might take him back to the previous destinations list. If he could get to that maybe it would have Luxor programmed in. Perhaps even the airport.

But all that happened when he finally touched it was that the screen froze.

Then he remembered Google Maps on his iPhone and pulled that out. To his relief there was a weak 3G signal. Enough for the app to work. But with his shaking hands it took him several minutes before he was able to enter 'Luxor Airport'.

To his amazement, the device found it. A round blue symbol with a white aircraft outline appeared. And a pulsing blue symbol showing where he was. Two hours and thirty-five minutes' driving time, it informed him.

And the route took him along the track he was already on.

He checked his watch. It was currently just after 3 p.m. His flight was 5.55 p.m. No chance. He looked around nervously. But there was no sign of any movement. The engine laboured and hot desert air blasted his face. He was thirsty. He lifted up the centre console and saw several small bottles of water in what looked like a built-in fridge compartment. Taking one out and unscrewing the lid, he drank the entire contents, followed by another.

Jumping down from the car, he walked round, inspecting each of the tyres, fearful they might have been shot out, but they all seemed properly inflated. He crouched underneath to see if any fluids were draining out, but everything looked dry. Then he stood back and stared at the shell of the car. It was not a pretty sight. The front was damaged from where it had struck the tail of the helicopter, part of the bonnet was buckled and one headlight was gone. The roof was dented, as was just about every panel of the bodywork.

Irrationally, he wondered if Hadidy had good insurance.

Anger flared inside him. Anger that his driver had bailed out and fled, leaving him to his fate. But could he blame him?

Then as he stood, staring at the car, he began to shake again, even more violently than before.

Afghanistan.

Trying to dispel those nightmare thoughts. To think clearly.

Who was behind this?

The same people who had followed him to Chalice Well and kicked him in the face there?

He looked around, turning his head steadily, slowly. He felt very scared now. He wanted to phone home, to hear a friendly voice. But maybe telling Imogen about this would not be smart. It would send her into total meltdown, and she would demand he dropped this, immediately. Instead he replied to her text:

Hot! X

But the signal had suddenly become crap. It didn't go through. He drove off, thinking hard about what he should now do. Contact the police? The British Embassy? But he'd have to tell them pretty close to the truth, and maybe there was some law preventing historical objects being taken out of the country. Besides, he didn't want to risk hanging around. If he stayed on here, he'd need to make himself very low profile. Better to get out, this afternoon, board a plane. If there wasn't one going to England, get one to somewhere else, and then fly on. Did the people in the helicopter have other accomplices in Luxor? Would they have contacted them already and put out an alert for him? A watch on the airport?

From the chaotic crowds at the airport last night, he recalled, it wouldn't be hard to move around it unnoticed. What did they know about him? If they'd had details of his flight out they'd be able to find out his flight back, and watch the gate. Better to fly to a different destination altogether, he decided. Paris? Berlin? Madrid? Anywhere. Somewhere he knew?

He just needed to get out.

The car he would have to worry about later. At this moment he was still angry with Hadidy for leaving him in the back seat of a driverless car. The Egyptian could damn well sort it out.

Sod him.

50

To the best of his knowledge, Ross had not been followed. And to his relief it was growing dark as he approached Luxor Airport, shortly before a quarter to six. It would make the damaged car less noticeable to any security guards.

He drove straight into the short-term car park, up a couple of levels and parked the Land Cruiser in a bay, leaving the keys in the ignition. He dusted himself down and wiped his face, then cleaned his sunglasses. To try to disguise himself a little he put his sunglasses back on, followed by his jacket, patting to check the cloth wrapped round the tooth was still snug in his inside pocket, picked up his overnight bag from the back and walked through into the airline ticketing area.

England was two hours behind Egypt; France and Germany one hour. Egypt Air had availability on a direct flight to Charles De Gaulle at 9 p.m. and Lufthansa had one shortly after to Berlin but it had two stopovers. He didn't want to get a through ticket to London, in case anyone was watching for just that. He would get an onward flight easily enough from either of these destinations.

He bought a ticket to Paris, then made his way through to the departure hall, picked up a departure card and filled it in. His hand was shaking badly. In addition to the trauma, he remembered he'd not eaten anything since breakfast.

If anyone was watching him as he stood in the passport line, they were doing a discreet job. The unsmiling passport officer looked at his passport then studied the card and gave Ross a strange look. 'You not stay long in Egypt.'

'Unfortunately. Would love to – it's still pretty cold back in my country.'

'You have business in Luxor?'

'I'm a writer. I came to meet with a writer friend who is working out here – we're discussing collaborating on a book about the Valley of the Kings. A kind of guide book – for tourism.'

He'd said the magic word. The officer stamped his passport, closed it and handed it back to him with a faintly discernible smile – possibly one of approval.

Once through security he found a bar. Perched on a stool, he ordered a cold lager and a double Scotch, and pointed at a tired-looking sandwich on a shelf, not caring what was in it. He swallowed the whisky in one grateful gulp. The burn as it went down felt good, and he ordered another.

The flight was delayed two hours, which meant they wouldn't land in Paris until past midnight. He'd have to overnight in an airport hotel and then travel on in the morning. He texted Imogen to tell her he was staying in Luxor.

Soon after the plane took off, he crashed out into a fitful sleep, and woke up with a blinding headache two hours later.

51

Tuesday, 7 March

In the boardroom on the top floor of the KK building, Ainsley Bloor stood icily by a window, staring down at the darkness of the Thames below as his trusted co-directors filed in. He was seething.

Finally, the last one entered, closing the sound-proof door behind him, and Bloor joined the six men at the table.

As was usual for the late-night, secretive board meetings of Kerr Kluge, no assistant had been invited into the room to take minutes. And no recordings would be made.

'Gentlemen, we have a monumental screw-up,' Bloor said. 'And that doesn't include the two and a half million in bribes we've had to pay to keep the Egyptian police and the aviation authorities quiet.' He looked at the Chief Operating Officer, Julius Helmsley. 'Money you're going to have to lose, Julius – we don't want any awkward questions from one of our shareholders at the next AGM.'

'It's taken care of, Ainsley,' he answered. Tall and gaunt with bad posture, floppy, thinning fair hair and a long face, the Chief Operating Officer wore absurdly fashionable glasses that would have looked more appropriate on an art-college student than a fifty-five-year-old bean counter in a grey suit. The accountant was well used to hiding large chunks of cash expenditure. One of the company's largest cost centres included bribes to the leaders of impoverished third-world nations.

'It had better be,' Bloor said, coldly. 'OK, a couple of you already know what's happened, but for the benefit of the rest of you, we've been outsmarted again, and in a very big way. It seems our security team couldn't organize the proverbial piss-up in a brewery. Firstly, they follow Ross Hunter to Chalice Well and they come away with fuck all. Now Hunter is on his way back to England from Luxor with, I'm presuming, what he went to get.'

'Do we know what that is?' another of his board asked.

'No, but we're going to find out fast. Something that might contain Jesus Christ's DNA,' Bloor replied. 'I don't know what exactly, apparently that crazy old man, Dr Cook, wouldn't say, however hard he was pressed. If those idiots had been more patient they might have got it out of him. All Cook would say, before he died on us, was that it was something significant relating to Christ Himself. And that no one, who wasn't destined to, would ever find it.'

'So somehow this journalist knew where it was?' said their Head of Research and Development, Alan Gittings. 'Do we know for sure he actually found anything?'

Bloor nodded at his most trusted lieutenant, Ron Mason, a sturdy, tough, no-nonsense Australian.

'What the observer in the helicopter saw,' Mason said, 'was an old woman come out of the cave with a package, which she handed to Hunter.'

'What kind of a package?' Gittings asked.

'They were too far away to see clearly. I have the video.'

Mason opened his laptop and they crowded round him. He set in motion grainy footage of what indeed looked like an old woman emerging from a cave and handing a package to Hunter. The reporter unwrapped it, as the woman and the two males with him looked on.

As Hunter revealed its content, even with the poor video image, all of the board members could see the excitement in his body language.

Ron Mason froze the recording.

'He's definitely got something significant,' Bloor said. 'No question. And we need it fast. We're aware someone else has a serious interest in what Hunter is up to, and also followed him to Glastonbury. These people may now even have the chalice in their possession – our observation team saw them grab a bag containing something that Hunter had apparently brought up from the well.'

'Do we know what, Ainsley?' Helmsley asked.

'No, but at least we know who we are up against – at this moment, anyway. The observers followed them to a tightly guarded estate in Surrey, near Guildford. The HQ of the religious organization the Wesley Wenceslas Ministries.'

'That guy's a complete crook,' Ron Mason said, in his Australian accent. 'Wesley Wenceslas. My nephew, who's into God, went to one of his services or whatever they call them, and told me you get asked to pay for a prayer! That guy's just a con artist!'

'A very successful one,' Gittings said. 'He's got millions of followers.'

'He'll have even more when he starts waving the Holy Grail around,' Helmsley said.

'We'll get Chalice Well to demand its return – stolen property,' Bloor said. 'Then I'm sure Julius can take care of it from there, as a trustee.' He looked at him. Helmsley nodded, looking uncomfortable.

'Let's just take a reality check here, Ainsley,' Gittings said. 'Firstly, we don't know what Hunter brought up from the bottom of the well, and that Wenceslas Ministries have in their possession. We now believe he has something – maybe a body part – found in a cave in Egypt. There's no certainty it comes from Christ.'

'There's no certainty that whatever Hunter may – or may not – have recovered from Chalice Well is the Holy Grail, either, Alan,' Bloor replied. 'But we strongly believe it might be. If there is a DNA match between the two items, then what?'

'That would be immensely strong evidence of the provenance,' Helmsley said.

All of his colleagues nodded.

'So, we'd have the DNA of a possibly mythological healer who may or may not have lived two thousand years ago and was capable of performing miracles?' said another of the board, Grant Rowlands, in his blunt Yorkshire accent. 'My view is this is too much of a distraction for us. We should be thankful for two lucky escapes from anything getting traced back to us, first with Dr Cook and secondly with today's Egypt fiasco. The two thugs who went to Cook's house are – ?' He left the question hanging.

'Safely back in the west of Ireland,' Bloor answered him. 'I'm not thankful at all. We've had no lucky escapes, just two total screw-ups. This, and someone else getting ahead of us at Chalice Well.'

'I'm minded we should drop this,' Rowlands continued. 'We're risking the entire reputation of our company – and our own personal futures in its share value – for what? The DNA profile of a charlatan? Come on, Ainsley, you're the biggest non-believer of us all here. Isn't that what your monkey experiment is all about? Proof there is no God?'

'Grant,' Bloor said acidly, fixing him with a cold stare. 'We all made this decision together. Regardless of any of our beliefs, we agreed that potentially over two billion Christian people around the globe would pay any amount of money they could get their hands on – and I mean *any* amount – for a cure for their ailments developed through the provenance of Jesus Christ's DNA. And consider this, too. How much would prospective parents around the globe pay to have some – or all – of Jesus Christ's DNA in their child?'

There was a long silence. Several of the directors smiled.

'If you have a problem with that, Grant, you'd better tell us.'

Aware of how Bloor dealt with problems, and of his own substantial shareholding, and his two-million-a-year bonus, Grant Rowlands shook his head. 'I don't have a problem, Ainsley. Just – you know – doing my job as a director. Checks and balances.'

Bloor gave him a withering look. 'Good to hear, I like my team to be diligent.'

'Absolutely.'

'Anything else, Grant, before we move on?'

'No, I'm good.'

'One quick question, Ainsley,' Julius Helmsley said.

'Yes?'

'How are your monkeys doing?'

Bloor turned his gaze on another of the directors, Kurt Iann, Director of Security, before replying.

'A lot better than one of you lot. Since you asked.'

Smarting from Bloor's harsh gaze, Iann said, 'Whatever Hunter has got, we'll get it off him, Ainsley.'

'Really?' Bloor retorted, sarcastically. 'You're actually going to do something right?'

52

Wednesday, 8 March

Ross checked in to the Ibis hotel at Charles De Gaulle Airport. It was anonymous and impersonal, all the guests strangers like himself, in transit. He'd not seen anyone who looked like they might be following him at Luxor Airport, nor on the plane.

Even so, he took precautions, double-locking the door and putting on the safety chain.

Although exhausted, he slept fitfully for a short while, then woke from a nightmare in which he was back in Afghanistan, running for his life, Taliban fighters shooting at him. He tore into a vast building and down, down, down into the dark vaults.

He had survived then by hiding, lying low, biding his time. Which was what he needed to do now, he thought, sipping some water and staring into the darkness. Whoever was after him would almost certainly have someone watching their house. Waiting for him to arrive home.

He cursed himself for not thinking about this sooner. About how the helicopter might have located him in the desert. Switching on the bedside light, he picked up his iPhone and began going through his settings. Within moments, he saw he had his geo mapping on. Which meant his phone was talking all the time to everything around and above it. Someone with the right software could track his movements in real time, minute by minute. To the middle of the desert.

Or here.

He disabled the function.

Afraid, he climbed out of bed, dressed, packed his bag, then walked to the door and peered through the spyhole. What he could see of the corridor outside was empty. Cautiously he removed the safety chain, and slipped out. Just in case there was anyone watching for him in the lobby, he took the stairs.

On the ground floor, three flights down, he pushed open the door and looked out. The lobby was empty, just a night clerk on duty. His room was already paid for, and he had opted for the express checkout. He walked over to the clerk and asked if he could get him a taxi to take him into central Paris.

There was a small boutique hotel where he'd stayed with Imogen two years ago, for their wedding anniversary, the Montalambert in St Germain. When the taxi arrived, he climbed into the rear and asked the driver to take him there.

Although small, it was a five-star hotel, with round-the-clock service and great staff. Hopefully, at this time of year, they'd have a room. If not, they would be able to find him somewhere, despite the hour.

As the taxi pulled out, he looked around, then double-checked his phone to ensure that the geo mapping was safely off. He settled back into his seat and dozed until the taxi came to a halt in the narrow side street outside the hotel. His luck was in – they had a room, and greeted him warmly.

He slept reasonably soundly, until he was woken by a text from Imogen, just after 7.30 a.m.

> Hope u slept OK wherever you are. Monty and I
> did not. Our wonderful new alarm went off
> three times in the night. Engineer came at 5
> am. Faulty box or something. Been awake since.
> X

He thought carefully before texting her back. Maybe their phones were being bugged or intercepted in some way.

> Poor you. Really hope it gets fixed quick. Had to
> stay on here. Call u later. X

Then he dozed again for another hour, before waking ravenous. He phoned down and ordered breakfast.

53

Wednesday, 8 March

After an omelette, two cups of strong coffee and a shower, Ross felt refreshed, and was thinking clearly.

Hopefully no one knew where he was. But whoever had been after him in Egypt wasn't going to go away and stay away empty-handed.

He tried to put himself in their shoes. What would they be expecting him to do? Get back to England as fast as possible?

There were worse places to have to kill time than Paris. He decided to buy himself a day, let them fret – and hopefully panic. People made mistakes when they panicked.

He rang around the airlines from his room. There was availability on several flights to Heathrow, where his car was parked, tomorrow. He booked a seat on British Airways.

After he put the phone down, he unwrapped the tooth from its bundle of cloth.

Was it this someone had wanted so desperately? Someone with enough money and contacts to hire a helicopter with a gunman?

So much trouble for such a tiny object with little or no provenance.

Nothing of significance?

Or the greatest relic ever found?

If someone had gone to the effort of trying to hijack him out in that desert – perhaps for this tooth – sure as hell they would be trying again. Should he go public now? Should he give the story to his editor, show the tooth, and the cup, in the hope of taking the curse off this whole damned thing?

It was too soon. He had to find out more first. Had to know how real or otherwise the items were.

But what was he going to tell Imogen – now the stakes had risen? Was it fair to be possibly putting his family's life at risk, too?

Was any story – even this one – worth that?

And yet he couldn't stop now.

A plan was forming in his mind.

He opened his laptop, logged on to the hotel's Wi-Fi, briefly checked his emails for anything urgent, then typed into Google the name 'ATGC Forensics'.

It was a company whose name he had come across several times in recent years. They were one of the secure independent labs used by police forces in the UK for DNA testing of evidence.

He got a result instantly.

ATGC FORENSIC SCIENCE – ATGC GROUP

www.ATGCgroup.com/sectors/forensic-science

ATGC is a world leader in forensic science and one of the UK's leading full-service forensics providers. We work with police forces in the UK and internationally to assist . . .
And we offer a 24/7 service.

He went to their Contacts page, found the number and dialled it on the hotel phone, aware how easy it was for anyone to listen in to a mobile phone conversation.

It was answered by a chirpy female voice.

'Hi, I wonder if you can help me. Do you do DNA testing for private clients?'

'Well, normally we only work with registered agencies, but we do have a facility for private client work. Can I put you through to someone?'

'Thank you.'

He was put on hold for a short while, then he heard a male voice. 'Peter Mackie speaking, can I help you?'

Ross had learned, years ago, that you got much more out of people if you said their name. A psychologist he had once interviewed had told him that a person's name was the most important sound in the world to them.

'Thank you, Peter,' he replied. 'I'm Ross Hunter, a newspaper reporter working on an article, and I have two objects, one wooden – a cup – and the other a tooth. I'm interested to obtain DNA profiles on each.'

'Under the Data Protection Act I wouldn't be able to tell you if there is any match to the UK DNA database.'

'It's OK, what I'm after is to see if there is a match between these two objects.'

'A wooden cup and a tooth?'

'Yes.'

'Do you know approximately how old they are?'

'No. Fairly old – centuries, I believe.'

'The cup wouldn't be a problem to test, but a tooth is more difficult. We would have to grind it down into powder.'

'All of it?' he exclaimed.

'Yes, I'm afraid so.'

Shit, Ross thought. This might be the only known remnant of Jesus that still existed. What would any archaeologist think about destroying it?

'There's no way you could retain even the tiniest bit?' he asked.

'Well,' Mackie said, dubiously. 'That would depend on its size and age. But unlikely.'

Ross stood, thinking hard. Could he do this? Could he take the responsibility – and the gamble? 'You'd do the work for me as a private client?' he asked, finally.

'Yes.'

'How much would you charge?'

Ross held his breath, worried that the man was going to come back with a figure that was out of reach.

'Well, I can't give you an exact figure, that would depend on how much work is involved. But the ball-park would be between three to five hundred pounds for each item.'

Ross felt a surge of relief. 'How quickly could you do this?'

'We're open pretty much around the clock. If you brought it in today we could probably get results back to you by sometime tomorrow, certainly within forty-eight hours.'

'I'm in Europe at the moment, flying back to the UK tomorrow. You're in Kingston?'

'We are.'

Ross thought for a moment. The security company where he had placed the cup in a safety deposit box shut at 6 p.m. If his flight was reasonably on schedule, he would be back in the UK by around 2 p.m. By the time he had retrieved his car and got on the road it would be 2.30 and then, depending on the traffic, he should just about make it in time. But then it would take him a couple of hours, he estimated, to battle through the London rush-hour traffic to Kingston.

'I could be with you by early evening tomorrow,' he said.

'I'll tell my colleague, Jolene Thomas, to expect you, Mr Hunter.'

Ross thanked him.

54

Thursday, 9 March

Ross's flight back to London was delayed over an hour, and then he was stuck in a tailback on the M25 motorway because of an accident. By the time he arrived at the U-Store Self-Storage warehouse, close to Shoreham Harbour, the sole, surly employee in the office was clearly in the process of closing up for the night and greeted his arrival, at less than ten minutes to 6 p.m., with a stony stare.

Ross apologized, signed the register, dating it and writing down his time in, then walked to the steel-shuttered door and entered his security code on the pad beside it. As it clattered up, he ducked under and entered the chilly, cavernous interior of the warehouse, with rows of locked steel doors, all padlocked, down each side and along the far end.

He found his number, 478, which he had protected with two sturdy padlocks. One had a six-figure combination, which he opened, and the other required a key. He inserted and turned it, feeling the cams of the well-oiled lock revolving smoothly.

He pulled open the heavy metal door and removed the bundle of cloth containing the cup, but left the two halves of the oak container in situ. Then he relocked the unit and, hiding the bundle beneath his bomber jacket, signed out and hurried back to his Audi in the empty customer car park.

He texted Imogen to tell her he was back in the UK and would hopefully be home as soon as he could this evening, around 9 p.m.

As he drove out of the entrance gates, two nondescript saloon cars were waiting for him, both parked a short distance along the road. One was pointing east, on the same side of the road as himself, the other west, on the far side. They were part of the surveillance team of eight vehicles that had tailed him here from the airport.

A small van slowed and flashed his lights. Ross pulled out, waving a thank you, and turned left, east, heading toward the A27 and from there to the A23. Thirty minutes later he was creeping north on the A23 in heavy, rush-hour traffic.

For the next hour and a half, as he continued through mostly crawling traffic, he passed the time by alternately listening to the news, and a recent George Ezra album, and thinking. All the time, mindful someone could be following him, he kept a careful watch in his mirrors. Watching for one pair of headlights that might remain steadily behind him. But to his relief, the lights behind him changed frequently.

His thoughts kept returning to the message that had appeared on Imogen's laptop. The attack on him in Egypt. Was it really worth the risk of carrying on? The risk to Imogen and their baby?

He thought back to his meeting with the Bishop of Monmouth. Benedict Carmichael had, in his own gentle way, attempted to warn and dissuade him.

Then he thought back to his grandfather. He had never been close to him as a child, but had visited every day during his last weeks in Brighton's Martlets Hospice. Bill Hunter had been a deeply unhappy man, with a whole raft of unfulfilled dreams, and long separated from his wife, who had left him then died in a car crash with her new lover. The last conversation he'd had with his grandfather had always stayed with him.

Ross, your dad and you are all I have left in the world – and all I have to leave. I was afraid to follow my dreams and took the secure path – well, the one I thought was secure. I've learned too late that security is an illusion, a dream we chase. Nothing matters, does it? Nothing except the one most important thing. That we don't die with all our dreams still inside us. Don't let anyone or anything ever stop you from doing what you believe in. That's the only thing that matters. I'd have lived my life very differently if only I'd had the courage. I'm going to die knowing I'm a failure, that I never amounted to anything. Promise me that whatever happens in your life, you will matter. That, in whatever small way you do it, you'll make a difference to the world.

Finally, just before 8 p.m., his satnav told him he was less than two minutes from his destination. A sign loomed ahead, on his left, ATGC FORENSICS.

He switched on the indicator and glanced in his mirrors. To his relief, the vehicle behind him, some distance back, was indicating right.

55

Ross drove into what looked like a residential estate, and arrived at a security barrier. A guard came over to him, and he gave his name.

The barrier rose and he went through and, as directed by the man, followed the winding road until he saw ahead of him a row of long, modern, three-storey red-brick buildings, all interconnected. Then a sign indicating VISITORS' CAR PARK in front of a glass atrium between two of the buildings, which was clearly the main entrance.

He pulled into a bay, and sat still, thinking. The tooth was going to have to be ground to powder. He'd taken numerous close-up photographs of it, but what if it really was Christ's tooth? The only surviving item of His earthly body, and its unique historical importance – and he was about to sanction its destruction. But without that, he would never know its provenance. Hopefully they might be able to retain a part of it. He climbed out of his car, with his holdall, and walked towards the entrance, passing a sign which read ATGC – BRITISH PHARMACOPEIA COMMISSION LABORATORY. MEDICINES AND HEALTHCARE PRODUCTS. REGULATORY PRODUCTS.

As he approached the doors they slid open and he entered a large reception area, with seating either side, and a curious spiky black sculpture sitting on a shingle base.

Ahead of him was a wide, curved reception desk with WEL-COME TO ATGC emblazoned on the front.

He walked up to the woman seated behind it.

'Hi, my name's Ross Hunter. Jolene Thomas, from the DNA lab, is expecting me.'

He was directed to a carpeted seating area in a recess framed by bare-brick walls. There were several round tables, at each of which were three turquoise upholstered chairs, and a line of screens beyond, on the far wall, displaying photographs of laboratory workers, gowned in white with protective gloves, some wearing face masks and others goggles, performing various tasks.

He placed the bag on the table then checked his phone. There was no message from Imogen. He felt bad, knowing she was so frightened. Maybe this lab would come back with a result showing nothing, and that would be the end of it. A short piece in the *Sunday Times* about his encounters with a religious nutter who had clearly convinced a lot of people – enough to pursue him to Egypt?

'Mr Hunter?'

He looked up, startled out of his thoughts, to see a young, attractive woman of about thirty in a bright green dress and black leggings, with silky, waist-length black hair.

'Yes.' He stood up and shook her extended hand.

'Jolene Thomas,' she said as she sat down opposite him.

'It's good of you to see me so late.'

'No, it's fine, really. We work mostly for police forces, so we operate on a twenty-four-seven basis. But I understand you've come as a private client?'

'Yes, I have. Can I ask how confidential and secure your work is?'

She smiled. 'The majority of our work involves crime-scene DNA – where the chain of evidence is crucial.

Everything in this company is security code protected. Anything we are given is immediately assigned a bar code, not a name. We are very mindful that we are a prime target for villains who would dearly love to destroy their DNA evidence. But even in the unlikely case they were to break in, they'd find it impossible to locate their samples. Even our individual laboratories here are coded.'

'Good.'

'So, what do you have for me?'

'Is there somewhere private we can go?' Ross asked.

She took him to a small room just off the reception area. Ross unzipped the bag, removed first the chalice and unwrapped that, followed by the tooth.

'I believe both of these are very old,' he said. 'Many centuries and possibly more – could be as much as two thousand years old. Is dating something you are able to do?'

'Not dating, no. We can hopefully obtain a DNA profile from each object, and we can get some clues from the degradation, but dating is not our field. We may be able to determine ethnicity, depending on what we are able to find. And we offer three kinds of DNA profile – standard, mitochondrial and Y-STR.'

'Which is which?' Ross asked.

'Well, standard would give you the current profile of the person. That's what the police tend to want – to see if there is a match to the suspected perpetrator. Mitochondrial, which is harder, and a different test, is the DNA passed down through the X chromosome – the female. That's the one that enables you to determine the historic bloodline as it doesn't change.'

'Doesn't change?'

'No.'

'Does that mean that someone born two thousand years ago, who had a line of direct descendants, could be identified today from their X chromosome?'

'It does, yes – barring any genetic mutations, which can occur. And the third one, Y-STR, which is more recent, achieves a similar result but down the male line, although it's not as stable as the mitochondrial, and there are fewer databases at present. The Y chromosomal Short Tandem Repeat.'

'And that does what?'

'Well, as I explained, it's the male equivalent to the mitochondrial. It goes down through the male line, through the Y chromosome, unchanged.'

'Brilliant, I would like that done too, please. What sort of money are we talking about for all three?'

'One thing I need to ask you first is whether these items have been handled by gloved or ungloved individuals?'

'I haven't touched them with my bare hands – always with gloves or a cloth – but I don't know who before me might have done.'

'OK, don't worry, we'll take your DNA profiles, which will add a little to the cost, to eliminate you. If you are happy with that?'

'Yes, fine.'

'I'll get these items priced. For the three tests on the two items it will be in the region of two thousand pounds total, plus another two hundred pounds or so for your elimination.'

'It's a little more than I'd expected, from my phone conversation earlier, but I can understand why,' Ross said. 'That's fine.'

She looked down at the two items on the table. 'Doing the tests on this wooden cup will be straightforward, but the tooth is more complicated. I think you were told over the phone that to obtain these results we'd have to crush it into powder, then put it through a sequence of chemical processes.'

'Do you have to destroy it completely?'

'I'm afraid so. With an item this small there is no alternative.'

'Would there be anything left afterwards that you could give me?'

'Yes, if you wanted, it would be a solution in a vial. And we could make a photographic record of the process, if that would be helpful?'

Ross stared at the tooth. Possibly, if it was real, it was the most significant item in Christian history. He would have to agree to it being deconstructed in order to establish its provenance. Could he do that?

But if he did not, the world would never know.

He felt trapped – a kind of Hobson's Choice conundrum. Could he do it? Who was he to make this decision? Was there no other way?

'Jolene, if you crush it, are you able to determine the normal DNA, mitochondrial and Y-STR?'

'Yes, all three,' she said.

'And there is absolutely no other way? No other technology in development that could read the DNA from this without having to destroy it?'

'Not that I'm aware of.'

He felt a lump in his throat. His hands were clammy. He was perspiring. What to do? What to do?

'OK,' he said, finally. 'Go ahead, and please make a photo record.'

'Just to confirm, how quickly do you need it?'

'As fast as you can.'

'We should be able to get you initial results back in about forty-eight hours – is that OK?'

'Perfect.'

She produced a bunch of forms, which he began to fill in.

56

The white Boeing 737, emblazoned with the Wesley Wenceslas Ministries logo, was starting its descent into Miami International Airport at the end of its flight from Denver. The jet carried the pastor's full entourage.

As much a nervous flier in his jet plane as he was in his helicopter, ordinarily the pastor's prayers to the Lord to keep him safe would have been augmented by a series of glasses of Krug. But at this moment he was too angry to be afraid, and had not touched a drop. Instead he downed several double espressos, in succession, for which Smilealot repeatedly chided him. His MD reminded him that too much caffeine made him hyper, and that when he was hyper he got increasingly angry, and being angry was bad for his blood pressure, which was already too high.

Seated opposite him in the luxurious, rear-facing seat in the office suite of the jet, Lancelot Pope, nattily dressed as ever, swigged smugly and virtuously from a bottle of mineral water. He stuck it on the table in front of him and made another note on his elegant Smythson's pad with his Montegrappa pen.

'What's that bloody smile doing on your face, Smilealot? It's not holy water in that bottle, you know,' Wenceslas said.

'You have to calm down, boss,' said his trusted MD. 'You know your doctor's orders.'

'Yes, oh wise man? Well, to paraphrase the exchange between the judge and Oscar Fingal O'Flahertie Wills Wilde, when the judge said, "Never mind your doctor's orders, Mr Wilde," he replied, "I never sodding do."'

'Tut tut!' Pope chided. 'Such language from a man of the cloth. Spiritual leader of millions. Imagine that leaking out onto Twitter!'

'That would be the least of our problems.'

'You really are in a bad mood.'

'And you think I should be in a good one? There is a reason to be in a good one?'

There was a cackle of girlie laughter from the entourage cabin, further along the aircraft. It was followed by a squeal, and then more laughter.

'Count your blessings,' Pope said.

'I don't have any blessings today.' He held out his hands in an empty gesture. 'See? Notice any blessings?'

'What I do notice is you are biting your fingernails again. Naughty boy!'

Wenceslas curled his fingers over and studied them with an expression of surprise. 'So I am.'

'And don't give me that stuff about the Lord wanting you to bite them as a show of humility again. I'll arrange a manicure for you when we get to the house. It's really not a good image for a leader of the Christian faith to have chewed nails.'

'Know what you are? You're a pain in the ass.'

'That's why God sent me to you. You want a yes-man, go find him. Until then, you're stuck with me.' He put the pen down and held up both his hands. 'See. Immaculate nails. They say a lot about a person.'

Wenceslas gave him a dubious look. 'I have bigger things on my mind than my fingernails. *We* have bigger things. At this moment a very big problem, don't you think? Possibly the biggest problem the world has ever known?'

The plane bumped a couple of times through small air pockets and the pastor went pale.

'I can't believe it's this scumbag newspaper reporter involved,' Wenceslas said. 'Carrying on the work of a dangerous, gullible old man, Harry F. Cook. You know your Bible?'

'Some of it,' Pope replied, evasively. In truth, he was well aware of his ignorance of the scriptures, and most of what he knew, he had picked up working for his boss.

'We know, from our phone taps, that Dr Cook went to a medium and believed that God spoke to him. In 2 Thessalonians 2:9, it says: "The coming of the lawless one is by the activity of Satan with all power and false signs and wonders." In 2 Corinthians 11, verses 13 to 15, is written: "For such men are false apostles, deceitful workmen, disguising themselves as apostles of Christ. And no wonder, for even Satan disguises himself as an angel of light. So it is no surprise if his servants, also, disguise themselves as servants of righteousness. Their end will correspond to their deeds."'

'Meaning what exactly?' Pope asked.

'1 John, chapter 4, verses 1 to 3: "Beloved, do not believe every spirit, but test the spirits to see whether they are from God, for many false prophets have gone out into the world. By this you know the Spirit of God: every spirit that confesses that Jesus Christ has come in the flesh is from God, and every spirit that does not confess Jesus is not from God. This is the spirit of the Antichrist, which you heard was coming and now is in the world already." And 1 John, 2, verse 18 tells us, "The Antichrist is coming, even now many Antichrists have come!"'

'So where is he?'

'He's clever, he's smart, he's a master of disguise. Maybe we are already too late.'

'Don't think negatively, boss. That's one of your mantras, right? Well, that's what you're doing now, you are thinking too negatively. Go for the positive. That bastard Ross Hunter is on a crusade, great, let him do the work for us. Let's see how far he gets. Imagine he finds conclusively that what he has is really Christ's DNA, fine, then let him lead us to this Antichrist.'

'How?'

'We're on it. Watching him twenty-four-seven.'

'So is someone else, right? The company, Kerr Kluge. Maybe with a very different agenda from ours – people who want to harness that power, not destroy it.'

'I've hired one of the top guys in the business, ex-Scotland Yard. What he doesn't know about surveillance isn't worth a can of beans. We've twenty-two experienced covert operatives on Hunter. Want to know where he is?'

'Yeah, I do.'

'He's three miles from home in Brighton, on his way back from ATGC Forensics where he has delivered whatever he brought back from Egypt and—'

'Whatever he found in Chalice Well that your team screwed up on,' Wenceslas interrupted. 'A biscuit tin and a christening cup.'

'Yep, well, OK, he made a mug out of us – so to speak. Fortunately, our friends in Kerr Kluge screwed up even more in Egypt, according to my sources. And all they have is a small team watching him.'

'You know, Smilealot, you are being pretty flip about everything. You understand what all this could mean, don't you? I'm wondering.'

'Loud and clear, boss. But what if it's not the Antichrist, but the true Second Coming?'

'If this smart alec journalist has really got what we think he has, and this gets out into the open – as it surely will – we won't be in just a two-horse race for it any more.'

Pope nodded. They'd talked it through a lot over the past few days. Christ's DNA. How many churches of the Christian faith would be after it – starting with the Vatican? How many of Christianity's ancient enemies? If Wenceslas could go on tour with the Holy Grail and proof of our Lord's DNA and his messages, they'd fill every football stadium on the planet. He couldn't even begin to calculate the revenue it would generate. Just supposing it wasn't the Antichrist but the real deal.

'We'd become richer than the goddam imposters of the Holy Roman Church! Praise the Lord!' Wenceslas said, answering his thoughts for him.

'Praise the Lord,' Pope echoed.

'But if the Vatican got hold of it, they'd exhibit it under guard, some place where people could form endless queues to venerate it in a glass display case, in exchange for a dona-tion and the possibility of answered prayers. Or more likely it would disappear. Be buried for ever in some deep vault.'

'Why do you say that, boss?'

Wesley Wenceslas looked at the man to whom he entrusted the running of his growing empire. 'What planet are you on? We are in the business of *faith*, not *proof*. If His existence is proven, why would anyone need us any more? They'd just go direct. It would have the same impact on providers of faith that Amazon's had on retailers. We'd be out of business overnight. You don't get it? Or what if this turns out to be the Antichrist that has been prophesied? And is already here?'

'The Antichrist is already here? You really think that? Or is that just your sales message, O Mighty One?' Pope feigned a bow of subservience.

'Cut it out!'

'Let's have a reality check, shall we?' Pope said. 'What is really upsetting you this time about Ross Hunter? Is it your true belief that because he's following directions given by a medium, it's the work of the Antichrist? Or is that your smokescreen?'

'Smokescreen?'

'Don't give me that angelic, innocent face, Pastor! I know you too well. You're afraid that this could be real, aren't you? That if this is the true Second Coming, then our Lord will expose you for the fraud you really are. That's your real agenda, isn't it?'

Without warning, the aircraft plunged for several seconds.

Wesley Wenceslas fell silent and mouthed a prayer.

The plane stabilized.

A minute later they touched down.

'Praise the Lord,' Wenceslas said, with relief.

'Praise the pilot, I'd say,' retorted Pope.

57

It was late when Ross arrived home. He pulled into the driveway, scanning all around, but could see no unfamiliar vehicles on the street. All the same he waited before getting out of the car, checking all the shadows. Then he removed his bag from the boot and walked up to the front door.

It was opened by a tearful Imogen before he reached it, with Monty right behind her.

He put his arms round her, hugging her tightly. 'Hey, what's up?'

She pressed her wet cheeks against his face. 'Thank God you're home. I couldn't stay here tonight alone. I was going to call the Hodges and ask if I could go over to their place if you weren't back.'

'What is it? What's happened?'

'Come and see what came in while I was at work today.'

He knelt for a moment, hugging and stroking the dog, as she secured the new safety chain, then followed her into the kitchen. Her laptop was open on the table. She tapped the keyboard and he saw the message on the screen.

THIS IS YOUR SECOND WARNING.
YOU DON'T GET A THIRD.

Turning to him, she demanded, 'Can you explain that?'

He studied the address of the sender. It was the same Hotmail address as the previous untraceable one – he recognized it from the '666' among the numbers.

'I think we should speak to the police,' he said.

'And tell them what? That you think you might have pissed Satan off?'

He smiled grimly, thinking hard. 'I tell you what, I'll call Jason Tingley.'

Tingley had been a young DC whom Ross and Imogen had first met during their days on the *Argus* and who was now a superintendent.

'I'm scared, Ross.'

'I'll call him now.'

He looked through his contacts until he found the name, Jason Tingley, and dialled the Detective Superintendent. It rang and after some moments he got Tingley's voicemail and left a message.

'Hi, Jason, it's Ross Hunter, could you give me a call, I need some help.' He left his number and ended the call.

'So, tell me about your trip. How did it go. What did you find?'

'I'll tell you all about it. I need a drink and I need to get something to eat.'

'I took a moussaka out of the freezer for you and there's some salad in the fridge.'

'Thanks.' He went over to the cabinet, removed a bottle of his favourite whisky, poured a large measure into a glass, added some ice from the fridge, splashed in a drop of water and sat at the table. Just as he did so, looking again at the email, his phone rang. It was Jason.

Putting the phone on speaker, for Imogen's benefit, they caught up briefly and he congratulated the detective on his recent promotion. Then he gave him a summary of what had transpired since his original call from Harry F. Cook, but omitting – for Imogen's benefit – the attempt on his life in Egypt. Tingley told him he would put out an alert to the Brighton Neighbourhood Policing and Response teams and a request for vigilance on his home. He asked him for the registration numbers of his and Imogen's cars. Then added he would ask someone from the Digital Forensics team to contact him, and take a look at the messages Imogen had been sent. He asked Ross to update him on any developments. Ross thanked him and they made vague arrangements to meet for a coffee soon.

As he ended the call, Imogen said, 'Is this how we have to live our lives from now on? Prisoners in our own home? In constant fear? Dependent on police protection?'

He stared back at her, and sipped some whisky. 'It's what I do, Imo. I've always taken risks with stories I've written, exposing injustice.'

'It's different. I'm now getting really scared for your safety – our safety. I think you're out of your depth. It's not just about you, think about our child – he'll need a father. You have a bigger priority than your next story now.'

'Imo, I want our son to be proud of me. When he grows up I want him to be someone who stands up for what he believes in.'

'You know what I want?' she retorted. 'Or rather what I don't want? I don't want our son to be an orphan.'

58

Thursday, 9 March

In the glare of floodlights from the belly of the helicopter, Ainsley Bloor could see the blades of grass, around the landing circle, bending in the downdraught from the rotor blades. Moments later the machine touched down and settled.

Thanking his personal pilot and wishing him a good night, he unbuckled his safety harness, removed his headphones and hooked them up behind him, then pushed his door open and clambered out. He kept his head ducked low until he was well clear of the still-rotating blades, although he could have stood safely at his full six-foot height.

The shadow of his mansion, with several lights blazing in windows, lay a couple of hundred yards in front of him. But he turned away from it, shouldered the strap of the bag containing his laptop and paperwork he needed to go over before tomorrow, and hurried across the lawn towards the orangery and the six cages containing his monkeys, eager to see if any progress had been made.

He switched on the lights and entered, wrinkling his nose at the sour stench, and inspected each of the cages, looking for pages of printout, which would have meant the monkeys had been tapping the keys. There was no printout in any of the first five. Just monkey shit and peanut shells on every keyboard and printer, and puddles of piss on the floor.

Then he peered through the bars of the sixth, Boris's. And saw, excitedly, that there were several pages of printout.

Murmuring platitudes to the monkey, he let himself into the cage and rushed excitedly across to the printer, tore the pages free and looked at them. Boris watched him from a perch, rubbing his chin like an ancient sage.

Bloor scanned through six pages of a meaningless jumble of letters of the alphabet, symbols and numbers. Then as he reached the seventh page, he froze.

And stared.

At the three letters staring out at him, like a gleaming nugget of gold in a sack of coal.

He wanted to high five the monkey.

'Yes, yes, yes, you good boy, you! Boris! Yes, yes!!!!'

And all the nightmare of the past few days was forgotten at this moment.

'Wow! You good boy, you! Wow!'

Shelling a peanut, the capuchin monkey gave him a bemused stare.

'You've done it! You've bloody done it!'

He took the printout and hurried towards the house, calling out to his wife before he'd even reached the door. 'Cilla! Cilla!'

She was in the drawing room, watching an orchestra on television.

'Look!' he shouted. 'Look what I have!'

'How about, *Hello, darling, how are you, how was your day?*' she replied, sharply.

'Look at this!' He grabbed the remote and froze the screen. Then he held the sheet of printout in front of her face. 'Look! Look!'

'At what, exactly?'

'The start of the proof! The absolute proof that there is no Creator. That the world came into existence through random chance. This is monumental! Remember tonight! It will go down in history.'

'The night a monkey typed the word "the"?'

'You just don't understand the significance, do you?'

'Actually, no. And there's something else I don't understand.'

'What?'

'You're an atheist. A hard-core atheist. You're conducting this barmy experiment because you have this weird notion that through these monkeys you can conclusively prove that God does not exist, right?'

'Correct.'

'In that case, why are you so keen to get hold of Christ's DNA? Or am I missing something?'

'No, you're not missing anything. That's called *business*, darling.'

'I have a different word for it. *Hypocrisy*.'

59

Thursday, 9 March

At a few minutes past 11 p.m., Ross was sitting alone in his den, his emotions in turmoil. Suddenly he saw headlights moving very slowly along the street and stopping outside his house. For a moment he stiffened, then relaxed when he saw it was a marked police patrol car. Detective Superintendent Tingley had been true to his word.

The car moved on.

As it did so, his phone rang, the display showing the number was withheld.

After a brief hesitation, he hit the green button. 'Ross Hunter,' he answered.

The male voice at the other end was so quiet he had to strain to hear it.

'Ross? It's Hussam Udin.'

'Hussam!' he said to the blind cleric. 'Hi.'

'Are you able to speak?'

'Yes, yes, sure.'

'Ross, I just heard from my cousin, Medhat El-Hadidy.'

'Thank goodness he's alive. I'm sorry, Hussam. I'm just so sorry to get your cousin involved in this, I really hope he's OK. I don't know what was going on or who was behind it. Did he say how he is?'

'He's OK but his car isn't. Ross, this is what I need to say to you – I do know what is going on. I must meet you very urgently. You are in much greater danger than you can possibly know.'

'What kind of danger, Hussam?'

'This is not a telephone conversation. When could we meet?'

'Tomorrow morning?'

'I think that would be wise.'

'I could be with you about eleven o'clock – would that work?'

'I am always here.'

'I'll see you then.'

The moment he ended the call, he sensed someone behind him and spun round.

It was Imogen.

'Who was that, Ross? Do you want to tell me? What danger are you in that I don't know about already?'

He took a deep breath and showed her the photographs he had taken in Egypt. Then he told her. Everything. Starting from the beginning.

When he had finished she asked, 'So what happens now, Ross?'

'I wait for the DNA results.'

'And then?'

'They're probably zilch. Nothing. End of.'

'But what if there's a match, between the tooth and the contents of the chalice? What then?'

'We'll have to see.'

'People tried to stop you in Egypt. People are threatening us here. What if it's all real? What if there is a match? What then, Ross? All those who claim to possess relics like the Turin Shroud, the Holy Tunic of Christ, the Spear of Destiny. I've been looking them up on the internet.' She tapped her iPhone and looked at her list. 'The Crown of

Thorns, the Iron Crown of Lombardy, the Veil of Veronica, the Mandylion, and all the rest. There are huge commercial interests involved, Ross. Their owners aren't going to want the DNA you have to disprove them. You're a newspaper journalist punching way above your weight here. I don't think you realize quite how deep in you are, nor what kind of a hornets' nest you're opening. Is any story worth our lives? And why is it *you* who's been chosen?'

She looked at the window and the darkness of the night beyond as if noticing for the first time, got up, walked over and pulled the blinds shut. 'Have you thought about that?'

'I don't know, Imogen. Maybe because whoever did choose me figured I had a chance of getting the story taken seriously. But you have to understand, nothing matters more to me than our baby. OK?'

'So, nothing matters more to you than our baby?'

'Absolutely.'

'What about me?'

'You're a given!'

'Then prove it to me.'

'How can I do that?'

'Go tell the world you're forgetting about it. Post it on Twitter and Facebook. Announce you're no longer pursuing the story. Post all the sodding coordinates. Give them to the world.'

'I can't do that – not yet.'

'Why not?' Imogen demanded.

'Because I don't have the final one – the most important one of all – yet.'

'Then get it and post it, as quickly as you can.'

'I'm not sure I can do that.'

She shook her head. 'Same old, same old. You come first, our son doesn't matter, I don't matter.'

'No, Imo, I don't come first. Mankind comes first.'

'And if you believe that, you're a bigger egotist and an even bigger fantasist than I ever realized.'

She walked out of the room.

60

Friday, 10 March

At 11.30 a.m. the next morning, Ross sat in the curtained privacy of Hussam Udin's office, gratefully sipping the strong, sweet coffee, his head pounding a little from too much whisky, which he had sat drinking into the small hours of last night. He was drinking too much, he knew, way more than normal, but nothing was normal any more.

The cleric sat regally, dressed as ever in a brown robe, dark glasses covering his blind eyes. A lit cigarette in his hand hovered over the Cinzano ashtray filled with stubbed-out butts. 'You've been through an ordeal, Ross, but you escaped.'

'Somehow. Not entirely thanks to your cousin.' He was beginning to see more as his eyes became accustomed to the darkness.

'Perhaps it was through the will of Allah?'

Ross smiled. And realized it had been several days since he had last smiled. 'You could say that.'

He could see the man was not smiling but looking worried.

'You were followed here today, Ross.'

'No,' he replied emphatically. 'I kept a careful watch.'

'I'm telling you, Ross, you were followed.'

'What makes you say that?'

'You sound tired, your judgement is impaired today,

perhaps. You are dealing with very clever people. They will be following you everywhere and you will never see them. They will have bugged your phones, also.'

'I checked under my car this morning for any tracking devices, and there was nothing.'

'I'm telling you, you will see nothing.' Udin's glasses fixed on him with uncanny precision, as they so often did. 'Ross, when you came to see me, you said that you needed a man in Luxor with a car, who could keep you safe. Now it is all very different. My cousin has a wrecked car that his insurance may not cover, but he failed to protect you, so I am not happy with him. More importantly, you are in trouble, am I correct?'

'It's not that simple. If I can, I will try to reimburse Hadidy. But listen, I thought, as an investigative journalist, I had a story to write based on the ramblings of an elderly, deluded widower who believed he had proof of God. But now it seems a whole lot bigger and more real than I could ever have imagined.'

'And more dangerous?'

'Indeed.'

'It involves conclusive proof of God's existence, if I am correct?'

'You are.'

Udin placed his hand on his chest. 'Sometimes, in my heart, I feel envy for those who have unquestioning faith. For them, provided they have lived their lives according to Allah's will, death holds no fears. It's the same for all other faiths. Everyone on earth who believes in one God. Muslims, Christians, Jews, Sikhs. They all just interpret him differently. Perhaps the Sikhs most of all. Their aim is to see the divine order that God has given to everything, and through it to understand the nature of God. Perhaps they are closest in their beliefs to my own – that of Intelligent Design. But no matter. What concerns me at this moment is that a friend of mine is in grave danger. That friend is you, Ross. This is what I hear.'

'What do you know, Udin?'

'I have many friends in my home country, Egypt. I am told by them that what you have brought back to England is an item of the greatest significance. For that reason, it puts you in very great danger.'

'Why do you say that?'

'I am told that you have brought back with you something that belongs to another religion altogether – one that is a sometime enemy of Islam and of other faiths. If this object is real – is what you believe it might be – it is a dangerous thing for you to possess. Many people will be after it. One group have already very nearly killed you for it. They are not going to stop until they have it, and their resources are infinite.'

'You know who they are?'

Udin put a fresh cigarette in his mouth and attempted to light it from the burning stub of the previous one. Ross watched him as the two ends kept missing each other, wondering if he should intervene. Then they connected. Drawing the smoke in deeply, Udin ignored the question. 'You brought home with you a tooth. It may or may not be one from your prophet, Jesus Christ. DNA testing may perhaps enlighten you.'

Ross, staring into the glasses, nodded, wondering. *How did he know this?*

'Imagine, my friend, you obtain DNA from this tooth, which turns out to have true provenance. And then with carbon dating you establish this did indeed come from two thousand years ago. You have another object, possibly the cup that Jesus Christ drank from at the Last Supper, and in which, when He was on the cross, some of His blood was captured. Imagine the DNA from this is a match to the tooth?'

'How do you know all this, Hussam?'

'I told you, my friend, Ross. I may be entombed in this house, and almost certainly will die here, but I have people out in the world who tell me things. They listen, they are connected, they know. What you have in your possession may turn out to be nothing at all or may be real. If these are real, there will be many people who will want them and are prepared to take them, and you will be the discarded pawn.'

'You say you know who tried to hijack me, Hussam. Who are they? I have to know. Tell me.'

'You do know who they are. You may not be aware, but for sure you know who they are. All of us do. We swallow their vitamins and pills; we might brush our teeth with their brand of toothpaste; take their cough medicine; swallow their laxatives when we are constipated; use their nasal sprays when we are congested with colds; some of us will use their stop-smoking aids. This company kills millions of people every year in Africa and other poor countries by selling them untested or out-of-date drugs, or powdered milk that does not contain the mothers' vital antibodies the babies need. Do you think they'll care about one English newspaper reporter's life?'

Ross stared at him. 'This sounds like any big pharma. Which one, Udin?'

'Kerr Kluge.'

'Kerr Kluge?' Ross echoed.

'Yes.'

'You're making these people sound like the Antichrist.'

'They only have one religion, Ross, and that is money. The bottom line, at all cost.'

'Are they worried about Jesus returning? That he might put them out of business because he can heal the sick without pharmaceuticals?'

Udin shook his head, drew on his cigarette and blew out a cloud of smoke. 'No, Ross, I don't believe they have this thought at all. What they see is the value of possessing the only items in existence containing Jesus Christ's DNA. The marketing value of this for them is incalculable.'

With a grin, Ross said, 'Maybe I should offer them a deal?'

'I think you will find that the Devil doesn't negotiate, my friend.'

61

Friday, 10 March

Driving back down towards Brighton, Ross kept an extra close eye on his mirrors. Several times he pulled over, at random. Waiting as the traffic roared past him. He could see no sign of anyone following him. Yet he did not dismiss Hussam Udin's warning.

But how did Udin know? How did his people know? Udin said the people who had tried to kill him in Egypt were in the pharmaceutical business. Was the blind cleric right?

How did these people, whoever they were, know about him or what he had?

Why would—?

A chill rippled through him as something came back to him.

Shit.

There was a lay-by a couple of hundred yards ahead. A bus stop. He pulled into it, shaking.

His conversation with Sally Hughes.

My uncle's a trustee of Chalice Well . . .

Julius Helmsley. He's a director of a pharmaceutical company . . .

Ross picked up his phone, googled the name Kerr Kluge and looked at the list of directors.

And saw the name, Julius Helmsley. Chief Operating Officer.

He sat thinking for some minutes. Were they the people in Egypt? Was it one of their henchmen who had kicked him in the face as he emerged from the well, and taken his bag? The one he had planted, containing the biscuit tin and christening mug he had bought in Lewes Flea Market?

He drove on, a plan forming in his mind. After a few miles, he saw a shopping mall coming up on his right, and turned into it. A short distance ahead he saw a large hoarding listing the stores in the mall. As he had hoped, one said CARPHONE WAREHOUSE. He parked, locked the Audi and entered the mall.

Fifteen minutes later he returned to his car holding a plastic carrier bag. It contained a roll of small stickers he had bought in a stationery shop and two fully charged and loaded pay-as-you-go mobile phones – 'burners' as criminals would call them, as they tended to make one call only and discard them, so they could not be traced.

He sat and labelled the phones, marking them 1 and 2. Then he removed from his wallet the business card Sally had given him, and with mobile 1 dialled her number.

It rang five times, then went to voicemail.

'Hi, this is Sally, I'm busy, please leave a message and I'll get back to you.'

'Hi, Sally, it's Ross Hunter. Could you give me a call back on this number – it should have come up on your phone.'

He drove out of the car park and pulled out back onto the A23, watching vigilantly once more for anyone who might be holding back, waiting to follow him, but saw no sign of anything suspicious.

As he drove on, he lapsed back into his thoughts. If the ATGC report on the DNA showed a connection between the tooth and the cup, what could he do? There had to be a way of writing his story that would take him and Imogen out of danger, surely? What about if he simply went public? Perhaps after getting the final set of coordinates from that strange old solicitor in Birmingham, Robert Anholt-Sperry? Put it all out into the public domain. Then walk away from it.

His iPhone began ringing.

'Ross Hunter,' he answered.

'Mr Hunter, it's DCI Martin Starr from Birmingham Major Crime Unit, we met briefly at the station when you gave your statement about Dr Cook.'

'Yes, hi.'

'Are you able to talk?'

'I'm driving but I'm on hands-free.'

'Would you prefer to speak on a landline when you have stopped?'

'No, I'll pull over. Hold on a sec, there's a turn-off just ahead.'

Ross pulled off the main road and halted the car. 'OK,' he said.

'Can you tell me again, Mr Hunter, why you entered the premises of Rose Cottage, Newhurst Village, rather than calling the police?'

He thought carefully before answering. 'Yes – I had met Dr Harry F. Cook, earlier that week. He had contacted me some days before, telling me he had been told I was the journalist who could help him regarding – this may sound strange to you – proof of God's existence.'

'I see.' Starr sounded deadpan. And a tad cynical. 'Told by who, sir?'

Ross hesitated. 'A representative of God.'

'A representative of God?'

'I did at the time consider Dr Cook a bit of a crackpot, but I was intrigued – enough to meet him and hear his story.'

'And you did?'

'He came down to my home in Sussex and told me more.'

'About proof of God?' The detective's voice was sounding more sceptical by the minute.

'Yes.'

'I see. And what happened?'

'I decided after meeting him that he was a bit – shall we say, politely – earnest, but –'

'But *what*, sir?'

'A bit of a – well, a bit *deluded*.'

'Yet you decided, subsequently, to drive all the way from Brighton to Worcestershire to meet him?'

'Well, I called him on Thursday night to tell him I didn't think I could help him. But he implored me to meet him. He said he had some information for me that would change my mind. I'm a journalist, so I thought I should at least hear him out.'

'Then you went to his house, where you found the deceased?'

'I did.'

'And the moment you found his body, you called the police?'

'Correct.'

'Did Dr Cook at any time mention any enemies to you, Mr Hunter? Any fanatics who might not share his views?'

'No, he didn't.'

'Are you aware of anyone who might have been upset by him?'

'I'm not, no.'

'I appreciate you've already given my colleagues a statement. If I require a further statement from you, would you be willing to talk to us again? We could come down to you if that is more convenient?'

'Yes, absolutely.'

'Thank you, Mr Hunter. That's all for now. I'll be in touch again.'

As Ross ended the call, and was about to drive off, he heard an unfamiliar ring tone. It was from one of his new burners. The one he had used to call Sally. He answered it.

'Hello, Ross!' Her voice sounded even warmer and friendlier than he remembered.

'Hi, Sally, how are you doing?'

'Yep, OK, you?'

'Well, fine – I think,' he replied.

'It's refreshing to hear a friendly voice. I just came off air with one of our great knights of the theatre. What a pompous prat – it was like having to be interviewed on provincial radio was beneath him. He gave me an evasive answer to every question. *So are you looking forward to your play coming to the Bristol Hippodrome, Sir William? Oh my love, should I be? I understand you've wanted to play the role of Archie Rice all your life? Not true, my love. Do you have any unfulfilled ambition, Sir William – is there a role you want to play? I've played them all, my dear.*'

'I hope you stuffed him.'

'I wish I had. There are a million things I wish I'd thought of at the time.'

'There's a great Oscar Wilde line about that,' Ross said. 'He was at a party with the painter, Whistler, and Whistler made a very witty remark. "I wish I'd said that," Oscar Wilde replied. To which Whistler retorted, "You will, Oscar, you will!"'

She laughed. 'I so much enjoyed our interview – lovely to talk to someone who is smart, fun and has no ego.'

'Sorry I disappointed you, in that case.'

'Not remotely. You were a lot more interesting than most of the people I have on my show.'

'You're very kind. So, the reason I called is I wonder if I could have another chat with you – off the record? Something very important.'

'Sure – over the phone or do you want to meet?'

'It would be better to meet.'

'I'm around this weekend, then I'm away skiing for a few days.'

He thought quickly. Bristol was about three hours' drive from home. They were going to a party at the Hodges tomorrow night – it was Helen's birthday and he would be in seriously bad odour with Imogen if he ducked out of that. 'How about I get to you around lunchtime on Sunday? Perhaps we could have a quick pub lunch?'

'A quick one?' She sounded disappointed. 'I think a long one would be much nicer.'

Again, he felt the same vibe he had as when he had first met her – that frisson of attraction between them. It excited him and he knew it shouldn't. But he didn't want it to stop. At the same time, he wondered what her real motives were. Was she being duplicitous in some way?

'A long lunch sounds very nice indeed,' he said.

62

Sunday, 12 March

As Ross expected, Imogen was seriously unimpressed that he was spending Sunday driving to Bristol and back. Her sister, Virginia, brother-in-law, Ben, and their three children were coming over for lunch and a walk, and secretly he was very glad to be missing them. Her sister was a virtuous prig who frowned on alcohol, and was always the 'designated' driver, and he had, years ago, run out of conversation with her heavy boozer husband who never had anything of interest to say, and repeated himself interminably the drunker he got.

Sally, dressed in tight jeans, suede boots and white blouse, looked stunning, and was already waiting for him at a wooden table in the busy modern pub. A bottle of Rioja sat in front of her.

'Sorry to be late,' he said.

'No need to apologize. Glass of wine?'

She poured it without waiting for a reply, and pushed a menu at him. 'There are specials on the board. I'm going to have French onion soup and the roast – they do a brilliant roast beef on Sundays.'

'Sounds good, I'll have the same.'

'So, Mr Ross Hunter, famous journalist, what is so important for you to give up a Sunday to come all this way to have lunch with a provincial radio hack?'

He found himself struggling to keep their meeting formal. 'When we talked before you mentioned your uncle, Julius?'

'Julius Helmsley?'

'Right. You said he's on the board of a pharmaceutical company?'

'Yes, pretty high up.'

'Remind me which company he's with?' he asked to double-check.

'Kerr Kluge.'

'Just a little outfit.'

'Indeed.' She smiled. 'I think they're ranked third in the world.'

'Can you tell me a bit about your uncle?'

'Sure, what would you like to know?'

He sipped some wine and nodded approvingly at her choice. He raised the glass. 'This is seriously good.'

'Averys of Bristol – this city's economy was partly founded on the wine trade.'

'Of course.'

He tried to avoid her gaze, but was finding it difficult. 'What kind of a guy is your uncle?'

'We're not close. He's my late mother's brother-in-law, I think I told you. She died last year.'

'I'm sorry.'

'No apology necessary. She had a virulent strain of breast cancer.' Sally poured more wine into her glass, which was nearly empty, and was about to top his up when he put a hand over his glass.

'Just the one,' he said. 'I've got a long drive.'

'Have you ever lost someone close to you?' she asked.

'I have, yes.'

'You told me when we talked after the show that

something had happened to you that turned you from being a sceptical agnostic into – maybe not exactly a believer, but had opened your mind. You said it was too personal to talk about. Are you ready to talk about it now?'

'How about I trade you?'

'Trade me?'

'If I tell you all I can about why I changed, will you tell me about your uncle – like – everything about him?'

She gave him another smile. 'OK.'

He told her about the morning Ricky died, and what had happened to him in the gym in Brighton, and she listened intently, almost spellbound. When he had finished, she said, 'Ross, this is incredible. I interviewed a doctor who'd made a study of near-death experiences and had written a book about them. A couple of the stories he told me were very similar to what happened to you.'

He nodded. 'Yes, I read up a lot about it at the time. There's all kinds of theories, about telepathy, about the brain's shutting-down processes.'

'And about life after death?' she queried.

He smiled. 'I guess one day we'll find out – or not.'

'I'd really like to talk more about this sometime,' she said. 'It really fascinates me, I think there's something in it.'

'OK, I'm happy to talk more.'

'I think you should write a book about it. Then I could have you back on the show promoting it.'

'Maybe I will one day. Right, your turn!'

'OK. The thing is, Uncle Julius was always a bit odd when I was a child. He liked to show me chemical experiments – such as making stink bombs and magnesium flashes. Like he was a magician. But more recently I've pretty much lost any connection with him. I've tried to get him on my show but he's not interested. They're a very

secretive organization – like most pharmaceutical companies. They're protective of everything – all their patents – and
what they have in development. Why are you interested in
him?'

'Just curious.'

She tilted her head. 'Really. You came all this way to ask
me about my uncle – I think that makes you more than *just
curious!*'

His phone vibrated in his pocket. Apologizing to Sally,
he pulled it out and answered it. 'Hello?'

'Mr Hunter?'

'Speaking.'

'It's Jolene Thomas from ATGC Forensics.'

'Oh, hi!' he said, giving another apologetic signal to the
presenter.

'I thought you would like to know. I've just heard from
the lab that we've the initial results for you on the two
items. Sorry it's a bit later than I'd hoped, the tooth took
more time. Could you come over tomorrow? We can go
through them and I'll explain what they mean.'

'Have you a match between them?'

'I'm afraid for security reasons I'm not permitted to say
anything over the phone.'

He thanked her and ended the call.

'Good news?' Sally Hughes quizzed.

63

Ross detoured via Lewes on his way up to the ATGC Forensics labs. He pulled into the Needlemakers car park, stuck a one-hour pay and display sticker on his windscreen, then hurried down again to the antiques emporium that he and Imogen loved visiting occasionally at weekends, round the corner.

Forty minutes later he was back in his car and heading north towards Kingston, south-west of London. As had become the norm, now – paranoia perhaps – he kept a careful check in his mirrors for any signs that he was being followed. He changed his speed frequently to try to flush someone out, accelerating up to 95 mph in short bursts, then dropping back to 50 mph.

He parked and walked through into the entrance to the main building, strode across to the reception desk and said that Jolene Thomas was expecting him. The receptionist tore off the visitors' form on which he wrote his name, car registration and time of arrival and folded it inside a tag on a lanyard. He put it on.

A few minutes later the young forensic scientist appeared, wearing an elegant green dress, and took him up in the lift to the second floor. They walked along a labyrinth of cream-painted corridors, through a series of double doors, then stopped outside another double doorway leading off to the right. On the wall beside it was a black sign with white lettering, headed SCENE OF CRIME.

Beneath was indicated: LABS 1/15, 1/18, 1/20, 1/21, 1/22.

Underneath were more: LABS 1/1, 1/5, 1/6, 1/7, 1/8.

And beneath that:

SPECIALIST DNA FORENSIC DNA DEPARTMENT

LABS 1/10, 1/12, 1/13

FNDAS

LAB 1/14

She saw Ross looking, baffled, at the signs and grinned. 'We deliberately don't make it easy for any strangers to navigate around here. All part of our security, as most of our work in this section is on DNA evidence for police forces.'

'Good to know,' he said, aware of the warning from Hussam Udin, and his recent experiences. 'Have you ever had any break-ins?'

'Touch wood, no. We're aware that plenty of criminals would dearly like to get their hands on some of the evidence we are processing – and destroy it. But everything that comes in here is allocated a code, and is only known to the staff by that code. Even if someone hacked our computer system, which is pretty secure, they wouldn't know where to start looking.'

'I can see that,' Ross said as he followed her into another labyrinth, glancing at the signs.

BONE EXTRACTION LABORATORY 1/22

DO NOT OPEN THIS DOOR WITHOUT GLOVES AND A FACE MASK

WARNING! DO NOT ENTER ROOM IF THE ALARM ABOVE THE DOOR IS FLASHING ORANGE

Jolene finally stopped at a door with a tiny glass and wire mesh panel. She held a tag up to a reader, tapped in a code and then went through, holding the door for him.

He entered a long, open-plan room, with about twenty people hunched over workstations, all seemingly deep in concentration. She walked across to a vacant terminal towards the far end, pulled up a chair for him and sat down beside Ross. She tapped in a password on the keyboard. Beneath the monitor on the cluttered desktop was a box of tissues, a stack of paperwork and a cardboard coffee cup with the plastic lid on.

The screen came to life. Down to the left appeared what looked like an index list, rows of figures that were meaningless to him. In the centre of the screen were several columns of pairs of spindly spikes, of different heights, each topped with a small disc with a number above it.

She turned to Ross. 'Have you ever looked at DNA before?'

'No.'

'OK, this is from the cup you gave us – we got a result from the coagulated blood inside it.'

'Blood?'

'Yes, definitely, it was confirmed by presumptive testing.'

'Blood?' he said again. *Was it Christ's blood? From when he was on the cross?*

'I'm afraid the DNA in that is pretty degraded. What we have from the tooth is better. Each pair of spikes you can see represents the male and the female pairing. We've done, as you requested, the standard, mitochondrial and Y-STR DNA on both the cup and the tooth. I'll show you the mitochondria and Y-STR in a minute.'

'Are you able to at all date this DNA from the cup?'

'No, you'd have to go to carbon dating for that. But I can tell you, in my opinion I believe this is very old.'

'Any sense how old?'

She shook her head. 'It would depend on how and where it has been stored. I'm guessing a few hundred years, minimum, and possibly much older than that. But I stress this is only a guess, based on what you've told me.'

She tapped the keyboard again.

A new image appeared. On this one, there were far more spikes, some so close together they resembled park railings, and too close to tell which were the pairs. Then a second image replaced it, this filled with rows of columns containing blocks of the letters *ACGT*, in countless permutations.

'This is the mitochondrial from the contents of the cup,' she said. 'Now this is where it gets very interesting.'

She tapped the keyboard again and more distinct pairs of spikes appeared, again with the numbered discs above them. There were many more than on the first image.

'This is what we obtained from crushing the tooth. You see?'

He peered closely, unsure exactly what he was looking at. 'I think so.'

Again, she tapped the keyboard and several columns of figures appeared, as completely meaningless to him as the previous ones. He stared hard at them.

'What am I meant to be looking at here, Jolene?'

She pointed to various pairings of figures on the columns. 'These are the points of match of standard DNA between the tooth and the cup. We have the same with the mitochondrial DNA – in fact, better. And we have, to my surprise, because it is the least stable of all, a very clear Y-STR match between the two items, also.'

'How much of a match is it?'

She looked pleased with herself. 'Well, if I was presenting this for submission in a court of law by prosecuting counsel, I would say there is a match between the two that is beyond any reasonable doubt, in terms of mathematical probability. Billions to one. There are seven specific mutations in the mitochondrial DNA – very rare mutations when compared to our database, and seven different ones in the Y chromosome, again very rare. Exactly the same mutations are present in the DNA from both the tooth and the cup.'

Ross felt a strange ripple, like an electrical current, running deep inside him. 'It's the same with both the standard and the mitochondrial – and the Y-STR?'

'Yes.'

'If I understand correctly from what you told me last time about mitochondrial DNA – that means it passes down through the female line, unaltered?'

'Yes, exactly.'

'And the Y-STR passes down through the male line, unaltered as well?'

'Correct.'

'How many generations could either go through, Jolene?'

'So long as the reproductive process continues, in which there is a female born, for the mitochondrial, and a male for the Y-STR, who each then in turn give birth, indefinitely.'

'Unchanged?' he asked, to verify.

'Unchanged.'

He was wary of saying too much, yet he felt he could trust this woman. 'OK, so let's say this DNA is two thousand years old. Am I right in understanding what you are saying, that you could identify someone alive today as being a direct descendant – from their mitochondrial DNA containing a unique genetic profile?'

'You could, Mr Hunter, a female. Yes.'

'And from the Y-STR?'

'A male, yes.'

He felt on fire. 'Do you have anything left from the tooth that you had to crush? Anything at all?'

'We do,' she said. 'It's in a glass vial, in liquid solution.'

He felt a massive sense of relief. 'That's great, fantastic!'

'I'd need you to sign release forms and I'll give you your receipt. Would you want the cup back, too?'

'Yes please.'

64

Monday, 13 March

Forty minutes later Ross turned off the M25 onto the M23, southbound towards Brighton. He was driving slower than normal on the quiet motorway because he was wrapped up in his thoughts, keeping to a steady 70 mph in the inside lane. The traffic was light and the sun was out, still fairly low in the sky above the distant hills of the South Downs and beaming straight into his eyes, dazzling him. He tugged down the sun visor and an old parking permit fluttered from it. Momentarily distracted, he grabbed it and put it on the passenger seat.

Then he noticed the articulated lorry thundering along on his offside, in the middle lane. It had drawn alongside him but was not making any effort to pass. It seemed to be pacing him. Why, when the road ahead was clear, did it not just go on past?

Then his rear-view mirror filled with the radiator grille of an SUV. The vehicle was inches behind him, tailgating him dangerously.

His second sense told him something was wrong. He floored the accelerator, felt the kick-down of the gear change, and the car surged forward – almost straight into the rear of a white van which had cut across the front of the truck and was now right in front of him.

He hooted angrily.

The van's brake lights came on. It began to slow down and the truck was slowing, too, holding its position beside him.

It took him a moment to realize what was happening. There was a classic manoeuvre the police used for stopping vehicles in pursuits, TPAC. Tactical Pursuit and Containment. Three or sometimes four vehicles would box in the target vehicle and steadily reduce their speed, forcing it to a halt.

An exit was coming up. Just as he decided to take it, the SUV behind him suddenly switched lanes, coming up on his inside, blocking his ability to turn off. Ross braked and the SUV braked.

Then he was past the exit ramp and the SUV switched to the inside lane again, right behind him.

He glanced at the hard shoulder. Could he swing left on to that and accelerate past the van in front of him, on the inside?

As though anticipating his thoughts, the van moved left a little, and an instant later the lorry edged closer towards him, and kept on edging. He was either going to collide with it or have to move over to the left, partly onto the hard shoulder.

Shit, shit, shit.

He moved over, and the lorry moved closer again, forcing him further over onto the wide hard shoulder.

The van's brake lights came on brightly as it slowed, forcing him to reduce speed steadily. 60 mph . . . 55 . . . 50. He had to do something. Had to.

Then he remembered something about brake lights. They came on with the brake pedal. But not with the parking brake.

Glancing in his mirror, bracing himself, he yanked up the parking brake handle hard, and held it.

Heard the scrubbing of his rear wheels locking up.

Felt the car zigzagging, the steering wheel jerking in his hands. Heard the scream of the SUV's tyres, then in his mirrors saw it swerving past him on the inside, missing the rear of his car by inches. A shower of sparks as the SUV struck the barrier; then an instant later it appeared to catapult off the barrier and shoot across the hard shoulder, striking the lorry almost broadside, before barrel-rolling.

Ross slammed the Audi gear shift into R and, craning his head over his shoulder, reversed as fast as he could, the car snaking wildly, back up the hard shoulder, his brain racing. The exit was only a couple of hundred yards or so back. What he was doing was illegal and dangerous. If the police came along, great, he would tell them what had happened. If not, he'd take the turn-off.

Allowing himself a quick glance down the road, he saw the SUV upside down on the hard shoulder, partly embedded in the side of the truck, like an animal feasting on prey. The white van had vanished.

He reached the turn-off, waited until there was a gap in the light traffic, which was slowing anyway, then made the dangerous manoeuvre, backing right across the slip road entrance and accelerating hard away.

His head was pounding, his hands shaking. He knew one thing, that what had just happened made it all the more imperative he get to his destination as quickly as possible.

Just under an hour later, still very shaken by the incident on the motorway, Ross pulled into the car park of the U-Store depot in Shoreham. He sat still, wondering if he should have called the police and reported that he'd been involved in an accident. Wasn't it an offence to drive away from the scene? Were there CCTV cameras that would have picked it up? Seen him reversing on a motorway? It was something he would have to deal with later.

Although had he actually been involved in an accident, technically, as his car hadn't been touched?

Jumping out, Ross hurried to the rear of the Audi. After looking around, warily, he grabbed the holdall out of the boot and carried it through into the security hut.

The grossly overweight, bored-looking slob of a man, in his thirties, with greasy, unkempt hair and a single gold earring, who Ross recognized from before, sat behind the counter in front of a bank of CCTV monitors. They showed static views of the exterior of the depot and the interior of the warehouse. The slob was reading a Terry Pratchett novel and eating a submarine with sauce leaking down the sides. The place reeked of curry. A name tag pinned to the lapel of his crumpled, ill-fitting uniform identified him as Ron Spokes.

'Hi, Ron!' he said, cheerily.

The miserable-looking guard looked up and gave no sign of recognition. 'Yes?'

'You're a Pratchett fan?'

'He's all right.'

'I like him too,' Ross said.

His response was a blank stare.

Ross signed in.

Ron Spokes pointed at the rear door, pressed a button and the lock clicked open. He took another bite of his monster sub and returned to his book, ignoring the trickle of sauce running down his chin. Ross carried his bag through the door and into the courtyard. A short distance in front of him was the metal shuttered door of the warehouse.

He punched his code into the entry panel and waited as the door clattered upwards. He was pleased that, just as on his previous visits, he was the only person in here. He waited for the door to lower again, and strode along through the vast area until he reached his own storage facility. He put the holdall down, entered the combination on the first padlock and inserted his key into the second one, then twisted it, springing it open.

Placing his bag inside, he locked the door again, checking both padlocks several times, almost obsessively, before walking back through the security hut, out into the visitors' car park and into his car.

He sat in the Audi, checking his email on his phone, but there was nothing of importance. He programmed the address of his next port of call into the satnav, drove out of the depot and waited for a gap in the stream of traffic along the busy main road beside Shoreham Harbour. Some distance to his right, parked across the road in front of an office building, was a white van bearing a satellite dish emblem and the name KEITH HAWKINS AERIALS.

As he turned left and drove off, heading home, a man in the back of the white van watched him with binoculars from behind darkened glass in the rear doors. A car, part of the current shift of surveillance vehicles that had been swapping places behind him from the moment he had left home this morning, began tailing him once more, carefully remaining several vehicles back.

65

Back at home and ravenous, Ross opened the Audi's boot and removed three huge carrier bags bearing the store's name, SAFE HOUSE SECURITY SYSTEMS. He carried them through into the garage and laid them gently on the floor. They contained five outdoor CCTV cameras and a control unit that would enable him to see the images on his phone or laptop from wherever in the world he was. Hopefully it would make Imogen feel a little safer, in addition to the alarm system that was now up and running – and himself, too.

He'd always been a bit rubbish at DIY, but the man in the shop assured him installation was easy; with the whole system being wireless and battery operated, all he had to do was fix each camera with a couple of screws, then follow the simple set-up instructions. Even so, he was dubious. From past experience, whenever anyone told him a job such as this was simple, it meant that it might be if you were a rocket scientist.

Whenever Imogen saw him with a hammer, a saw or a screwdriver in his hand, she gave him a worried look. So he decided he would get straight on with it after a very quick bite of lunch and a couple of urgent phone calls, and surprise her when she arrived home this evening.

He made himself a Cheddar and Branston pickle

sandwich, much to Monty's delight, as he gulped down several chunks of cheese which his master slipped him.

'You know, Monty, you're meant to taste food, right? You just swallow it down – it could be bloody anything.'

The dog barked at him.

'You want more?'

He barked again.

'No begging!' Ross said, dutifully, knowing Imogen did not approve of the dog doing that.

Monty sat and stared at him expectantly, tongue hanging out.

'So now you're playing the tugging-on-heart-strings ticket, right?'

Monty cocked his head, looking all mournful.

Ross cut off a large chunk of the cheese and handed it to him. It was gone in two bites.

'Just don't tell your mum, OK? Deal?'

Monty barked again.

'No! Enough, OK? That's it! No more! I'll take you for a walk later on – I've got stuff to do.'

Ross sat at the kitchen table and picked up his sandwich. As he ate he glanced through the papers. A couple of pages into *The Times*, a headline caught his eye.

PASTOR WARNS BEWARE THE GREAT IMPOSTER

Below it, he read:

Pastor Wesley Wenceslas, the UK's most popular ever evangelist, claims the world political climate of fragmenting established order, anger and the rise of aggressive politicians is all predicted in the Bible – and heralds the perfect environment for the arrival of the Antichrist.

He gave this warning to a packed congregation of his Kensington church, yesterday: 'The Bible tells us that ancient serpent, the Devil, who deceived Eve in the Garden of Eden, will appear masquerading as God or the Son of God. The Devil will appear in all of the great cities of earth, one at a time. When he appears the world will be in a desperate position and cries of suffering will be everywhere. The father of lies and misery, the enemy of all humanity, will feign sympathy for the terrible human suffering he sees. To make his deception believable he will perform great signs, such as healing the sick and feeding the hungry. Many people will be duped into believing the Devil is Almighty God. My path is the right path, beware the Great Imposter.'

Pastor Wesley Wenceslas has four churches in England and a further three in the USA. His YouTube channel, Wenceslas Ministries TV, has over 5m subscribers from around the globe. Last year he appeared at 830th on the *Sunday Times* Rich List with a personal fortune of £172m.

During our exclusive interview, Wenceslas gave guarded answers to questions vetted in advance by his publicist, who remained present. When queried about his need for a private Boeing 737 – and his current 'Pray For A Sky Mile' fund-raising appeal to his worshippers, to replace it with an even larger aircraft – the publicist answered it was in the skies where the pastor felt closest to God and he needed to spend more time up there, away from earthly interference.

Ross tore the page out of the paper, and folded it. Not much had changed since his article on the pastor, a few years ago. The old fraud was still reeling in the suckers – he had some nerve talking about imposters.

As he made himself a coffee, he wondered if Wenceslas might possibly have got wind of Harry Cook's story. He carried the mug upstairs, along with the article, sat at his desk and checked his emails, still pondering. There was a request from his *Sunday Times* editor for him to fly to Strasbourg to interview a cross-section of Euro MPs on their views of the UK's latest Brexit negotiations.

It was a lucrative gig, but it would take him away for several days. And he could not let go of what he had. He emailed back a reply.

> Natalie, I'm on the trail of a story which, if it pans out, will blow you away. I can't let go of it at the moment – you'll understand when I file it. Reluctant to turn work down but can you give the Strasbourg one to someone else? Ross X

She replied instantly.

> Need a big story for next Sunday – when can I see it? Can you get it to me by Thursday? X

Ross stared beyond his screen, out through the window, down at his grimy Audi on the drive in front of the house, and at the street beyond. Thursday? His editor had no idea just how big this could be.

Nor, he thought ruefully, did he.

The DNA match, from a tooth that might have come from Jesus Christ, with a cup that might have contained Christ's blood.

What odds could there be on a tooth from a cave in a mountainous region of Egypt providing a DNA match with a small wooden cup he had recovered from a well in Glastonbury, England?

He was about to reply when another email pinged in. This one from Imogen.

> So how did it go at the lab?

He replied:

> Interesting! Tell you all later.

Then he replied to his editor:

> Maybe Thursday week – if I'm still alive.

The reply came back seconds later.

> I trust you are joking.

He typed back:

> I wish I was.

Opening his address book, he looked up the number of the Birmingham solicitor, and dialled it, recognizing the voice of the battle-axe who answered. He gave his name and asked if he could speak to Robert Anholt-Sperry.

'I'm afraid he's in conference with a client – may I ask him to call you back? Will he know what it is about?'

'Yes,' Ross said. 'He will.'

Next, he made a call to attempt to contact a man he had not spoken to since around the time of his return from Afghanistan. He didn't even know for sure he was still alive. He googled the website of the place where his uncle Angus resided, and found a phone number. He dialled it.

'Is it possible to speak to the Prior?' he asked the calm, surprisingly jovial-sounding man who answered.

'You're speaking to him.'

Ross explained who he was and what he wanted.

'Mr Hunter, you realize that our brothers here are hermits residing under a collective roof? They have chosen the silent life of prayer and contemplation secure from the distractions – and intrusions – of the world. All I can do is to ask Brother Angus – I will do it via a note with his evening meal. But I cannot promise you a response.'

As Ross ended the call he had a thought, and entered into Google the words 'laboratory test tubes'.

After a few minutes searching through three sites, he found exactly what he wanted.

66

It wasn't until he got two hundred pages into the Pratchett novel that Ron Spokes began to figure out he had read it before. Stuff like that was happening all the time at the moment. And his stomach was going thermo-nuclear, fizzing and gurgling. There had been something in that curried sub that had tasted strange, he should have spat it out. Was he now going down with food poisoning, on top of everything else?

The only good news was it was 5.55 p.m. Just five minutes to go. Then he could head home, via the kebab house – or maybe not, the way his stomach was feeling. But perhaps more food was what it needed. He could give it a try – and spend the evening as he had planned, bingeing on skewered lamb and honey-and-pecan ice cream, watching the old movie *The Matrix*, which his mate Mick, at the darts club, had been raving about.

6 p.m.

We're done!

He levered himself off the stool, his knees complaining at standing up after sitting down too long, and waddled over to activate the night-time alarm system. As he left the front entrance and walked into the damp, misty darkness of the car park he had an attack of stomach cramps. He could feel the build-up of wind inside him as the cramps tightened for a moment, and he doubled up, with tears of pain in his eyes, until the cramps finally relaxed their grip.

He walked on towards his shit-box, rust-bucket of a car. The twenty-year-old Honda Accord that hadn't been serviced in over a year. The MOT deadline was in four days and there was no way it was going to pass. Three bald tyres and a knackered exhaust system. Without the car, he didn't know how he was going to get to work. And there was a new lady he had started seeing, Madeleine. Was he going to have to take her out on a date by bus – how impressed would she be?

He put his key in the lock, not that there was much point in securing the vehicle – it would take an even sadder loser than himself to steal it, he thought. He eased himself into the driver's seat, pulled the door shut and fumbled in the darkness to get the key into the ignition. Then he let out a massive fart.

'Charming,' said a male voice behind him.

As he jumped in shock, Spokes felt something hard and cold press into the back of his neck.

'This is what you think it is,' the voice said. Then an instant later, 'Jeez, what have you eaten?'

'What do you want?'

'I'm here to give you a choice. I can either be your executioner or your fairy godmother.'

'Very funny.'

'I'm not joking.'

The cold barrel of the gun pressed harder into the security guard's neck.

'I know how much debt you are in, and I have with me enough cash to clear all your credit cards – ten thousand pounds in folding – so we could do business if you like?'

'What business?'

'I just need you to let me in, deactivate the CCTV and take me to the locker of one of your customers, Mr Ross Hunter.'

'I can't do that.'

'Oh yes you can, I promise you, you can, and you are going to, aren't you?'

'You know the trouble I'll get into?'

'Not as much trouble as being dead.'

67

Monday, 13 March

'Ross, what on earth are you doing?' Imogen asked, climbing out of her car.

He stood at the top of the ladder, which was leaning precariously against the front wall of the house, struggling to fix the CCTV camera to the wall just beneath the eaves.

'Nearly done!'

'Nearly done what? Killing yourself?'

The screwdriver, along with the two rawlplugs he had been holding in his mouth, fell to the ground. They were rapidly joined by the electric drill, which fell off the top rung. 'Shit, shit, bugger!'

'Get down!' she said, sounding furious and gripping the ladder.

Sheepishly, he clambered back onto the ground, holding the camera in his left hand. 'I bought these this afternoon – I thought it would make us feel safer.'

'Coming home and finding you at the top of a ladder is going to make me feel safer? I don't think so. You and DIY do not go together. You have a great talent for writing – you're not a bloody electrician.'

'It's not difficult to put these up.'

'So I can see.'

He shrugged. 'Yep, well maybe they are a bit harder than I thought.'

'Why don't we phone the electrician and ask him to deal with it tomorrow, if he can?'

'Maybe that's a good plan.' He smiled. 'How was your day?'

'It was fine until around midday when I got a craving for salt and vinegar crisps.' She gave him a guilty look. 'I've eaten three packs of them. Like, large packs. Now I'm parched.'

They went inside. Ross closed the front door and slid home the safety chain.

As she knelt and stroked Monty, Imogen asked, 'So, the lab, what happened?'

'Well,' he said. 'The DNA is a match. It's crazy, can you believe it?'

'Between the tooth and the cup?'

'Yes.'

She blanched. 'Saliva on the cup?'

'No – from what they identified, it's quite degraded blood.'

She stared at him in silence. 'I need a drink,' she said. 'A small glass of white wine – that would be OK, wouldn't it?'

'On the evening you discover your husband is possibly in possession of Jesus Christ's DNA, I think a small glass of wine is permissible.'

'Don't be frivolous.'

He went to the fridge, in silence, took out a bottle of Albarino and began to open it. 'I'm not being frivolous.'

'I don't like it. I said it before, you are punching way above your weight here, Ross.'

He brought her glass over, handed it to her and sat back down.

'Dr Cook was killed over this,' she said. 'You were nearly killed in Egypt. I've had threats. Is any bloody story worth risking our lives for? You're into crackpot territory here. Religious fanaticism.'

'Come on!'

'No, Ross, you *come on*. Get real.'

'Is there anything more real than a DNA match between a tooth in the back of a cave in Egypt and a cup I found sealed in an ancient container in Chalice Well? Just supposing it's true, that Cook really did get a message from God. And I was the person chosen to tell the world – and I walked away from it. I don't think I could live with that.'

'You'll be a fat lot of use to the world dead,' she said.

'I've got to see this through. I have to, OK?'

'Why? Because you owe it to Dr Cook? You said yourself he was a nutter.'

He sipped his wine. 'He's not seeming such a nutter any more.'

'No?'

Ross went up to his den and returned with the printouts that Jolene Thomas had given him. He laid them out on the table and talked Imogen through them.

'So what am I supposed to say?' she said, when he had finished. 'That I'm impressed?'

'Tell me what I'm getting wrong here, Imo. This is dyna-mite. It's possibly the biggest story ever. Can you imagine the headlines?'

'Yes, and that's what scares me. You told me what your bishop friend told you. All the religious factions out there – and the non-religious ones.'

'Potentially delivering to the world proof of God? Could we really ignore that?'

'I could,' she said. 'I'm sure if God cares that much about saving the world he could find someone else.'

'You have faith, Imogen. Far more than I do. You go to church regularly.'

'I do. But I don't have faith in this madness you've got yourself into.'

He stared at her and could see the fear in her face. He was fully aware of the danger they were in. He was still shaken by what had happened on the motorway earlier. And yet. It was bigger than just a newspaper story, way bigger. There was just one key piece to the whole thing he had yet to obtain – and with luck he would get that tomorrow.

'I'm going to Birmingham tomorrow, to see Cook's solicitor again. Come with me, see for yourself.'

'I can't, Ross, you know that, I have to be in the office.'

'OK. He has the final piece to this puzzle that he's going to give me. That will show, for sure, whether there is any real substance to this story or if it's just a crazy old man's delusion. I'll make the decision after that.'

'And if there is substance, what then, Ross?'

He stared down at the table for some moments before looking her in the eye again. He had no answer.

68

Tuesday, 14 March

Lancelot Pope had no answer either. It was 10 a.m. He sat dumbfounded opposite Wesley Wenceslas, in the white-carpeted boardroom at Gethsemane Park, with the view through the grand, first-floor windows across terraces of perfect green lawn leading down to the lake. There was a man-made island, in the shape of a cross, in the centre of which stood a twenty-foot-tall white marble statue of the pastor, with his arms open, expansively, as if gesturing to the heavens.

Around the walls hung the Wenceslas collection of icons, acquired during the past decade from auction sales all over the world. A small tooth and a wooden cup sat on the twenty-seater table. The silence was broken momentarily by the buzz of Pope's mobile phone vibrating. He muted it, and gave Wenceslas an update from the surveillance team of the previous day, including how their rivals had nearly run Hunter off the road.

'Well?' said Wenceslas, furious. 'I don't see my Smilealot smiling a lot. Do you?'

Pope stared again, dumbly, at the two objects.

'I'm waiting for your explanation, Lancelot. Meantime my personal cup of bounteous patience is running dry.'

Pope picked up the wooden cup and turned it round in his hands for the third time. He had a sheepish expression.

'This is what – what was in – in Ross Hunter's storage locker at the depot.'

'And you paid ten thousand pounds for it.'

'You did authorize it, boss.'

'I authorized you spending ten thousand pounds to secure the Holy Grail and the tooth belonging to Jesus Christ, so we could protect and guard them in the name of our Lord.' He reached across the table and snatched the cup out of his MD's hand. He turned it upside down and held the base up close to Pope's face. 'I do not think that the authentic chalice of our Lord, the *Holy Grail*, would have a "Made in China" sticker on the bottom. Do you? Is it really likely China was exporting wooden cups to the Holy Land two thousand years ago?'

Pope hesitated. 'Probably not.'

'Probably fucking not, no!' Wenceslas exploded, banging the cup down hard on the table.

'We're dealing with someone very smart here, boss. It could be that Hunter took this label off something else and stuck it on the chalice to try to fool everyone.'

'Is that what you really think?' He picked up the tooth. 'And you think that Jesus Christ our Lord was a vampire, do you?'

'A vampire?'

'I don't know what dentists were like back in the days of our Lord, but I'm doubting they carved teeth into fangs. Or am I missing something here?'

Pope stifled a nervous grin. 'No, you're not, you could be right, boss.'

'This is not a human tooth, this belongs to an animal, a wild animal. I don't know anything about teeth, but I know one that isn't human when I see it. We've just paid ten thousand pounds, that could have gone to help the poor, on a crap wooden souvenir and the tooth of a dead dog. We've been had.'

'Maybe Hunter has been had,' Pope replied lamely. 'This is what was in his locker.'

'Then the Holy Grail and the real tooth of our Lord Jesus Christ are somewhere else. Not in Mr Hunter's locker. Find them, and find them fast.'

'Leave it with me, boss.'

Wenceslas stared at him. 'We do not have long. Word will be getting out about what this man, Hunter, has. He is still being followed and observed?'

'Twenty-four-seven.'

'So where is he right at this minute?'

Pope consulted an app on his phone. After a few moments he gave Wenceslas a wary look. 'He left Brighton twenty minutes ago and drove through the village of Henfield, approximately ten miles north of there. The team have momentarily lost visual on him.'

Wenceslas banged both fists on the table, repeatedly. 'What? What? What?'

'It's OK, they're not far behind, they'll find him again.'

'Sure they will. Just like you found the Holy Grail. I'll tell you where they should start looking – how about a souvenir stall in a Shanghai street market?'

69

Ross had driven past the sign countless times, as had hundreds of thousands of others, barely noticing it. And he almost missed it now.

ST HUGH'S CHARTERHOUSE

A small white board on the grass verge, in front of an unruly hedge, discreetly marking the entrance to the monastery.

He braked hard, putting out his hand to stop his clinking bag tumbling off the passenger seat into the footwell, and turned sharp left onto a paved driveway. He drove past a small cottage, with no sign of life. The driveway curved before straightening out and passing under the archway of a gatehouse. Straight ahead was an imposing-looking edifice that reminded him of one of the grand Cambridge University buildings. The tallest part, topped with three spires, was flanked on both sides by glassed-in, cloistered wings, and had a grand oak door.

He pulled up, climbed out and lugged the clinking carrier bag from the passenger seat, collecting his rucksack from the boot.

The door opened and a chubby man in his sixties with white robes, a white skullcap and wearing Birkenstocks appeared. He strode across with a friendly smile, exuding more the air of a bon viveur than an ascetic monk.

'Mr Hunter?'

'Yes.'

He held out his hand. 'I am Father Raphael, the Prior – we spoke yesterday. Welcome to our humble abode.'

Ross responded, smiling. 'It doesn't look that humble!'

'Well, actually, we are rather blessed. Among other things we have the longest cloisters of any monastery in the United Kingdom.'

'Is that so?'

'Indeed. As the actor Michael Caine might say, "Not a lot of people know that!"'

Ross grinned, surprised to find the Prior so worldly.

'But I don't think you have come, Mr Hunter, to hear about the length of our cloisters. Let me take you to your uncle Angus. He was very pleased to have word from you – much to my surprise – but that's good. I believe contact with the outside world is not always a bad thing. Even for those leading the cloistered life. He is not enjoying the best of health, so I hope your visit will cheer him up.'

Ross followed him along a paved, high-ceilinged corridor with stark, bare stone walls and frequent columns. They passed a wooden noticeboard with a list of names. He only had time to absorb a few of them: Bro William; Dom Pachomius; Bro Alban; Dom Ignatius; Dom Henry; Dom Stephen Mary. Then a small, cream sign: HAIRCUT 9.30–10.

They turned a corner and entered a long, narrow, cloistered walkway. It had a grey flagstone floor and white walls criss-crossed with cream vaulted arches which stretched away, seemingly, to the distant horizon. Every twenty yards or so was a closed, ornate wooden door, with a Latin inscription above.

A short distance along, the Prior stopped outside one of these doors. Ross looked at the Latin , but had no idea what it meant.

Mihi enim vivere CHRISTUS est, et mori lucrum.

The Prior rapped on the door.

Ross tried to remember the last conversation he had had with his uncle. Angus had long been referred to by his parents as the black sheep of the family. In photographs Angus had shoulder-length hair, tinted round spectacles, and was dressed in a black T-shirt, skinny jeans and Cuban-heeled boots. Ross used to think it was cool to have an uncle who was a rocker.

Now he had no idea what to expect, but even so, as the door opened very slowly, as if by an elderly woman afraid of an intruder, he was shocked by the gaunt figure that appeared. With his sallow skin and shaven head, wearing a robe with a pointed hood, his uncle looked like a ghost.

Those once mischievous, twinkling nut-brown eyes were now like burned-out stars in a collapsing universe, and the grin he remembered, the confident grin as if the world was all one big joke, was now a thin, sad smile.

'Ross? Ross? It is you, isn't it! Oh, Ross!' he said in a voice that still retained some of its old ebullient energy. He held out a frail, bony hand and Ross shook it gently. His uncle peered at him closely. 'Please come in – I'm afraid it's not the presidential suite at the Four Seasons.'

Ross looked at the Prior, who beamed, beatifically. 'I will leave you together.'

As his uncle closed the door, Ross found himself in a narrow, tiled hallway, at the end of which, ten metres away, sat a painted statuette of the Virgin Mary on a piece of tree trunk. A framed icon hung on a wall at the far end, bathed in light from a window.

'I've not resided in many other monasteries but apparently I'm very lucky, Ross,' his uncle said. 'They built this place to accommodate two hundred monks and there are only twenty-three of us here. I have two whole floors, a nice workshop and a garden all to myself. It's like my own house – and with no noisy neighbours to worry about! Come on in.'

It was only a short, stone staircase, but Ross could see how sick his uncle was from the length of time it took him to climb the steps, frequently stopping for breath.

At the top was a spartan room with bare floorboards. The only furniture was a desk and chair, on which sat an anglepoise lamp, a few books including a Bible, and a calendar. There was an unlit wood-burning stove and a recess with a crucifix on the wall that looked, to Ross, like a prayer area. Through an open doorway he could see a turquoise hot-water bottle hanging from a hook, and a narrow, recessed bed.

'I've brought you a gift, Uncle Angus,' he said, and handed him the carrier bag.

'A gift?' The monk held the bag with a faraway smile. As if a distant memory had been triggered. Setting the bag down on the floor, its weight seeming too much for him, his uncle looked close to tears. 'I don't remember – the last time – I received a gift. This is kind. Very kind.'

Ross was so touched by his genuine astonishment, he felt tears welling in his own eyes. 'I thought – I didn't know if you were permitted –?'

The monk removed the four bottles of claret, one at a time, holding them up to the light and inspecting them with an expression of sheer joy that shed years from his countenance. 'Red wine? French? It is years – years – since I drank anything other than communion wine!' He delved further into the bag and removed an item, holding it up. 'A corkscrew! You are so thoughtful, bless you!'

Ross stood, awkwardly, unsure how to react to the old man's pure happiness. He now wished he had brought him more bottles.

Then he opened his rucksack and removed the carefully wrapped wooden cup, back in its wooden container, and a small glass vial, containing a few drops of opaque fluid and sealed with a white plastic cap. He placed them on his uncle's desk.

Looking at the items with curiosity, Angus said, 'Please sit down, Ross. I'm afraid I don't have much furniture – we don't do much entertaining in our cells!' He smiled. 'You are actually the only guest I have ever had.'

Ross grinned. 'I'm fine standing.'

'You know, I always liked you, Ross. I was certain you would amount to something in life. We have so many years to catch up on! We should drink, I think.'

'No, please, keep these for yourself – to enjoy.'

'Well, I don't know if my medication – or my vows – permit. But perhaps the Lord will forgive an old, sick man for a small indulgence.' He looked at the bottles again. 'This is such temptation! You are so kind.' He opened the wooden container and peered inside. 'And you provide me with a wine glass, too.'

'Actually, Uncle Angus,' Ross said, his tone serious now, 'that cup is not for you to drink from. And the vial does not contain something to get you high on.'

'You remember! The old days, yes, when I had my group? Satan's Creed? We toured as the warm-up band for Black Sabbath.'

'I do, my dad told me all about it. I was very proud of you – you were my cool uncle!'

The old man smiled, happiness creasing his face. 'So tell me, why has God brought you here to see an old man who once embarrassed your family, and who is now not long for this world?'

Ross pointed at the two items on the desk. 'Uncle Angus, I need you to keep these safe for me, as a favour. To hide them. Put them somewhere very safe.'

'They are important to you?'

'Not me, they are important to the world. To mankind. I don't want them falling into the wrong hands. There are a lot of people who want these very badly.'

Brother Angus frowned. 'How much do you want to tell me?'

'Perhaps I should leave it for God to tell you.'

His uncle led him across to the window by the desk and pointed through it. Down below was a walled garden. Beyond was a long, rectangular graveyard, with neat rows of plain wooden crosses planted in well-tended grass, bounded by the cloisters.

'Soon, I will have one of those crosses, Ross. I don't know how long the Lord will spare me. I have a cancer that is, unfortunately, rather an adventurous one, so the doctor told me. It has managed to travel to just about every part of my body. I've named it Marco Polo.'

Ross smiled again. 'Are you having any treatment?'

'No, it is beyond that. But it's OK, I've had my life. I have a mission still to complete, and I believe our Lord will allow me to complete it.'

'I'm sorry to hear that, Uncle.'

'Don't be. But what I'm saying is that if you need something important to be protected, I'm probably not the best person.'

'You are. If you could do me this one favour – as I'm not

sure how much longer I have to live either. I'm sure you will know where to keep these items safe and hidden.'

'You are ill, Ross? You don't look sick to me.'

'Not ill – but in danger. Very big danger.'

'Oh? Tell me?'

Ross pointed at the cup and the vial. 'I don't want to put you in danger, too, on top of what you are already going through.'

'What can harm a dying man?' The old monk fell silent for some moments. Then he put the corkscrew and one bottle on the desk, went out of the room and came back with two mismatched glasses. 'It's a long, long while – many years – since I drank with anyone other than at communion. I feel this is the moment. God will forgive us both.'

'But I do have to drive to Birmingham, unfortunately.'

Brother Angus replied, 'What was that expression we used to have – so many years ago – *one for the road*?'

A few minutes later they clinked glasses. 'God bless you,' his uncle said.

Before he left, Ross told his uncle the whole story. He felt he needed to know what he had to safeguard. His uncle told him he had an idea.

70

Two hours later Ross pulled into a motorway service station to refuel. The satnav told him he had a further one hour and twenty minutes to his destination. The effect of the small glass of red wine had worn off a long while ago and he was badly in need of a pee, a caffeine hit and something to eat. He drove from the pumps into a parking bay and entered the garish, rammed interior of the service station.

Since leaving the monastery he had been feeling a strange mix of emotions about his uncle. It had been hard to reconcile the frail, lonely man in his stark, surprisingly spacious accommodation with the former wild rocker. Yet his uncle's clear faith touched him deeply. As had the sheer glee on the old man's face at seeing the bottles of wine.

How could a hedonist like Uncle Angus closet himself away from the world and live a solitary life of constant prayer, with rejection and denial of all pleasures? Could anyone, if they were buoyed up by their faith? If it was strong enough?

His uncle was no fool. He was like countless intelligent people around the world who had faith – a belief that remained intact no matter what happened to them. In some ways, they were lucky.

He thought back to Harry Cook. Two sets of compass coordinates. Taking him to a cup in a well in Glastonbury and a tooth in a cave in Egypt. An attempt on his life. His wife threatened.

The warnings of Benedict Carmichael.

The message from his dead brother.

This planet that he was stuck to like glue, by gravity. One of a hundred billion trillion perhaps – and counting – in the universe. This beautiful planet. This dog-eat-dog, polluted, miraculous place, torn apart daily by hatred born so often from different religious beliefs. Different factions of the same belief.

Such minuscule differences between so many of the religions; semantics between some others. All of them ultimately believing in a supreme God.

Sunni. Shi'ite. Roman Catholics. Anglo-Catholics. Free churches. Charismatic and conservative Evangelicals. Salvation Army. Exclusive Brethren. Quakers. Jews. Hindus. Sikhs. The list was endless. Would they be divided until the end of time? Until every different faith on this amazing planet was consumed by nuclear dust?

Or did Harry F. Cook truly have something that could change our world, as he had suggested?

He thought of the words of the astronaut, Frank Borman, on Apollo 8: 'When you're finally up at the moon looking back on earth, all those differences and nationalistic traits are pretty well going to blend, and you're going to get a concept that maybe this really is one world, and why the hell can't we learn to live together like decent people?'

That was how Ross felt, looking around at the signs inside the service station. Burger King. WHSmith. Costa. And at all the other travellers coming in and walking out, many of them looking fatigued by whatever journey they were on. Someone bumped into him, hurrying on without apologizing. A couple walked past him, pushing a baby in a buggy. That would be himself and Imogen in a few months' time. What world would their son be born into? he wondered, as he entered the main restaurant area, wrinkling his nose at the ingrained smell of fried food.

A world that might not last unless something changed, dramatically. A change that, however improbably, he might be the person to unlock. He owed it to his unborn son to see through this strange mission. He knew, deep in his heart, that if he walked away from it he would never be able to look his son in the eye as he grew up.

Taking a tray, he wandered along the line of counters, passing the salads and the other healthy options. He was in need of something warm and filling, something to give him energy. He asked the server for fish and chips and mushy peas, and then, further along, he requested a large coffee and helped himself to a bottle of mineral water.

He paid, then went over to another counter, took a knife and fork, poured some milk into his coffee, took several sachets of ketchup, vinegar, salt and pepper, and carried his meal over to a table by the window. Outside, through the window, he saw two women standing, smoking in the falling drizzle. He set everything down and put the tray into a rack close by, then sat and picked up a ketchup sachet.

As he was about to tear it open, a slim man in his forties, with short, neat, dark hair, wearing a trench coat over a suit and holding a cardboard cup with a lid on, slipped purposefully into the empty chair beside him.

Annoyed at the invasion of privacy, when there were plenty of empty tables all around, he glared at the man. But the man merely smiled back at him as if in recognition. He had a strong face with a serious expression, and Ross noticed he wore a signet ring on his wedding finger.

Not interested in engaging in conversation with a bored

fellow traveller, Ross was about to stand up and move to a vacant table nearby when the man spoke, in a silky, assured voice.

'Ross Hunter?'

'Yes?'

The stranger shot a glance around him before speaking, and lowered his voice. 'Stuart Ivens, from the Ministry of Defence.' He discreetly flipped open his wallet, displaying an ID card in a plastic window inside. 'I'm sorry to interrupt your lunch,' he said, politely. 'Would you mind if we had a quick chat?'

'What about?' Ross stared at the ID, reading the small but clear 'MI5'.

A few years ago he'd written a piece about the mysterious death of a man suspected of being an MI5 agent who had been found dead in a London flat, zipped into a holdall bag, dressed head to toe in latex and wearing a gimp mask. All his attempts at establishing the facts from the security agency had been stonewalled. He had never managed to establish whether the man had died as a result of a bondage game gone wrong or whether he had been murdered. But this could not be related to that piece, surely not after all this time? He had a pretty shrewd idea what the man was going to talk to him about and he was right.

'I believe you were acquainted with the late Dr Harry Cook,' Stuart Ivens said, pleasantly.

'What do you know about him?' Ross asked, suspiciously.

'Probably not as much as you do, Mr Hunter,' he said, removing the lid of his carton to reveal steaming coffee. 'But enough for us to be very concerned for national security – and for your own safety.'

Ross stared at him.

'Look, let's cut straight to the chase. Following your encounter with Dr Cook, you now have in your possession some items you believe might relate to proof of God. Correct?'

'How do you know what I have?'

'In these days of heightened security, it is our business to know – call it national security, a watching brief,' he said calmly, maintaining his courteous tone. 'You think you have a potential story, but it has far-reaching consequences that you may not realize. And it poses a very real threat to your own life.'

'I'm aware of that.'

'Are you?' Stuart Ivens gave him a quizzical stare. 'If what you have is indeed genuine, do you really understand the ramifications? Even if it's not authentic, but you produce a plausible story, the potential consequences are a nightmare scenario of civil unrest in our country – and beyond.'

Ross looked at him. 'What is it you think I have – or might have?'

'Some things that might prove God's existence, Mr Hunter.'

He was making Ross feel very deeply uncomfortable. 'I don't have proof, not yet, I'm still a long way from it – if it's real at all, or even possible to prove. And even if I could prove it, would the world believe me? I may be on a wild goose chase. Are you planning to arrest me or something? Lock me up and torture me?'

Ivens smiled thinly. 'Not at all. Nor am I here to threaten you in any way. You're a respected journalist, you know as well as anyone just what a sensitive topic religion is in our country today – and throughout many parts of the world.'

'So, you want me to forget it?'

'That's not what I'm here to ask you. I would just like you to think about the responsibility you have. To consider the consequences of anything you may go public with. Would you be willing to run your story by us before publishing?'

Ross looked at the man. This whole thing felt surreal. 'I'd have to think about that and talk to my editor. I can't make any promises.'

Ivens blew calmly on his coffee, then sipped it.

Was this for real? Was he in a motorway cafeteria, talking to a spy?

'You're a very intelligent man, Mr Hunter. How many places can you name where they have faith in God? And where that very faith is ripping them apart and has been doing so for years – decades? Belfast, Yemen, Syria, Iran, Iraq, Nigeria? How far back in history do you need to go?' Ivens sipped more of his coffee. 'Did Dr Cook tell you exactly whose God it was that he was going to give you proof of?'

After some moments Ross replied, 'No.' He was feeling an uncomfortable reality check going on inside him.

'Exactly. Every division of every faith has its own interpretation.' Ivens pulled out a business card and slipped it to Ross. 'You're an influential journalist and the UK press will publish much of what you write. You've covered many important topics in your career, including embarrassing the government over equipment for the military in Afghanistan.'

'Which they fully deserved.'

'I couldn't possibly comment on that.' Ivens gave him a strange smile.

'Really? Do I take that as a positive?'

Ivens smiled again. 'Let's not go there, other than to say

I respect your guts. We are dealing now with something very different. Just consider this. Maybe – and I don't want to cast any aspersions on your integrity or intelligence – you don't completely comprehend quite how far out of your depth you might be here. The world of religious faith is not a rational one, and never has been. There are religious divisions in this country and around the world on a scale that is unprecedented. As you must be well aware, our national security is under severe threat from these divisions. You may be under the impression that proving the existence of God could restore balance in the world. Consider if it had the reverse effect. That's all I'm saying to you. If you want to discuss anything with me, you have my contact details on this card. You can reach me twenty-four-seven.'

Ivens handed him his card, stood, picked up his cup and gave Ross a wry smile. 'I'm sorry to have interrupted your lunch.' He began to walk off, then stopped and turned back. 'Oh, by the way, a word of advice. Never a good idea to leave rucksacks lying around in cafes. Especially not these days.'

71

Tuesday, 14 March

For some time after his nephew had departed, Brother Angus felt sad, knowing it was unlikely he would live long enough to ever see him again. He also felt an immense weight of responsibility as he stared at the wooden cup and the glass vial with the small amount of fluid it contained.

He carried them into his cubicle, closed his eyes and knelt, asking for strength from God to protect them, as he had been bidden by Ross, and he prayed for Ross, too.

He thought about Ross's words.

Perhaps God would explain what he should do.

But after an hour, God said nothing more to him.

He had a feeling – just a sense – nothing that was coming to him loud and clear, though, that this visit from Ross, and these items, were connected to the doubts he had been having about faith – and his concerns for the world.

He felt an overwhelming sense of duty to his nephew to protect these two items. Yes, he knew, he could request them to be buried with him. But equally he was aware of the parlous state of the finances of this monastery. Just twenty-three monks, including himself, in a monastery built to accommodate very many more. In a few years perhaps it might be sold. Perhaps turned into a country house hotel with a golf course? He understood how the world worked. A property developer would not care about the graves. Brother Angus needed to do something to respect his nephew's wishes. To ensure the preservation of these two items, undisturbed, for ever.

Perhaps it was God now telling him. Or was it his own common sense?

The idea he'd had earlier was taking root. The one person he knew whom he could trust and was in a place of complete safety. As he laid the objects in the cupboard by his bed, the more he thought about it, the more he liked the idea.

He would go and ask the Prior. If he said no, so be it.

But God would surely guide him to agree.

72

The green line on the map on Ross's satnav screen directed him round the maze that was Spaghetti Junction. Was this the world's ugliest and most complicated road junction ever constructed? Surely, somewhere in the heart of the person who designed it, he pondered, must have resided a sense of basic decency and community spirit – however much that was lacking in the end result.

The map vanished and was replaced by a fat white line curled round on itself and pointing backwards. It was accompanied by the stentorian satnav female voice ordering him to make a U-turn.

Yep, great. 'I'm on a sodding motorway!' he replied to her, feeling frazzled from his long drive – and having his lunch interrupted by smooth Stuart Ivens from MI5. The pelting rain wasn't helping his mood, either.

His phone rang. He hit the button to answer it on hands-free.

'Ross?' It was Imogen, her voice sounding uneasy.

'Hi! How are you?'

'Where are you?'

'Somewhere outside Birmingham and about to drive up my own sodding backside. What's up?'

The map reappeared and the satnav arrow indicated the turn-off coming up; it was accompanied by the woman's voice ordering him to turn at the next left. He did so and then saw he was heading exactly where he did not want to go. On the southbound M6. The direction he had just come from. *Damn.*

'There's a man turned up at the office,' Imogen said.

Had she had a visit from the MI5 guy, Stuart Ivens, too?

'Who was he – what did he want?' Ross peered through the windscreen for any sign of the next exit.

'Someone called Monsignor Giuseppe Silvestri, it sounded like. He arrived in a chauffeured car and claimed to be representing the Vatican. He said he needed to speak to me in private, so I took him into a conference room.'

'And?'

'He told me if you can prove what you have is real, they would be willing to buy the items. He pretty much implied you could name your price.'

'The Vatican?'

'Ross, why don't you do that? See what they offer – then we can distance ourselves from this whole thing.'

'Name my price?'

'Yes! I got the feeling they would pay serious money – very serious money.'

'Imo, look, I don't have—'

'Ross,' she implored. 'Please, listen. Whatever you – we – are into, this is scaring me witless. You're smart, and a great reporter, but whatever the truth of this story you're pursuing, it's too dangerous. At least meet with him tomorrow and listen to what he has to say.'

'Let me have this meeting up here in Birmingham and then I'll see, OK?'

The next exit was coming up.

'I'm not sure I want to be a part of any of this any longer, Ross.'

'Look, I'll call you as soon as I've met Anholt-Sperry again, OK? I've got to focus on the road.'

'OK,' she said, bleakly. 'Call me back when you can. When will you be home?'

'I should be back by seven or so.'

'You'll be home before me. Take Monty out for a walk if you can. I won't be back until after ten – I'm having a bite with an old school friend who's in town for a conference.'

'Who's that?'

'Jennie Elkington – haven't seen her since sixth form.'

'OK, great, have fun,' he said. He'd never heard her name before, and however much he tried there was always the nagging doubt in his mind. Wondering just who she might really be meeting.

There was something about the way she had started behaving – quite some months ago now – that brought back memories of the time she'd had the affair. She'd confessed some while later that it had been going on for many months and, thinking back through that time, as he had done often in the aftermath, he realized he had seen the signs before he'd gone to Afghanistan, but ignored them. The same signs he was seeing again now, even though she was pregnant.

Or was he seeing ghosts?

73

Twenty-five minutes later, Ross pulled up in a parking space a short distance along the road from the offices of Anholt-Sperry Brine. He stepped out and hurried along the pavement, ducking his head against the rain. He passed a parked Ducati motorcycle with two panniers, ran up the steps to the entrance porch and pressed the buzzer.

Almost immediately there was a sharp click; he pushed the heavy black door open. A figure who looked like a courier, clad in black leathers, wearing a full-face motorcycling helmet with the visor down, and holding a small briefcase, barged past him without any apology. As he did so, Ross felt a strange, invisible pull towards the man, like an unseen hand, just for a brief instant, and the St Christopher's medallion that Imogen had given him years ago felt as if it was tugging against the front of his shirt. Or had he imagined it?

The reception area was rammed, with every chair taken, reminding him of a doctor's waiting room. Several members of an Asian family were seated in a group, all in earnest discussion. A gloomy young couple sat holding hands and staring vacantly ahead. An anxious-looking man in his fifties was surreptitiously holding an e-cigarette and vaping. On another chair sat a woman in a burqa, with a screaming baby.

The same harridan he recognized from his previous visit was perched behind the tall wooden counter, and gave Ross a frosty look as he walked up to her.

'Yes?'

'I have an appointment with Mr Anholt-Sperry.'

She riffled through an appointment sheet. 'Three o'clock?'

'Yes.'

'It's chaos here today and his secretary never turned up. I just saw his last appointment leave.' She pressed an inter-com buzzer. Then she shook her head, her expression thawing a little. 'He has no idea how to work this. You'd better go up – you know the way.'

'I do.'

He strode up the three flights of narrow, rickety stairs, and knocked on the right-hand door when he reached the top.

There was no answer.

He knocked again, harder, and waited. There was still no response. He pushed the door open, slowly, and saw the same cluttered office he remembered from his previous visit, with stacks of files scattered around the floor and piles of papers on the desk.

Robert Anholt-Sperry himself sat very upright behind it, with his heavily jowled face, moles and threadbare comb-over, his hands resting on the leather top of the desk. He was dressed, as before, in a frayed checked shirt and badly knotted Old Harrovian tie, and was staring, blankly, ahead of him, with a bemused expression.

'Oh – sorry to barge in – your lady downstairs said to come up.'

There was no response from the solicitor.

The man was utterly motionless. His eyes unblinking.

'Mr Anholt-Sperry?'

He took a step closer. And now he could see the man wasn't breathing.

Ross felt as if he had stepped into a deep freeze and someone had closed the door behind him. He raced downstairs to the receptionist.

74

As Brother Angus entered the Prior's grand office – he'd never stepped foot in here before in all the years he had been in this monastery – he stared around in awe. At the book-lined shelves, the comfortable leather chairs, the computer, printer and the wall-mounted television.

It could have been the office of the chief executive of a multi-national corporation, rather than of the man who was the custodian of twenty-three disparate monks. It reminded Brother Angus of all he had left behind when he entered holy orders. But it also served to remind him that he missed none of this.

The simplicity of his life of contemplation – or to be exact his *second* life, after his wild youth – had given him a peace and contentment he had never found in all the drug-fuelled years of playing gigs, sleeping with groupies and earning ridiculous amounts of money. There had been a time, back then, when the idea of death had terrified him. It had all changed when he entered the monastic commune of Mount Athos and discovered his faith, and that had strengthened even further when he had come here after burying his mother.

No fears. No anxieties. No responsibilities beyond his daily prayers for the world. Soon his body would be buried, too, like his mother's. Just an empty shell. His spirit, his soul, called to a higher purpose.

'Your silent contemplation has been interrupted already today, Brother Angus,' the Prior said in his richly engaging voice. 'Please take a seat at my desk. Make your phone call. Something is happening in your life, is it not?'

'Something, yes, Prior.'

Angus sat down, grateful to be able to conserve some energy.

'I feel it also, Brother Angus. The Lord told me today in my morning prayers that you are tasked with something extremely important for all of us. Would I be correct?'

'I believe so, Father Raphael.'

The two men were silent for some moments. The Prior knew the rules of privacy here, and did not try to pry.

'Brother Angus, my door is always open. I will leave you alone to make your phone call. If you ever wish to talk, please come to me. Don't leave it too late. Will you assure me?'

'I assure you, Father Raphael.'

The Prior went out of the room and closed the door.

Brother Angus stared at the modern handset lying in its base unit. It was a long time since he had last made a telephone call. He opened out the piece of folded paper he had carried in his hand, flattened it on the desk, and then picked up the receiver with trepidation and dialled the overseas number.

There was a long silence. Perhaps it was no longer in service, he thought.

Then he heard a single beep. Followed by another. Then another.

Finally, he heard a click, followed by a gruff, suspicious Greek voice. During his years in the monastery of Simonopetra on Mount Athos, he'd had to learn basic Greek in order to communicate with most of the monks there.

In Greek he said, 'Hello, my name is Brother Angus, I was a resident some years ago. I need, very urgently, to speak to my cousin, the American, Brother Pete. He is still with you?'

The voice remained gruff and suspicious, as if irritated by the intrusion. He informed Brother Angus that Brother Pete was indeed still with them, still the monastery's Guest Master.

'It is very important,' Brother Angus said. 'This is ordained by God.'

After a long silence the monk at the other end said, 'You may call at ten minutes to seven this evening, after our evening meal. I will tell Brother Pete he has permission to speak to you – if he wishes to.'

Brother Angus thanked him profusely.

75

Pastor Wesley Wenceslas sat in his suite at his Leeds hotel, accompanied by Lancelot Pope, watching the final edit of his weekly YouTube broadcast on Wesley Wenceslas Ministries Faith TV. The pastor was drinking Krug, with the bottle in an ice bucket on the table, and Pope was sipping a single malt. The remains of their hamburger dinner lay on the dining table.

The video, with soul music playing over, showed Wenceslas, his prematurely greying hair beautifully coiffed, elegantly attired in a black, mandarin-style Armani suit, with a black shirt and white dog collar. He was holding a microphone and pacing around in front of the seventeen-hundred-strong congregation that packed his Leeds church. It was intercut with carefully selected tight close-ups of people there, and relayed on huge screens behind him. Faces of people of all races, ages and genders, either singing hymns, praying or listening with rapt expressions.

'And the Lord saith thou shalt not take the name of the Lord thy God in vain. And the Lord saith, love money, yes, he does! Because One Timothy Six, verse ten, tells us that the love of money is the root of all evil, but – listen good! *If the Lord's money is sowed back into the Lord's ministry, our Lord, being no man's debtor, has promised us in the Holy Gospel of Mark, chapter 10, verse 30, that he will give us one hundred times more than the amount we put in the offering plate!'*

The pastor continued to pace around in silence, allowing time for his worshippers to absorb this very important fact. Then he continued. 'Marriage is ordained by God and it allows a holy sexual union between just a man and his wife. Any other sexual union thy God saith is an abomination.'

He paced around again in silence, turned away, then turned back to face, challenge and exhort everyone in the room.

'Join hands!' he said. 'You want it? Take it in Jesus! The glory of the Lord will descend on us tonight in waves. Take it, take it.' He began singing, 'Hallelujah! Hallelujah!'

The crowd joined in as one.

'Who wants anointing tonight?' he asked.

A middle-aged man in a blue suit stepped forward.

Two of Wenceslas's minders moved discreetly forward, also. One positioned himself behind the man.

'Your name is?' the pastor asked him.

'Brian.'

'Are you ready to embrace Jesus tonight, Brian?'

The man nodded in supplication.

Moving his hands round Brian's bowed head, Wenceslas said, 'Brian, what God will do with you now will stay with you for the rest of your life. Oh, Jesus all-glorious, prepare in us your temple!' He tapped the man on each of his shoulders, and he bowed even further forward. 'What the Lord is telling me now is precious, totally precious, Brian! Put your faith in the Holy Ghost, He is with us all tonight.'

Wenceslas turned round to face the altar, which was covered in huge floral displays and crystals, and illuminated in shades of fluorescent blues and greens. To one side sat a fifteen-piece orchestra. He was snapping his fingers. 'Jesus, all-glorious, create in us your temple!'

He turned back to the man and tapped him again on his shoulders. 'Are you ready to receive him, Brian? What the Lord is telling me is so precious.' He stifled a sob. 'So precious. Totally precious!'

With his hands clasped together, the man tumbled onto the floor and lay on one side, motionless.

'What God is doing with him now is completely precious!' Wenceslas continued, his voice in a high pitch of emotion. He paced around, wiping tears from his eyes with the back of his hand and sniffing. He pulled out his handkerchief and wiped his eyes, sniffing again, and addressed the congregation. 'Lift your hands and pray, please. Come on! Sometimes we plan things but God changes it. All of you lift your hands and pray to the Holy Ghost, God is not done yet. God has saved Brian here tonight, but can He save all of you? Only those of you who want to be saved. Those who do, God and Jesus and the Holy Ghost ask that you step forward but first hear me. Hear what is happening. The Great Beast – the Antichrist – may already be among us, masquerading as it says in the Bible as our saviour. I have to fight him, for Brian, for all of you, for all of mankind. Who among you will help me expose this Beast?'

He jabbed a finger at random members of the audience, to rapturous cries of 'Me! Me! Me!'

'Matthew 24, verse 24, tells us, "For false Christs and false prophets will arise and perform great signs and wonders, so as to lead astray, if possible, even the elect."' He opened his arms wide. 'That's you all here. The *elect*. But I know I can trust you because you are the Lord's Soldiers! When you go home tonight, mail me a handkerchief and a cheque for twenty-five pounds and I'll pray over it and send it back to you, and you keep that with you always, it will be your soldier's shield. And don't forget my special "Pay for a Prayer" service. Every penny we raise goes towards keeping this ministry going. Always remember, by sowing seeds into the ministry you will reap the harvest of God's blessing.'

On a wide screen behind him flashed the message, along with a phone number: PAY FOR A PRAYER. ALL MAJOR CREDIT CARDS ACCEPTED.

'And now let us pray to our Lord and protector!'

As the video ended, Pope looked at his boss. 'Good performance – what do you think?'

'It's fine,' Wenceslas said, still angry at the man over the ridiculous cup and tooth he had presented to him this morning. 'You know what I really think?'

'I'm all ears, O Great Master.'

'I think I deserve to unwind with some pretty company tonight.'

'Well, in that case, it seems like Divine Providence! I have two very lovely young ladies currently sequestered in a room two floors above us.'

For the first time today, Pastor Wesley Wenceslas smiled. Then, with a frown of caution, he said, 'And you are confident they do not know who I am?'

'Absolutely they know who you are. Your name is Maurice Winters and you are a very successful London property developer, up here in Leeds to look at a development opportunity.'

'Praise the Lord! I think you may be redeeming yourself, Smilealot!'

'You're a very naughty boy,' Pope retorted, wheeling out one of the few Biblical quotes he knew by heart, which he liked to use occasionally to taunt his boss. 'Revelation. "Then one of the seven angels came and said to me, 'Come,

I will show you the judgement of the great prostitute who is seated on many waters, with whom the kings of the earth have committed sexual immorality, and with the wine of whose sexual immorality the dwellers on earth have become drunk.""'

'Up yours.'

'That's exactly what I'm hoping will happen tonight.' Pope smiled and rolled his eyes, dreamily. 'Each to his own.'

76

The Ducati's engine burbled on tickover as the fatigued rider leaned across and pressed the button on the panel beside the tall white gates of the house on Richmond Hill, in south-west London. He was conscious of the camera pointing at him, and kept his visor lowered.

'Hello?' a female voice said.

'Delivery,' he said, masking his American accent as best he could, the helmet helping to muffle his voice.

The gates swung open. Gravel. Big Tony hated gravel. The sight of it added to his filthy mood. Stuck two hours on the M40, thanks to an idiot overturning a caravan and the police totally closing the road. He rode slowly up the drive, keeping his legs out wide, ready to dig in his boots if the machine tried to get away from him. As he approached the large, modern red-brick mansion, floodlights came on.

Dismounting outside the front door, he switched off the engine, kicked down the stand and propped the bike carefully, making sure it was secure before stepping away. He took care of his machines. Checking that the Monaco licence plate was still fully covered by the false English one, he walked up the imposing steps to the entrance porch and rang the front doorbell.

Another security-light beam shone at him.

Inside he heard ferocious barking. Then a redhead in

her early forties, in a tracksuit and trainers, opened the door and peered at him. 'You have a delivery?' she asked in what sounded to him like a posh English voice. The barking continued somewhere behind her.

'For Mr Brown. I have a collection to make first,' Big Tony replied.

'I think my husband was expecting you quite a bit earlier.'

'Is that so? Maybe he should have fixed the traffic for me.'

'He's just on a conference call – can I sign for the delivery? What is it you are here to collect?'

'I need to see your husband, but I don't wait for people on phones, lady,' he said, letting his American accent slip out. 'Guess what I have for him isn't important enough.'

He headed back down the steps. At the bottom he turned round and called out to her, 'Tell Mr Brown that Big Tony swung by – he knows how to get in touch with me.'

'Wait!' she called out. 'He's just coming – Mr Brown, did you say? I think you have the wrong –'

Big Tony saw the tall, gangly man he knew as Mr Brown, in suit trousers, red braces over an open-neck business shirt, red-framed glasses and monogrammed slippers, hurry out of the door.

'Tony, hi! Sorry to keep you! You had a bad journey?'

Turning his back on him, Big Tony swung a leg over the saddle. The man came running up to him. 'You have it – the memory stick?'

'Yeah. Thought you might want it, went to a bit of trouble for you, but you don't seem to want it that urgently. Maybe I'll take it away, charge you storage, you can let me know when you want to come and collect it.'

'No, please, we really need this.'

'Maybe I should put the price up some more then?'

'I have the money for you. I got it out of the safe, it's in my study. Just wait one minute.'

'I told the lady I don't wait ever, for anyone. I'll give you one minute, exactly.' He peeled the cuff of his glove back to check his watch.

The man ran back up the steps and went sprawling. Big Tony smiled. The man's fancy glasses had come off. As he stood up, pulling them back on, the motorcyclist could see blood running down the side of the man's cheek. He didn't like Mr Brown, he really didn't like him at all. He'd been around plenty of evil people in his life – people as evil as they get, like himself. And this man, limping away down the hallway of his house now, was like he had been marinated in evil, like he had let it seep into every pore of his skin.

Big Tony checked his watch. Fifty-five seconds gone. Fifty-eight. Sixty.

He pressed the starter button, rolled the bike forward off its stand, engaged first gear and, in a hail of gravel, the rear of the bike slewing wildly, accelerated hard down towards the still-open gates.

77

Tuesday, 14 March

Ross was tired, hungry and very shaken as he drove south on the M40 motorway, in darkness and rain that was still falling heavily, and a new hazard that was slowing his journey even more than the traffic – steadily thickening fog. He was playing some of his favourite Glen Campbell tracks on the music system to cheer himself up. At the moment, it was 'Rhinestone Cowboy'.

'Now I really don't mind the rain . . . And a smile can hide all the pain . . .'

Sorry, Glen, he thought. I am minding the rain and I ain't smiling.

And his wife wasn't returning his calls. He'd left two voicemails and sent a text.

He overtook a lorry, the spray momentarily blinding him, then he was past and the wipers cleared the screen enough so he could see the tail lights some distance in front of him.

As he drove, keeping a safe distance from the car in front, he was thinking constantly about the events of the past few hours.

The receptionist had called the police as well as an ambulance because of the strange and suspicious way the previous client had rushed out. Ross had waited, then accompanied her and the two paramedics upstairs. He'd watched from the doorway as they attempted CPR, while the woman stood beside them, distraught and sobbing her heart out.

During all the distraction, Ross had taken the opportunity to slip, unnoticed, behind the desk and read the names on the files piled on it. He saw his own name almost immediately, on a green folder. Making sure no one was looking at him, he flipped it open. It was empty.

After about ten minutes the paramedics stopped their attempts, finally declaring the solicitor dead. There were no apparent marks on the man's body and their initial conclusion was he had suffered either a massive heart attack or stroke.

Despite the apparent natural causes, the previous client aroused the police's suspicion – as he did Ross's, although he'd not said anything about that. Had the solicitor died whilst the client in motorcycling leathers had been in there? If so, why had he not immediately rushed and told the receptionist? And there was a mystery over the man's identity.

He had booked his appointment with the solicitor under the name Terence Dunn, as a new client purportedly seeking legal advice over a disputed legacy. A swift check by the police had revealed the number was a pay-as-you-go phone. There was no answer when they rang it.

Given he had seen the man leave and found the solicitor dead, Ross had agreed to accompany the two detectives to the police station to give a witness statement.

He had been unsure how much he would tell them, but then, sitting in the waiting area, a man in his late thirties, smartly dressed, had walked across to him. 'Nice to meet you again, Mr Hunter. DCI Martin Starr from Birmingham Major Crime Unit. Looks like you're making a bit of a habit of this, arriving at meetings with dead people.'

The DCI was at pains to reassure him he was not under arrest, nor a suspect, he just wanted Ross to tell him everything he could remember. He was joined by a female detective constable, Maria Stevens, who clearly thought differently and treated him more like a suspect than a witness.

The first question Starr asked him was whether he had seen anyone actually leave Robert Anholt-Sperry's office. He'd replied he had not, but a motorcyclist, whom he had assumed was a courier, had rudely barged past him as he arrived at the building – and fitted the description of the solicitor's previous client given by the receptionist. Ross was not able to give any description, because the motorcyclist's dark visor had been down, but he – or it could have been a she – had been holding a small briefcase, and there had been a Ducati motorcycle parked outside the building. He told the two detectives he'd noticed it because he had always fancied owning one.

Starr's questioning became awkward when he asked how much he knew of the connection between the dead solicitor and Cook.

From his journalism training, Ross knew there were strict rules of client confidentiality around solicitors, and decided to use that if need be.

'So, there was no connection between Dr Cook's claims of proof of God and your visit to Mr Anholt-Sperry?' Maria Stevens had quizzed.

'I had decided to meet Mr Anholt-Sperry to try to find out more about his deceased client, for a piece I'm working on for the *Sunday Times*,' Ross had replied, evasively.

He signed a brief statement and agreed, if required, to make a fuller statement. Finally he had left for the long drive back to Brighton, shortly before 8 p.m.

Was the old solicitor's death connected to all that was going on? Or just coincidence? Anholt-Sperry was elderly and overweight with a heart problem; and he hadn't looked a healthy specimen when he had last seen him. It could have been the stress.

Or?

He'd covered a news story some years back about a solicitor who had been killed by a disgruntled client. Perhaps Robert Anholt-Sperry had angered someone in the past.

But he doubted that. He was certain that the deaths of Cook and Anholt-Sperry were connected. Yet there were no apparent injuries, certainly none visible, on the solicitor.

He thought about the empty file with his name on, sitting on the desk. Had the motorcyclist taken the contents? Or had the solicitor been about to put something inside it?

The crucial third set of compass coordinates?

Remembering Imogen had said she would be home late – that she was meeting a friend – he tried calling her again now, dialling her number on his hands-free. To his relief, this time she answered almost instantly.

'Hi!' he said. 'I've been so worried – I phoned and texted you. Are you OK?'

She sounded shaken to the core. 'No, Ross,' she said, breaking into a hysterical shout. 'I've just got home and I am very not OK. I AM NOT AT ALL OK.'

78

Tuesday, 14 March

Boris seemed to be getting the hang of things, Ainsley Bloor thought, as he watched the monkey hammering away at the keyboard. He was hitting the keys 'a' and 'i' with increasing regularity, greedily grabbing the peanut, grape or banana treat that was delivered down the chute each time. And from the pages of printout spewing from the printer, Boris seemed to have figured that typing the entire word, 'the', delivered an extra special treat of a whole apple, orange or banana.

None of the other five monkeys had yet figured out any of it. And the complete works of Shakespeare were a long sodding way off.

Bloor had been working on a new algorithm to reward Boris when he typed a longer word, but so far, the dumb creature hadn't responded. He just kept hammering out those single 'a' and 'i' letters, and the occasional 'the'.

But at this moment, shivering from the damp cold, the experiment was the least of Bloor's problems. He yawned, tired after a long and frustrating day, looking forward to going indoors and pouring himself a stiff drink. His pilot had advised him that the fog was too thick to risk flying home, so he'd travelled down by car, his chauffeur driving at a ridiculously slow speed in the poor visibility. It was gone 8.30, and early tomorrow morning he had a Radio 4

Today interview on his company's work in the field of gene therapies to prepare for, and a board meeting in London later.

Adding to his anger was the fact that the phone call he had been awaiting hadn't come. Was everyone in his organization as incompetent as his sodding monkeys?

'Come on, Boris, you can do it!' he shouted.

The monkey turned for an instant in his direction, then as if hearing his master, tapped the keyboard again. A grape came down the chute.

Another letter 'i'.

'You cretin!' his master yelled at him – and at all six of the monkeys. 'You don't know how good you have it, you dumb dwarf apes!'

As he turned away in anger, and began striding across the wet grass towards the house, which lay some distance beyond the wall of fog, his phone rang. His display showed the caller's name.

'Yes, Julius?' he answered. 'You've got it?'

'Houston, we have a problem,' Helmsley said.

79

It was 11.15 p.m. when Ross, barely able to keep his eyes open, pulled up alongside Imogen's car outside their house. Despite his exhaustion, it was second nature now to check carefully all around before getting out of the Audi. The street was deserted. He'd seen no sign of anyone following him throughout the journey.

Lights were on in the house. Too many. All of them, blazing through the windows of every room, which was odd, he thought, apprehensively, as he pressed the key fob to lock the Audi's doors. He looked up at the three CCTV cameras just below the eaves, which had been fixed by their electrician. And frowned, a sick feeling in the pit of his stomach.

The lens of each was shattered.

The front door opened before he reached it, and Imogen was standing there, in dungarees and a white T-shirt, hair ragged, her complexion deathly white, her face tear-stained.

'Hi!' he said, striding towards her with his arms open, but she shrank back as he reached her.

'You'd better take a look at what's happened to your home, Ross. Our home. What *was* our home.' She was shaking.

He entered, and stopped in his tracks. Spray-painted in

black on the hall wall were two inverted crucifixes. Across one of the crosses was scrawled, in blood red, ROSS HUNTER, FRIEND OF THE ANTICHRIST, and across the other, IMOGEN HUNTER, EXPECTENT MOTHER OF THE ANTI-CHRIST.

His blood ran cold.

All the drawers of the hall table had been pulled out and lay on the floor, the contents scattered around.

'It's not just here, Ross, it's everywhere. This is what I came home to.'

He went through into the kitchen. Monty, who would normally have come running over to him, sat cowering in his basket.

STOOGES OF THE DEVIL was scrawled across one wall, in large writing. Everything in here had been pulled out of the drawers and taken off the shelves and just strewn about.

He went back into the hall and looked up the stairs and saw more writing.

AND BEHOLD, IN THIS HORN WERE EYES LIKE THE EYES OF A MAN, AND A MOUTH SPEAKING GREAT THINGS.

He tried the integral door to the garage and it opened. He switched on the garage light. His tools and golf clubs lay scattered around, and his road bike lay wrecked on the floor, its cross-bar hacked open.

He ran back inside and up to the landing. There was more religious scrawl on the walls. And in their bedroom across the wall to the left of their bed, in large black writing:

LET HIM THAT HATH UNDERSTANDING COUNT THE NUMBER OF THE BEAST . . .

He went into his office. Every wall there was covered in writing, too. All his filing cabinet drawers were opened and his papers strewn everywhere. His computer backup, he saw, was no longer on his desk.

If there was one thing he could salvage from this horror, he thought, one small speck of relief, it was that he had taken his laptop with him in the car. Otherwise, for sure, that would be gone, too.

He turned to Imogen who was standing behind him in the doorway. 'Seen enough?' she said.

'How did they get in – did they break a window?'

'Does it matter?'

'Does it matter?' he echoed. 'Yes, I want to make sure the house is secure, in case they decide to come back. Did you call the police?'

'Of course I called the police. They came within minutes. They pointed out that our wonderful CCTV cameras are all broken. One of them said it looked like they'd been shot out with an air rifle. There are detectives or CSIs or whatever coming round to take fingerprints. They said they'd try to get someone over tonight, or else it would be in the morning.'

'Babes.' He tried to hug her but she shrank away from him.

'I've phoned Virginia,' she said. 'I'm going to stay with her and Ben tonight. You can come too, if you want.'

Her sister and her brother-in-law lived with their three children in a small village about fifteen miles north of Patcham.

'What about Monty? Ben's allergic to all dogs, isn't he?'

'I don't care about the dog. Our baby's what matters to me at this moment. If I have to commute, I'll do that. I'm not staying here another night until –'

'Until?'

'Until you forget all of this. I can't believe you turned down that job to interview the Euro MPs in Strasbourg, which would have paid you three thousand. We need the money – why do we have to go through this hell? Let's sell whatever you have to the Vatican if they're serious. Maybe we'll get enough money to pay off the mortgage.'

'I can't do that. Not after –'

'After what, Ross? After we're both dead? Is this crazy story worth risking everything you – we – have?'

'Crazy story? You're a *believer*. You're a Christian. What's crazy about this story?'

She threw her arms open, pointing at the writing on the wall. 'This is not crazy? I don't need proof, I don't need absolute proof, I'm a believer, yes, that's enough for me. The world's in a fragile enough state as it is without you stirring up a religious storm – thanks to the ramblings of an elderly loony.'

Ross stood still, staring at her. 'If Cook was such a *loony* how come the Vatican – what was the guy who came to see you called – Spinoni –?'

'Silvestri. Monsignor Giuseppe Silvestri.'

'How come he was prepared to offer us money?'

'Only if it's *real*, Ross.'

'Fine, that's just what I'm trying to do, find out if it is real.'

She pointed at the walls again. 'Isn't this real enough? Weren't the messages I had on my computer screen real enough? Someone's sending some pretty clear signals they don't like what you're doing, Ross.'

The image of Robert Anholt-Sperry at his desk came flooding back, shaking him to the core.

Then the rheumy, pleading eyes of Harry Cook.

You and I have to save the world.

He looked at his wife. And at the small bulge in her midriff. Their child.

Could he argue with what she said?

He stared up at all the crazy shit scrawled around the walls of his home, and anger rose inside him. He thought about the helicopter in Egypt. Harry Cook's tortured body. The dead solicitor.

The world that awaited his unborn child.

His dead brother.

The bastards who had kicked him in the face as he'd emerged from Chalice Well.

Who could he trust? Stuart Ivens, from MI5?

Or the man Imogen had told him about earlier, Monsignor Giuseppe Silvestri, claiming to represent the Vatican?

Could he just drop this story, walk away from it and go back to writing about politics, war and climate change? Did any of that matter in the bigger picture he potentially had?

Possibly the biggest story ever?

Big enough to try to kill him, to murder Dr Cook and perhaps his solicitor in Birmingham? Had the man in motorcycling leathers taken the final piece of the puzzle? The one that Anholt-Sperry was planning to hand him?

He found it hard to look back at Imogen. To tell her what he had to. He knew it sounded absurd to anyone. Except the evidence that it might not be absurd was written all over the walls of their house, their home, their sanctuary.

They'd been invaded.

By whom?

Religiously motivated fanatics? Was he going to permit himself to be cowed by them? Maybe that was just what they had wanted. For him to be cowed. To walk away. But he didn't walk away, could never walk away, from anything.

He turned to face his wife. 'Imo, I understand, I get how you are feeling.'

'You do? Great. Then we leave now. I'm already packed. Go and throw some stuff in a bag, I'll wait.'

'And put Virginia and her family in danger, too? And what would we do with Monty?'

'Put him in kennels.'

'Babes, look –'

'Look *what*?'

'I need you.'

'You do? I don't feel I know you any more, Ross. You're a man on a mission. And it's not a mission I want to be on any more. You're on your own now.'

80

Wednesday, 15 March

Ross woke in the morning, tired, his head muzzy and filled with a sense of dread. He lay still for some moments before opening his eyes and reaching out to touch Imogen, but all his hand felt was a cold pillow.

She really had gone.

He felt hollow.

It was a bright, sunny morning. Full daylight was streaming in through the curtains. He heard the voices of workmen across the street.

It hadn't all been a bad dream. The writing was there on the wall beside the bed.

LET HIM THAT HATH UNDERSTANDING COUNT THE NUMBER OF THE BEAST . . .

Who had done it? The same creep who had sent the emails?

But this was more than the work of a solitary person. There were at least two and possibly three different hand-writing styles across all the walls. How had they got in without triggering the alarm or being captured on CCTV? Had they sat in a vehicle outside and calmly and silently shot out the CCTV cameras before disabling the alarm?

Who knew about what he was doing?

How many people might Cook have contacted before approaching him? Clearly people at Chalice Well – and in turn Kerr Kluge had learned about it. Now MI5 knew and apparently the Vatican. Could last night's intrusion be the work of KK? Trying to scare him? Or a gazillionaire evangelist like Wesley Wenceslas? Some other fanatic religious sect?

He doubted it was the same people who had tried to kill him in Egypt. Who'd tracked him to the cave then tried to take the tooth. It was likely to be those people who had tortured Cook, too. This trashing of the house was an altogether different style. It smacked of someone trying to put the frighteners on them for a reason.

To make him sell the information?

Someone like Monsignor Giuseppe Silvestri?

He rolled over and to his shock the clock radio showed 7.20 a.m.

Normally, Radio 4 woke him sharp at 6.30 a.m.

Shit.

The radio was on, and must have come on nearly an hour ago. He'd slept through it. A Radio 4 presenter was interviewing an arrogant-sounding scientist.

'We have identified the genes responsible for empathy,' the scientist said. 'We believe that in a short while – within many people's lifetimes – parents will be able to choose the levels of empathy of their child. Do you want a sweet, gentle little boy? But he could be trodden on later in life. Do you want a strong, tough little chap? But he could end up being the school bully – and perhaps a sociopath.'

'And where does God fit in with all this?' the presenter asked.

'Well, that depends on which side of the faith fence you are sitting,' the scientist continued, smoothly. 'Intelligent Design or Natural Selection.'

'So, on which side are you sitting?'

'Ask me that question in a few months' time and I might have an answer for you.'

'Really? Can you expand?'

'Not now.' The aloofness, the arrogance in his voice was palpable.

'Well, you are leaving me – and many listeners, I'm sure – intrigued. Your company is today announcing a major breakthrough in gene therapy treatments. Can you explain what this will mean?'

'Certainly. The breakthrough in gene therapy treatments that Kerr Kluge is announcing is a game-changer for medicine.'

Ross sat bolt upright, and increased the volume. *Kerr Kluge*. He could hardly believe his ears.

'It will mean two things, John,' the man answered calmly and confidently. 'The first is that within ten years we will be able to cure many of the world's biggest killer diseases. I'm not talking about extending life expectancy of, say, cancer victims, through pharmaceuticals. We're looking at total cures through changes in DNA structures of individuals.'

'Speaking cynically, Dr Bloor, you are running a company dependent on the global sales of pharmaceuticals. The medical conditions that are the most profitable for a company like yours, I believe, are the chronic ones, where people are medication-dependent for years or decades. Wouldn't you be shooting yourself in the foot to offer an instant cure for these?'

'Quite the reverse. And the second thing, John, is how we will be creating a massive paradigm shift in the way we all regard human existence. For the first time in the history of the human race, thanks to the work we are doing at Kerr Kluge, humans will be freeing themselves of all kinds of the tyranny that has dominated human existence since intelligent life, as we know it, began. Through identifying the ageing genes and reversing them we will no longer have to suffer the indignities of old age or of incapacitating ailments. We will be liberating everyone from the tyranny of Mother Nature. We believe that Kerr Kluge will be the forerunner of a whole new age of man.'

'For those who can afford to pay?'

'The choice will be there for everyone,' Bloor answered glibly.

'Everyone who can afford to pay? Isn't this going to create a two-tiered world – for the haves and have-nots? Are you not in danger of creating a genetic underclass? I'm afraid we're running out of time. Can you give us a very quick response?'

'On the contrary, John, to what you are saying, we will be offering a kind of equality the world has never seen before.'

'Ainsley Bloor, Chief Executive Officer of Kerr Kluge, we'll have to leave it there. Thank you for talking to us.'

'Thank you, John.'

'And now here's Rick Anderson with the latest sports news and racing tips.'

Ross turned down the volume.

Ainsley Bloor. The CEO. The man running the company which may have been behind trying to kill him in Egypt. For what reason?

It was making more sense now. He could more clearly see the value of what he had, to Bloor and his company. How much did Sally Hughes's uncle, Julius Helmsley, know about this?

He could imagine the cynical marketing campaign.

Brought to you by the custodians of Jesus Christ's DNA!

He stared at the graffiti on the walls of the bedroom. It

was obviously an attempt to frighten him off. It had certainly succeeded in frightening Imogen.

Was he being stupid not to be frightened off himself?

In truth, he was concerned. Equally, he was angry and determined not to be cowed. He'd been threatened before in the course of his investigative work. A few years ago, he'd door-stepped the owner of a fraudulent Spanish timeshare scheme at his Essex mansion. The man had punched him in the face, giving him a black eye, and set two Rottweilers on him, one of which had bitten a chunk out of his leg, drawing blood, which required him to have stitches and a tetanus jab. Another time, investigating a child-sex ring involving Romanian street kids being made to work in a Bedford nightclub, he'd been threatened with a handgun, beaten up by two henchmen and thrown out through a back door into a rear yard. That had cost him two broken ribs and fifteen hundred pounds in dental repair work.

But maybe his brief time in Afghanistan had hardened him to fear.

Instead of scaring him away, such reactions just made him even more determined.

And at this moment, that determination was stronger than ever. Whatever the cost.

There was a new text on his Apple Watch. It was from Imogen.

> Miss you. Come to your senses and join me. I love you. XX

Picking up his phone, which was easier to reply from, he messaged her back.

> Love you, but I have to deal with this. X

He went downstairs, his anger at KK intensified by the smug arrogance of its CEO's voice just now. As he entered the kitchen, Monty climbed out of his basket and walked slowly, almost hesitantly, towards him, his tail down. The dog's behaviour was strange, totally uncharacteristic. Normally in the morning Monty would come flying to him, tail wagging and with a big, soppy grin.

He knelt and put his arms round his neck. 'What happened, boy? Who did you see last night? Who came here? How did they get in? You didn't let them in, right? You didn't open the door for them?'

Where was the police patrol Tingley had arranged, he wondered?

The creature was shaking.

'Don't worry, I'm not putting you into kennels. I'll take care of you, we'll get through this together. Right?' He pressed his face close and felt the dog's damp nose against his cheek.

What had the bastards done to Monty that he was still so freaked out? Had they given him something doped or poisoned? Not that they would have needed to, he was a total softie and would have welcomed any intruder as a long-lost friend.

'I love you, Monty.' He pressed his face close to the dog's again. 'I really love you.' He smelled his warm fur. 'Calm down, it's OK. It's OK. It's all OK.'

He wished he could believe it.

81

Ross stood in the shower, turning the heat up as much as he could bear. Despite his exhaustion, he was beginning to think with more clarity.

He'd been all around the house looking for signs of where the intruders had broken in, but could find nothing. No broken windows, no forced door frames. He had checked underneath a flowerpot in the toolshed in the back garden, where they kept a spare key hidden, and that was undisturbed, the key still there. Then he had gone around again photographing every graffitied wall.

A bunch of weirdo fanatics would have probably just smashed their way in. The fact that the entry was skilful indicated even more to him that this was professional. The work of people with resources behind them.

The whole place was going to have to be redecorated, every room, and that would run to several thousand pounds. Plus anything that he and Imogen discovered had been stolen, in addition to his computer backup. Hopefully the insurance would cover it.

He stepped out of the shower and began to dry himself. The doorbell rang and Monty barked.

Wrapping the towel round his midriff, he hurried downstairs as the bell rang again, and across the hall to the front door. He peered through the spyhole and saw a man standing there, with a van parked behind him. He checked the safety chain was in position and pulled the door open a few inches.

'Delivery,' the man said in an Eastern European accent, holding up a cardboard box with AMAZON stencilled all over it. It looked like a book – he had several orders with them for a variety of religious books he wanted to read.

He slipped the catch, took the package, signed electronic-ally then closed the door. Stroking the dog with one hand, he watched through the spyhole again as the man walked back to his van and drove off. Then he carried the box through into the kitchen and put it on the table. It felt quite light, almost too light to contain a book, unless it was a very slim volume. He shook it and something inside rattled. And as he looked at the parcel more closely he recognized that this wasn't the normal, neat Amazon package. There was black gaffer tape round it, as if it was old wrapping being reused.

Hesitating, he stared at it uncomfortably. Could it be a bomb?

He turned it over, examining it carefully for any clue as to the sender. But there was nothing. Should he leave it, call the police? Let them come and make their own decision about it?

Maybe he was being paranoid.

He took a knife from a drawer and carefully slit through the black tape, then prised the two halves of cardboard apart, very slowly. Stupid, he knew, he should call the police and ask them to deal with it. Yet he was almost at the point of not caring. He tore the packaging open, and stared at the object it contained.

A small plastic crucifix. With an envelope pinned to Jesus's heart by a broken-off cocktail stick that resembled a dagger.

He quickly took a picture on his phone, pulled the dagger out and opened the envelope. Inside was a typed note: *For the wrath of God is revealed from Heaven against all ungodliness and unrighteousness of men, who hold the truth in unrighteousness. Romans 1:18.*

Turning the note over, he saw typed on the reverse: *I did not appreciate your post on Twitter. You are in dangerous, blasphemous waters, my friend. I suggest you return to your day job.*

Ross had long been immune to nasty tweets and had been trolled several times in the past over controversial pieces he had written. But this note, particularly, disturbed him and he was glad Imogen wasn't here to see it. He put it all inside the Amazon packaging, carried it up to his office and slid it into a drawer in his desk. It might be something to show the police or just to keep as evidence in case . . .

Back in the bathroom he wetted his face, patted gel onto his stubble and began to shave, thinking about what to do next. He had to assume that the coordinates Robert Anholt-Sperry had been going to hand to him were now in someone else's hands.

He had a pretty good idea whose. Kerr Kluge's.

The crucial third set of coordinates that Cook had implied were related to the Second Coming.

But without the DNA results, were they of any real value to the company? Perhaps there was a negotiation to be had? Playing off MI5, the Vatican representative, Monsignor Giuseppe Silvestri, and Kerr Kluge?

How dangerous would that be? The Vatican had a reputation for not taking prisoners. Reforming popes were short-lived. Roberto Calvi, known as God's banker, was found in 1982 hanging from Blackfriars Bridge in London.

His death elegantly removed the prospect of an unpleasant scandal for the Vatican Bank.

Was Imogen right when she told him that he was punching well above his weight? Was there any way out, other than to keep going forward?

He dressed, then went up to his office and picked up the black leather wallet Imogen had given him two Christmases ago. He ran his finger along the dark-brown lining and felt the reassuring crinkle of the piece of paper he had put inside, along with the minute, sealed test tube, and then glued the lining back.

It contained, reduced to little bigger than a postage stamp, details of the standard DNA, mitochondrial and Y-STR that Jolene Thomas at ATGC Forensics had obtained from the cup and the tooth, along with a tiny amount, as a backup, of the remaining fluid from the crushed tooth that Jolene had returned to him, and which he had subsequently given to Uncle Angus for safekeeping.

The DNA of Jesus Christ?

Could he ever find out without the missing third set of coordinates?

Would anyone let him live long enough?

He called the electrician's mobile and the man answered almost immediately. Ross gave him a quick summary of the break-in and vandalism, and asked him if he had any time today, or in the next couple of days, to get the CCTV camera lenses repaired or the cameras replaced. The electrician said he would take a look at them sometime today, and sort them first thing tomorrow morning.

He went downstairs, fed Monty, made himself a strong coffee, then put a bowl of porridge in the microwave. Whilst it was cooking, he sliced an apple and put a Berocca tablet into a glass of water – Imogen had recently convinced him to take one daily. It was a fine, sunny day. He took his drinks out onto the patio, then went to the front door and picked up the bunch of newspapers lying on the mat and carried them outside, too, glancing at a newspaper headline:

MOTHER MURDERED BABY

His phone rang. The display showed a number he didn't recognize.

'Ross Hunter,' he answered, guardedly.

'Mr Hunter, my name is Quentin Grieg, and I do apologize for the intrusion of this phone call. I'm calling on behalf of the Archbishop of Canterbury. Word has reached our team of a story you are working on.' The man sounded immensely courteous and friendly.

'Can you give me a number and I'll call you straight back?'

After a moment's hesitation, Grieg gave it to him and Ross wrote it down. He called him straight back on his burner phone. 'What story is that?' Ross asked. 'I'm actually working on a number of stories at the moment.'

'This one is of a religious nature, if we are correct?'

'Yes,' Ross replied. 'Correct.'

'The Archbishop is intrigued. We only have very scant information at this stage, but he wonders if you would be prepared to spare some of your precious time to discuss it with him?'

Ross, astonished to get this call, thought quickly. This was a golden opportunity. The Archbishop of Canterbury, the Head of the Anglican Church in the UK, wanted to meet him. Whichever way this story ended up, to be able to put in one or two quotes from the Archbishop would give it enormous credibility.

'Yes, I'd be very happy to meet him.'

'I have a couple of dates when he will be at Lambeth Palace in London, with some availability in his diary. But I'm instructed to tell you that if these are not convenient for you, the Archbishop is prepared to cancel appointments in order to meet.'

Ross felt a strange tingling inside him. The Archbishop of Canterbury was prepared to cancel appointments to meet *him*? He could scarcely believe what he was hearing. Could it be a hoax of some kind? Or was there some agenda going on? Had Benedict Carmichael alerted the Archbishop?

'He could see you at 3.30 p.m. this afternoon or at 11 a.m. tomorrow.'

'I could make this afternoon,' Ross said.

Grieg gave him directions and told him a car-parking space would be reserved for him, if he required one.

Ending the call, he heard the microwave ping.

He went inside and removed the bowl of porridge. He carried his breakfast back out, sat down, and began flipping through the pages of the *Argus*.

And stopped, drawn out of curiosity to one headline a few pages in.

DIVORCED BECAUSE HE PRESSED
TOO HARD

He read the story. It was an accountant who had been married for twenty years, until his wife had suspicions he was being unfaithful. For some while she had been unable to get any concrete evidence. Then she had seen indentations on a notepad, from which the previous page had been removed.

Unable to decipher them, she remembered a programme she had seen on television about a facility at a forensics laboratory the police used, where there was a piece of kit, called ESDA, that could recover handwriting from even the faintest of impressions left on a pad.

The firm was ATGC Forensics.

Suddenly, he had a light-bulb moment. Thinking back to when Dr Cook had visited him.

Thinking about the manuscript that he had left with him.

I have of course inked those compass coordinates out, Mr Hunter, in case this fell into the wrong hands.

He grabbed his phone.

Monty trotted up to him with his lead in his mouth.

Ross put down the phone and patted him. 'I'm sorry, fellow, no big walk yesterday and none so far this morning. I'll make it up to you later when I'm back, I promise. We'll go for a long walk this evening, OK?'

The dog gave him a look that said it wasn't really OK at all.

Then the doorbell rang. He hurried in, cautiously peered through the spyhole and saw a young man holding a bag. It was a Crime Scene Investigator, who introduced himself as Alex Call.

For the next hour, Call dusted for prints around the house. Ross left him to it. When he had finished, the CSI told him that so far there had been no matches to anyone they had on record.

As soon as Call left, Ross grabbed his car keys, went outside, opened the garage door and drove his Audi in, then climbed out and pulled the garage door shut behind him. There was something he wanted to load into the boot of the car that he did not want to risk anyone seeing who might be watching out in the street.

82

Julius Helmsley limped into his CEO's office at a couple of minutes to 10 a.m., holding a bag of croissants in one hand and a stiff brown envelope in the other. 'Good radio interview, Ainsley. Very good,' the Chief Operating Officer said.

'Huh.'

Before sitting down at the meeting table by the window, Helmsley said, 'You're not recording this?'

'I'm not mad, Julius. No. Coffee?'

Helmsley nodded and Bloor poured. 'What have you done to your face?'

Helmsley, embarrassed, touched the sticking plaster across his left cheek. 'I tripped.'

'Tripped? Tripped up? Hurt your leg, cut your face? Good party, was it?'

'Very amusing.'

A launch, with a blue and yellow Battenberg-painted superstructure and the word POLICE stencilled on its hull, cruised along the Thames beneath them.

Bloor slid the cup, followed by a jug of milk, towards Helmsley. 'So, what happened?'

'We've made a mistake, we hired a wild animal who is now holding us over a barrel.'

'Not *we*, Julius. *You*. This man in Monaco?'

He nodded.

'The one who doubled his price on us when you went to see him?'

'Yes.'

'He's the man you recommended.'

'He was recommended to us. Blue-chip credentials. Pretty impressive track record.'

'Yep, well I'm very impressed. So far he's taken us for eight million and now he's going to hold us to ransom.'

'I'll fly to Monaco and sort it with him.'

'Monaco doesn't have an airport,' Bloor said, testily.

'I'll fly to Nice and take the helicopter.'

'No, you won't take the helicopter and you won't fly in luxury. This is your screw-up. You can fly easyJet and take a sodding bus.'

Helmsley grinned, then saw Bloor wasn't joking.

'Do we even know he's actually got it?'

'He's got it, I'm sure of that. The third set of compass coordinates. The ones the Birmingham solicitor, Robert Anholt-Sperry, was due to hand to Ross Hunter yesterday afternoon,' Helmsley said. 'Or rather I should say, the *late* solicitor.'

'Ross Hunter,' Bloor said the name acidly. 'I'm minded of the words of Henry the Second – "Will no one rid me of this turbulent priest?"'

'I believe he actually said *meddlesome*,' Helmsley said. '*Turbulent* is a misquote.'

Bloor gave him a querulous stare. 'I don't think this is the moment for semantics.'

'Sorry, boss.' He poured some milk into his coffee. 'But killing Hunter at this stage wouldn't be smart. I'm pretty certain he holds the key.'

'Do you think he'd do business with us?'

'Hunter?'

'He's struggling financially and has been for a couple of years. Journalism is paying less and less. We know he's got a big mortgage; credit cards close to the limit and a child on the way.'

Helmsley gave him a strange look. 'While we're on quotations, "He who sups with the devil should have a long spoon." Hunter is wily and dangerous – we've already seen that. He has powerful press connections and all our research on him shows he's not a man motivated by money. Several people and organizations who've tried to buy him off in the past have ended up with egg on their faces. One thing we are certain of is that he has, concealed somewhere, part or all of what we believe is Jesus Christ's DNA, and we need that.'

'What about this manuscript he's rumoured to have in his possession – that Cook gave him and we couldn't find in Cook's house?' Bloor reached over and grabbed a croissant from the bag. 'These always remind me of crabs,' he said, tearing off one end and holding it up. 'Like a pincer, don't you think?'

'That's never occurred to me.'

'Do you find a lot of things don't occur to you, Julius?'

'How do you mean?'

'Sometimes I feel you treat everything as a game. We're not playing a game here. If we get what we're after, you realize what it can do for our company, don't you? Jesus Christ's DNA informing our products? You have a handsome shareholding. It's already made you a wealthy man, on paper. But this could take us to a whole new level – it could make you a billionaire, right? So, get real.'

'How are the monkeys?' Helmsley answered, like a petulant child. And then, for a moment, thought his CEO was about to have a heart attack.

Bloor rose from his chair and thumped both fists on the table. 'What have my bloody monkeys got to do with anything?'

Helmsley raised his hands in the air, in a pacifying gesture. 'Just trying to figure out how you square them with this.'

'Square them with what?'

Peering at him through his red-rimmed spectacles, Julius Helmsley said, 'The experiment you're conducting with the monkeys is designed to prove – or at least suggest – how the world might have originated by pure chance rather than by intelligent design. And yet you believe the future growth of our company could be linked to the DNA of the Son of God. A slight contradiction, isn't it?'

'I call it *business*, Julius. There are 2.2 billion Christians in the world. If you were a Christian—'

'I am,' Helmsley interrupted.

'Good. Then maybe you'd like to tell me something. Imagine you are afflicted with an incurable disease. Are you going to go for gene therapy treatment from the company that possesses Jesus's DNA or from another that doesn't?'

'There's no contest, Ainsley.'

'My point exactly. So, let's get real. This third set of co-ordinates must be in that damned manuscript of Dr Cook's as well as on that memory stick.'

'And do we think this journalist has a copy of the compass coordinates? In the manuscript?'

'I don't think he can have, Julius. That's what he went to Birmingham for, yesterday. If he had the coordinates in the manuscript, he wouldn't have needed to go there.'

'OK, so he doesn't have them. Let's assume they're in the pannier of a motorcycle somewhere between here and Monaco – in the hands of a crook of a hitman who doesn't actually realize what he has got. Ross Hunter has been to ATGC Forensics – whatever they've given him, they must have records on file.'

'Could we try hacking or breaking in to them, Julius?'

He shook his head. 'I've looked into it. They're a fortress. One of the main DNA resources for many of the UK's police forces. There's plenty of villains who would dearly love to penetrate them – and it's never happened. We've tested them, and their security is strong – everything is coded and not even their lab staff know the identity of their clients beyond a coded number.'

'There must be someone working there who has access to Hunter's files whom we could bribe – or kidnap?' Bloor said.

'I don't think that's a runner. We're better off to stay cool, get whatever our friend in Monaco has off him, watch Hunter round the clock and see where he leads us. I have that sorted.'

'And just where do you think he is going to lead us?'

Julius Helmsley smiled. 'To the promised land.'

83

Wednesday, 15 March

Shortly after 10 a.m., Ross sat in a small, first-floor meeting room, in his solicitor's modern offices. He was staring out of the window at Brighton's Jubilee Library across the road, a building he was very fond of, sipping a cup of tea the receptionist had brought him and waiting for his document to be brought in, when his phone pinged.

It was a text from Imogen.

> Need to pick up some stuff from the house on my way back from the office. What time u there? Don't want to go alone. X

He replied.

> Dunno – have meeting in London this after-noon. Probably around 6.30 pm. Can call you when I'm on my way, if you like? X

The door opened and his lawyer's legal assistant came in carrying a large box file, which she showed to Ross. 'I think this is the one you mean?'

It was labelled ROSS HUNTER – PRIVATE.

He opened the lid and peered inside. Then he turned to her. 'Yes, this is it, thank you.'

'I'll leave you to it.' Pointing at the phone on the end of the table, she said, 'Just dial 21 when you're ready to go – or if you need anything– and I'll answer.'

'I might want to get something photocopied.'

'No problem at all, just shout.'

As she closed the door he lifted the manuscript out of the box file and placed it on the shiny tabletop. Then as he removed the first of the two elastic bands, it snapped, the rubber perished. He removed the second carefully, then set about the arduous task of going through it, one page at a time, thinking about Cook's words.

I have of course inked those compass coordinates out, Mr Hunter, in case this fell into the wrong hands.

It took him just under an hour to find them, on page 565. He missed them the first time through because the inked sections were so small.

On one line, the name *Chalice Well* was followed by an inch and a half of something inked out with a felt-tip pen. Two lines down, *Egypt, Valley of the Kings*, was followed by a similar deletion. And a further two lines down he saw words that he was looking for.

Second Coming.

Followed by an inch and a half of something again inked out.

Gingerly putting this sheet of paper to one side, he picked up the one directly below, page 566, and raised it to the overhead light. It was faint, but there was very definitely something there, visible across the ink scrawl. The imprint of the writing on the previous page.

The coordinates?

84

Julius Helmsley, still smarting from his CEO's anger, and uncomfortably aware of how he had screwed up big-time, sat in his office, staring at the computer screen. On it was a road map, showing a section of the M25 London orbital road. A small red dot was moving steadily along in the light late-morning traffic. He watched it turning off onto the M3, heading north towards London.

Ross Hunter's Audi.

The journalist who figured he was so smart would not find the tracking device even if he took the car apart. It was concealed inside a brake-light bulb in one of the rear lamp clusters.

Thirty miles away, in his first-floor office in the west wing of Gethsemane Park, Lancelot Pope sipped his herbal tea. He watched the dot moving north along the M3 on his iPhone, from the data fed back to him by the eight-car surveillance crew currently on shift.

He was still furious at the idiots who had failed to box Hunter in on the motorway as he was returning from ATGC with the red-hot goods in his car. But it taught Pope, if he didn't have it already, respect for Ross Hunter's cunning. Like the bloody fox that had managed to break into his fenced-off garden at his weekend cottage in Dorset and kill all the Pochard and Whistler ducks on his pond.

He continued to watch the dot as it travelled towards Kingston.

Heading back to ATGC Forensics, straight from his lawyers in Brighton?

What was going on?

Yesterday Ross Hunter had been to a law firm in Birmingham for the second time. Then in the local news, only as a minor item, had been the sudden, unexplained death of the managing partner, Robert Anholt-Sperry. A suspected heart attack or stroke.

Dr Harry Cook's solicitor.

Thirty minutes later, Pope's assumption proved right. Ross Hunter pulled up in the car park of ATGC Forensics. As he did so, Pope's phone rang.

'Yes?'

'Just to let you know, boss, that the subject has pulled into the car park of ATGC Forensics.'

'I can see that. What's he doing there?'

'He's out of his car. Walking in with an envelope under his arm.'

'Follow him! Find out what the hell is in it.'

85

Ross returned to his car after his brief meeting with Jolene Thomas, by the reception desk of ATGC Forensics. She was going to take the page he had removed from Cook's manuscript, page 566, to the ESDA team. Even just holding it up to the overhead lights in the reception area she could see there were clear indentations from the handwriting on the sheet above. From what limited amount she knew about the ESDA abilities, she was confident of a positive result.

He switched on the engine, then programmed the satnav for the route from where he was, in Kingston, to Lambeth Palace, tapping the postcode in carefully. SE1 7JU.

The journey time read forty-seven minutes.

It was now 1.15 p.m. and his appointment was not until 3.30 p.m. That gave him ample time to grab a bite of lunch en route and to still carry out his plan.

The traffic was much heavier now he was on the outskirts of London. With the satnav giving him an arrival time of 2.21 p.m., he headed west, crossed the winding Thames for the first time, close to Twickenham, again at Richmond and then again at Kew. The phone now gave his arrival time as 2.48. Then switched to 2.37.

Thirty minutes later, heading along Chelsea Embankment, the device told him to turn right onto Vauxhall Bridge.

As he crossed the winding Thames once more, he pulled over. Then he entered a search on the satnav for car parks. There was one directly ahead as he reached the busy Elephant and Castle gyratory. He missed it the first time round, got himself into the correct lane and managed a neat exit into the multistorey on his second circuit, driving up to the fourth floor before the sign showed there were available spaces.

Reversing into one, he waited for the beepers to go off, then drove a couple of feet forward – enough, he estimated, to be able to reach the boot. He switched off, climbed out, walked to the rear of the car and lifted his heavy, folded Brompton bicycle out. He slammed the lid shut and locked the car, lugged the bike out into an open space then swung it open, locking the frame, the front wheels and the saddle into place, and flipped down the left pedal. He pulled on his yellow cycling jacket, wrap-around sports glasses and helmet, jammed his phone into the cradle in front of the handlebars and whizzed down the circular ramp, free.

Free from anyone following him!

He pedalled out into the street, mindful of the traffic. It had been a few months since he had last ridden in London, but with the growing network of bicycle lanes and general awareness of drivers – apart from a few idiots – he always found it enjoyable. Particularly today with a clear blue sky above him.

And with a sense, of glee, at what he might have left behind him.

He rode along the Albert Embankment, with the Thames and the glorious Houses of Parliament on the far side. Then, after several modern buildings blocked his view, he started to see the imposing, twin-towered edifice of Lambeth Palace rising up.

Glancing at his watch, he saw he had less than an hour to go till his meeting. He pedalled on, then spotted a cafe on the far side of the road. Dismounting, he waited for a gap in the traffic, then hurriedly pushed his bike across, folded it back up and carried it inside. He chose a seat that gave him a view of the front door and the street.

The printed menu on the wall offered an all-day breakfast, followed by a range of healthy options. Had he been here with Imogen he would have gone for the vegan, or the vegetarian, at least. But on his own, and figuring he needed an intake of carbs, he ordered ham, egg and chips.

As he waited for his order, keeping an eye on the street and passing traffic, he checked his phone but there was nothing new. His hands were shaking, he realized. He was feeling the pressure of the past few days and wondering what was going to happen next. What would be the end game? Could things get worse? Perhaps Imogen had a point. But he could not quit now.

He was intensely curious to find out why the Archbishop was so interested to meet him, personally, and he knew that, whatever the purpose, it would add gravitas to his eventual story. Equally importantly, with the Head of the Church of England on board it must surely give him a little more protection. Could he trust the Church of England more than, perhaps, the Vatican?

Then just as his food arrived, his phone rang, the display showing the number withheld.

'Hello?' he answered, cagily.

A smooth, overtly friendly voice, with a faint Italian accent asked, 'Am I speaking to Mr Ross Hunter?'

'Who is calling?'

'My name is Giuseppe Silvestri. Your wife gave me your number. Is this a convenient time to speak?'

The man from the Vatican. He recognized the name instantly.

'Actually, I'm busy at the moment.'

'It is a matter of extreme importance, Mr Hunter. May I contact you a little later, perhaps?'

'Sometime this evening.'

'I cannot stress how important it is.'

He found the man's voice irritating. Jamming the phone to his ear with his shoulder, he picked up a tube of mustard and squeezed some out onto his plate. 'Then, Mr Silverstone, I'm sure if it is so important you will call me back.'

He ended the call.

86

Wednesday, 15 March

Three-quarters of an hour later a polite, neatly dressed man ushered Ross in to a beautiful book-lined office with a fine antique carpet. Oil paintings hung on the walls and a window gave a view across the Thames to the Houses of Parliament and Big Ben.

A fit, energetic-looking man of sixty, whose face was very familiar from many appearances in the media, stood up from behind a grand desk. His grey hair was thinning and he wore round, wire-framed spectacles, a purple shirt with a white dog collar beneath a grey suit jacket, and a large gold cross on a heavy chain.

He came round his desk, outstretched hand sporting a gold episcopal ring with a purple stone and a welcoming smile on his face. His voice was strong, English public school. 'Mr Hunter! This is extremely good of you to see me!'

'On the contrary, sir, I feel very honoured to be invited here.'

And he genuinely did. It was a strange, almost over-whelming sensation to be here in this office, meeting the Most Reverend, Right Honourable Tristram Tenby, the most powerful church leader in the United Kingdom, and he was feeling instantly charmed by the man's whole demeanour.

But mindful of maintaining his guard.

The Archbishop ushered him to a comfortable chair facing the window, at a small, low meeting table, and Ross wondered if he had deliberately been placed so he could see the magnificent view.

Moments later a male assistant came in with a silver tray on which was a pot of tea, china cups and a plate of biscuits.

'Tea all right for you or would you prefer coffee?' the Archbishop asked.

'Tea is perfect.'

A couple of minutes later when they were settled and the assistant had left and closed the door, Tenby gave him a warm smile. 'I imagine you know the reason I wanted to have a chat with you, Mr Hunter? Or may I call you Ross?'

'Ross is fine, sir – Archbishop.'

'Tristram is good, too,' he replied, giving him an almost conspiratorial wink.

'Thank you. Well – I do have an inkling as to why I might be here.'

'I believe you and the Bishop of Monmouth are friends?'

'Very old friends, sir – Tristram – yes. Benedict and I go back quite a while, to when he was a vicar in Brighton. I'm very fond of him.'

'Well, I am too – I have a strong belief in his abilities. So, he told me about your recent meeting, because he was left both intrigued and deeply concerned by what you told him.'

'In what way concerned?'

'Well, I suppose firstly because of how this information came to you, from a gentleman, Dr Harry Cook, who had obtained some of it through consulting a spiritualist medium.' The Archbishop picked up his cup and saucer and placed them on his lap. 'I'm sure you know what the

Bible says about mediums, and how we in the clergy view them?'

Testing him, Ross replied, 'Is that, possibly, because they challenge your lines through to the Other Side? Could it be that the Church feels it has a monopoly on communicating with the spiritual world, and uses all the dire warnings in the Bible to try to dismiss them?'

Tenby smiled. 'I won't argue on that or we would be here for days. Let's park it for now and get into the deeper questions regarding proof of God. I'm sure you are familiar with the old saying that science asks *how*, religion *why*?'

Ross nodded.

'Scientific tests are all about trying to *prove*, faith tests are about trying to find *meaning*. In our modern world, I see the duty of the Church to try to bring the two together. They are very different discourses. *Meaning* and *Values*. The recent controversies we've seen in the US and Europe show that a sea change is wanted by people, a change from the previous model we have lived by, to the values they feel we should be embracing. Relationships, freedom, equality. Human community. The world order that we have known for a long time is breaking down, and a new order is coming to the fore. Will it be better or worse?'

Ross stared at him. 'Does anyone know at this moment?'

'I would say the jury is out. If I'm correct, Dr Cook claimed to have three sets of compass coordinates that would provide proof of God. But Benedict told you that for such proof, he'd be looking for evidential quality beyond that.'

'He did, yes. But we didn't get into what those sets of compass coordinates might lead to.'

'Of course.' The Archbishop paused to sip his tea, and then fell silent for a brief while. 'You know, throughout time, many of the monotheistic religions have believed in a saviour coming to the world. Muslims believe that Jesus Christ will return, but as a prophet, not *the* Prophet – that prophet will always be Mohammed for them. The Jewish faith believes in the Messiah coming. We Christians believe in the Second Coming of Christ, but we have always been wary of imposters masquerading as Him. And when the message that God is concerned about the state of the world comes through a spiritualist medium, that does ring alarm bells I'm afraid, Ross.'

Tenby put his cup and saucer back on the table. 'That's not to dismiss out-of-hand what Dr Cook has told you. It could be genuine, a salutary reminder of the importance of God during a time when the world is changing so much. Perhaps a changing order to make this world more respect-ful of human beings and of communities. Tell me what you feel, in your heart, Ross? I've read many of your articles. You are an extremely intelligent and perceptive man, tell me what you really feel.'

'I think Dr Cook was a decent man, perhaps a little too obsessive to be taken seriously, and the death of his wife might have unhinged him slightly. But since taking up the baton he passed on to me, frankly, I'm scared.'

'Scared for what reason?'

'To be honest, I was sceptical at first – and ready to dis-miss him as a bit of a loony. But subsequent events have changed my mind. Two people I've met, one being Dr Cook and the other his solicitor, have died. I've been attacked in Glastonbury, chased and shot at in Egypt by people in a helicopter. My house has been trashed and religious slogans written all over the walls, and my wife has been threatened.'

Tenby looked genuinely shocked. 'Do you want to tell me the details?'

Ross felt comfortable enough with the man to tell him the entire story, from his first call from Cook to his visits to Egypt and to Chalice Well. And even why he'd travelled the last leg of his journey here by bicycle.

When he had finished, the Archbishop, apologetically, stood up, went over to his desk, lifted his phone and asked his secretary to warn the next scheduled meeting that he might be delayed. Then he sat back down.

'Ross, what has always struck me in articles of yours that I've read is your apparent humanity. All religions, ultimately, are about faith in the same God. At their very core, what they are about is living well. Equality. Freedom. The Common Good. It takes some longer than others to get to that point, and I'd be the first to admit that Christianity has a very dark past. Wind the clock back a thousand years to the atrocities committed during the Crusades; the torturing or burning at the stake of heretics for centuries after. We've evolved since then into something very different – for the most part – into a tolerant and positive social structure. A kingdom of justice and truth. We give hope to the world. It's a glorious and positive image. At the end of the day, what we try to offer to people is meaning. Religion is about meaning. As I said earlier, science may ask how, but what we search for is the answer to *why*.'

'Have you found that answer yourself, Tristram?'

'No, I haven't. I have my faith and I keep looking.'

'So, does it bother you if I keep looking, too?'

The Archbishop looked deeply serious. 'I would be untruthful if I said I was not worried for your safety, Ross. Many people before you have searched for our Lord's DNA. Maybe you truly have found it. But I am concerned that some of the source has been through a medium – regardless of your feelings on that subject. There are many people, with immense power and resources, who would want to get their hands on it. And equally these people would have vested interests in not wanting you to go public.'

'I'm not a stranger to danger. I've had many threats during my career.'

'This is on a different scale to anything you've delved into before. You are tackling the most fundamental question for humankind. And there are a lot of people in the world who would use religious belief to legitimize violence – people who are not only prepared to die for their beliefs, but to kill to protect them.' He paused and his expression softened into warmth.

'I sense in you, Ross, a decent man in a dark, troubled world, searching for the elusive light. Tell me if you find it. Until then, I'll be praying for you. Please know I'm here anytime you need me – or any of us. May God be with you. Shall we say a prayer together now?' He placed his hands together and closed his eyes.

Ross, despite feeling awkward, did the same, not wishing to offend him.

87

As he drove back home in the stop-go-stop rush-hour traffic, Ross spent the entire journey thinking about his meeting with the Archbishop. Tenby had given him a lot of time and wisdom, but how seriously, he wondered, had the Archbishop actually taken him?

Had he been, very subtly and very intellectually, swept aside? Was Tenby's caveat about the information having come through a medium just a smart bit of pro-Church of England PR, to make him doubt his sources?

His phone rang. He glanced at the hands-free display on the dash. It was an 0121 number. The Birmingham prefix.

'Ross Hunter,' he answered.

He heard a female voice, with a faint Brummy accent, that he recognized. It was Anholt-Sperry's elderly receptionist, who had become considerably more friendly in the immediate aftermath of the solicitor's death. He'd given her his personal number, and they'd exchanged a couple of texts.

'Mr Hunter, it's Irene Smither.'

'Hello, Irene,' he said, gently. 'How are you?'

'Well, I'm bearing up. We are all in shock here, as you can imagine.'

'I can indeed.'

'I thought you would appreciate an update.'

'Yes, thank you, what have you heard?'

'I've just had a visit from Detective Chief Inspector Starr. He's had the provisional result from Mr Anholt-Sperry's postmortem – it appears his pacemaker stopped working.'

'Pacemaker? I didn't realize he had a pacemaker.'

Then he recalled Anholt-Sperry mentioning his 'ticker' problem.

'Yes, he has had one for several years; in fact this is his second, it was fitted eighteen months ago. It's being sent off for examination to see if –' Her voice broke, and he heard her sniffing, as if regaining her composure. Then she continued. 'To see if it was faulty in some way.'

Ross felt strangely cold as he remembered something. The motorcyclist who had barged past him in the front doorway of the solicitor's. The strange, pulling sensation he had felt at that moment. His St Christopher medallion feeling as if it was tugging against the front of his shirt.

He remembered a recent article he had read on the internet, about methods of killing that could be undetected. Some modern types of pacemakers could be hacked and their electrical pulses altered or halted.

Powerful magnets would affect them also.

Had the motorcyclist, possibly Robert Anholt-Sperry's previous mystery client, been carrying such a magnet?

He heard the woman's voice distantly, faintly, like an echo. 'Hello? Hello? Mr Hunter, are you still there?'

'Yes – yes, sorry, bad reception – I'm driving.'

'Oh, perhaps I should call you later.'

'It's OK, I'm on hands-free. Did the detective say anything else?'

'Yes, he said they have still not been able to trace the client who came in before you, Mr Dunn – Terence Dunn.'

'Does he think there might be a connection with Mr Anholt-Sperry's death?'

'He said they are not ruling anything out at this stage. I – it – it's just terrible.'

'Robert was a nice man,' he said, lamely.

'I'll let you know if I hear any more.'

'I'd appreciate that.'

As he ended the call his phone rang again. It was Imogen.

'Where are you, Ross?'

He glanced at the car clock. 6 p.m. 'Just at the junction of the M25 and the M23. The traffic's horrible.'

'How long will you be?'

'Forty minutes to an hour.'

'I'll wait.'

'I've got Gordon, the electrician, coming tomorrow morning to sort out the CCTV cameras.'

'That's my Ross,' she said bitterly. 'Always do everything after the horse has bolted.'

'Hey, Imo – that's not—'

She had hung up.

88

Wednesday, 15 March

Seated at the table in the main boardroom of Gethsemane Park, alone with Lancelot Pope, Pastor Wesley Wenceslas stared out into the falling darkness. He was not happy.

His wife, Marina, buzzed him on the intercom. 'Are you coming to say goodnight to the children and read to them, darling?'

'No, my sweetheart, I have a little problem I need to deal with. Say goodnight for me.'

'What time would you like supper?'

'I don't know, I'll call you, OK, my sweet?'

'Try not to be too late.'

As Wenceslas ended the call, Pope grinned at him. 'Domestic bliss, eh?'

Ignoring the comment, Wenceslas launched into him. 'Smilealot, Ross Hunter did not spend two and a half hours this afternoon sitting in his car in a multistorey car park in the Elephant and Castle with his thumb up his jacksie. So where did he go?'

'I don't know. He gave us the slip. But we're on him again now.' Pope nodded at the computer screen. The blue dot was moving steadily south along the M23 towards Brighton, currently passing the turn-off for Gatwick Airport.

'I can see that.' Wenceslas pointed two fingers at his

own eyes. 'I've got these things in my head that the Lord gave me – at the same time as he was filling your head with sawdust. What I can't see is what Hunter did during those two and a half hours.'

'Can't God tell you?'

Wesley Wenceslas glowered at his MD. 'How much longer are you going to let that reporter run rings around you? There are times when I think you're treating this all as one big joke. How about I fire you – would that be so funny?'

Smilealot looked at him and smiled, very smugly. Both men knew that Wenceslas could never, in a million years, fire Lancelot Pope. Not if he didn't want his entire empire to crash and burn, when Pope ran to the press with a closet full of skeletons. 'Calm down, boss, this is not good for your blood pressure.'

'You're not good for my blood pressure.'

'Be happy! We've got his every move covered – his conversations, his movements, his whereabouts, twenty-four-seven. And we're following the followers. We know he took *something* to ATGC, and this time, when he goes to collect it, we'll have it off him before he even gets out of the car park.'

'If we don't, your neck's on the block.'

Pope shook his head. 'No, my neck is never on the block. Don't threaten me, I don't like it. I think I should get you a book on anger management. Really.'

'Lancelot, you know what the source of my anger always is? It's you.'

'You're just transferring your frustrations onto me. *Blame culture*. It's one of the things you preach against, Pastor. Tut, tut.'

'I could actually throttle you.'

'Thou shalt not kill – the sixth commandment.'

Wenceslas looked back at the screen. 'You do really appreciate the seriousness of this situation, don't you?' he asked.

Pope turned to him. 'You're forgetting something in all your anger, OK? I found you preaching to a congregation of fifty people in a rusty shed in Tooting, when I was down on my luck. I'd just been made redundant and I'd come home to find my partner had gone off to Ibiza with another bloke. I was wandering down the street wondering what the hell I was going to do, when I heard your voice coming through the open door.'

'The Lord brought you to me.'

'No, He didn't dislike me that much.'

Wenceslas had the grace to smile.

'I watched you preaching and I thought to myself that you had potential. I saw the rapt faces of your audience.'

'Congregation,' Wenceslas corrected him.

'Whatever. I saw a business opportunity. OK? Simple as that. Your skills as a preacher and my business head. All these years later, we're doing pretty OK, aren't we?'

'And now we're teetering on the brink. Ross Hunter is about to unveil the Great Imposter to the world. Do you realize what this means? He is going to unleash Satan upon us!'

'Come on,' Pope said. 'You're not talking to one of your suckers. You know you don't believe that bollocks. You have a much deeper worry, don't you, you old fraud!'

'Who's the bigger fraud?' Wenceslas retorted. 'The failed accountant who saw the road to a fortune through manipulating a humble preacher man? Eh?'

'Or,' retorted Pope, 'the phoney man of the cloth who saw a way to turn worship into a global empire? And is now terrified that the real Lord is about to return, or may already be here, and will find him out? Pastor, you're behaving like a spoilt kid. This is not the time for throwing your toys out of the pram. We need to be serious. To get real.'

After some moments, Wenceslas nodded, calming down. 'You're right.'

'I'm always right.'

89

Thirty miles away, on the forty-fourth floor of the KK building, Ainsley Bloor and Julius Helmsley stared at the red dot, on the large screen, that was moving steadily south on the A23, approaching Brighton.

'No way did Hunter spend two and half hours sitting in a multistorey car park in Vauxhall,' Bloor said, angrily. 'What a bunch of assholes you've hired. How could he have given them the slip for all that time – and more importantly, where did Hunter go? What's around there?'

'The South Bank?' Helmsley said.

'Oh sure – what did he do – go to a theatre and watch a play?'

'I don't think so.'

'The Houses of Parliament? Or Lambeth Palace – maybe he went to see the Archbishop of Canterbury! And His Holiness the Pope while he was at it?' Bloor snorted.

'I wouldn't rule that out, either,' Helmsley replied.

'Ha ha. So why did he go back to ATGC Forensics? What was he doing there again?'

'I'll find out.'

'With the same ruthless efficiency with which you found out what that Birmingham solicitor was going to hand to Hunter?'

'I'm flying to Monaco in the morning to get that, Ainsley.'

'With the price raised by a further million, at least.'

'Small beer. Very small beer compared to what it is worth to us.'

'Our friend in Monaco knows that.'

'He's not a fool. He also knows that it has no value to him – he'll have to do a deal. Leave it with me.'

Bloor stared at the screen. 'Where did Hunter go in those missing two and a half hours?'

'Look at the positives. He's a man on a mission. Whatever he's doing, it is ultimately for us. We just have to keep our cool. And when the moment comes, we'll jump one step ahead of him.'

'As of this moment, Julius, we are two steps behind him.'

Helmsley smiled at his CEO. 'Never forget that old saying: "It's the second mouse that gets the cheese."'

'Stinking Bishop?'

'All bishops stink.'

90

As Ross drove down his street, he saw Imogen's car parked outside their house. She had reversed onto the drive, presumably so she could keep an eye for anyone approaching.

He pulled up alongside her and climbed out.

She opened her door and swung her legs out, then stood up. She looked terrible, with rings round her eyes, her hair a mess, wearing a baggy jumper and badly creased jeans. She gave him a strange look.

'Hi,' she said.

Instead of hugging or kissing her, he just nodded at her and walked towards the front door. Unlocking it, he pushed it open and instantly Monty came rushing towards them, holding a squeaky toy duck in his mouth, almost ignoring him and making a beeline for Imogen.

As she knelt and hugged the dog, Ross scooped the post up from the floor and dumped it on the table without looking at it.

'Good boy, you've brought me a present!' she said. 'Good boy!'

Monty then bounded over to Ross, showing him the squeaking duck, proud as punch, his tail wagging wildly. Out of the corner of his eye he saw Imogen having a quick rummage through the post. She picked up an envelope, opened it and removed a letter. Then she crumpled it into a ball.

'You buy a bloody dress in a shop and five years later they're still pestering you with special offers.'

'You shouldn't have given them your address,' Ross said. 'You're not under any legal obligation to.'

'We all do a lot of things we're not under a *legal obligation* to do,' she said, her voice brittle, walking over to the integral door to the garage, unlocking it and entering. She returned with a suitcase and closed the door behind her. 'You're not under a *legal obligation* to come and stay with me at Ben and Virginia's, but it might be nice if you did.'

'This is our home, here.'

She looked around at the scrawl on the walls. 'It doesn't feel like our home any more, Ross. It was our sanctuary. It's been invaded, it feels horrible. I don't feel safe here now. I won't feel safe until you forget this whole Harry Cook business.'

'Is that why you gave that creepy-sounding Vatican man, Silvestri, my number? In the hope that I might just roll over, give him everything I have?'

'Ross, we have to get out of this danger. Let the Vatican take it over, they're big enough to deal with it – you are not.'

'You said Silvestri was offering to buy the items if I can show the evidence that what I have is real. He's not making any kind of unconditional offer from the sound of it.'

'Did you at least talk to him, Ross?'

'He rang when I was having lunch. I told him to call me later.'

'It never normally bothers you to talk on the phone when you're eating.'

'Yep, well, Silvestri did bother me.'

She shook her head. 'Jesus, I can't believe it. Our lives

are in danger, out of the blue comes a possible solution – and you're dismissing it.'

'I'm not dismissing anything, Imo.'

'So where are you at with the evidence?'

'I'm getting closer to – I don't know – getting closer to the final piece of the puzzle.'

'Getting closer,' she said, nodding her head in the very irritating way, for Ross, that she did whenever he said something she did not believe. 'If they let you live long enough.'

'If *who* lets me live long enough?'

'You know what I'm talking about, Ross. You know exactly. It might be nice if you lived long enough to see your son born – and perhaps help me to raise him.'

'Imo,' he said, taking a step towards her. 'Look, I know how this all appears to you, and I don't blame you for going to the safety of your sister until it's over, but I think you're overreacting, I know you're stressed because you're pregnant.'

'What?' She practically shouted at him, her eyes blazing. 'Don't you dare try throwing that little number at me. I'm trying to be a realist here.'

'I'm being a realist too, Imo. We've a huge mortgage on this house, and you're not going to be bringing in any income for many months.'

'So, maybe, just maybe, a deal with Silvestri could solve all our problems at once – our financial and our safety ones.'

'Fine, why don't I go to Kerr Kluge, tell them we're holding an auction. Them and the Vatican and anyone else who's interested. We'll flog Christ's DNA to the highest bidder. Is that what you want?'

'I just want to feel safe,' she replied. 'I just want

everything to be how it was, before you had that call from that damned man.'

'It can't be.'

'No, of course it can't,' she said, picking up the suitcase. 'Not now you have to save the world.'

91

Wednesday, 15 March

After Imogen had driven off, Ross felt very lonely. And exhausted.

And empty.

He sat down at the kitchen table, trying to ignore the scrawlings across the walls, and, as if sensing his mood, Monty came over, sighed and flopped down beside him.

Ross leaned down and stroked him. 'You know, Monty, you probably don't realize it, but you have it pretty cushy. You get fed and you get loved, and the only thing you have to worry about in the whole world is when your next walk's going to be. Right?'

The dog sighed again, then let out a small whine and looked up at his master.

'You want a walk now, is that what you're telling me? You've been here all day just sleeping and chewing bones and you're bored, right? OK! I think we both need some air.'

Ross jumped up and Monty barked excitedly.

He fetched the lead, pulled on his scruffy dog-walking coat and a baseball cap, stuffed a couple of plastic bags in his pocket, grabbed a torch, then took several goes to clip the lead onto Monty's collar because the dog was so excited.

They stepped out into the damp darkness and Ross looked around, carefully, before he closed the door behind them. Turning left, he headed up the hill, waiting as Monty stopped to check out every other lamp post, sniffing and giving it a quick squirt of pee. Imogen once suggested, humorously, it was the dog's version of email, picking up the scent of other dogs and leaving his own.

At the top of the hill was a small park, long and narrow, bordered by trees. He bent down and unclipped the lead. Immediately and excitedly, Monty bounded off. Just as he did so, a foreign accent, right behind Ross, startled him.

'Mr Hunter?'

He turned, pulling the torch from his pocket, snapping it on and pointing it at the stranger who was just a couple of feet away, with both hands in his pockets. He was standing too close, right in his personal space, and Ross backed away a couple of steps. The man stood still.

In his forties, smartly dressed in an expensive-looking belted raincoat with epaulettes, the man was handsome and very assured.

'Yes – who are you?' Ross demanded.

'Forgive me interrupting your evening walk, Mr Hunter. My name is Giuseppe Silvestri. We spoke earlier, you will remember?'

Ross recognized the cultured Italian accent. 'I thought you were going to phone me?'

'I do apologize,' he said with such charm and sincerity Ross almost thought that he meant it.

Silvestri pulled a gloved hand from his pocket and held it out. Ross stared at it for a moment then shook it reluctantly, at the same time glancing around, checking on Monty. To his relief he saw a dog-shaped shadow loping along a short distance away, sniffing the ground, picking up the scent of something.

Next, the Italian proffered a business card. Ross shone his torch on it. It was embossed with a gold, crossed keys coat of arms and a Latin inscription, and bore the name Monsignor Giuseppe Silvestri, with a title below, Special Vatican Emissary.

'Is this a convenient moment to talk, Mr Hunter?'

'What about?'

'Perhaps you would rather we went into your house – or my car – to be more private?'

'Here is fine.'

'Of course.' He continued the charm offensive. 'I think you know, perhaps, why I have come to speak with you?'

'My wife only told me a little. Would you like to start from the beginning?'

Monty began barking. A woman, who Ross didn't recognize as one of the regulars here, had come into the park with a schnauzer. She walked right past them. Both men fell silent for a moment.

'Good evening!' she said.

'Good evening,' Ross replied.

When she was out of earshot Silvestri said, 'There is much talk of the mission you are on, Mr Hunter. Discoveries you have made. Objects that might be of great historical significance. But which might place you and your wife in very great danger.'

'Are you saying this to threaten me?'

'Please do not take what I am saying the wrong way. But if what you have is what I am told it is, you must understand the consequences are immense – and extremely dangerous. Not just for you and your family, Mr Hunter – far beyond. It is necessary for you to understand this.'

'Who has told you – and what have you been told?'

The Italian smiled. 'Please, Mr Hunter. With something so important, believe me, I know. There are many people who know.'

'How? How do they know?'

There was a long silence. Silvestri looked at him, still smiling. 'Mr Hunter, discoveries like these do not stay quiet.'

Ross was momentarily distracted by a vehicle driving down the street, slowly. He glanced over and saw it was a police car.

'Wooky! Wooky!' the woman called out.

He turned and saw Monty play-wrestling the smaller dog.

'Wooky!' she called again, imperiously.

'You're going to tell me that God told you?' Ross said.

'You have a mortgage you are struggling with, I am informed,' the Italian said. 'And people have been inside your house and written bad things.'

'What else did my wife tell you?'

'She did not tell me, Mr Hunter. I have been sent by a very high authority to help you.'

'Sure, the Pope himself?'

'Wooky!' The woman walked towards them as the dogs continued wrestling. 'Excuse me, could you please control your dog?'

'Monty! Monty!' he called. 'Monty!'

After some moments the dog broke cover again and bounded over to them.

Ross knelt and clipped his lead back on.

'I think it might be better to continue this conversation somewhere more private, perhaps?' Silvestri suggested.

Ross turned away from him and, gently tugging the lead, headed out onto the pavement and back down the hill. The Italian maintained a steady pace beside him.

'Please understand, I mean no harm and no offence. I wish to help you, that is all.'

'I'm fine.'

'No, I don't think you are, Mr Hunter, if what you have in your possession is genuinely a tooth belonging to our Lord, Jesus Christ, and the vessel from which He drank at the Last Supper – and into which His blood was poured, whilst He was on the cross – then I am authorized to pay you a great deal of money. Sufficient not just to clear your mortgage, but to make you a wealthy man. It would be discreet, of course. Payment could be made into a Swiss account. No one would ever know.'

'Really? If God is informing you what I have, then why do you even have to question its provenance? And if you *are* questioning its provenance, why should I believe you?'

'I would like to understand a little more. A little more information. To see these items, of course. To have them examined.'

'Your religion is the richest on earth,' Ross replied. 'The Roman Catholic Church has assets greater than all the Russian oligarchs combined. Are you worried that proof of God might impact on that? That your religion would no longer be, to all your followers, the exclusive gateway to God?'

Silvestri smiled. 'Not at all. Proof of God would be a wonderful thing. But, to come to know God is not to *know* God.'

'So, you have to be a Catholic, not an Anglican or a Muslim or a Jew or a Sikh or a Hindu, to *know* God?'

'The human experience of love, truth and beauty – these are what are required to know God,' Silvestri replied, calmly. 'The Second Coming will be the moment when no one will be able to deny God's existence for better or worse. It will be unmistakable. The absolute proof of who Jesus claimed to be. If there were an absolute proof, we would like to think that everyone would rejoice.'

'So long as you – the Catholic Church – owned the news and delivered it?'

'No, Mr Hunter, this is not at all what I'm saying.'

'So why are you offering my wife and me vast amounts of money?'

A couple of hundred yards ahead, Ross saw the police car had pulled alongside a large Mercedes limousine, with diplomatic plates, parked outside his house. A female officer stood on the pavement, talking to the driver.

'Your car?' Ross asked him.

'Yes.'

As Ross approached the officer, he said, 'Good evening, I'm Ross Hunter.'

'Is everything OK?' she asked.

'Actually no,' he said. He nodded at the Italian. 'I'm being harassed.'

'Is this your car, sir?' she said to Silvestri.

'It is, yes.'

'You've heard what the gentleman said.' She gave him a polite but firm stare.

The Italian opened the rear door of the car and climbed in. Looking at Ross, he said, in the same polite and charming tone of voice, 'Mr Hunter, you have my card. I believe we should continue with our discussion.'

As the car glided away, Ross turned to the officer. 'Thank you.'

'We're on shift until 11.30 p.m. tonight,' she said. 'If you have any concerns please dial 999 right away. I'll make sure the next shift is briefed, too.'

Ross thanked her then went into the house. He unclipped Monty, who shot off into the kitchen and out through the dog flap, with a loud clatter. He looked up at the scrawl on the walls, with its spelling error.

ROSS HUNTER, FRIEND OF THE ANTICHRIST

IMOGEN HUNTER, EXPECTENT MOTHER OF THE ANTI-CHRIST

He went through into the kitchen, made himself an espresso then called Imogen and sat down at the table.

She answered almost immediately. 'Hi, you OK?'

'Not really. Tell me something. That Italian creep who came to see you yesterday, Giuseppe Silvestri?'

'He wasn't a creep, I thought he was very charming.'

'Yep, sure. I could have scraped enough oil off his face and hair to fry an egg. What did you tell him? About our financial position? About the house being vandalized?'

'I didn't, Ross, honestly. He just seemed to know about – about our finances – that they're not great. Did you say he mentioned the house being vandalized?'

'Yes.'

'Ross, I couldn't have said anything about that, I didn't know then – how could I? I hadn't been home.'

Was the house bugged? Ross wondered suddenly. For the next half an hour he searched high and low, but found nothing. He went back into the kitchen.

92

For some while, he sat very still, shaken. As the implications dawned on him, he called Imogen.

'Maybe the police told him – perhaps he has some contact with them and they told him?' she ventured.

Ross did not reply. He was thinking. *Had Silvestri been responsible? Part of his intimidation tactics?*

'Look, Ross, why don't you come over here, it can't be nice sitting with all that horrible writing all over the walls? There's that great pub, the Cat, if we're quick we could have supper there.'

'I've got stuff I have to do,' he said, aware he was sounding distant.

Because he was feeling distant.

'Ben's away on business, you could use his office.'

'I've got so much to do here, including the painters coming to give me a quote.'

'Will the insurance cover everything?'

'I don't know, I hope so.'

'You haven't spoken to them yet?'

'No,' he said, her voice irritating him. 'I'll do it tomorrow. And I've told you, I've got the electrician coming to get the CCTV sorted.'

He ended the call.

Silvestri.

People have been inside your house and written bad things.
Silvestri's people?

He sipped his coffee, pulled a fish pie out of the freezer, read the instructions and put it in the microwave. Then he noticed the light winking on their landline answering machine. One new message. He played it.

'Hello, it's Detective Constable Harris from Brighton CID. I'm calling to follow up on the reported vandalism incident at your home. If Mr Hunter could call me back to make an appointment or speak to one of my colleagues if I'm not here and give them the following reference.'

Ross wrote down the phone number and the reference number, then went up to his den.

There was an email from Jolene at ATGC.

> Hi Mr Hunter,
> We have a result for you from the ESDA on your document. Will be here all tomorrow from early.

He thought for some moments and had an idea. He emailed her back asking if she could courier the result and the manuscript sheet to his lawyer in Brighton.

Then his eye was caught by the folded copy of the page he had torn from *The Times*.

PASTOR WARNS BEWARE
THE GREAT IMPOSTER

He typed the link for Wesley Wenceslas's YouTube channel into Google and waited.

A white Boeing aircraft appeared, decorated with a logo showing a winged fish entwined round a cross. Superimposed were the words:

PRAY FOR AN AIR MILE. HELP OUR PASTOR WESLEY WENCESLAS COMMUNE WITH GOD FOR YOU – AND TO SPREAD THE GOSPEL WIDER AROUND THE WORLD. ALL MAJOR CREDIT CARDS ACCEPTED.

Then the pastor himself appeared. Along with the wording, superimposed:

PRAY FOR PASTOR WESLEY WENCESLAS. HELP HIM PRAY FOR YOU!

The plane disappeared and was replaced by sharp-suited, dog-collared Pastor Wesley Wenceslas, microphone in hand, strutting around in front of a huge congregation. Behind him was a twenty-foot-tall illuminated cross, an orchestra and a dazzling lighting display.

He was speaking quietly, sincerely. His flock was silent, enraptured. The camera singled out faces. All of them nodding, as if the pastor was speaking to each and every one of them individually.

'How important is your soul to you? Do you ever think about that?'

He paused to let that sink in, then went on. 'I want to talk to you tonight about the man who came here to save you. His name is Jesus. Jesus Christ, who was crucified, dead and buried. And on that third day he rose again. He rose, ready to come back to save you. And He is coming back, will He save you? Where do you think He will come back to? One of the great Christian cities? Or to a place that needs saving first? You are all here because you believe in Jesus.'

There was a chorus of cries from the room, 'Hallelujah!'

He nodded, a humble, pious expression on his face. 'Read the Book of the Lord, Matthew 24. He tells us what to expect before the Lord gets back.' He lowered his voice, staring at his congregation, imploringly. 'He said we must expect trouble. Great tribulation. Jesus is honest, He has told us the truth about the future, He hasn't hidden things.'

Then Wenceslas clasped his hands together and raised his head. 'Thank you, Jesus, for being honest.'

He paused as there were more cries of 'Hallelujah!'

He smiled and took a few steps across the stage, closer to his worshippers. 'Look, I'll level with you. We are all facing big trouble until Jesus comes back. There is nothing without suffering, no crown without the cross. There is trouble coming. Matthew 24 gave us a clear picture, when the disciples asked what the signs of His Coming would be. He gave four clear signs – and a warning about deception. Remember the first? Sign one: you will see disasters in the world. Earthquakes, wars, famines.' He paused again and once more expanded his arms, speaking gently. 'Don't be troubled, these are not death pains, they are birth pains! When non-Christians say they do not know what the world is coming to, Christians say, as one, *We do!*'

Ross watched, feeling angry at the way the man was manipulating his audience, and waiting for the next cash call to come.

'There will be false messiahs who claim to be the Saviour. Daniel wrote about the *abomination of desolation*. In it is a man who thinks he is God, who rises. He is lawless, promises peace and security. But he is the Beast. A very dangerous figure. A political dictator. Fortunately, his reign will be brief.'

He paused again, to increasing cries of 'Hallelujah!'

'You will read in Revelation of the Four Horsemen of the Apocalypse. The first is white, symbolizing military aggression. The second is red, for bloodshed. The third is black, for famine. The fourth is pale, for pestilence. Instead of Father, Son and Holy Spirit you will be offered Satan, Antichrist and False Prophet. I am telling you, it has all been foretold in the Bible. Every single prophecy in the Bible so far has come true. But as true Christians, you can be saved!'

He turned back to the altar, knelt and raised his hands in suppliant prayer. Then he stood and addressed the crowd.

'One day soon you will look into the sky and you will find the sun, the moon and the stars switched off. Daytime will be like the middle of the night. God is going to switch the house lights down. But then! There will be a sudden blinding light. Curtain up. You will see Jesus and a blaze of angels!'

Hundreds of people cried out together, 'Hallelujah!'

He ran off the stage as if drawn by an invisible force. On the wide screen appeared the words:

DONATE NOW TO BE SAVED. CASH BUCKETS ON THE WAY OUT. VISIT MY WEBSITE FOR MIRACLES PRICE LIST. ALL MAJOR CREDIT CARDS ACCEPTED.

Then the video of the Boeing 737 appeared again.

PRAY FOR A MILE!

Ross logged out, seething at the man. Didn't they realize what a fraud he was? How stupid people could be. He had tried to expose Wenceslas previously, but it clearly hadn't had much effect.

He looked back down at the *Times* article on Pastor Wesley Wenceslas. It just amazed him how people were taken in.

Then, he reflected, perhaps the same way he had been taken in by Cook?

He was startled by the ping of an incoming text, and picked up his phone. It was from Sally Hughes.

Hi Ross. How are you? XX

From the moment he and Imogen had started dating, he could honestly say he had never strayed, nor, as some of his friends had crudely put it, had he ever been window shopping. But there was something, he had to admit to himself, about this radio presenter that he was finding increasingly attractive. Apart from that, he was intrigued as to what she might be up to.

He typed a guarded reply.

> I'm feeling a bit like that old Chinese curse.
> 'May you live in interesting times.' X

A few moments later she texted back.

> Oh? Tell me more? XX

He replied:

> Rather too much happening to put in a text.
> Meet for a coffee or drink sometime? X

She replied:

> Have to come to Brighton 2morrow. Doing a
> piece on how many writers live in your city. If u
> have time? Caffeine v alcohol? Alcohol wins
> every time in my book! XX

He frowned. Hadn't she told him she would be away skiing this week? Was there a more sinister reason for this visit? Something connected to Harry Cook and her uncle?

> I like your style. Call me when you're in town. X

93

Thursday, 16 March

It was still dark when Ainsley Bloor, in jogging kit, let himself out into the dry, mild, morning air. He did some stretches, switched on his head torch and started his route, pounding along the cinder path which he'd had laid down some years ago, and which meandered around the boundary of his estate.

Beating the bounds, he liked to call his morning run. Streaks of red and pink speared the sky. No fog or mist. Good, his helicopter would be able to take him to the office, landing on the roof of the KK building, which meant he'd get there at least forty minutes sooner than going by road.

As he ran through the deer park, he was thinking about Ross Hunter. How the hell to deal with him? How best were they going to get what they wanted from him? He ran around the great lake, then sprinted the final quarter of a mile, flat out. He finished, panting and perspiring, at the orangery, where lights stayed on throughout the night. An idea was forming in his mind.

He entered and walked along the six monkey cages, peering inside each. As he expected, the first five capuchins still had produced nothing, but it looked as though there were several pages of printout in the collection box of his star.

The monkey, perched high up, eyed Bloor suspiciously as he entered, walked over to the printer and opened the lid of the collection. 'Have you been brilliant, Boris?' he asked. 'Let's see how brilliant, eh?'

The monkey remained still as Bloor looked at the sheets.

Bloor remained still, too. Every page was covered in the repeated word, 'the' – *the the the the the the the the the the the the the the the the the* . . .

All eight pages.

'Tut tut tut!' he said. 'Boris! I want better than this!'

As if in dismissive reply, the monkey leaped from his perch onto his trapeze and let out a screech.

Bloor folded the pages and carried them back towards the house, annoyed and very deeply disappointed. He went downstairs to his indoor pool, stripped off, pulled on his goggles and began his daily twenty-minute swim. As he did lap after lap in a fast crawl, his mind was all over the place. He put Ross Hunter temporarily aside and concentrated on Boris.

the the the the the the the the the the the the the the the the the . . .

Out of fear of ridicule, he'd kept this experiment totally quiet. Few of his work colleagues knew about it, and only one trusted member of his staff here at his home did – his head gardener. Every day the man cleaned out the cages and kept the monkeys' food topped up. Bloor's wife, Cilla, thought the experiment was bonkers.

Maybe she was right.

But she had never read Richard Dawkins, other than *The God Delusion*. It was *The Blind Watchmaker* which had been Bloor's inspiration for this experiment. Dawkins had come the closest to anyone in showing how evolution took place over millions – billions – of years. How the human eye had developed, through evolution, from a single cell.

Philosopher Antony Flew, at one time the world's most notorious atheist, was the last public figure to have taken a serious interest in the monkey and typewriter experiment – at least, that Bloor was aware of. That had ended in disastrous failure, and had contributed to Flew's conversion to belief in Intelligent Design.

Now his own experiment, although only six months old, was at the moment heading for failure, too.

the the the the the the the the the the the the the the the the the . . .

Was it the reward system that he had got wrong, he contemplated? Was it simply chance, because the keys for the letters 't', 'h' and 'e' were close together, and Boris liked the pattern? Or was something else going on in the monkey's brain?

And how did he change the creature's mindset? Bigger rewards for different words? But that wouldn't count as random.

He parked it, because at this moment he had a bigger problem to worry about. And bigger rewards. The monkey experiment was his personal interest. Ross Hunter was his company's future.

Bloor switched his focus to the board meeting in a few hours' time. A big decision needed to be made.

94

Unable to sleep much, Ross got up shortly before 6.30 a.m. and took Monty out. With daylight breaking, he crossed the footbridge over the A27 dual carriageway, checked there were no sheep around, unclipped the dog and let him run free over the fields on the far side.

Then, hands in his tatty old Barbour's pockets, he walked slowly, trying to take stock of everything. So many things to weigh up, but much depended on what result the ATGC laboratories had for him. He needed to see that and, afterwards, he'd make a decision.

Returning home, he watched the 8 a.m. *Breakfast* TV news headlines, showered and made breakfast for himself and Monty. There was no text from Imogen, so he sent her one.

Hope you're OK. X

He scanned through the papers whilst Monty gulped his food, his dog tag clattering against the side of his bowl.

As soon as he had finished his granola, Ross hurried upstairs. He called the number Detective Constable Harris had left yesterday, and arranged an appointment for 10.30 a.m. Next, he had a quick glance at Twitter. Nothing new. He still had the same number of followers as last time he'd looked: 7,865. He took a look at Instagram on his phone, realizing it had been over a month since he had posted anything there. The one Imogen had taken of him trying to read a Sunday paper with Monty's head in the way was still there with his caption, *Newshound?* It had forty-seven likes.

The front doorbell rang. It was the electrician, come to replace the damaged CCTV cameras. Ross made him a mug of tea and himself a strong coffee, and went back upstairs.

An email from Jolene had just come in. A courier would be no problem, she said. Could he call her to arrange payment?

Concerned about the possibility of his landline and personal phone being bugged, he texted her using one of the burners, giving her the address of his solicitor and asking her to use the same credit card details she now had on file.

Next, he texted his solicitor, told him about the expected delivery and asked him to photocopy what came in, put the copy in the same vault as the manuscript and courier the original to him, urgently, at his home address.

Scanning his overnight emails, he binned a couple of obvious scam ones, then saw one from Natalie at the *Sunday Times*.

> Hello Mr Stranger. Any chance of seeing that big story you said you're working on sometime this century?

He got up and checked the street below. A builder's van was parked opposite, with a flatbed behind it, from which they were unloading scaffold poles. There were no other unfamiliar vehicles that he could see. He sat back down.

The big story.

Where actually was he on it? What would today bring?

When the package arrived from his solicitor he might know a lot more.

He reflected on some of his conversations in the past couple of days: the MI5 man, Stuart Ivens, in the motorway service station, the Archbishop of Canterbury, the Italian last night, Giuseppe Silvestri.

That man bothered him. There was something deeply sinister beneath his charm.

Vatican Emissary.

What did that actually mean? Henchman to the Pope?

When he had been studying journalism at college in London, back in his late teens, many of his fellow students had dreamed of *the big story*. One of the lecturers there, whom he had really liked, Jim Coheny, was a laid-back guy with an impressive track record himself. One rather drunken evening in a pub, Coheny told him there were a million stories to write about every day. But a really big one only came along once in a decade or maybe even once in a lifetime. It wouldn't always be immediately obvious. Intuition, tenacity, perseverance, belief in yourself and gambling everything, in equal measure, were what it took to get that one, Coheny told him. Coheny cited every reporter's dream, the scoop of Woodward and Bernstein in 1972, when they'd exposed the Watergate scandal and brought down the US president, Richard Nixon.

Then Coheny had looked him in the eye. 'If that opportunity ever falls your way, Ross, no matter what the cost, seize it. That will be your chance for your day in the sun. You'll know it in your heart when it comes. It could be the difference between you having, one day, your own column in *The Times* or the *Guardian* or whatever, or ending your career writing about village fetes and lost dogs for some provincial rag on its last legs. You have it, kid. You have the cojones. I sense it in you. Don't let me down.' He had put his pint down, then tapped his own ears. 'Listen.' Then he pointed at his own eyes. 'Watch.' Then he raised his arms and curled his fingers into claws and hissed, 'Pounce!'

Ross would have liked to talk to Coheny now, get his advice on what he should do, but the reporter had been killed in Syria five years ago, working on a piece about ISIS. His *big story*, Ross wondered?

Thinking of Coheny reminded him of his grandfather's words shortly before he died, telling him never to be frightened to make the right choices.

But he was feeling deeply depressed. And in a strange space. Alone.

Imogen had fled and their home had been trashed. Their finances were bad. The *Sunday Times* editor was clearly running out of patience. The events of the past weeks had been traumatizing and he realized he should be more scared himself. But he wasn't. Perhaps he was too tired to think straight, just operating on autopilot?

Should he call Silvestri and negotiate?

And then? Perhaps walk away financially secure?

Could he ever live with that?

Live with the memory of those wistful eyes of Harry Cook, just weeks ago? And the knowledge that he might have done something of real value for mankind, but instead took the money and ran. And just how far could you run in a world that was falling apart?

He thought of Coheny's words again.

Intuition, tenacity, perseverance, belief in yourself and gambling everything, in equal measure, is what it takes.

The *big one*. Imogen knew his dream and had always supported him – until the break-in.

His mobile phone rang.

'Ross Hunter,' he answered.

'How's your day looking?' said a breezy female voice he instantly recognized.

'You're here already, Sally?'

'On the train.'

'Do you have lunch plans?'

'Nothing I can't move for the man who has proof of God.'

He smiled, his spirits instantly lifted. 'Anything you particularly like to eat?'

'Born-again Christians. Grilled, preferably.'

'Fishy ones?'

'Fish is good. Very Christian.'

He arranged to meet her at English's restaurant at 1 p.m. After he ended the call to Sally he rang and booked a table.

95

Thursday, 16 March

The directors of Kerr Kluge were assembled in the top-floor boardroom. Each of them had a copy of the document, downloaded from the memory stick Julius Helmsley had finally obtained from his Monaco contact.

Ainsley Bloor read out the coordinates on it.

34°4'56.42''N 118°22'56.52''W

The computer screen on the wall above them showed a street map of West Hollywood, Los Angeles.

'Nice work, Julius,' Bloor said, his voice laced with bitterness. 'Do you realize how big this area is? Anything you'd like to add?'

'This is what the Birmingham solicitor, Anholt-Sperry, had in his file, presumably to give to the reporter Ross Hunter,' Helmsley replied.

'Can you refine the search area? What exactly are we supposed to be looking for?'

'We know one thing, Ainsley,' Helmsley said. 'We've thwarted Hunter by getting this.'

Bloor stared at him. 'So far we've failed to get what Ross Hunter was after in Chalice Well. We've failed to get what he was after in Egypt. Now we have something he was after but we don't know what it is, right? A map without a key.'

'Perhaps Mr Hunter has the key but not the map?'

suggested Alan Gittings, the Head of Research and Development.

'Look, has it occurred to any of us we might be going about this the wrong way?' said Ron Mason, the director Bloor most trusted on his team.

'In what sense, Ron?' Julius Helmsley asked.

Mason laid in front of him a sheet of printout. 'This is Ross Hunter's current financial position. Have a read.'

Helmsley turned the document round and studied it. 'Mortgage of four hundred and fifty thousand and he's asked his bank for a repayment holiday. He's almost at his overdraft limit of ten thousand. Eight hundred pounds of credit left on his AmEx. Fifteen hundred on his Visa.'

'What does that tell us?' Mason pressed.

'As we already knew, he needs money. Badly,' Helmsley replied.

Bloor smiled. 'What is our company motto, Julius?'

'*The company that cares.*'

'So, go and talk to him. Offer to pay his mortgage off, clear his cards and a nice lump sum on top; way more than his paper would ever pay him.' Bloor smiled, baring his immaculate white teeth. 'To show we care.'

96

Detective Constable Mike Harris was shocked and sympathetic in equal measures about what he saw on the walls of the house. He'd heard back from CSI Alex Call that there was no new evidence, and asked Ross what he thought might have provoked this.

Because of his worry about bugs, Ross took Harris outside and told him the truth about Harry Cook's original call and visit, and what he had found at Cook's home – and gave him the name of the Birmingham DCI, Martin Starr. He also told him what he knew of Robert Anholt-Sperry's death. Harris said that he would follow up with DCI Starr.

Moments after the detective left, the envelope arrived from his solicitor.

He opened it in the kitchen and removed the document that had been enhanced by ATGC onto a plain sheet of paper. On it were handwritten compass coordinates:

34°4'56.42''N 118°22'56.52''W

He went up to his office, opened up Google Earth and entered the coordinates in the search box. After some seconds, a section of West Hollywood zoomed in. It showed as the intersection of Fairfax and Melrose. Were the coordinates deliberately vague, he wondered, as they had been for Chalice Well, putting him in the vicinity but not the precise spot?

He went to the street-view setting and navigated around. He saw a small shopping mall; the Fairfax Farmers Market; a cosmetic dental lab; a gas station; then a large complex of buildings and open space, Fairfax High School; cafes; bars; shops; a shabby blue structure, like a large shack, with a yellow hoarding advertising itself as CENTER-FOLD NEWS STAND.

What was he supposed to be looking for? This didn't exactly look like the area where a tumultuous event would occur. But then neither had a stable in Bethlehem, most probably.

He stopped and thought back to Anholt-Sperry. Remembering his words.

Come back to me once you have found what awaits you at the second set of coordinates. Then you will know for sure . . . With the third you will find the location of the Second Coming of Christ himself.

He felt a sudden beat of excitement. An idea that might work. Could it?

He looked up Jolene Thomas's number, went outside and dialled it on one of his burners. She answered after just two rings.

He identified himself.

'Hello, Mr Hunter!' she said, breezily. 'Did your documents arrive safely?'

'Yes, thank you,' he said. 'There's something I wonder if you could help me with.'

'I'll try!'

'DNA databases. Can you tell me, are there separate national and international databases for standard DNA, mitochondrial DNA and Y-STR DNA?'

'Yes, there are, completely. By far the most comprehensive are the standard DNA databases – there's pretty much worldwide coverage with these now among law-enforcement agencies – subject to the privacy rules of certain countries, and certain states within the USA. Mitochondrial databases are less comprehensive. And the Y-STR is sort of the new kid on the block – that has the fewest databases currently. It will change, but it will be several years before it catches up with standard DNA.'

'To make sure I have it absolutely clear in my head, standard DNA is different for every human being?'

'Correct – except for identical twins and, in rare cases, identical triplets.'

'And mitochondrial is the female DNA – and that passes down through the female line unchanged?'

'Yes.'

'For generations, right?'

'Yes, it does, it goes down through the bloodline. Mother to daughter to granddaughter ad infinitum, completely unchanged.'

'And the Y-STR does the same thing, but down the male line?'

'Yes, for as long as the male line continues. It has a great deal of value in paternity testing – and in genealogy. But you have to be aware there can sometimes be mutations – and the longer the line, the more chance there is.'

'How big is that chance?'

'Pretty small.'

'Small enough to be unlikely?'

'Yes, very. But you need to be aware of the possibility, always.'

Ross was jotting down notes. 'You said that there are not that many Y-STR DNA databases at present.'

'Correct.'

'Where are the biggest databases, currently?'

'For Y-STR?'

'Yes.'

'There are a few in the UK now, and growing. A number in Europe – and the Czech Republic, for some reason, has been very progressive in this area.'

'What about America?' he asked.

'Yes, there are quite a number there. New York State, Illinois, Florida; the biggest actually is in Southern California.'

'Southern California?'

'Yes.'

'Do you know if they have an equally big mitochondrial database there?'

'Yes, they do – actually much bigger at this stage than their Y-STR.'

'Can anyone access these databases? Would I be able to?' he asked.

'No, they are all strictly protected. Here in the UK they fall under the Data Protection Act – for instance, I wouldn't even be permitted to let you have your own DNA if it was on a database. The overseas ones would depend on the individual laws of each country – or American state. In some places law enforcement agencies can access them freely, in others they'd require a court order.'

As Ross thanked Jolene and ended the call, excitement thrummed inside him.

Southern California.

Los Angeles was in Southern California.

97

Thursday, 16 March

Ross looked down at the notes he had just made from his conversation with the DNA scientist. *All strictly protected.*

He looked at his watch. 11.55 a.m. He had to leave in a quarter of an hour, latest, to get into town and park in time for his lunch meeting with Sally. He needed to access the databases. Somehow.

How?

Then he thought of someone who could help him.

He was aware that although it was approaching midday, it was still the middle of the night for the nocturnal computer hacker. The oddball didn't like to be disturbed until late afternoon, at the very earliest. Too bad. He looked up Zack Boxx's number, went out into the garden and dialled it on a burner.

After several rings, it was answered by a very bleary-sounding voice.

'Yrrr?'

'Zack, it's Ross Hunter.'

'Yrrr.'

There was a long silence. Ross waited patiently but there was no sound.

'Zack?'

'Do you have any idea what time it is?'

'Midday.'

'Not in San Francisco. It's four in the morning, for God's sake, Ross!'

'Are you in San Francisco?'

'No, I'm not, I'm in Brighton. Trying to get some sleep. What do you want?'

'I need some help.'

'I already gave you some. Shit. You want free help?'

'I'm willing to pay.'

'That would be a first.'

'I'm serious. Can I come over and talk to you? I don't trust the phones. Are you in the same place?'

'You mean mentally? Physically? Geographically? Astronomically? Astrologically?'

'Residentially.'

'Actually, I'm living in a nice condominium on Mars, since you asked. Seems to be the smart place these days. My earthly residence is still Elm Grove, Brighton, but for hopefully not too much longer.'

'Long enough for me to get over to see you? Urgently?'

'Can it wait till four o'clock this afternoon?'

'That would be good.'

'Fine. Until then, sod off and let me go back to sleep.'

98

Thursday, 16 March

A large, round platter of West Mersea oysters was placed in front of them, on a tall metal stand, along with lemons, dishes of vinaigrette with chopped onion and buttered brown bread.

Sally looked great. Raising his wine glass, Ross said, 'Cheers!'

They clinked glasses.

'It's very good to see you again,' he said.

'Funny you should say that, I was thinking the same thing.' She gave him a cheeky grin.

'So, you're in town, interviewing writers,' he fished. 'Who have you talked to so far?'

'William Shaw and Elly Griffiths – they're both lovely. And a wonderfully whacky food writer called Andrew Kay. Do you know any of them?'

Ross nodded. 'Yep, Andrew Kay does a lot with the local media and he's an interesting novelist, too. I've read both Shaw and Griffiths – very good writers.'

'So, how is Mr God?' she asked. 'Or is it *Mrs*?'

'Good question.'

'What's happening with your article? Have you written it yet?' She picked up a shell, squeezed lemon onto the oyster, spooned on some vinaigrette, then tipped the contents of the shell into her mouth, chewed once and swallowed.

'Wow!' she said. 'Sensational!' She raised her glass and drank some more. 'OK, *Interesting times*, you said in your text. So?'

Guardedly, Ross brought the radio presenter up to speed, telling her as much as he wanted to share with her. He was careful to keep back the LA coordinates.

When he had finished she looked at him in silence. 'So where do you go from here?'

'Honestly?'

She nodded.

'I'm increasingly getting the strong message from my wife that if I want to save our marriage, then I should sell out.'

'To sleazy Mr Silvestri?'

'Take the Vatican's shilling.'

'And will you?'

'I'm not a quitter, Sally. Everything is totally surreal at the moment. But I can't stop now – I think I'm in too deep.' He looked hard at her, smiling, then took a sip of his wine. 'Tell me, have you spoken to your uncle again at all?'

'Creepy Uncle Julius Helmsley?'

Very interested in this comment, he asked, 'Why do you say *creepy*?'

'Have you ever seen a picture of him?'

'Yes, I googled the board of Kerr Kluge.'

'He's one of those people that kind of make you want to wash your hands – or have a bath – after you've been in his company. He's pervy.'

'Oh?'

'He's never come on to me, but I just feel it – always have. It's the way he looks – with those ridiculous red glasses and his stupid hairstyle, and he never makes eye contact when he talks to you – he sort of stares past you.

Uggggh! He always seems so superior and condescending. Whenever he used to come to our home when I was a child he would arrive all la-di-da aloof. Him with his grand London house and his weekend country estate, and all of that.'

'What's his wife like?'

'An ice queen. Mum was arty, a bit chaotic – bohemian. My aunt Antonia was always cold and hard – very into science. My mum tolerated Antonia because she was her sister, but I don't think they ever got on that well.' She hesitated and blushed. 'Actually – this may sound pathetic – but my uncle Julius pretty much killed Christmas for me when I was six.'

'I love Christmas – that doesn't sound pathetic at all. What happened, what did he do?'

'He and my aunt had come over to spend Christmas Day with us. We had the tree, all the presents under it, you know, all the fun stuff. He took me aside, sat me down in a quiet room and spent half an hour very solemnly explaining, scientifically, why Santa Claus could not exist. He went through the lot – how reindeer did not have wings, so they couldn't fly. And he'd done the maths, which he showed me in elaborate, easy-to-understand diagrams. He pointed out just how many homes there were in England alone – something like twenty-five million – and that if Santa spent just two minutes at each of them, it would take him 34,000 days – about ninety-five years. I can still remember his expression – it was really cruel, as if he was getting huge pleasure from telling me.'

'What a bastard. I hate it when people rob kids of their fantasies.'

She nodded. 'Totally. So, would that include hard-core atheists like Dawkins?'

'You know, even when I was having my most atheist leanings, in my agnostic phase, there was stuff about the reductionist scientists that bothered me. There's a really big paradox for scientists.' He drank another sip of wine.

'Which is?'

'OK, you have scientists stating categorically how the world began, the Big Bang theory, right?'

'Yes. My uncle is right up there with that one.'

'So, here's the paradox: a tenet of science is that any experiment should be repeatable in a laboratory. It's one of their big arguments against ghosts, mediums, telepathy and anything else paranormal. Do you know the term "methodological naturalism"?'

She frowned. 'No.'

'It's what your uncle and a number of other scientists follow: it's the term for scientifically studying the world, totally excluding any possible supernatural causes. It is the absolute assumption that God should have no part in scientific phenomena.'

'And the paradox is?'

'Methodological naturalism requires scientists to seek explanations in the world around us that are based on what we can observe, test and replicate. They might try to replicate the Big Bang in a particle accelerator but –' he expanded his arms – 'are they going to replicate this universe? This restaurant? You and me sitting here? This bottle of Pouilly-Fuissé?'

'So, the paradox is that cosmologists don't tick the boxes required by science? Don't you think some of them might be a bit peeved to be told their work does not qualify as science?'

'I think it's time the arrogance of some militant atheists did get lanced. When they can replicate the world, exactly, and whatever state of evolution everything is at, at this moment in time, then I'll accept them unconditionally. Until then they need to cut other possible explanations – including God – some slack.'

'Provided they can replicate these West Mersea oysters, too?'

'Of course!'

'What about the Higgs boson?' she asked.

'The God particle, which they discovered at CERN? Does it actually prove anything? There's still the question of who made it.'

Sally took another oyster.

Ross took one, also.

Staring at him with twinkling eyes, she said, 'You know these are meant to be aphrodisiacs?'

He smiled back. 'Yep. They also used to be peasant food. Staple diet for monks, because they were cheap protein.'

'Are you deliberately trying to kill a romantic moment?' she tested.

'I'm a married man.'

'And I would never, ever attempt to lead you astray.'

'And I believe that.'

There was a moment of comfortable silence between them.

They clinked glasses again.

'Another bottle, sir?'

He looked up at the waitress. Had they really downed an entire bottle already? Maybe, he wondered, if Sally had a little more to drink she might let something slip.

'I think so,' he said. 'Would be rude not to.'

Sally Hughes agreed.

Ross stood up and excused himself for a moment. 'Just going to have a pee, I'll be right back.'

As he walked out of the room, Sally was startled by a ping from his phone. A text.

She saw Ross disappear down the stairs and quickly, out of curiosity, turned the phone round. It was a text from a travel agent called Travel Counsellors, confirming a flight she was holding to Los Angeles. She turned the phone back round and sat waiting for his return.

She said nothing as he sat back down.

99

Imogen pulled up outside their house shortly after 3 p.m. She wasn't sure whether she was glad or sad that Ross's car wasn't in the drive. As she went in, Monty padded excitedly towards her and she knelt down and stroked him.

'I've missed you, my lovely!'

After some moments of doggie worship, she went upstairs to their bedroom to grab some more clothes that she needed. As she entered the room, the front doorbell rang. She hurried back down, across the hallway and opened the door.

A tall, equine-looking man in a business suit stood there. He wore rather arty red-framed glasses, a modern hairstyle that was twenty years too young for him and had a patch of sticking plaster on his cheek.

'Oh, hello,' he said. 'Would Mr Ross Hunter be in, by chance?'

'No, but I'm Mrs Hunter – by chance.'

He gave an awkward smile.

'How can I help you?'

'Er –' He hesitated. 'Perhaps I should come back?'

'Can I give my husband a message?'

'Well, yes.' He handed her a business card. 'My name is Julius Helmsley, I'm the Chief Operating Officer of a company called Kerr Kluge.'

She tilted her head. 'A company *called* Kerr Kluge. Do you think I've never heard of you, or something?'

'Well – I – I imagine we are a bit of a household name.'

'You could say that.' She smiled. 'So, are you here to sell me toothpaste? Soap? Sleeping pills?' She looked at the card.

'No – actually – it's a financial matter.'

'Is Kerr Kluge a very sexist company, Mr Hamley?'

'*Helmsley*,' he corrected. 'Not at all – not remotely. Far from it, we are one of the pioneers of sexual equality in the workplace, Mrs Hunter. All our female workers earn the same as their male counterparts.'

'Good. In that case you can tell me anything that you were planning to tell my husband. Would you like to come in and have a cup of tea?'

'Well, if it's no trouble.'

'It's no trouble.'

100

Thursday, 16 March

Sally could sure drink – and hold it – and Ross liked that, as well as her gusto for food. She seemed to have gusto for life itself, and it was infectious.

Imogen had been like that too in their early days, he thought ruefully.

They'd finished the second bottle of wine and then, not wanting the dialogue to end, he'd ordered a cognac and she'd had a Cointreau on the rocks. As they left the restaurant with their coats on, just after 3.30 p.m., the last people in there, and negotiated their way past the outside tables, he was feeling a little unsteady on his feet. And he still hadn't worked her out yet.

They stopped and stared at each other. Sally was giving him a warm come-on smile.

'That was fun!' he said.

'We should do it again.'

'We should.'

There was an awkward moment.

'I think –' he said, and hesitated.

'You think?'

Ross gave her a quizzical look. 'I do think sometimes, yes!'

She leaned forward, spontaneously, and planted a kiss on his cheek. Then she turned away, waved a hand in the

air, called out, 'See you!' and walked off, her elegantly
tailored white coat clinging to her body, her tight jeans
tucked into her leather, high-heeled boots.

He stood there, feeling a tad giddy.

He had drunk far too much to drive. He would take a
taxi up to Zack Boxx and then return tomorrow to the car
park beneath the Waterfront Hotel.

He headed along towards the East Street taxi rank. As he
walked he was trying to focus his mind on what he had to
ask Boxx about. But he was a little distracted by the scents
of Sally's perfume and her hair.

Warning bells ringing in his head.

His phone pinging in his pocket.

He pulled it out and looked at it.

It was a text from Sally.

> Now that's what I call a lunch! Next one is on
> me. X

All his instincts told him not to respond until he was
sober. But, a few moments after he had climbed into a taxi
and given the driver Zack Boxx's address, he texted back.

> Make it soon. ☺

101

Zack Boxx hadn't changed. He still lived in the same, dark, chaotic pad that he had been in a decade back as a student, which he shared with the same hostile Siamese cat. It was the basement of a terraced Victorian house, close to Brighton's racecourse, and the blinds were permanently drawn. The place smelled stale, slightly rank, badly in need of daylight and fresh air, and there was a faint hint of weed.

Boxx was wearing a faded Gandalf T-shirt, unfashionable jeans and a pair of slippers he might have inherited from a dead grandfather. His lank hair was in the same shapeless style, but starting to thin and grey, Ross noticed. The bumfluff on his face from a decade ago had matured into an apology for designer stubble and it looked odd on his slightly pudgy, baby face. He had the complexion of a ghost.

As Ross stepped through a maze of computer monitors, keyboards and server towers that covered almost all of the living-room floor, as well as empty mugs and takeaway cartons, Boxx pointed him towards a semi-collapsed sofa against the far wall. The only things obviously new from his last visit that Ross observed were two vast television screens, one switched off, the other almost the entire width of a wall, on which a video of the galaxy was playing.

'So, you weren't joking about Mars, Zack?'

'It's a direct feed from the British observatory on Mauna Kea, in Hawaii. And it is actually still night-time there – since you asked,' he added sarcastically, reaching out to stroke the cat, which arched his back and slunk away from him. 'I'm looking for somewhere to move to before it's too late. Just got a few technical issues to sort out, like finding somewhere else that supports carbon-based life forms – and a way of getting there.'

The geek, who could speak seven languages fluently, still had the same hostile attitude; just like his cat. And the same distinct lack of social graces. It was as if the whole world was against him and everyone had better keep their distance.

Ross reached the sofa and sat down on it, feeling a busted spring beneath him. Boxx totally ignored him for several minutes, kneeling on the floor, logging on to first one, then another computer and studying what were, to Ross, totally meaningless rows of algebraic figures on both, all the while muttering, 'Idiot . . . I can't believe this . . . what have you done there? You cretins! Honestly! . . . What – what is this?'

After a while he turned to his visitor. 'Be with you in a minute. Got to help GCHQ out with a problem and the CIA have some issue in Iraq.'

'It's OK, you go ahead and save the world.'

'Honestly, you'd think sometimes – you know – these guys – they –' He fell silent, tapping at the keyboard and peering intently. 'I mean, like – you know? Ridiculous.'

Ross was still feeling a little drunk. 'Any chance of a coffee?'

'Kitchen. Help yourself. There's a kettle or Nespresso machine. By the way, you smell like a pub.'

Ross went through into a kitchen that looked like it had

recently been hit by a tornado. After rummaging around, he found what looked like the only clean mug in any of the cupboards and a small stack of coffee capsules next to the coffee machine.

He made himself a tripple espresso and carried it back into the living room. As he sat back down, Boxx turned to him.

'So?'

'How's life?' Ross asked.

'A bit shit. Working on my evacuation plan. We've all got to get out of here, pdq.'

'I wouldn't disagree with you.'

'I'm telling you. Armageddon. Find a planet, for real. This isn't a social visit, is it?'

'No, I wondered if you can help me. I need some data-bases hacked.'

'Uh-huh?'

Keeping back some details, Ross told him what he wanted.

Zack Boxx tapped out notes on a keyboard in front of him as Ross talked. When he had finished, he said, 'OK. Right. Standard DNA, mitochondrial DNA and Y-STR, Los Angeles – or rather, Southern California. You want me to look into their databases?'

'Yes.'

'Break the law?'

'Whatever you need to do. I'm guessing you know how to cover your tracks.'

'I don't do this shit for fun any more, Ross, or because I can. It's business now, my livelihood. Know what I'm saying?'

'I understand.'

'I really do want to get out of here. I'm saving.'

'Out of this flat?'

Boxx looked at him as if he was mental. 'This fucked planet. If you've got any sense you'll come with me.'

'I'm trying to save it.'

'Good luck with that one.' He tapped some more keys and his screen changed. 'OK, what I'll do is try to get into each of these three databases, and leave something there that will look for a match or notify me if a match pops up in the future.'

'How long in the future?' Ross asked.

'As long as you want.'

'How quickly can you get a result?'

'It depends what's there, and I've got some stuff to do for my employers – quite a big program to write. Maybe later tonight or tomorrow.'

'OK.'

'And before I start – no offence but I'd need payment upfront.'

'How much are you charging?'

Boxx smiled for the first time. 'Mates' rates? Two thousand for the searches. One thousand bonus for each hit I get – maximum bonus three thousand. All right?'

'Do you take credit cards?'

'Ha ha.'

102

Thursday, 16 March

The Abbot sat behind his desk, a frail man with bottle-lens glasses and an unruly crescent of a white beard. Behind him was a narrow window, open to the elements. Its edges were uneven, hacked out of the wall by a craftsman back around 1366 AD, when this monastery was built on the escarpment then known as Simon's Rock, perched high above the Aegean Sea.

Brother Pete stood in front of him, hands behind his back. Both men were attired identically, in their heavy black habits and their Eastern Orthodox headdress, the *kalymafki* – a round black hat with a veil falling from either side of the face and down the shoulders. The only distinguishing feature the Abbot had was the heirloom ancient gold cross hanging down almost to his midriff from a chain round his neck.

It was the same cross that had been worn by another, now long dead, Abbot, in the framed black-and-white group photograph on the wall opposite the window. It showed three rows of monks, the rear two rows standing, the front seated, in the courtyard of the monastery. They were all heavily bearded, only the top part of their faces visible, a few wearing glasses. Their ages ranged from early twenties into their nineties and all of them looked solemn and dutiful.

Brother Pete had seen the photograph before; it had been taken over fifty years ago. All the monks today looked exactly the same, as did the courtyard. It would have been pretty much the same image if it had been taken five hundred years ago. And it would look the same in five hundred years' time, if –

If everything stayed the same. If time here remained standing still.

If the funding continued to come, through God's guidance.

If the world –

The Abbot was nodding at him, as if reading his thoughts and agreeing with him. After a long silence he said, 'Brother Pete, if I do give you permission to go, how will I know for sure you will return?'

'Why would I not, Father Abbot? I don't have anywhere else I want to go or be. This is my home, here, it always will be, blessed by the Virgin Mary until I am called to a higher place by the Lord.'

The Abbot looked pensive. 'So, tell me, why exactly do you wish to make this journey?'

'My cousin Angus is dying. You will remember Brother Angus, he was the reason I came here.'

'I remember him well. I gave him permission to go and visit his mother, who was sick, and he never returned.' He gave a wan smile. 'He did not need to visit her; his journey was not necessary. His prayers from here would have been as effective, I'm certain. Why do you wish to trouble yourself with travelling – why don't you just pray for your cousin?'

'I think this will be the last time I see him, Father Abbot. He does not have long to live.'

'The last time you see him?' There was a strange twinkle

in the old man's eyes. The hint of a smile. 'Surely not. Surely just the last time *here*, Brother Pete? Until the day you are both reunited in the glory of God's sight?'

'My cousin has something he needs to give me for safe-keeping. That telephone call I had from him two days ago, which you kindly permitted me to take. That is what he was asking. A dying wish. He has been entrusted with the protection of two items, which he tells me are of the greatest imaginable significance to the Christian faith. He is worried what will happen to them after he dies.'

'Do you know what they are? Are they genuine?'

'He believes so.'

'You need to be careful, Brother Pete. The history of our faith has been mired with fake relics, forgeries of all kinds, and hoaxes. Some are the work of the Antichrist. Some are just the work of opportunists and chancers – people trying to make money from those who are gullible.'

'Brother Angus believes we will see the evidence of how real these are very soon.'

'Should we wait for that evidence before you go? Should we test it?'

'I'm afraid that if he dies, Father Abbot, these items may be lost forever.'

The Abbot nodded, thoughtfully. 'Do you not think, if they are truly from God, they will find their rightful place through Him without intervention?'

'Perhaps, Father Abbot, it is our destiny that our monastery is their rightful place?'

The old man gave a sad smile. 'Please, explain to me what these items are and then I will make my decision.'

Hesitantly, Brother Pete told him.

103

Thursday, 16 March

As Ross sat in the rear of the bouncy, uncomfortable people carrier, on his way home from Zack Boxx, the taxi driver drove recklessly fast, arguing with someone on his phone, which he held to his ear, seemingly oblivious to the law.

A text pinged in from Imogen.

> Hi stranger! How's your day going? Why don't we meet this evening – come over and join us?
> XX

He stared at it, feeling guilty about Sally. Standing on the street outside English's being kissed by her. His wife expecting their child.

'So the Seagulls doing well, yes!' the foreign driver shouted at him, unexpectedly, over his shoulder, still holding his phone in one hand.

'Yep, great, they are!'

He looked down at the text.

Seconds later it was followed by one from Sally.

> Think I was a bit smashed after our lunch and never thanked you properly. Hope your meeting went OK? ☺

He frowned, trying to recall the details of their lunchtime conversation and what he had told her about Zack
Boxx, hoping he hadn't given away too much. From the
disparaging things she had said about her uncle, Julius
Helmsley, she didn't sound like she was about to run to him
and tell him anything. But he couldn't be sure.

He replied to Imogen.

> Thanks but can't. Have spoken to the decor-
> ators and they are coming over to give an
> estimate – and let me know when they could
> start. X

Then he looked at Sally Hughes's text and replied.

> Managed to stay awake, though not sure how
> coherent I was. But lunch was great! Definitely
> again, soon! XXXX

Another text pinged in from Imogen.

> Glad to hear lunch was great. So who was it
> with that deserved four Xs?

He felt a cold flush of dread. Shit, shit, shit.

How did that happen?

He looked at the thread. And sure enough, he'd sent the
reply to Imogen in error.

A reply came in from Sally.

> Ermmm? Decorators?

He cursed his stupidity again, his brain racing. Very carefully he tapped out a reply to Imogen.

My editor! XX

Seconds later another reply back from her.

Oh right. Didn't realize you had to shag her to get your commissions.

104

'So?' Wesley Wenceslas asked.

'So?' Pope replied.

'Tell me. Give me an answer,' the pastor said into the microphone of his headset, looking out uncomfortably at the rain sliding down the helicopter's window and at the darkness beyond.

'That would depend on the question,' Pope said. 'If you want to know the capital of Peru, it's Lima. Or the meaning of life, according to Douglas Adams? In which case, it's the number forty-two.' He looked back down at the crib sheet for the pastor's address to his faithful, tonight, in Leicester.

'This is not the moment to be frivolous,' Wenceslas said.

The helicopter bumped and yawed in turbulence, on its descent to East Midlands Airport. The pastor clenched his eyes shut, his hands clasped in front of him.

'Oh? You never read Kurt Vonnegut?' said Pope.

'Who?'

'Tut tut.'

'Kurt who?'

'A great American writer. He got it, he understood. He came up with some of the wisest words ever written: "Listen, we are put on this earth to fart around, and don't let anyone tell you any different."'

Wenceslas looked at him. 'Did it ever occur to you that

one day you might be a bit too irreverent for your own good?' He shook his head. 'What did I do wrong to deserve you?'

'God chose me for you, remember? Put it down to His sense of humour.'

There were landing lights now, directly below them. The helicopter was hovering just a few feet above a marked area and Wenceslas relaxed, finally. He shot a glance at Pope. 'All I can say is, if God chose you for me, He must have been having an off day.'

As the machine settled on the ground, both men pulled off their headsets. 'So, let's be serious, Smilealot, where are we with this Ross Hunter? It's worrying me a lot, I keep—'

He was interrupted by a *ting-ting*. Pope glanced down at his phone, then studied a message. 'From our electrician.'

'Electrician?'

'He gave the man fixing the CCTV cameras at Ross Hunter's home a bung. Five years' earnings for him. Probably could have got him cheaper, but hey, we don't do cheap, do we, Pastor?'

'Easy for you to say when you're spending my money.'

'*Our* money.'

'You're a crook.'

'Oh, right, pardon me. When was the last time you actually prayed over a handkerchief, which you charged twenty-five pounds for?'

'It's symbolic.'

'Of course it is! Is that what you will explain to God on Judgement Day? Assuming He happens to be in when you arrive up there at the Pearly Gates.'

'He will understand that I was truly a man of the people, who brought millions of human beings closer to Him through filling them with the Holy Spirit.'

Pope looked at him. 'That's a big part of your problem, isn't it? That you really believe your own press release.'

'And a big part of your problem, Mr Pope, is that if you continue being frivolous, that little creep of a journalist, Ross Hunter, could seriously disrupt your pension plan.'

'And yours.'

'So, you gave Hunter's electrician a bung?'

'To allow *our* electrician to help him. We now have control of his external CCTV cameras, and a tap on his landline phone. As soon as he arrives home this evening, from a lunch in central Brighton followed by a meeting near Brighton racecourse, we should be able to remotely monitor his mobile phone communications, too. That is, if he is dumb enough to leave his Bluetooth on.'

'And if he isn't?'

Smilealot lived up to his nickname with a big smile. 'Then we'll switch it on for him.'

Wesley Wenceslas wagged a finger. 'You're a very naughty snooper!'

'Isn't that just what your God does?' Pope retorted. 'Snoop on all of us?'

The pastor looked at him. 'You need to be careful about saying things like that. You are verging on blasphemy. Did it ever occur to you that you could end up in Hell?'

'Should I worry about that? You keep assuring everyone that the afterlife is so much better than here. I'm thinking Hell must be, too. Bring it on, I say!'

'Smilealot, sometimes I despair of you – and I pray for your soul.'

'Which makes me unique.'

'Unique? In what way?'

'I get your prayers as a freebie!'

105

The house was in darkness when Ross arrived home. He paid the taxi, got a receipt and walked up to the front door, as ever looking around, carefully. From inside he heard a desultory bark.

As he entered, Monty bounding up to him, his phone rang. The display showed the number was withheld.

'Ross Hunter,' he answered.

'Good evening, Mr Hunter, I apologize for the intrusion. I am wondering if you had any thoughts following our conversation last night?'

It was Giuseppe Silvestri.

'No further thoughts at all,' he replied.

'I would really like to meet up with you again and put a proposition to you. I am authorized by my superiors to make you an unconditional offer.'

Jamming the phone against his ear, Ross knelt and stroked the dog. 'For what, exactly?'

'For the chalice and for the tooth that we believe you have in your possession.'

'An unconditional offer – how much exactly are you talking about?' he asked.

'How would three million euros, paid to a bank account of your choice anywhere in the world, sound to you?'

Ross was silent for some moments, somewhat astonished.

Three million euros was close to three million pounds at current exchange rates. Serious money. More than he could ever hope to get, even with multiple spin-offs, from his eventual article. Even after tax, it would clear their mortgage and give them a massive cash surplus. And remove all the threats. And yet . . .

He tried to think clearly. Then he said, 'Mr Silvestri, yesterday you were questioning the provenance of what I have – or might have. Now you are not?'

'Can we meet and discuss this further, Mr Hunter? I could come to your house now, if convenient?'

'You need to understand this is not about money. I appreciate this is an enormous sum you are offering. I am not going to reject it out of hand, but I need time to think. I have your contact details. I'd like time to consider it.'

'Mr Hunter, this situation is too important to wait for very long, and the danger of these items falling into the wrong hands is increasing all the time.'

The man's tone verged on belligerent.

'Really? I'm not prepared to be bullied by anyone, I think you should know that. I've been attacked, threatened and my home has been trashed. Let me tell you something, I don't do threats. Do I make myself clear?'

'Let me make something clear to you, please, Mr Hunter. I have direct authority to talk to you from His Holiness, the Pope, the Vicar of Christ, the Bishop of Rome, the Holy See. Our Pope is the symbolic descendant of the apostle Peter. Head of the Catholic Church.'

'I appreciate your credentials, Mr Silvestri. But you are talking about the Catholic Church, which is just one of many – like the Anglican Church – and what about the Jehovah's Witnesses? Or the Presbyterians? What about the Eastern Orthodox Church? The Baptists? Lutherans?

Quakers? Plymouth Brethren? Methodists? The Pentecostal Church?'

'Mr Hunter,' Silvestri said, calm and polite as ever. 'Let us not get bogged down in semantics. If what you truly possess is the Holy Grail and a tooth from our Lord Jesus Christ Himself, their rightful home is in Rome, in the seat of Christianity.'

'That is your opinion.'

'Mr Hunter, what I am telling you is fact.'

'I can assure you, Mr Silvestri, that these items are in safe hands. I respect them, and I have taken steps to protect them. If and when I decide you would be the right custodian, I will tell you. I will consider your offer. All right?'

'You may believe you have protected these items, but perhaps you do not realize there are people with, permit me to say, fewer morals than His Holiness. They are determined to get their hands on them at all cost – even if that cost is your life, Mr Hunter. You have many enemies out there. We will try to protect you until you have passed them to us. Of course, you do understand that when you have done that, you and your family will be safe.'

'You *are* threatening me, Mr Silvestri?'

'Please do not misinterpret me.'

'How should I interpret you?'

'Regard me as a friend.'

'OK, my friend. I'm hanging up now, and I'll call you if and when I'm ready to talk more.'

Ross ended the call and stared around at the stark messages on the walls. Then he took Monty out and walked him through the darkness. Deep in thought. And completely sober now.

When he reached the park and let the dog off the lead he looked again at the text from Imogen.

Oh right. Didn't realize you had to shag her to get your commissions.

He texted a reply.

Charming. Actually, it doesn't work that way. X

Then he texted the radio presenter.

Meeting afterwards was not as fun as our lunch. X

Almost instantly a text came back from Sally.

Decided to stay in Brighton tonight. Out at dinner. If u fancy a drink later let me know. XX PS I'm a dab hand at decorating.

He grinned, and stared at it. Then, making a decision to rein it in, he replied:

I wish I could join u. Have fun! X

He wasn't hungry but knew he needed to eat something. Rummaging in the freezer when he got back, he found a mushroom risotto and pulled it out. He would put it in the microwave later. Then he went up and checked his social media. There was an Instagram post of Imogen and Virginia sharing a sofa with the children, happy families style.

He went back down into the kitchen and made himself a coffee. He opened the window, removed a pack of Silk Cut and a lighter from a kitchen drawer and lit a cigarette. As he smoked he was thinking about Sally. Then about three million pounds. He tapped the end of the cigarette against the ashtray that lived on the windowsill.

Last year he'd written a piece on the Russian oligarchs. One of them, Boris Berezovsky, had decided he could not make ends meet on one and a half billion pounds, and one theory had it that he topped himself.

Three million seemed pretty small beer compared to that.

Compared to, potentially, the greatest newspaper story of all time.

Although it would get rid of their mortgage and give them a very nice cushion going forward.

Accept it?

Pass the buck to Silvestri, take the money and run? Maybe negotiate the price up a bit?

Or risk, as Benedict Carmichael had warned, being killed.

He stared up at the clear night sky. At the stars above. The heavens. The firmament.

All of this from two bits of dust that collided and set off the Big Bang?

If that was truly the case, the whole reason for all existence, then did any of this matter a hill of beans? Was all of human life just a random, insignificant happening?

One day, the collection of cells inside Imogen would be a walking, talking human being. Their child. That child would sit on his knee and look into his eyes and ask him questions. The same kind of questions he used to ask his mum and dad.

Where did I come from?
What happened before I was born?
What will happen after I die?
Why do I exist?

Was he going to be able to look his son in the eye and say to him, 'I might have been able to give you the answer, but instead I took the cash'?

106

Thursday, 16 March

'I was rubbish tonight, wasn't I?' Wenceslas said, freezing the playback of the recording of his service earlier this evening at his Leicester church. He lounged back on a sofa in the vast hotel suite and stared across the coffee table at Lancelot Pope.

'They loved you! They always love you, Pastor. Even when your performance is – how should I put it – as I often remind you, perhaps more about *profit* than any Biblical *prophet*?'

'Don't screw with my head, Smilealot.'

'I leave that to God.'

After some moments, Wenceslas said, 'And the correct church term, Smilealot, is not *profit*, it is *collection plate*.'

'Pardon me.' Pope focused back on his own laptop. 'Good comments on Twitter – nothing but good ones. Listen to this:

> O how I pray peeps wld understand the true power of the #HolySpirit (God) wow! Powerful preaching @PastorWenceslas. Amen

And this:

Wow. So intense. Thank you @PastorWenceslas

And I like this one:

Sir I am having a wonderful time taking in all
the Holy Spirit is impacting in me through you.
#Godbless.'

'How deeply touching,' Pope said, rolling his eyes. 'You should be pleased.'

'What about Facebook?'

'I've just been checking, more of the same. They love you. Adore you!'

'I'm just a humble conduit, Smilealot. Always have been. They love me because the spirit of our Lord flows into their hearts through me.'

'Long may our Lord keep topping you up.'

Wenceslas gave him a friendly glare.

'Just on something more mundane for a moment, boss. I've ordered room service to bring your breakfast at 6 a.m. – the forecast is not looking good for flying so I've arranged the car to be on standby – as we've a board meeting at Gethsemane at 9 a.m. You OK with that?'

'Do I have an option?'

The bell rang. Lancelot Pope closed the lid of his laptop, jumped up from his sofa and went over to the door.

A nervous-looking room-service waiter wheeled in a rattling trolley. It was accompanied by the aroma of French fries. Two round metal covers sat on the white linen cloth, along with a bread basket, a bottle of mineral water and two glasses.

'Gentlemen, would you like me to set this out next door in the dining room?'

'No, just here is fine,' Wenceslas said.

The waiter flipped down both ends of the trolley, converting it into a table. He lifted one metal cover to show the steak and chips Wenceslas had ordered, and the other to reveal Pope's quinoa salad.

Wenceslas stood up, closing his eyes and raising his hands towards heaven, and prayed with the voice that was usually reserved for preaching. 'Thank you, good Lord, for this food, and also for your anointing tonight that confirms to me, your most humble and faithful servant, that you have chosen to raise me above other men. Amen.'

Amen seemed to act like a wake-up call to Pope. He leaped up from his seat and asked, 'Where's the champagne?'

'Champagne?' The waiter looked puzzled.

'I ordered it at the same time I ordered the food.'

'I'm so sorry, I will see what has happened and fetch it right away!' Then he turned to Wenceslas. 'Sir, I would have been worshipping with you tonight, but my boss would not give me the time off.'

'What is your name?' the pastor asked him.

'Melvin,' he replied.

'Melvin, would you kneel in front of me.'

The waiter obeyed.

Wenceslas stood and placed his hands on the man's head. 'My child, are you ready to receive the Lord here? Are you ready for Jesus?'

'I am, sir.'

'Do you not feel His spirit? Do you feel His power and warmth entering your body? Your heart and your innermost soul?'

'I do, I do, I do.'

'Praise the Lord!'

Wenceslas gave his head a firm, but gentle push. The waiter crumpled to the floor and lay still.

The pastor knelt beside him. 'Oh Lord, bless this man! Forgive him his sins! Fill him with your spirit! With your boundless generosity help him to be a great waiter. A man who will one day wait on your right hand at your table in Heaven!'

Slowly the waiter came out of his trance and looked around, dazed.

'Melvin, be thankful you are now not only one of God's children, you are also one of my sons!' Wenceslas said.

The young man climbed, dizzily, to his feet and looked at the pastor.

'Thank you,' he said. 'Thank you, Pastor.' He made his way, unsteadily, towards the door. 'Please – please telephone – the room-service number – when you would like your trolley removed.'

'The Lord will let you know, my son. Just remember to donate on the Wesley Wenceslas Ministries website, so you can be truly blessed tonight. Whatever you can afford.'

The waiter lowered his head, looking overwhelmed. 'Yes, yes, I will.' Then slipped out of the door.

Pope shifted the food and drinks off the trolley onto the coffee table, and poured out two glasses of water. 'Got to admire you, boss. Most people give the room-service guys a tip. You've got him paying you.'

'Paying his respects to our Lord,' Wenceslas corrected.

Pope sat back down opposite him. 'Yep, right. And in turn our Lord passes the cash to you. Showing His bountiful mercy or whatever?'

Ignoring him, Wenceslas said, 'So, you said you have an update?'

'I do. Seems like we have a rival for our affections – none other than my namesake, the Pope himself.'

'What?'

'I've had a report in from the bugging of Hunter's home. A man called Giuseppe Silvestri, if I'm pronouncing it right, Special Vatican Emissary, appears to be negotiating with Hunter for two items in his possession, the Holy Grail and a tooth from Jesus Christ. Offering him three million euros.'

'So, go offer him more.'

'It sounds like he's not motivated by money.'

'Everyone has a price.' Wenceslas held his water glass and seemed to be staring at it.

'Waiting for Jesus to come along and turn that into wine?' his MD jibed.

'Smilealot, I despair of you. Shit, where's that champagne? I need a proper drink.' He squirted ketchup on his steak and across his chips. Nodding at the salad, he added, 'And why are you eating that rabbit fodder?'

'Quinoa – didn't God tell you about it? The new super-food.'

'Didn't He tell you about the fatted calf? Which I'm eating now. The return of the Prodigal Son. My problem is the Prodigal Son never left, and now he sits eating rabbit food and judging me.'

'Did they have French fries at the Last Supper?'

Wenceslas gave him a sideways look. 'No, they had them at the Penultimate Supper – before the deep-fat fryer blew a fuse and screwed up the menu.'

'So, no Judas and chips?'

'I tell you, Smilealot. One day you will be struck dead. Now get real. Ross Hunter.'

'A man we do want struck dead, right?'

There was a long silence. Wenceslas looked at him. 'If we need to. If it gets us the items.'

'Tut tut. The sixth commandment?'

'The Great Imposter, Smilealot. Do I need to remind you? What Ross Hunter is doing is all about heralding in the Great Imposter. He's going to make claims about the Second Coming. He'll find the Great Imposter and give him the oxygen of publicity in all the world's press and media, legitimizing him. You know what happens when oxygen meets flames? They burn more fiercely. Hunter must be stopped. Do you understand what I am telling you? Ross Hunter has this fantasy of revealing to the world the Second Coming. But this deluded man, in reality, is giving oxygen to the Antichrist. The most dangerous being in the world. A total imposter. You hear what I am saying? An imposter.'

'Takes one to know one,' Pope retorted.

Wenceslas glared at him. 'What is your problem tonight?'

Pope smiled back, disarmingly. 'You and I both know the real reason you want Ross Hunter stopped – gotten rid of. I've said it before. Quite apart from him writing that stinking piece about you, you are worried this Second Coming could be real. That it might not be the Great Imposter at all, but Jesus Christ come back. And just as last time He was here, when Christ had a go at all the money-lenders in the temple, this time He might just have a go at all the phoney charismatic evangelical preachers who've been cashing in on the God business for so long. And you know fine well you are going to be near the top of that list, Pastor.'

'And that's amusing you? If I go down, you go down. Everything we have goes down the Swanee.'

Pope looked at him with a sudden, dark chill in his eyes.

'It's not amusing me, Pastor. I'm totally with you – and ahead of you. I think the only certain way to stop Hunter is to nix him.' He drew a finger, theatrically, across his throat. 'And quickly.'

Wenceslas looked back at him, equally seriously. 'You have someone in mind?'

'I do. Someone I've been recommended highly. Very discreet, lives in Monte Carlo. I've already briefed him, paid the money into his Swiss bank account and he's on the case.'

'No possible connection back to us?'

Pope looked him in the eye. 'Nope. This guy's the top.'

'He's expensive?'

Pope smiled. 'Reassuringly so.'

'An eye for an eye?'

'I think a tooth for a tooth might be more appropriate, in the circumstances.'

The bell rang again.

Pope went over to the door and opened it.

Another room-service waiter entered. He held a tray containing an ice bucket with the neck of the bottle protruding from it, two champagne flutes and a white napkin folded over his arm. This waiter was older and smarmier than the one the pastor had just saved, with slicked-down hair and an Eastern European accent.

'Krug, gentlemen? I apologize for the delay. May I open and pour?' He bowed obsequiously.

'Thank you,' Pope said, indicating the coffee table.

The man set the bucket down on it. Then, with a flourish, he covered the bottle with his napkin and raised it from the bucket. Water dripped from the base. He pointed it in Wenceslas's direction.

There was a muted *pop*.

Wesley Wenceslas jerked back in the sofa.

For a horrified instant, Lancelot Pope thought the pastor had been struck in the face by the cork. Then he froze, staring in numb disbelief at the small round hole in the centre of his forehead. At the trickle of blood running down from it.

'Jeeee—' Pope screamed.

The napkin pointed at him.

There was a second *pop*.

107

Friday, 17 March

Ross had a restless night, with constant nightmares. When the clock radio came on at 6.30 a.m., with the news headlines, he instantly pressed the snooze button, feeling in need of more sleep, not ready for the day ahead that awaited him.

It seemed only seconds later that the radio was on again. He pressed the snooze button once more. Then the radio came on again. It was now 6.50 a.m.

He sat up, drank some water and picked up his phone. There was a text from Sally, which had been sent just before 11 p.m.

> Hope you are having a good evening. Sleep tight.
> XX

Nothing from Imogen.

Hadn't he sent Imogen a text before going to sleep? He checked.

> Sleep tight, and Caligula. Monty sez hi. X

No reply.

Great.

Maybe she'd gone to bed early.

Or maybe she was still pissed off at him for the text he'd sent by mistake.

Get over it, Imo. I have lunch with people all the time, it's part of my job; to meet people and probe. Doesn't mean I'm shagging them.

Even if I happen to fancy them. We're not all like you.

The doorbell rang. Monty barked.

7.00 a.m. He felt a stab of unease.

Grabbing his dressing gown and wrestling it on, he hurried across the landing into the spare room, at the front of the house, and peered out and down at the street. The two painters, Dave and Rob, who had decorated the house for them when they had originally moved in, were standing there. And now he remembered, they'd said they could call in early on their way to a job. He went down, patted the dog trying to calm him, removed the safety chain and opened the door.

As they stepped into the hallway, both decorators looked at the walls in disbelief.

'Blimey,' Rob said.

'Ignorant twats, can't even spell!' Dave added, looking around, pointing.

'Spell?' Ross said.

ROSS HUNTER, FRIEND OF THE ANTICHRIST, IMOGEN HUNTER, EXPECTENT MOTHER OF THE ANTICHRIST

'I may be just an ignorant house painter, but I know how to spell. *Expectent?*'

'He should know about expectant mothers,' Rob said. 'He's had five kids.'

'Should be an "a", last vowel. Not "e",' Dave said.

'Very helpful,' Ross remarked.

'You know me, Mr Hunter, from when we did this place before. Helpful is my middle name.'

'Mine, too,' added Rob.

'If I find out who did it, maybe they can come back and correct it,' Ross said, drily.

He showed them around each of the rooms.

'I didn't know newspaper reporters had fan clubs,' Rob said.

'Ha ha,' Ross retorted.

'It's a lot of work,' Dave said. 'Can't just paint over that writing, it would take too many coats. We're going to have to strip the lining paper off. Insurance job?'

'I bloody hope so.'

'We'll work out a price and let you have it later today or tomorrow. If it's for the insurers, we could give you two quotes. Know what I'm saying?' He winked.

Ross grinned and thanked them. Having shown them out he pulled on a tracksuit and trainers and took Monty for a run, to try to clear his head and think.

He returned shortly after 8.15 a.m., switched on the television to the *Breakfast* news and began to mash up a disgusting-smelling roll of raw dog food – a supposedly healthy diet Imogen had recently started buying for Monty.

A battery of flashing lights on the screen caught his eye, and he looked across. He saw the entrance of a large conference-style hotel cordoned off by crime-scene tape, with a cluster of police vehicles haphazardly assembled outside, along with a crowd of reporters and photographers. A ticker ran along the bottom of the screen announcing, *Breaking News.*

The scene changed to the studio and the neatly dressed presenter, Charlie Stayt, looking solemn. 'In breaking news, the bodies of two men were discovered earlier this morning in a hotel suite occupied by the popular evangelical preacher, Pastor Wesley Wenceslas. We are going live, now, to the scene at the Hinckley Point Hotel, near Leicester, where police are about to make a statement.'

A stocky, confident-looking man in his forties, with gelled black hair and wearing a dark suit and tie, was standing in front of the cordon, with the hotel behind him. His tie flapped in a strong wind, amid a steady stream of flash-lights.

A banner across the screen read, *Detective Inspector Paul Garradin, Leicestershire Police.*

'I can confirm that two men have been found dead, from suspected gunshot wounds, in a suite at this hotel,' he said. 'We are treating these deaths as a double murder. We will hold a full press briefing later today after the victims' identities have been confirmed. I have no further informa-tion at this point. Thank you.'

There was a barrage of shouted questions, which he ignored.

Ross continued to stare at the screen. *Pastor Wesley Wenceslas.* He remembered door-stepping him outside his London church, when he was working on his piece on evangelists, and one of the pastor's minders pushed him away so hard he fell over. And he remembered Wenceslas's attempts to sue the *Sunday Times* and himself after the huge piece was published.

Pastor Wesley Wenceslas was a total shit, a very clever and charismatic con man. Getting, finally, his just desserts? No doubt it would be all over the news in the coming hours.

But there was something about this report that made Ross feel deeply uncomfortable. He thought back to his conversation with Giuseppe Silvestri last night.

You may believe you have protected these items, but perhaps you do not realize there are people with, shall I say, fewer morals than His Holiness. They are determined to get their hands on them at all cost – even if that cost is your life, Mr Hunter. You have many enemies out there, we will try to protect you until you have passed them to us. Of course . . . when you have done that, you and your family will be safe.

As he had wondered earlier, was Pastor Wesley Wenceslas one of these enemies?

Was that who the Italian was referring to?

Wild speculation, he knew, but was there some link between these shootings and himself? A Silvestri connection?

Monty whined at him.

'Sorry, boy!' He finished preparing the food, trying to avoid breathing too much of the stink, then put the bowl on the floor.

Instead of falling on it ravenously, the dog walked across the floor and curled up in his basket.

'Hey, what's up? I thought you were hungry? What is it? Are you missing your mum?'

Ross went to the front door, scooped up the papers which had just arrived, then poured himself some cereal. He chopped up an apple, added some blueberries, grapes and Greek yoghurt, mixed them together and sat down.

He stared at the television. Waiting for another development on the murders. But there was nothing further. A mention of an EU protest against US policy on climate change. An MP tabling a no-confidence motion against the Speaker of the House of Commons. More issues on the National Health Service, and the defiant Health Secretary heatedly defending his latest actions.

Then he felt a vibration on his left wrist from his Apple Watch.

He looked at it and saw an email from Zack Boxx that had come in during the night.

> Hi Ross, I told you I'd charge you £2k for the search. And a bonus of £1k for each of the results? Well I've got good news – or maybe it's bad news – for you. You owe me £5k!

Aware he was unlikely to be up at this hour, Ross emailed him back anyway, excitedly.

> What do you have?????

He waited several minutes, but there was no response. Impatiently, he picked up his burner phone, found the geek's number and dialled it.

After four rings, it went to voicemail.

'Hi, this is Zack Boxx. If you want to get any sense out of me, call me after 4 p.m. Sleep tight! And if you're really desperate, leave a message.'

He left a brief message.

Then sat still, wondering. Eating his cereal with no appetite. What did Boxx have?

On the 9 a.m. news, the BBC ran the same story about the double murder he'd seen at 8.30 a.m.

He decided to take a look on Twitter and rapidly found a lot more information, put out by what sounded like a member of the hotel staff, in a tweet that had already gone viral. A room-service waiter taking the pastor's pre-ordered breakfast found the two men both dead, each with a single gunshot wound to the head.

He shivered.

His iPhone rang. The display showed it was Imogen.

'Hi,' he answered.

'Have you seen the news?' she said.

'About Pastor Wesley Wenceslas?'

'Yes.' Her tone was grim. 'A member of his staff has already put up a Facebook memorial page – and it's getting hundreds of posts.'

'What does that crook's death have to do with anything?'

'You don't get it, do you, Ross? Two more murders. I'm really worried we'll be next.'

'But, Imogen, they've got nothing to do with me, those guys – other than I tried to interview them, years ago.'

'Ross, come on, get real! This isn't coincidence. There are fanatics out there; religion's a bloody minefield. Come and stay here until we are safe.'

'Imogen, I don't think I'm in real danger. I've got what they're after, and all the time I have it I'm safe. And you are a lot safer if we keep apart – and I'm not putting Monty in kennels just because of Ben's allergies. Let's talk later in the day, OK?'

'Sorry, didn't mean to interrupt your love nest.'

'Hey – what do you mean?'

There was no response. She had hung up.

He dialled her number. It went straight to voicemail. 'Imogen, I'm here alone. OK?'

After quickly showering, shaving and dressing, he checked his phone. Imogen had still not called him back. He tried her number again. And again, got her voicemail.

He hung up, angry at her. Angry at himself.

At his desk, he continued to work on his story of the events to date.

At 4 p.m., on the dot, he rang Zack Boxx, and got his sleepy voice.

'Yeah?'

'It's Ross.'

'Oh right, yeah.'

'You said you have a result for me.'

'I do. Yep.'

There was a long silence. Ross wondered if he had gone back to sleep.

'You there, Zack?'

'I'm here. You'd better come over, I think it would be easier to show you.'

'Now?'

'Now's good, I suppose,' he said, sounding reluctant.

Then Ross remembered his Audi was in the underground car park beneath the Waterfront Hotel. 'I'll be with you in an hour.'

'I'll still be here, unfortunately. Trapped on earth.'

108

Just after 5 p.m. Ross Hunter crouched down uncomfortably beside Zack Boxx on the manky beige carpet. The cat was prowling around at the far end of the room, looking unsettled. Ross had never seen Boxx so animated.

On the screen in front of them were rows of numbers and letters, totally meaningless to him. Boxx pointed at some of them, excitedly, running his finger along a row. 'See that DNA match?'

'Not really,' Ross replied.

Boxx refreshed the screen and a new set of figures, equally meaningless to Ross, appeared. 'How about this?'

'Nope.'

He again refreshed the screen. 'Any of these?'

'Nope.'

Boxx pushed his mop of hair back and looked at Ross as if he was a simpleton. 'OK, let's go back to the first image.'

He tapped the keypad, and within seconds the screen filled with rows of figures. 'You're lucky, Ross. I think we've got really, really lucky! With the standard DNA, the mitochondrial and the Y-STR.'

'In what way?'

'In every way! OK, the first is through the mitochondrial DNA database held by the Los Angeles Police Department.

I've got a match with the mitochondrial you gave me. The seven mutations are present in both profiles.'

'You have – with whom?'

'A lady called Arlene Katzenberg.'

'Arlene Katzenberg?'

'Yes. Does her name mean anything to you?'

'Not immediately. What did she do to have her DNA on file with the LAPD?'

'All will become clear.'

Ross stared at the screen in silence. Mitochondrial. DNA that went down through the female line, unaltered. If the DNA from the chalice and from the tooth were really from Jesus Christ, this meant that Arlene Katzenberg, whoever she might be, was directly descended from the bloodline of Jesus.

'Brilliant work, Zack.'

'OK, now take a look at this. You gave me Y-STR – the Y-chromosome short tandem repeat DNA – which descends unaltered, like the mitochondrial, but from the male bloodline. I've got a profile match here too, again with the seven mutations, to a doctor called Myron Mizrahi, born in La Jolla, California. Also on file with the LAPD.'

'What's the reason they have his on file?'

'All will become clear.' Boxx gave him a smug look. 'You're going to see that I've earned my money.'

'I think you have.'

Ross's brain was racing. Dr Myron Mizrahi. Direct descendant, through the male bloodline, of Jesus Christ. So many possibilities were occurring to him.

'What's your view on religion, Zack? Do you have any beliefs?'

'Quantum physics is kind of my religion.'

'Not an area I can get my head around.'

Boxx rocked his head backwards and forwards, excitedly. 'You should try. Study it. It's like – probably the key to everything.'

'If anyone could understand it!'

'There's all kinds of stuff going on in quantum physics no one can understand, yep? Connections across the world that no one can explain. Stuff that is beyond coincidence, beyond chance. Supernatural? Could it be the work of an Intelligent Designer?'

'Is that what you think?'

'You know the multiverse theory?'

'I've heard the term but I don't know what it means.'

'For life to exist on our planet it requires an unbelievably intricate number of elements all combining. The simplest example is this: if we were only a small distance closer to the sun we'd be fried – life on this planet could not exist. A bit further away and it would be too cold to support life. And there's endless more. The mathematical, physical and chemical calculations required for life as we know it to exist are just – mind-boggling. So, the *multiverse* theory is that when the Big Bang happened it created hundreds, maybe millions, maybe billions of universes just like ours. The theory holds that in just one of them it's possible that all the elements combined, by sheer chance, to enable life as we know it to exist. Our planet, earth.'

'You subscribe to that?'

'Nope, I think it's bollocks. There's a category mistake here. The much more interesting stuff for me, in quantum physics, is the effect of the observer. That if you look at something, the fact that you are looking at it changes it.'

'God watching us? Changes us?'

'Who knows? Either that or human life is the result of a pretty big coincidence.'

'What did you mean by a *category mistake*?'

'Yep, OK. So, it's kind of a Paley's Watch kind of a thing –'

'Paley's Watch? You're losing me again.'

'OK, take a Ford motor car dropped into a remote part of the world where a man who has never seen a car, and knows nothing about modern engineering, looks at it. He might imagine there is a god – Mr Ford – inside the engine making it go. He might further imagine that when the engine ran sweetly, it was because Mr Ford inside the engine liked him, and when it wouldn't start it was because Mr Ford didn't like him and was angry about something, OK?'

Ross frowned, wondering where this was going.

'So, if he subsequently took engineering classes and dismantled the engine, he'd find there was no Mr Ford inside,' Zack continued. 'He'd also learn the real reason it worked was through internal combustion. But taking it a stage further, if he then decided that because he now knew how the engine worked, he had no reason to believe in the existence of Mr Ford, he'd be making a *category mistake*. Because if Mr Ford had never existed to design the mechanisms, none would exist.'

Ross let it sink in. Then he asked, 'What do you really believe yourself, Zack?'

'I haven't figured it out yet. Coincidence is kind of interesting, that draws me. Einstein named coincidences *God's calling cards*. I'm about to give you a coincidence that's about as close to God's calling card as you are ever likely to get. You ready for this?'

Ross smiled. 'Yes, I think so.'

'OK. Arlene Katzenberg and Myron Mizrahi met!'

'What?'

'They met.' He smiled.

'When? How do you know?'

'In 1946. Arlene Katzenberg and Myron Mizrahi got married.'

Ross looked at him, totally and utterly stunned. 'Married?'

He nodded. 'Yep. And they had a son, born in 1947.'

109

Ross stood up, feeling elated. A woman, with a DNA match to Jesus Christ, married to a man who was also a DNA match to Jesus?

And had a son?

'Zack,' he asked, with urgency in his voice. 'The son – do you have any idea if he is still alive?'

'He was, certainly, as recently as three years ago.'

'How do you know that?'

'All in good time!'

What were the chances of these two meeting, Ross wondered? Both descended from an ancestor born and living thousands of miles away, over two thousand years ago. What were the odds?

Billions to one? Trillions to one?

They were utterly incalculable.

'How did you get this information, Zack?'

'Anything you'd care to share with me, Ross?' He gave him a knowing look.

'Tell me about the parents, are they still alive?'

Boxx shook his head. 'That's how I was able to get this information from the police records – they were murdered soon after moving to Los Angeles in 1957, and it was never solved. A kind of ritual killing – at least that's how it looked, apparently. Luckily for us – well, for you – the LAPD reopened the case recently, as part of their examination of historical unsolved murders – cold cases – and obtained fresh DNA from their preserved blood samples.'

'Ritual killing? What happened – how did they die?'

'It looked like there were religious overtones, right? They were naked, each nailed to the floor of their home face up, side by side, arms outstretched, a nail through each hand and one through both feet. Like they were crucified.'

Ross looked back at Boxx, horrified. Silent for some moments. 'Was this in the files you hacked?'

'All there.'

'So – what happened to the son – what's his name?'

'Michael. The police records show his birth parents were killed when he was ten. He was taken into care, but there is nothing more on him after then.'

'But you say he's still alive – or was in 2014?'

Zack Boxx was grinning and nodding his head. 'Here's the bit I think you are really going to like – and where I really earn my money!'

Ross looked at him, expectantly.

'In March 2014, in West Hollywood, a sixty-seven-year-old man, Michael Henry Delaney, was arrested for the suspected misdemeanour of Driving Under Influence. A blood sample was taken by the police, and DNA was obtained from that.' Boxx looked up at Ross, almost gleeful. 'Michael Delaney's DNA, with the seven unique mutations on the mitochondrial and on the Y chromosome, is a one hundred per cent match to the profiles you gave me.'

Ross stared back at him. 'The missing son?'

He fell silent, thinking of the implications of this. His heart was pounding.

'So, is there?'

'Is there what, Zack?'

'Something you want to share with me on this?'

'Maybe one day, Zack. But not now. You're safer not knowing.'

110

Ross drove away from Boxx's flat in a daze. The geek hadn't wanted to let it go, so he'd fobbed off more of his questions about why he was so interested in all this DNA. He'd told him he was researching historical genetic links relating to the Jewish diaspora and emigration to the United States.

His mind was spinning.

Michael Delaney.

Michael Henry Delaney.

If what he had in his possession was authentic, the chalice and the tooth, that would mean Michael Delaney had the identical mitochondrial and Y-chromosome DNA to Jesus Christ – like a unique genetic fingerprint. Everyone knew Jesus hadn't married, but his Y chromosome would be the same as his brothers, who had wives.

His phone pinged with a text, but he ignored it, not wanting to disrupt his thoughts. Delaney's parents, direct descendants of Jesus Christ, down the female and the male lines. Meeting. Having a child.

He tried to think through the implications.

Arlene Katzenberg and Myron Mizrahi.

Total strangers to each other. Both Jewish names.

Meeting and marrying.

Murdered a decade later in a symbolic, ritual killing.

Did that mean someone back then knew? But if so, why had they killed the parents and not the son?

Had someone who knew the boy's provenance taken him away and hidden him? People called Delaney? Changing his last name from a Jewish one to an Irish one? He remembered in the Bible about King Herod and the Massacre of the Innocents. Slaughtering every male child under the age of two, in an attempt to kill the baby Jesus.

He wished he knew his Bible better.

He was drawn back to the coincidence. Two people meeting. OK, so they both lived in the same county of Southern California. But carrying that DNA, those genes? And then producing a son with an exact match to the DNA he'd had identified by the ATGC laboratory? How could that be? Every parent carried male and female bloodline genes. They would be randomly mixed in the nuclear DNA of a fertilized egg. Yet this Michael Delaney was carrying identical mitochondrial and Y-chromosome DNA to Jesus Christ – the unique genetic fingerprint. How could that have happened? Destiny?

If Delaney was still alive now he would be in his early seventies.

The Second Coming?

But if so, why had no one heard about it?

Or had they?

Delaney's parents murdered in a ritual killing mimicking the crucifixion. The boy possibly taken into hiding, terrified. Was he still terrified today – assuming he was still alive? Keeping low, under the radar, carrying a secret he was too scared to reveal.

Or, Ross suddenly thought, what if he didn't know?

Another, perhaps simpler explanation, was that the cup and the tooth he had were just not the real deal.

Or was Jesus Christ simply not the Saviour that some religions believed? Just a man who was a conjuror and illusionist, who was written about erratically by various people, including some of the Apostles, who believed they could found a religion by creating a myth around him?

If that was the case, he had to hand it to them. Their press releases had been pretty good to have lasted over two millennia.

But if Michael Delaney was the true Messiah, what were the implications – for the world?

He thought about the potential story he could write if he could find him.

The greatest newspaper scoop of all time?

111

At a few minutes to 6 p.m., Ross entered his house, crouched down and stroked Monty. 'We'll go for a walk later, OK? Promise!'

He hurried upstairs, sat in front of his computer and logged on. The moment the screen came alive, he did a Google search on the name 'Michael Delaney'.

Hundreds of matches appeared.

He narrowed the search by changing it to 'Michael Henry Delaney Wiki'.

The Wikipedia entry appeared and his hopes rose as he got a hit.

Michael Henry Delaney (born 18 April 1947) is an American close magician. Under the stage name Mickey Magic, he had his own prime-time show on ABC Television from 1994 to 1997. Formerly represented by Creative Artists Agency. As a child, he was put in the care of foster parents, adopting their last name, following the (unsolved) murder of his parents, Myron and Arlene (née Katzenberg) Mizrahi.

He then clicked on Images. But only one series of photographs appeared. They were of a flamboyant man in his late forties, with flowing brown hair. He was wearing a fancy white suit in each photo. Some of the images showed him performing magic, his head surrounded by rays of light, creating a halo effect.

There were no other photographs of Michael Delaney, and no indication he had died.

So where was he now? And by having these details up on Wikipedia, did it mean Delaney was no longer afraid?

Was he really a direct descendant of Jesus Christ? Alive somewhere in Los Angeles, the coordinates seemed to indicate, and unaware of who he really was?

And hadn't Jesus, in his own way, been a magician, too, back when the world had been a lot less sceptical?

Ross dealt with a few emails that needed quick responses. On his iPhone was a text from Imogen, suggesting they meet tomorrow for lunch if he was free – and not 'editing' – and there was one on his burner from Sally Hughes, asking how his day had been.

He did not reply to either. Instead he went downstairs, tugged Monty's lead off the back of the kitchen door and headed off with him into the darkness.

Thinking. A plan forming.

An hour later, when he returned, he went up to his den and typed an email to his editor.

> Hi Natalie, I have total dynamite on my story. You're going to have to trust me on this. I need expenses. Got to fly to LA asap. Have a flight on hold at a good price. Can you call me when you get this?

To his surprise, she rang back five minutes later on the burner phone number he had given her.

'Hang on one sec,' he told her, and hurriedly went outside to talk. 'OK!' he said.

'Ross, you are in the last-chance saloon. You're turning down every story I suggest – I'm getting nothing back from you. I'd really like you to write a follow-up piece on Wesley Wenceslas's murder. Could you do that for this weekend?'

'I can't, I need to go to LA.'

'This had better be good. What can you tell me?'

'Well, I'm not sure you would believe me if I did.'

'Try me.'

Ross tried her.

112

Big Tony lounged back in the curved window seat of his twelfth-floor apartment in Monaco. He was drinking his preferred single-grain Scotch, whilst listening through his headset to Ross Hunter, who was talking on his phone in his bugged home in Brighton, Sussex.

The colours in here were bright and sunny; the drapes and the cushions yellow, the carpet and furniture white. After his years in the darkness of his supermax cell, he liked brightness. He liked the sun shining in. For over two decades he'd not seen the sun.

Outside, a blue and white Héli Air Monaco shuttle was lifting off for its seven-minute flight to Nice Airport. He watched its winking lights as it climbed away into the darkening sky above the Med, then puffed on his Cohiba Robusto.

He liked Cohibas, the only cigar that controversial character Fidel Castro used to smoke. The Cuban dictator had been paranoid in his early days about being poisoned, so he had employed personally selected cigar rollers to work exclusively for him.

Big Tony figured the dictator of the world's premier cigar-manufacturing nation would have had the pick of the crops. If they were good enough for Castro, they were good enough for him. He liked to know stuff. He knew everything

511

about this whisky, too. The Haig distillery was founded in 1824 and was the first distillery to produce grain whisky using the column still method. It was important to know everything you could about who you were connected to, he believed. And he had learned a lot through his headset in the past few days.

The conversation was interesting. Ross Hunter was talking to a lady – maybe his editor, from the way it sounded – asking for funding for a trip to Los Angeles. Seemed like he wanted to go pretty urgently. But his voice was very faint, as if he had stepped outside and Tony was only picking up part of the conversation. It was enough for him to know what he needed to do next.

It was strange the way things worked out, he reflected. Banged up for twenty-five years in his mid twenties, life in that supermax had been hell. But since then it had been sweet. And now he was on a roll, and when the dice were rolling right, stuff worked out for you in ways so good it felt almost like there was a helping hand up there, somewhere.

Albeit a somewhat warped hand. First, he was hired to kill the man he was listening to on the phone, Ross Hunter, some kind of journalist scumbag. Everything agreed, the cash safely banked, payment in full. Then he'd been asked to kill the two men at the top of the company – Wesley Wenceslas Ministries – which had hired him to kill Hunter. His employees had of course tried to keep their identity secret, but not many clients succeeded in keeping secrets from him for very long.

Professional morality had prevented him from personally carrying out the executions of Wenceslas and Pope, but not enough for him to want to lose the business, so he had made a rare exception to his rule of never trusting anyone and engaged an associate for the task.

A reliable source in Bucharest. For less than ten per cent of the $5m fee he'd demanded, his Bucharest fixer had sent someone to England who had done the deed and was out of the country the next morning. On his share of the deal, the assassin could live like a king in his own country for the next decade. And it would be a decade before the fixer sent him to England again.

You could almost believe there was a God!

The shenanigans over the Wesley Wenceslas Ministries had left him wondering whether his professional services were still actually required. But if not, that meant he would have to return the money. So, he decided to continue as instructed.

He rattled the ice cubes in his glass and sipped some more. Shame he couldn't have the same happen to loathsome Julius Helmsley aka 'Mr Brown'. But hey, that was something to stick in his back pocket, maybe for the future. At this moment, he had his fish to fry. His mark, Ross Hunter.

Hunter was negotiating an allowance for this trip to LA. Sounded like the lady on the other end had agreed, if a bit reluctantly. The trip was on. Big Tony was happy about that. LA was a familiar hunting ground.

Besides, he rather liked the idea of a visit back to America. He might be living in a kind of exile but he still remained an American citizen, through and through, although Monte Carlo was his home now. He was comfortable here. Rich beyond his wildest dreams as a kid.

With just one problem: he had nothing he really needed or wanted to spend his money on.

Hunting down folk and killing them. That was what he liked doing best, however much he had tried denying it to himself.

It was the buzz. Each hit was a fresh challenge, fresh adrenalin rush. The moments in his life, on the hunt, the chase, when he truly felt alive.

The laptop on the table in front of him displayed dozens of mugshots of Ross Hunter. There was a particularly nice one on the journo's byline on the *Sunday Times* columns he wrote. Lean, smiling face. Short hair. Penetrating eyes.

He'd memorized the face. With sunglasses, without. Baseball cap, no hat. Stubble, no stubble. Beard, moustache, clean shaven.

LA would be nice.

Might be fun to travel there together, catch the same flight. Although, from the sound of the conversation, Hunter looked like he was doomed to a Coach seat. Hey, maybe he'd ask the stewardess in First Class to take the guy slumming it in the ghetto back there a glass of vintage champagne.

But maybe he wouldn't.

He picked up his phone and dialled a contact in Syracuse, New York, who owed him a favour. The guy ran a confidential service monitoring airline bookings. He could tell you what flight anyone was booked on, and if they were in the air, at what time they would land. Big Tony fed him the name Ross Hunter and asked him to let him know the moment Hunter booked on a flight from the UK to Los Angeles.

113

'Take a card! Any card, don't let me see it, just take a card!'

Friday night on St Patrick's Day in the half-full Fairfax Lounge. It was a tired room, old-fashioned but not in any fancy, retro way – just plain old. The smell of stale beer was ingrained in the fabric of the place. A long, shiny bar ran the length of one side, and a row of curved leather banquettes down the other. Dim green lampshades hung low, giving the feel of a 1930s speakeasy. A television on the wall behind the bar showed a ball game that a handful of guys and a couple of women, hunched on stools, were watching. At the far end of the room was a small stage on which stood microphone stands, various musical instruments, a tangle of wires and two speakers the size of fridges. The green-and-white flags dotted around the place, brought out annually, were limp and dusty.

The musicians had taken a break, the guitarist, drummer and saxophonist, along with the superannuated platinum-blonde singer who'd had so much facial work it looked like the surgeon was now pretty much down to bare bone.

'Any card, sir! That's right, any card!'

Mike Delaney, a gaunt man with a booze-veined face, stood in the one suit he possessed, light grey with some of the stitching gone and the elbows frayed, a sharp black shirt and badly scuffed desert boots. A lock of his overly long, threadbare grey hair hung over his forehead, partially obscuring his right eye.

He fanned out the full deck of cards, face down, with trembling hands. A group of four people sat at a banquette in front of him, one man drinking a Bud, the other with a tumbler of whiskey on the rocks, the ladies drinking cocktails from Martini glasses. One of the men, with a shaven head, wearing a singlet, had a belligerent expression. Looking reluctant to have this intrusion from the house magician, he reached forward with a tattooed arm on which he sported a large Breitling watch, and tugged out a card.

'What's your name, sir?'

'Billy.'

Delaney's voice was reedy and urgent. 'Take a look at it, Billy, don't let me see it. Show it to the others but don't let me see it!'

The man obliged. It was the eight of hearts.

Delaney handed him a marker pen. 'Would you write your name on the back of it, please, Billy.'

Billy obliged, scrawled his name in black ink on the card then returned the pen, which the elderly magician pocketed.

'Now put the card back in the pack – anywhere you like!'

The man slipped it back in, giving his companions a sceptical shrug.

Delaney closed the deck. Then, as he fanned the cards out again, he fumbled and dropped the entire deck on the floor, all the cards falling face up.

'Shit, man, you're a goddam cheat!' Billy said, loudly.

Both couples were leaning over the table looking down at the floor. All the cards were identical. Each one was an eight of hearts.

Hastily, Mike Delaney knelt and scooped the cards up, clumsily. 'Which was the card you chose, Billy?'

'Goddammit, you know which card, asshole.'

Delaney handed him the pack. 'Show me it, would you, sir.'

'What the fuck?'

'Show me the card, please, Billy.'

The man turned the pack over. To his surprise the bottom card was the queen of clubs and not an eight of hearts. He frowned and slid the card onto the low table in front of him. The next card in the pack was a two of spades. Frowning again, he continued through the pack. Each card was different. And now his other three companions were looking on with interest.

'Do you see your card, Billy?'

'Goddammit.' Silently the man worked his way through the entire deck. Then when he had finished and they all lay face up on the table he said, 'Ain't there.'

Delaney looked surprised. 'Well, OK, let's try something different. How about instead of you telling me which card you chose, I tell you where it is?'

'Yeah, right.'

Delaney produced a small spoon from thin air. 'Would you mind passing me your glass, Billy. If I spill any I'll get you another, fair dues?'

The man reluctantly handed him his tumbler.

Delaney spooned out a cube of ice and placed it on the table. He then produced, again from seemingly thin air, a small, silver hammer. Holding the ice cube with one hand, he struck it with the hammer, shattering it open. Inside lay a folded-up playing card. 'Could that be the one you chose, Billy?'

The man leaned forward, picked it up and unfolded it. Then he raised it, dumbfounded, showing it to his friends.

'That your card, Billy?'

'Well, it's the eight of hearts.'

'Turn it over.'

He did. On the back, in his handwriting in black, was the name 'Billy'.

'Jesus!' he said. 'How the heck did you do that?'

His companions looked amazed.

Delaney smiled. 'Guess I'd better be going, it's getting late, leave you guys to your party.' Then he hesitated. 'Oh, Billy, could you tell me the time?'

'Sure,' he said and glanced at his watch. Or rather, where his watch had been. He was staring at his bare wrist.

Delaney dug his hand into his inside breast pocket and pulled out the man's Breitling. He held it up by the strap. 'This what you're looking for, Billy?'

114

Ross sat opposite Imogen in their favourite vegetarian restaurant, Terre à Terre. At home neither of them drank at lunchtime, but Imogen said she fancied a glass of wine, and he certainly fancied one also.

He'd ended up ordering a bottle of Albarino.

'Cheers!' he said, after an awkward silence waiting for the waiter to return with the bottle and pour it. It felt strange sitting here with her.

Imogen raised her glass. 'Cheers,' she replied, with a total absence of cheer. She sipped some of the wine. 'Very minerally,' she said, flatly.

'You like *minerally*, normally.'

'Is anything *normal* right now, Ross?'

'Listen, I know things have been difficult. What would you say if I told you Jesus Christ was back on earth and I might have found him?'

'That you should be sectioned under the Mental Health Act?'

'I'm serious, Imo. I know you've been through hell – don't think I haven't either. But what I've got is pure dynamite. I have a story that could blow the human race's mind. I just need you to cut me some slack and trust my instincts, OK? This story is going to make us rich – richer

519

than we could ever have imagined. We'll clear all our debts and have masses to spare.'

She tilted her head and sipped some wine. 'Are you going to tell me about it?'

'Of course!' He raised his glass and clinked it against hers. Then he told her everything that had happened in the past two days.

'So, you fly to LA tomorrow?'

'Yes.'

'And where are you going to start looking? It's a vast city, and you've got compass coordinates for a part of it, nothing more.'

'I have some contacts there – an old friend of mine is now on the *LA Times*, and I know a guy in the LAPD who helped me a lot on that piece I wrote on celebrity stalking a couple of years back. I've emailed both of them.'

She nodded. 'What time are you flying?'

'Midday.'

'What are you going to do with Monty?'

'I've had to book him into kennels and I've found one I'm happy with – that one we see each time we drive past Lewes.'

'So, you're flying to LA to meet Jesus Christ?'

'That's my hope.'

'What if he's out?'

He smiled. 'Come on, stop being so cynical.'

'I'm sorry, Ross, you ought to try dictating all this into a machine and then playing it back to yourself, and seeing how ridiculous it sounds.'

'Did Jesus not originally die on the cross because a lot of people didn't believe him – or were scared of him? You're a believer, Imo. Your entire faith is founded on belief in the Resurrection, so what's your problem?'

'My problem is, Ross, in my faith we believe that before Jesus Christ returns – the Second Coming – we'll know about it, loud and clear. What you are doing is potentially giving air time to a nutter – with consequences that could damage the Christian faith badly.'

He looked at her. 'I can't believe you're not supporting me now. You're my wife, we're a unit. A supposedly inseparable unit. *What God has joined together, let no man put asunder.*' He gave her a hard, knowing stare and she had the grace to blush.

'I'm sorry,' he said. 'I didn't mean to –'

'To rake up the past? The glowing embers that never quite die out for you, right?'

'Imo, I've potentially got the biggest story of my life.'

'I can't support you any more, Ross, because your story means more to you than me and our baby do. I fell in love with a man I thought would put me above everything else in his life. But no, I was wrong. I understood early in our marriage that your work – your stories – would always come first. Over everything. Does nothing else ever matter to you?'

He glared at her. 'You know what? I'll tell you what matters more to me than anything, and that is that our child has a future, and in the world's current fucked-up state I'm not sure he does. This isn't just any old story, Imo, I'm talking about potentially changing and saving the world here.'

'You really believe that? The ramblings of a mad old man? Did you ever read the author E. M. Forster?'

'*A Room with a View? A Passage to India?*'

'Yes. "If I had to choose between betraying my country and betraying my friend, I hope I should have the guts to betray my country."'

'You'd rather I betrayed the world, just to make you feel

a little better?' He picked up his glass. 'What does that say about your faith?'

'My faith?'

'You're saying that I should dismiss the chance to prove God's existence to the world, in order to not upset my family?'

'It's not about upsetting your family. It's about caring whether the baby and I live or die. About putting us before your story.'

'It's also about supporting your partner, Imo.'

'So, we agree to differ.'

He shook his head, anger rising inside him. 'No, Imo, we don't agree on anything.'

115

Saturday, 18 March

As soon as Ross arrived home after his lunch with Imogen he went into his bedroom to pack. Monty followed him and stood beside him, tail down, as it always was when he saw suitcases.

'It's OK, boy, you're going to go to kennels, but only for a few days, I promise.'

It was strange, he thought, that he really didn't care if he'd upset Imogen. He should, but he didn't. Instead his mind turned to his packing. Thinking about speed and mobility, he wondered if he should try to cram everything into a carry-on, rather than taking the check-in suitcase he'd laid on the floor.

As he was pondering, his phone rang. He answered and heard a voice with a broad Midlands accent he did not recognize.

'Mr Hunter? I apologize for this intrusion, sir. My name is Detective Inspector Simon Cludes, from Leicestershire Police Major Crimes Branch.'

'Yes?'

'Sir, you may be aware of the double murder of Pastor Wesley Wenceslas and Mr Lancelot Pope.'

'Yes, I could hardly miss it – it's been all over the news.'

'May I ask if you were acquainted with either of these gentlemen, sir?'

'Not at all, no. Well, I tried to talk to Wenceslas once, but never got past a minder. I did subsequently refer to him, fairly scathingly, in a piece I wrote – about five years ago – on the world's richest evangelist preachers.'

'Might you have upset them, Mr Hunter?'

'Yes, they threatened legal action against myself and the paper. Then I think they thought better of it.'

'Might you have upset them enough for them to want to kill you?'

'I'm afraid I upset a lot of people in my work,' he replied. 'But that was a good five years ago, maybe six. I think if I'd pissed them off enough to want to kill me, they'd have done it by now.'

'I'm afraid that's not the information I have, Mr Hunter. From what our digital forensics team has been able to recover from their computers, so far, we believe your safety may be threatened.'

'What information do you have?'

'I'm afraid no more than that, at this stage, sir. You've not had any recent contact with the pastor or the Wesley Wenceslas Ministries which might have rekindled their anger against you?'

'No, none. So presumably now Wenceslas is dead, that threat is over?'

'We would hope so, sir, but we don't know. We will require you to give a statement, and I'm arranging for Sussex Police to send two detectives to see you.'

'Yes – I – I could see them, but I'm flying to America tomorrow.'

'I'll give you my number, Mr Hunter, if you could call me when you are back in the country.'

'Sure. Can you tell me – are you saying there is a contract out on me? What do you know about it?'

'Nothing more than I've told you, sir. It is alluded to, but the digital forensics team have not recovered any details. I don't want to worry you unduly, but I would be failing if I did not warn you. I suggest you be extra vigilant until we have been able to find out if there is anything more. I will of course notify you the moment we find any further information. Will you be contactable on this number in America, sir?'

'Twenty-four-seven.'

Ross ended the call. Pastor Wesley Wenceslas had put a contract on his life? Five years after his article on phoney, profiteering evangelists? Revenge might be a dish best eaten cold, but five years was far too long for this to be connected to that story. Everything was telling him it must be related to what he was doing now.

He looked at the pastor's Facebook page and saw an outpouring of grief. Post after post expressing shock, disbelief and sadness. Then he went to Wenceslas's website. A link took him to the pastor's YouTube channel. There was a prayer service at his London church being conducted by one of his minions, the camera panning across a sea of weeping faces.

He stared down at the street. All was surprisingly quiet for a Saturday afternoon, probably because Brighton and Hove Albion were not at the Amex stadium, but were playing away.

Why would Wenceslas or his organization have wanted him dead?

Was the pastor worried about the consequences of what his findings could do to his empire?

He opened up his file on the story, and for the next two hours he sat typing. He continued with the log of events that he had begun on the train to Birmingham – that felt like an eon ago. Then he sent what he had written, along with an accompanying email, to his editor.

> Hi Natalie, this is not for publication, only for safety. I've had a credible warning of a death threat against me. Hopefully I'll be filing more copy soon. Just hold this for now, and if anything happens to me you'll have some good material here!

He sent the email and attachment.

Then he went downstairs, pulled on his boots, put on Monty's lead, picked up his torch and went outside into the falling dusk.

He took the dog across the road bridge, then let him roam loose in the fields on the far side, walking along behind him in the blustery wind.

We believe your safety may be threatened.

He thought back to his meeting with Benedict Carmichael, the Bishop of Monmouth. His warning.

Do you know what I really, truthfully think, if someone credible claimed to have absolute proof of God's existence, Ross? I think that person would be killed.

Now Wenceslas was dead. Murdered. Who had killed him and why?

As he walked, breathing in the country smells and looking towards the lights of a distant farmhouse, he felt very alone. He thought back to his lunch with Imogen. With the angry stranger who was his wife. The angry stranger carrying his child.

Take Silvestri's money? End all their financial problems and try for a new start? They could put their house on the market and move out into the country, which had been their dream for a long time. But he came back to the same place. Could he spend the rest of his life wondering what might have been because he had sold his soul for thirty pieces of silver?

116

Saturday, 18 March

An hour later, guided by his torch, Ross headed back across the fields. As he reached the fence before the main road, he called Monty and clipped his lead back on. They crossed high above the dual carriageway and threaded their way through the network of Patcham streets back home. As he reached the front door of the house, bright headlights shone behind him.

He spun round.

A limousine pulled up. It was the same Mercedes with the diplomatic plates from three nights ago, he recognized. The rear door opened and Giuseppe Silvestri alighted.

'Ah, Mr Hunter!'

'Good evening, Mr Silvestri.'

'Would this be a convenient moment to have a chat?'

'Not really, no.'

'Perhaps I could have just a few minutes?'

'I'm sorry, this is not a good time.'

'Mr Hunter, I know what you are doing.'

'Is that right?'

'Do you not realize the damage you will cause? Please listen to me.'

'I'm listening. Damage to what?'

Silvestri looked around him, uncomfortably. 'I don't think this is such a good place to talk. I would like to continue our discussion from before.'

'What damage are you talking about? Damage to what, exactly?' he repeated.

'To all of our religions, all belief systems in our world.'

'Really? To Sikhs? I don't think they would be damaged by proof of God's existence. Their God is in everything. They *know* he exists.'

'The Roman Catholic Church is not an organization you should upset, Mr Hunter.'

'Are you worried about losing your monopoly, Mr Silvestri? You sound more like a Mafia negotiator, come to make me an offer I cannot refuse, than a man of God. I thought the days of the Inquisition were long past.'

'Mr Hunter, the world is in dark times. We hear things, we know things, we have ears everywhere. We are the direct channel to God.'

'What is it you want from me? The chalice and the remains of the tooth, that may or may not contain the DNA of Jesus Christ? Why are you so keen to have these?'

'Jesus Christ is fundamental to the Christian religion. To our existence.'

'What if He is back here now?'

'On earth?' Silvestri looked at him dubiously. 'Jesus Christ back on earth? I think, Mr Hunter, that we would be the first to know.'

'In which case, you have nothing to worry about.' Ross gave him a polite smile, opened the front door, let Monty in and followed him, then closed the door behind him and slid the safety chain home.

He unclipped the dog's lead, then ran up to his den, entered without turning the lights on, peered out of the window and down at the street. He watched Silvestri stand for some seconds, hesitate, then walk slowly back to his limousine and climb in.

The car drove away.

He switched his desk light on, sat down and logged on.

There was an email from his LAPD contact, Detective Investigator Jeff Carter.

> Ross, call me when you get into town. I think I've found your guy.

117

Sunday, 19 March

Not knowing how long he might have to be in Los Angeles, Ross had finally decided to take a decent-size suitcase and check it in. With an hour and a bit to go before the flight, he went to the WHSmith shop and bought several Sunday papers, then carried them over to a cafe, where he grabbed a coffee and a Danish.

He found a table, sat and scanned the front page of the *Observer*, then flipped through it.

And stopped.

A whole page on Pastor Wesley Wenceslas. Pictures of grief-stricken men and women attending a service at his London church. And the story beneath, which included several quotes from Detective Inspector Simon Cludes.

At this moment, we have no leads on who might have committed this terrible crime against such a popular man of the cloth and his loyal right hand. I would appeal to anyone who has information to come forward, or if they would like to remain anonymous, to call the Crimestoppers number below.

Ross could not help his natural scepticism. *Such a popular man of the cloth.* Really?

How about instead, Detective Inspector Cludes, *Such a*

ghastly old money-grabbing fraud who charges you £25 to
pray over a bit of cloth?

A few moments later he was interrupted by a familiar
voice behind him.

'No oysters today?'

He spun round on the stool.

It was Sally Hughes.

'Hey!' he said. 'What are you doing here?'

'Probably the same as you – catching a plane.'

'Let me get you a drink. Have you got time? Tea, coffee?'

'I'm good, thanks.' She jumped onto the empty stool
beside him, wearing a suede jacket, jeans and boots, with a
large, smart handbag slung over her shoulder.

'This is a bit of a coincidence! So where are you off to?'
he asked.

'LA. You?'

'You're going to Los Angeles?' he said, astonished.

'My radio station wants me to get soundings on how
people are feeling about the current political climate.'

'LA's pretty hard-core Democrat terrain. I don't think
you're going to find too many happy Trumpers there.'

'So where are you going?' she asked.

'Believe it or not, LA too!'

'No way! What flight are you on?'

'BA 201,' he replied

'Seriously?'

'Yep!'

'Me too. You're probably in First or Business – or at least
Premium Economy,' she said.

'You have to be joking. I'm Coach, Economy or whatever they call it. Back of the bus. You?'

'I'm in the ghetto, too.'

He grinned. 'So where are you sitting?'

She pulled out her boarding card. '43B.'

He pulled out his and peered at it, then showed it to her.

'I'm right in front of you!' she said.

He was in seat 44B.

This was too weird, he thought. It was beyond a coincidence – she had to be up to something.

118

Sunday, 19 March

'What is this?' Bloor said, disdainfully, as the stewardess on the Gulfstream handed him a tray of sandwiches.

'Your lunch, sir,' she replied politely. 'Smoked salmon, chicken salad, egg mayonnaise and hummus and tomato.'

'I'd expect this in Economy on a commercial airline, but on a private jet? Jesus!'

Julius Helmsley, seated opposite him, began to remove the cling film from his tray. 'It's different on a small jet, boss.'

'Yes?' Bloor retorted, angrily. 'We pay all this money for a private jet to get bloody sandwiches?'

'I didn't have time to organize a five-course banquet.'

'We'd have had better food First Class on British Airways, at a quarter of the price of this!'

'You wanted to arrive in LA ahead of Hunter, Ainsley. That's what we're doing. Relax. Chill! Next time maybe we should charter a bigger plane.'

'Is Hunter yanking our chain again?'

'Wait until we yank his back,' Helmsley said. 'Hard enough so his damned head comes off. But not yet. We have our ducks in a row. We know where he's staying and we know where he plans to go.'

'Approximately,' Bloor reminded him.

'Well, we have our informant and she is being well rewarded.' Helmsley smiled.

'Very nice work that, Julius.'

'We're in a pretty good place to keep track of him and, with luck, when we need it at some point in the next day or so, one crucial step ahead.'

'And then?'

Helmsley smiled again. 'We know that he believes Jesus Christ is back and in LA, and that someone he knows in the LAPD is helping to track him down. If Christ himself, or a credible imposter, is truly in LA, Hunter is going to lead us straight to him.'

Bloor nodded. 'And our plan is then?'

'Goodbye, Hunter.'

'And then negotiate with Jesus Christ to become the public face of Kerr Kluge?'

'We see how real he is.' Helmsley bit into a sandwich and some egg fell out and dropped on his napkin. 'How significant the DNA is.'

'I actually can't believe what we're doing, Julius. Is this the world's biggest ever wild goose chase? Flying halfway round the globe to find someone who might or might not have some of Jesus Christ's DNA?'

'That's not what we're doing, Ainsley. We all have some of the DNA from our distant ancestors. What we're talking about here is a unique genetic signature in the mitochondrial and Y-chromosome DNA of Delaney that's identical to the DNA of Jesus. Big difference.'

'Yes, and isn't there a one in ten billion, or something like that, chance of that happening?'

'The probability's even less than that. But yes, I agree, this could be just the wildest imaginable coincidence. However, realistically, the chances of the matrilineal and patrilineal lines converging in the same individual more than two thousand years after Christ are vastly small.'

'The thing I keep coming back to,' Bloor said, 'is that if this truly is the Son of God, and He's pushing seventy years old, how come He's spent his life being invisible? That ridiculous book of fairy tales that Christians read says that the Second Coming will be heralded by all kinds of signs. Portents. Wars. Catastrophe. Impending doom. Whatever.'

Helmsley looked at him with a serious expression. 'Don't you think that's pretty much where the world is?'

'It's where it's always been.'

'I disagree. The whole world order is crumbling. It's back to how things were in the 1930s. Discontent, anger, people feeling disenfranchised, despots gaining power over the world's nations, religious foment. General turmoil. Perhaps He's been biding His time – and now is the time.'

'Julius, I seem to remember in one of the fairy tales that the Second Coming is regarded as the literal return of Jesus Christ to earth as king in power and glory to rule for a thousand years. If He's nudging seventy He'd better get on with it.'

'He's done better than last time round. He only made it to thirty-three then.'

'Yup, well I think in the next day or two we're going to find out just how real or otherwise he is,' Bloor replied.

'Yes.'

'And if He is real, Julius?'

'You'll have a bit of a problem as an atheist, won't you?'

119

Big Tony was feeling very chilled as he finished his third glass of vintage Roederer. Earlier, whilst boarding, he had noticed Ross Hunter standing in the long Economy line.

Have a good flight, buddy. Enjoy your last hours on earth!

He dug a chilled prawn out of the salad and forked it into his mouth. It was a bit too cold for his liking, but the rich bubbly washed it down nicely.

He was so tempted to take a walk down the plane and see how his target was getting on. But caution got the better of him. No point in taking unnecessary risks. Ross Hunter wasn't going anywhere. He had all the time in the world.

He clicked his fingers at a stewardess. Another glass of Roederer appeared.

Magic!

'Magic!' Ross said to Sally, who had managed to swap seats with another passenger, raising the plastic glass of champagne she had treated him to. 'So how exactly did this happen?'

'I don't know, but it's very nice,' she said with a grin. She rolled her head over towards him. 'Maybe fate put us together? I'm pretty happy about that.' She laid an elegantly manicured hand on the armrest between them.

He took it and squeezed it, playing along. 'Me too, if only I wasn't married. Hey, I think we could make quite a team.'

She grinned. 'I understand and I respect your morals. Let me know if you ever change your mind.'

'Deal!' He grinned back. 'Never say never . . .'

Their food trays arrived.

Soon after he had finished his meal, Ross fell asleep. When he awoke two hours later, Sally was sitting, headphones on, watching a movie he did not recognize.

He pulled his laptop out of the pocket in front of him, his legs feeling stiff, and flipped open the lid as far as he could with the seat in front of him partially reclined. Awkwardly, he read through the story he had written so far, then began to type, starting with the email from the LA detective who reckoned he had found Michael Delaney.

He omitted any mention of meeting Sally Hughes on the plane.

Then he pulled up the map of the section of West Hollywood he had downloaded from Google Earth and studied the vast network of streets. Thinking.

Los Angeles?

If Jesus Christ had really returned, why had he chosen LA over the Mount of Olives in the Holy Land, as prophesied in the Bible?

Holy Land. Holy Wood? Hollywood? Was there some significance?

Then he noticed Sally peering at his screen.

She removed her headphones. 'What are you looking for? You're being very mysterious about your reasons for flying to LA. Can I try to guess?'

'Go ahead.'

'The third set of compass coordinates from your friend, Dr Cook?'

'Could be.' He smiled, evasively.

'The location of the Second Coming?'

'Do you seriously think He would come back to earth in Los Angeles, of all places?'

'Actually, yes,' she replied.

'Why do you say that?'

'If I were Jesus and I wanted to make the maximum impact on the world, then America is a good choice. My options would have narrowed a lot in the past two millennia. I think I would choose the nation that maintains one of the strongest Christian traditions and has the most influence on the world. If I were God and I wanted my Son to have the maximum possible exposure, I think I would send Him down to one of the media capitals of the world. LA is all of that.'

'And if I were Satan and wanted to send the Great Imposter to somewhere on earth where he could get the maximum global exposure, I might choose the same place,' he replied.

'Is that what you think, Ross? The reason you're going to LA? To expose an imposter? Satan posing as the Second Coming?'

'I'm a newspaper reporter, Sally, not an oracle. I just follow leads, stories. I don't know what I'm going to find. If anything.'

'So, if you do find who you are looking for, how will you know what's the truth?'

'There's an ancient saying among the people of Mesopotamia, that *four fingers stand between the truth and a lie*. If you measure that, you'll find it's the distance between your eyes and your ears.'

She looked at him. 'Between what you hear and what you see?'

'Exactly. It's a principle I've adhered to throughout my career. The rumours you hear and the truth you actually see.'

'Will you tell me if you find the truth?'

He stared back at her. As he did so, the man in front lowered his seat further, pushing the lid of his laptop down so far, he could no longer read the screen. 'I'll tell you and the whole world.'

She raised a cautioning hand. 'Promise me something?'

'What?'

'Just in case it's a truth that isn't palatable. I don't want to see you have a fatwa against you – what happened to that writer, Salman Rushdie. Please run it by me first, OK?'

'OK.'

'I'm serious.'

'I am too.'

'Promise?'

He raised his right arm. 'Scout's honour!'

120

Brother Pete Stellos stepped off the plane at Heathrow Airport in the late afternoon. In his hand, he carried the same small leather bag that he'd had with him when he first arrived at Mount Athos. It was lighter than back then, because it now contained little other than his Bible, toothbrush and toothpaste. Pretty much all the clothes he had in the world, he was wearing. His black habit, *kalymafki* and black shoes. That was all.

Now heading into passport control, he was bewildered. The crowds around him. The signs, the cordoned channels. It was strange being back in a world full of colour and noise. To see women again. Until he had arrived at the airport at Thessaloniki earlier today, he had not seen a woman for ten years. Or a child. Or people running. Or a dog.

He stood still. Rooted to the spot. Not daring to take another step. He felt the bustle and swarm of the crowds around him like a vast, suffocating weight. In a moment of near panic, he struggled to breathe.

His first instinct was to turn and run back to the aircraft from which he had just disembarked, and beg them to fly him back home.

But he had made a promise to his cousin, Brother Angus.

There was no greater sin, he believed, than to break a promise.

A promise under God's eyes.

'Can I help you?' a woman in a uniform asked.

He held out his arms. 'I – guess – I – I'm a little confused.'

'Do you live in the EU, sir?'

'Yes, yes I do, but I have an American passport – a new one – issued through the Pilgrim's Bureau in Thessaloniki.'

She pointed. 'Go down that way and join the queue there.'

He thanked her and shuffled along the line. Twenty minutes later he stepped forward to the Border Control officer's booth, and handed him his passport.

The man studied it carefully. Then he said, 'Peter Stellos?'

'Yes.'

'OK. Tell me about your outfit.'

'I'm a monk, sir. In the Greek Orthodox monastic commune of Mount Athos in Greece.'

'And what brings you to England?'

'I've come at the request of my cousin who is also a monk, who is dying.'

'I'm sorry to hear that.'

The officer handed him back his passport and waved him on.

He walked through the 'nothing to declare' channel and entered the duty-free section, where he was stopped by a man who was selling Heathrow Express tickets into central London. He bought one.

As he emerged into the arrivals lounge he stood for some moments, bewildered. Passengers hurrying past him, all urgently going somewhere, many talking on their little phones, some looking worried, some happy. He stared at a sea of placards held up by men in business suits. Arms were being thrown round loved ones. Business travellers headed towards their drivers. There was a sense both of anticipation, reunion and urgency.

He had no such urgency.

Time stood still for him.

Ten years that had flashed past in silence.

Ten years in which the world had changed so much. And he was exactly the same. Ten years of serving God. Of praying for the world.

He looked around, feeling a sudden, irrational flash of his old anger returning. Did any of these people know he prayed for them? Every day. Fourteen hours a day. Did they appreciate it?

He looked up at the noticeboards, trying to spot a sign for the trains. As he did so a large man towing a suitcase barged into him, almost knocking him over, and strode on without apologizing.

For an instant, he wanted to shout at him, but then he remembered something the Abbot had told him a while ago, after he had punched the journalist. A Buddhist saying: 'Everyone you meet is fighting a battle of their own you know nothing about. Be kind to everyone.'

Pete calmed himself down. Then felt a sudden chill ripple through him. As if something very bad had happened.

His cousin?

When they had spoken on the phone just a few days ago, Angus had sounded a very different person from the man he remembered. His voice was weak, without energy or joy.

He closed his eyes for a moment and prayed. Prayed that his cousin Angus would still be alive.

Tonight, he was staying at a hotel that the Mount Athos

Pilgrim's Bureau in Thessaloniki had kindly found for him, close to Victoria railway station where, in the morning, he could catch a train to Sussex. He had told his Abbot he hoped to fly back tomorrow afternoon.

Although Pete had other plans.

121

Sunday, 19 March

Ross felt slugged by tiredness as he disembarked and began the long walk through to the immigration zone.

Ordinarily, a text from Imogen would have pinged in when he switched his phone on after a flight, but there was nothing from her now. And ordinarily, he would have sent her one saying he had landed safely, followed by kisses. But he didn't feel in the mood to. Whether it was because he was still angry at her after their lunch yesterday or enjoying himself too much with Sally, he wasn't sure.

As they stood together at the baggage carousel, waiting for it to start moving, he mentally calculated the time difference. An eleven-hour flight, 4 p.m. Los Angeles time. Late evening in the UK. Too late to text her anyway, he justified to himself.

A short man in a tweed jacket, polo shirt and chinos was standing unobtrusively right behind them, holding his phone. He had his Bluetooth setting on and it was doing a scan for other devices. Among the list of over twenty that popped up on the screen was one that read: *Ross's iPhone*.

Big Tony smiled and pressed a couple of keys.

'Do you have dinner plans for this evening?' Sally asked.

He shook his head and stifled a yawn. 'I guess it's heading towards midnight, body-clock time. I hadn't thought about food. But a cocktail would be good, maybe.'

'There was a time in my previous job, at CNN, when I commuted back and forth across the pond. I found the way to beat jet lag is to stay up as late as you can, then get up early and go out into daylight and take a long walk. If you go to bed now, you'll wake up at 3 a.m. and feel like shit later on. Go and check into your hotel then meet me in the lobby bar there – you're staying at the Beverly Hilton, right?'

'Yep.'

'A couple of cocktails and you'll sleep like a lamb, I promise.'

'You do?'

'Trust me, I'm a radio presenter.'

'And international authority on jet lag?'

'That too.'

Ross had a rental car booked at the airport, and he offered Sally a lift. As he drove, following the satnav and trying to get used to the car and different roads, he stared out at a landscape so different from the UK. He'd been here once before, five years ago, and liked it a lot. Images from so many movies and TV series he had seen set here replayed in his mind.

He dropped her at a very posh hotel called Shutters on the Beach in Santa Monica. Before setting off again, he dialled the number of his detective contact.

It was answered after two rings by a curt but friendly voice. 'Jeff Carter.'

'Hi, it's Ross Hunter.'

'You in town, buddy?'

'Just landed.'

'Welcome to LA! Do you have plans this evening?'

'No – not anything I can't move around.'

'Good stuff. Where are you staying?'

'The Beverly Hilton.'

'Meet you there for a beer at 7 p.m.?'

'That would be great, thank you.'

'You got it, pal.'

Ross ended the call then sent Sally a text.

> So sorry, tonight not good, my cop contact wants to meet with some news – tomorrow – dinner?

Moments later she replied.

> Sounds good. Call me after, would love to hear what he says. Perhaps a late drink after if you're still up for it? Take care. XX

After he had checked in to his hotel room, he decided he ought to send Imogen a text.

> Arrived safe. X

He was surprised when she called him almost immediately.

'Hi,' she said, sounding friendlier than at their lunch.

'You're up late.'

'I'm worrying about you, Ross. So, what's happening – did you hear from your cop?'

'I'm meeting him here later.'

'Great, call me after?'

'That could be three or four in the morning, your time.'

'Good point. Email me, will you? I want to hear all about it.'

'Sure.'

He unpacked, undressed, then stood in the shower for

several minutes to refresh himself. Six floors above him, in a larger, grander room, Big Tony was taking a shower, too. With the unpredictable traffic in this city, he thought it would be convenient to keep close to his target, even though Ross's phone was now his eyes and ears on the man. Big Tony could listen to every conversation and see on his map exactly where Ross Hunter was. Accurate to within ten feet. He just had to hope the man didn't lose it or drop it down the toilet. That had happened to him once before.

At a few minutes before 7 p.m., dressed in fresh clothes, Ross went downstairs and into the bar. He sat in a studded leather corner seat, glanced through the cocktail menu for some minutes and then ordered a beer.

A few minutes later a lean man in his early fifties, with a crew cut, a bomber jacket over a black T-shirt, jeans and trainers that looked fresh out of their box, sauntered in and stared around. His eyes fixed on Ross and he made a bee-line for him.

'Ross?'

Ross stood up. 'Jeff?'

Although he had spoken to the LAPD detective a couple of times, when he'd been working on his piece on celebrity stalkers, they had never actually met.

He ordered Carter a beer then they sat down opposite each other. Until the detective's drink arrived they made small talk, about his flight over, about the weather in England. Ross tried to probe him on his views on gun control, but the detective was evasive on that topic. Then, finally, when Carter had a glass in his hand, he said, 'Michael Delaney? Right?'

'Yup.'

'Tell me your interest in him, buddy?'

'Oh, it's a piece I'm writing for one of my newspapers, the *Sunday Times*.' He hesitated. 'About rogue evangelical preachers who use magic – conjuring tricks – in their work.'

'Well, I've checked out the name, Delaney, and there are no evangelical preachers by that name. The match we have – and it's a pretty significant one – is for a former close magician and sometime lay preacher with that name. Mike Delaney – born 1947. Used to have his own prime-time television show under his stage name, Mickey Magic, until he got pushed out, about twenty years back.'

'Do you know why?' Ross asked.

'Off the record, drink problem. That's what I hear. He was on the sauce. Could only face his audiences if he was tanked up. But don't quote me on that, OK?'

Ross moved his fingers in a zipping motion, across his mouth.

'March 2014, he was arrested in West Hollywood and charged with Driving Under Influence after an automobile wreck – he ran a red light and T-boned a garbage truck.'

'Not the best thing to hit.'

Carter gave a sardonic smile. 'I guess if you're gonna be T-boned, a garbage truck's about the most solid vehicle to be in. The driver was lucky. No one was hurt apart from Delaney and his driver's license.'

'You said in your message that you had found him – you know where he is?'

'So, what I can tell you from Social Security records,' the detective said, 'is that Delaney is working for a charity close to the Farmers Market over on Fairfax and West Third.'

'A charity?'

'It's a drugs rehab centre run by nuns. La Brea Detox Sisters.'

Ross wrote it down. 'Interesting, thank you. That's great. Fantastic.'

The detective gave Ross a studious look. 'Not sure you're gonna get much mileage out of him for your paper.'

'Doesn't sound like it.' Ross smiled, but Carter wasn't smiling back. 'This is really helpful, Jeff.'

'It is? If you want rogue evangelical preachers, we got a whole ton of them on our radar.'

'I may come back to you on that.'

Carter stared at him. 'You got some other reason you want to see this Delaney character that you're holding back from me, Ross?'

'No, it's my editor, she has a bee in her bonnet about my talking to him. Editors get that way – they latch on to an idea and that's it.'

The detective nodded. 'So, anything else I can do for you while you're here in the City of Angels?'

'Do you have a residential address for Delaney, Jeff?'

'I spoke to the nun in charge of the detox centre. She thinks he has a room he rents somewhere in the neighbourhood. But doesn't know where.'

'Thank you again, I really appreciate your coming out on a Sunday night like this.'

'Not a problem.' Carter drained his beer.

'Another?' Ross offered.

'Thanks, but I guess I'd better get going. My kid's just started school and he's not too happy – Sunday-night thing. Promised him I'd get back in time to read him a story. You have kids?'

'One on the way.'

'You got it all to come.'

They shook hands and the detective left. Ross ordered another beer then went out, into the mild evening air, to smoke a cigarette. He watched the traffic passing on Wilshire Boulevard and the steady stream of cars and cabs pulling up at the hotel.

When he had finished, he called Sally and updated her, to check her reaction.

'Sure you don't feel like a nightcap?' she asked.

He hesitated. Tempted. But he was really exhausted now. 'I'd love to but I'm really zonked. I wouldn't want to fall asleep on you.'

'I wouldn't let you!' she said, teasingly.

He grinned. She made him smile and he liked that a lot. 'Dinner tomorrow?' he said.

'I've already made a reservation – somewhere the concierge recommended,' she replied.

'Can't wait.'

'Me too.'

He went back inside and finished his beer, reflecting on what the detective had told him, before heading up to his room and emailing Imogen with all he had been told. Then, totally exhausted, he peeled off his clothes, brushed his teeth, set the alarm and crashed out.

Big Tony listened to his heavy breathing for some minutes until he was satisfied he was asleep. He switched off, took a miniature whiskey from the minibar, then made a couple of calls.

122

Shortly before midday, the taxi Brother Pete had taken after arriving at Horsham station slowed down. They were driving along a two-lane country road, bordered on both sides by hedgerows.

Ahead was a white sign sticking out of an unkempt grass verge.

Above the wording announcing ST HUGH'S CHARTER-HOUSE was the simple cross and orb symbol of the Carthusian order. Brother Pete remembered the words this stood for.

Stat crux dum volvitur orbis.

The cross is steady while the world is turning.

The taxi turned right onto a driveway. After a short distance it curved right, through the archway of an ornate gatehouse. A couple of hundred yards in front of them, straight ahead, was a vast, magnificent-looking building. The central part was a tower with three spires, with a wing stretching out for several hundred yards on either side.

They pulled up outside the oak front door.

Brother Pete paid the driver, walked up to the door and pulled the large bell-handle beside it.

He heard a faint jangle. Followed by another. The door was opened by a rotund man in his sixties, in a white habit. He smiled. 'Hello, I am Father Raphael, the Prior, can I help you?' he asked.

'My name is Brother Pete – Pete Stellos – from the monastery of Simonopetra in the monastic commune of Mount Athos. I've come to see my cousin, Brother Angus.'

'Indeed, we've been expecting you.' His expression changed, becoming more serious. 'Please come in.'

Brother Pete followed him along a long, stark corridor, up a flight of stone steps and then along another corridor and into a large, cosy-feeling, book-lined office. The Prior ushered the monk to a chair.

'You have travelled a long way, Brother Pete.'

'I have, Prior.'

'You must be thirsty and hungry. May I offer you coffee, tea? Something to eat?'

'Coffee would be good, please. No milk.'

The Prior went out of the room, returning some minutes later with a tray containing two cups of coffee, a plate of biscuits and another plate on which sat a chunk of Cheddar cheese, several slices of bread and a knife. He set the tray down on the table in front of them. 'Please, help yourself.'

Pete helped himself to a chocolate digestive. As he bit a piece off, the Prior said, 'I'm afraid I have sad news for you.'

Pete stopped in mid-bite, his eyes locked on the Prior's.

'Your cousin, our dear Brother Angus, passed away last night after a long battle with cancer.'

'I'm too late. I –'

The Prior looked at him, sadly and expectantly.

'I had a feeling,' Pete admitted.

'You need to know that he was truly a man of God.'

Brother Pete nodded. 'I do. It was he who brought me on this path.'

'He asked you to come here because he had some very important things that he wanted you to keep safe.'

'That's what I have come for.'

'I have them. He was so happy that you were on your way. And relieved. I think he did his very best to hold on for you, but our Lord decided otherwise.' The Prior lifted up a small hessian carrier bag. 'They are in here. I don't know what they contain, and I did not ask, because we are all private here. But please take this and keep its contents safe, as he asked you.'

Brother Pete put the bag inside his own.

'I'm very deeply sorry for your loss. And for our loss. He was a real visionary.'

'May I see his body?'

'Of course. I will take you to him. Will you stay for his funeral, tomorrow? I can give you lodgings here.'

'Thank you, I'd appreciate it.'

'So, tell me, Brother Pete, how are things on Mount Athos?'

'Yup, uh-huh, all good,' he replied, a little non-committal. 'The number of monks is increasing for the first time in many years. In my monastery, Simonopetra, thirty years ago when the previous Abbot died, there weren't enough monks to carry his coffin. The only way we get new monks to join us is the way I came, through word of mouth. I guess with the way the world is these days, we offer a safe future for anyone troubled by what's happening.'

'Our late Brother Angus talked to me about you. Your former life as a long-distance truck driver and then doing night shifts in McDonald's restaurants. What have your years as a monk in a closed order taught you?'

'Honestly?' Brother Pete stared hard at him.

'No other answer is of any value.'

'I keep being told that to be a monk you have to believe, absolutely, unconditionally. That if you have doubts, you are in the wrong place. Have you ever had doubts, Prior?'

'We are all born knowing one certainty, Brother Pete. That one day we will die.'

Pete nodded. 'And the question on all our lips is what will happen after we die.'

'Will we sit at God's right hand?'

'Or rot in that graveyard I can see through your window.'

The Prior smiled. Brother Pete could see his eyes looking heavenwards.

'I pray fourteen hours a day, every day, Prior. Sometimes I feel a connection with a higher power, other times I feel – I'm sorry to say this – a total asshole. I feel like I'm just growing old without ever having lived. That one day I'm going to wake up at eighty – if I get that far – and wonder just what I did with my life. Do you ever feel that?'

The Prior shook his head. 'My faith came to me after years of abusing my body with pleasure. Life is not a gift, it is a responsibility. Something that intelligent people are charged with. There is just one thing that God expects of us in return for His gift of life. And that is for each of us to leave the world a better place than when we arrived here. Are you able to say that, Brother Pete?'

'I'm working on it.'

'So am I. So was Brother Angus, God rest his soul.'

123

Monday, 20 March

The room in the La Brea Detox Sisters Rehab Center had a red tiled floor. Running around three sides were stainless-steel work surfaces. Laid out along them, like place settings in a restaurant, were neatly set-out spoons and syringes on paper napkins.

The smell in here was rank, a mixture of disinfectant and un-washed clothing. Ross stared at a man in a grungy tracksuit, with greasy, greying hair cut like a monk's tonsure; he was probably forty but looked sixty. He sat on a stool, stooped in feverish concentration, cigarette papers lying around him, holding a lighter flame beneath a crackling fluid in his spoon.

One floor up on the observation level, Sister Marie Delacroix, dressed like an earth mother, said to Ross in a soft, southern drawl, 'We allow them to do this. We got volunteer doctors here, twenty-four-seven. We give them clean syringes and if they overdose we can help them. We'd prefer, if they are going to take drugs, that at least they do it in an hygienic, safe environment, with medical help on hand.'

Ross stifled a yawn. He'd been awake since 4 a.m., tossing and turning, until he'd finally had enough and went for a walk in the breaking dawn. It was now just after 10 a.m.

'And the police are OK with this?' he asked.

'They understand our work. Yes, they are, they turn a

blind eye. I've seen the work done in Germany and in Holland with this kind of clinic. They save many lives.'

'I should write a piece on them – on your work and the clinics in Europe.'

'You should, really, we need all the good press we can get. So, what can I do for you, Mr Hunter?'

'I'm told you have a volunteer here called Michael Delaney.'

Her reaction surprised him. She looked like she was going into rapture. 'Mike Delaney!' she said with deep reverence. 'This man is – how do I say it – a saint!'

'Really?'

'Truly, Mr Hunter.' She lowered her voice, conspiratorially. 'I'll tell you what my staff here call him – *Mr Miracle Worker*!'

'*Mr Miracle Worker?*'

'Truly! This guy is astonishing, it's like he has some magical power. He cures everyone he talks to. Within weeks, no matter how long they've been taking drugs, they're clean. He has a one hundred per cent success rate. He just walked in the door a couple of years back asking if he could help out in any way. He's astonishing. If you believe in miracles, that's what he is. A true miracle worker.'

'How does he do it?' Ross asked, trying not to let his excitement show.

'He just lays his hands on them, honey. That's all he does. Just lays his hands on them.'

'When are you expecting him in?' Ross asked.

She shrugged. 'That's the problem. He shows up when it suits him.' She lowered her voice again. 'When he hasn't drunk too much the night before.'

'So, he might not come here today?' Ross pressed.

'No, honey, he's a little unpredictable.'

'Do you know where he lives?'

Her demeanour changed and she looked uncomfortable. 'He moves around, different rooming houses. But I couldn't give out his current address, not without his consent.'

'Of course.'

'If he doesn't show here today, you could try the Fairfax Lounge this evening.'

'The Fairfax Lounge?'

'It's a bar a few blocks away. Mr Delaney used to be a pretty famous magician, I think until the demon drink got him.' She held her hand up and rolled it from side to side as if it were wobbling. 'The bar pays him a retainer to go round working the tables with his tricks. That and the tips he gets is enough to keep him in booze. We give him a pittance, too. I always try to bring him something to eat at lunchtime, a sandwich, something like that.'

'He's at the Fairfax Lounge every night?'

'Most nights, so he tells me. Although I think some evenings he has so much liquor on board he doesn't know what day of the week it is. Good luck interviewing him.'

'Sounds like I'll need it.'

'You will, honey. He doesn't speak much at all. I think he's a pretty sad guy. No family, I don't think. He seems a lost soul. And yet –' She hesitated.

Ross waited patiently.

'Sometimes when I look at him,' she said, 'I feel like I'm staring into a bottomless well. There's hidden depths to him that perhaps only God can see.'

'Perhaps,' Ross concurred.

124

Ross was glad to leave the oppressive smell and atmosphere of the rehab centre, and to step out into the warm sunshine. His mind was reeling.

Miracle worker!

He just lays his hands on them, honey.

He glanced around, checking, to see if anyone might be watching or following him. He was in a busy, wide street, with signs everywhere. A huge billboard on a scaffold gantry was advertising a movie. To his right the word MARKET was spelled out in flashing lights, with several bulbs blown. Suspended across a marked section of the road was a small, familiar yellow sign, PED XING.

He moved into the shade, entered 'Fairfax Lounge' on Google Maps, and after a few seconds it appeared, along with the option to request directions. He clicked on the button and the route appeared. It showed fourteen minutes on foot.

Following the directions on his phone, he turned into a palm-lined boulevard, with tall apartment blocks on either side. At the next intersection, he made a left into another busy street, four lanes wide, with cars parked along the far side. He passed a kosher supermarket, a bakery, a Starbucks, a burger joint, a Duane Reade and a store selling creepy-looking dolls. A few minutes later he found himself on Fairfax, with the instruction to turn left.

He walked past the Farmers Market and shortly after reached the intersection with Melrose. With the Fairfax High School complex on the far side, he crossed, walking down past the school and then past the blue shack he recognized from Google Earth. There was a Council Thrift Shop on the far side, a luggage store and medical office. Then he saw it, directly across the street on the far side of a pedestrian crossing, between a bakery and deli and a lamp store with a closing-down sale sign in the window. There was a large, old neon sign on the wall, FAIRFAX LOUNGE. Below, much smaller and unlit, were the words MAGICIAN NIGHTLY!

He waited for a line of traffic to pass then strode over. The exterior didn't look like it had seen a lick of paint in several decades, and the windows were grimy. Ross guessed the interior was going to be just as lousy.

He opened the door and was immediately hit by the ingrained smell of stale beer. It took some moments for his eyes to adjust to the gloom. There was a long bar to the left, with an old, miserable-looking guy in shirtsleeves wiping a row of cocktail glasses. Curved banquettes to the right, the leather peeling off in places. A stage at the far end with a microphone stand and a couple of speakers. Lights, most of them switched off, hanging low, with tasselled green shades. A Sinatra song was playing through a bad sound system. The carpet felt sticky underfoot.

Next to a large NO SMOKING sign on the wall was a small, faded poster in a cheap frame. In the centre was a face he recognized from his internet trawl. The flamboyant, long-haired man in his late forties, with rays of studio light creating a halo-effect round his head. The captions read:

MICKEY MAGIC – MAN OF MYSTERY!

A NEW ABC FAMILY ORIGINAL SHOW

ABSOLUTE PROOF

SUMMER PREMIERE. 16 JUNE.

FRIDAYS 9 PM / 8 PM CENTRAL TIME

Ross leaned forward as far as he could over the bar counter and took a photograph on his phone. Then he turned to the barman. 'Hi,' he said. 'Do you know if Mike Delaney will be here tonight?'

'Do I look like I know?' he replied without lifting his head.

'You look like the only person in here,' Ross retorted.

'Mebbe he will, mebbe he won't. If he's gonna show it'll be around cocktail time – Happy Hour.'

'What time's that here?'

He jerked a finger over his shoulder, and Ross saw the sign on the wall. Happy Hour was 5.30 to 7.30 p.m. Clearly really happy.

He thanked him, got an 'Uh-huh' grunt of a response, and went back out into the street. He was feeling badly in need of a caffeine hit and hungry, too. It was early for lunch, but a long time since he'd eaten breakfast at around 7.30 a.m. Looking about, he didn't see anywhere that appealed. He remembered how much Imogen had liked Melrose Avenue when they'd been here together, and the numerous cool cafes and delis along it. With plenty of time to kill, he crossed back over and walked up to it, then turned right, passing the school again.

Pulling out his phone, he dialled Sally. He got her voice-mail and left a message. He walked on, immersed in his thoughts but enjoying the warmth of the sunshine. Melrose Avenue. It had the kind of smart, funky neighbourhood atmosphere that reminded him of parts of Brighton. He walked past a shouty sign above a smart ladies' clothing store, HOT PINK. Then one above its neighbour, SHOWTIME. Past a large, white CVS pharmacy and a black storefront bearing the sign TATTOO.

He was trying to remember where they'd had a Sunday brunch, with one of the best egg dishes he'd ever eaten. He saw on the far side of the road a cool-looking cafe, with an awning, and crossed over to it. Stepping past a free-standing HAPPY HOUR sign on the sidewalk outside, he stopped at the entrance, looked all around him carefully, then went inside.

It was a large room with a Bohemian feel, and was almost completely empty. He sat at a table in the window, giving him a clear view of the street – and anyone who might be following him – and ordered a double espresso, Diet Coke, cheeseburger and fries. Then he sat watching the passing traffic and collecting his thoughts. Planning what he was going to say to Mike Delaney tonight – if he showed up.

What did you say to – the Son of God?

His brain was swirling with the enormity of it, and he was trembling.

And at the same time, he was conscious of the voice inside his head telling him that this wasn't real. Could not be real.

He looked across at the Glass Hookah Lounge, at the shop next to it, Nail Nation, at the Manic Panic Style Station and La Crème Cafe.

His vibrating phone broke into his thoughts. It was Sally.

'Hey!' he said.

'So, what's happened?'

Ross gave her a quick update.

'Want me to come over and be there with you? Maybe two can break the ice better than one?'

'No, that's good of you, but I need to do this alone.'

'Will you call me, straight after? God, this is incredible, Ross.'

'Or an incredible let-down?'

'I don't think so.'

As he hung up, his drinks arrived and, shortly after, his food. He raised the salt and was about to shake some onto his fries when a woman walked past on the opposite side of the road who bore an incredible likeness to Imogen.

His arm stopped in mid-air.

She was the absolute double of Imogen.

Was he hallucinating? His tired, addled brain making things up? Impossible.

Or was it?

He put down the salt, picked up his phone and dialled Imogen's number. Seconds later the woman stopped in her tracks, pulled her phone out of her handbag and peered at it. He watched her stab a button, keeping it well away from her ear, and return it to her bag.

She had redirected the call straight to voicemail.

125

Monday, 20 March

Ross jumped up from his seat, about to run for the door and chase after Imogen. But instead he sat back down, mystified.

His number would have shown on her phone display, for sure. So she saw it and hung up on him, why? Because she was out on a busy Los Angeles street instead of in the quiet of rural Sussex with her sister.

Her being here explained why she had called him – at what he thought was around 1 a.m. UK time – last night. Why was she here then? What was she playing at? What was her agenda?

He felt totally and utterly baffled.

The sheer coincidence of even seeing her in this vast city was massive. Although on reflection, perhaps not such big odds, as this had been one of their favourite areas when they'd been here together, so perhaps it was natural she would gravitate to it.

But coincidences seemed to be racking up, one after the other. The coincidence of meeting Sally Hughes, whose uncle was a trustee of Chalice Well, the day after he'd met Harry Cook for the first time. The coincidence, if that's what it was, of being on the same flight as her, one row apart. Now the coincidence of seeing Imogen walk past. Just five minutes later and he might not have seen her.

Or might have bumped into her in the street.

Einstein's words on coincidence came back to him again.

God's calling cards.

He ate his meal, barely noticing the taste of the food. He was totally immersed in his thoughts.

What was going on? What on earth was Imogen doing here? Was she spying on him? Suspicious about his reasons for coming here? The last conversation they'd had was all about danger. What had changed? Just what was she doing? And why hadn't she told him?

Still fretting, he left the diner, looking around, carefully, for any sign of Imogen before stepping out. This felt very weird, hiding from his wife. But then he thought, *what the hell.* If they bumped into each other it would be mightily interesting, and he'd look forward to her explanation – especially as she had been going on about how tight money was for them. Not so tight she couldn't buy an airline ticket to Los Angeles?

With a few hours to kill before there was any point in going to the Fairfax Lounge, he took a walk around the Farmers Market, got tempted by a huge doughnut, ate it and immediately regretted it, big time. He left the market and walked up towards the Hollywood Hills, keeping a fast pace on the increasingly steep incline, trying to burn the damned doughnut off. But an hour and a half later he still had a dull ache in his stomach, and the sensation of having swallowed a cannonball.

As he walked back towards his car, parked in a far corner in a lot off La Brea, a text pinged in from Sally.

Be careful he doesn't recruit you to be one of his disciples. Though I'm sure you'd look great with a beard and sandals LOL ☺ XX

He grinned and replied.

Ha ha! XX

126

Ross climbed into his car and closed the door. The clock on the dash read 3.50 p.m.

Happy Hour at the gloomy Fairfax Lounge began at 5.30 p.m. Would Mike Delaney show up today?

A wave of tiredness washed over him. He could do with a catnap, but his mind was whirring too much.

Imogen had flown all this way – when money was tight – without telling him. Was she planning to surprise him in some way? Well, she sure had.

He looked on his phone at the list of recent numbers dialled. *Imogen Mob* was at the top. He hovered his finger over the dial button.

It was almost midnight, UK time. Would she answer pretending to sound all sleepy? Or again not answer at all? And what would he say if she did pick up?

He still had not decided as he pushed the button.

It rang four times then he got her voicemail message. Short and no-nonsense.

'Hi, it's Imogen, leave me a message.'

'It's me,' he said, tersely. Then, sarcastically, 'Sorry it's so *late*. Give me a call.'

For the next ten minutes he checked his emails on his phone; there was one from his editor asking if he had arrived OK and how it was going. He looked at Twitter and

Facebook, then at Sky News. A London tube strike was looming, along with another Southern Railways strike that would hit trains to Brighton. Hitler's wartime telephone was coming up for auction. Great, he wondered – who would want such a ghastly trophy? Church of England weekly attendance had fallen below one million for the first time.

No wonder God was concerned, Ross thought.

It reminded him of something that the Nobel Prize-winning quantum physicist, Max Planck, once said: Science moves forward one funeral at a time.

Was science replacing the Church by stealth? Playing the long game?

Another wave of tiredness sapped him, despite his nervous energy, and he yawned. He set the alarm on his watch for an hours' time, reclined his seat the few inches it would go, then closed his eyes.

But all he could think of, and all he could see behind his closed lids, was Imogen walking past on Melrose.

What was she doing?

Was she having an affair? It was awful, he thought, that he didn't really care if she was. That didn't say much about the state of their relationship, he knew.

Even if she was, she wouldn't have been dumb enough to have flown to the same city he was in, surely? Unless she was spying on him?

She knew where he was staying and hadn't contacted him. She hadn't taken his call – twice. Hadn't called him back either.

After the alarm rang, he climbed out of the car, utterly mystified, locked it, then made his way back towards the Fairfax Lounge.

127

It had clouded over in the past hour, and a wind had got up, tugging hard at Ross's jacket as he crossed the street to the bar. With no sunlight shining on it, the place looked even gloomier and less inviting than earlier.

He pushed open the heavy door and entered. Most of the ceiling lights were now on, but the weak bulbs in the dusty shades cast only a faint glow. The television was showing a ball game, although no one was watching it, and Dolly Parton's voice was coming through the crackly sound system. The grumpy old bartender had smartened up and was wearing a crimson tuxedo with a bow tie. He stood still, hands on the bar surface, with seemingly nothing to do except glower at the world. Another bartender of a similar vintage, a small, slight man, identically attired, was stirring a long spoon in a silver cocktail shaker.

Two business suits sat at a banquette, phones clamped to their ears. Both had Martini glasses in front of them. The only other customers were a middle-aged man, also in a suit, with a provocatively dressed redhead. They sat at the bar engrossed in each other. The man wore a ring, Ross noticed; the woman sported a couple of rocks but not on her wedding finger. He wondered what their story was.

Another barman carried a bright green cocktail to the woman and a beer to the man, then approached him.

'Yes, sir, good evening, sir?'

Ross could have done with a stiff drink, but he had no idea how long he might have to wait and he didn't want to risk making himself more tired. 'Could I have a water?'

The bartender frowned, disapprovingly. 'Tap?'

'No, bottled, please.'

'Still or with gas?'

'Do you have Evian?'

This seemed, mysteriously, to hit the right spot and instantly the old man brightened. 'Evian. We sure do. Slice of lime with it?'

'Perfect, thank you.'

'OK, you got it.'

'Would you happen to know – will Mike Delaney show up tonight?' Ross asked.

'There's only two folks know the answer to that, sir. Mr Delaney and the Lord God Almighty himself.' Then he leaned down, glanced conspiratorially over his shoulder at his colleagues as if to make sure they weren't listening, and in a lowered voice said, 'Sir, if it's a magic show you're after, word is that the hottest place in town is Black Rabbit Rose on North Hudson. I'm afraid our Mr Delaney – you know – he's a little tame perhaps by today's standards.' Then he touched his lips. 'But I didn't tell you that, sir. OK, sir, you got it, one Evian water with a slice of lime, coming up!'

A handful more customers trickled in during the next hour. Ross munched on the peanuts the bartender brought with his drink, had a second Evian, then went to the gents. When he returned to his seat he was really struggling again to keep awake.

His thoughts turned to dinner, later, with Sally. He was going to be great company if he was like this, he thought. Got to perk up!

Where was Imogen dining tonight, he wondered? With whom? What would be the chances of them ending up in the same restaurant?

Well, hey, that would make for an interesting conversation.

He sipped his drink and as he put the glass back down he noticed a tall, elderly man with a slight stoop walking across the bar. Dressed in a fraying grey suit, scuffed boots and a black shirt with rhinestone buttons, he had a long face beneath a mane of thinning grey hair, a large nose and cheeks that were mapped with thin red veins.

He was approaching the two business suits, who looked to be in deep discussion, their phones on the table in front of them. On their second Martinis now, or maybe their third.

As he reached them, he fanned out a deck of cards in his right hand. 'Take a card, sir,' he said to one of them. 'Any card you like.' He had a courtly, engaging voice with a Californian accent.

One of the suits waved the magician away, dismissively. The old man raised an arm apologetically and moved on towards Ross, with an agility that seemed to belie his age.

128

Ross began to shake, his nerves out of control. He took several deep breaths in rapid succession as the realization hit him that this was the moment his entire life might have been building up to.

I've recently been given absolute proof of God's existence – and I've been advised there is a writer, a respected journalist called Ross Hunter, who could help me to get taken seriously.

He was seldom lost for words, but at this moment he was. Remembering his plan just in time, he discreetly hovered his hand over his phone and tapped the Voice Memos app, activating the recorder.

Despite his broken appearance, the conjuror exuded a strangely powerful presence. Ross's skin was tingling as he grew closer. The man's hazel eyes seemed much younger than the rest of him and they shone, filled with zeal and magnetism, from behind glasses with bent frames.

Closer up now, Ross could see the resemblance to the much younger person in the poster on the wall across the room. It was there, clearly, inside the shell of this old man. As if he were wearing a suit and a mask, but there was someone else inside.

Ross felt a strange, powerful aura, the sensation of

being sucked into an airlock. He found himself wanting to kneel in front of him.

'Mike Delaney?' he asked, his voice sounding disembodied.

'That's me, sir,' the man replied, fanning out a deck of cards in a shaking hand. There was alcohol on his breath. 'Sir,' he asked, 'may I show you a trick?'

Ross could see the young eyes twinkling through the mask. Twinkling with humour, with mischief. Twinkling with a shared secret.

He felt the hairs rising on the nape of his neck. He shivered, awed and excited, but at the same time feeling he was dreaming. This wasn't real, it couldn't be.

But he was here. Delaney standing in front of him.

The man with Jesus Christ's DNA.

Delaney continued smiling, eyes boring into him as if reading his mind. Encouraging him. And almost without realizing, Ross began to feel an immense sense of calm. Of wellbeing. Of energy.

'Sir, may I show you a trick?' the man repeated.

You are showing me one, Ross wanted to say. *You are showing me something incredible.* Instead, returning the man's smile, he pointed at his glass of Evian. 'Could you change that into wine?'

Their eyes locked. Ross had the strange sensation of being drawn into them, deep in through the lenses of his glasses, deep into the pupils, deep into the man's very soul. He saw the trembling smile. Despite his frail, threadbare appearance, there was something quite majestic and commanding about him.

About the presence inside the shell, behind the mask.

'Pinot Noir or Merlot, sir, or perhaps a nice Chablis?'

'Did you give them a choice last time?' Ross responded.

Delaney frowned, fleetingly, then smiled again, even more warmly. Ross was feeling a strange sensation of complete and utter wellbeing. All his tiredness had gone, and he was now as wide awake as it was possible to feel. Then he suddenly broke into a cold sweat and felt giddy, as if the room was moving around him.

'Very good,' Delaney said, approvingly. 'But I'm guessing you didn't come all the way from England for a free glass of wine, did you, Mr Hunter?'

It surprised him that Delaney knew his name. He smiled, shaking his head. 'I was hoping for a little more than that.'

'I've been kind of expecting you. The old guy came to see you, right?'

Ross nodded. The whole room seemed to be rotating round him. 'Dr Cook.'

'Dr Harry F. Cook.'

Inside the young man inhabiting the old man's shell, it seemed there was an even younger man. And a younger man still inside that, as if it were another shell. As if he were staring into the souls of an infinite number of beings, each inside the other, like Russian dolls. Drawing him in. Enveloping him. Protecting him inside this airlock.

'Why him?' Ross asked. He felt a catch in his throat. 'Why did you choose him?'

'Why anyone else?' Delaney replied, simply.

There was a moment of silence between the two men as they just looked at each other. Ross felt strangely comfortable. It was as though no one else beyond them existed at this moment.

'Will you join me, Mr Delaney, let me get you a drink?' Ross suggested.

Delaney perched down beside Ross on the curved

banquette, keeping a space between them. 'I can't stop too long, they don't like it, you see, they want me moving around, working the tables. But I guess it's pretty quiet right now, so we can talk a while.'

Ross ordered him a Jim Beam, and a beer for himself. Then as the bartender walked away, he turned back to Delaney. Despite his shabby appearance, he smelled clean, freshly showered.

'I feel like I'm in some kind of dream,' Ross said. 'I – I just – just want to ask you –' He fell into a long silence, unsure how to say what he wanted to. There were so many questions he wanted to ask him. About the past, about the future.

'I know who I am,' Delaney said, 'if that's the question.' He looked at Ross. 'That's what you want to ask me, isn't it?'

Ross stared back into his eyes, mesmerized. 'Why Harry Cook?' he asked again. 'Why did you choose a modest, humble old guy like him when you could have chosen –' He fell silent again, lost for words.

'When we could have communicated in all other kinds of ways? Found someone more savvy? More media friendly? Who would anyone have believed? Not the Pope, not the Archbishop of Canterbury, not any of the imams, the Sikh leaders, the Hindu Brahmans, the rabbis. All of them already have their faith, they *know*. It's not them who need to believe. They're not going to stop humankind going over the precipice.'

The warning words, *The Great Imposter*, kept coming into Ross's mind. Was he sitting here with an old fraud, *Mr Ten-Billion-to-One* who happened to have the same DNA as Christ?

Or the genuine article?

He was having difficulty believing Delaney was real.

That it wasn't just his imagination in some kind of wild overdrive. But as he looked back at the man he felt the magnetism. As if he were staring into infinity. As if he were staring into the souls of everyone who had ever lived on this planet.

But how does he know about Harry Cook? How does he know my name?

'So who is capable of stopping – as you put it – humankind falling over the precipice, Mr Delaney?' Before giving him a chance to reply, Ross went on. 'Dr Cook told me God believed that if we could have faith reaffirmed, it would help steer us back onto an even keel. But in the Middle Ages almost everyone had religious faith. That didn't stop all the centuries of terrible wars, the Holocaust, the dropping of nuclear bombs on Hiroshima and Nagasaki. Why would it make it any different now?'

Delaney smiled, wistfully, momentarily turning back into a single person, an old man, the skin creasing around his eyes. 'Perhaps because too many people are listening to a handful of arrogant, influential people. Smart scientists and the cognoscenti, all with their hubris, who believe there cannot be anything more important than themselves in the universe. These same people who are so certain, yet still cannot explain how the world began. They talk convincingly of the Big Bang. But they can't explain how it actually happened. Two bits of dust collided and set it off? So who put those two bits of dust there? That's the subject they always duck. Along with the question *why*. *Why* did anyone put those two bits of dust there? No one can answer that, Mr Hunter, because the only possible answer is someone bigger than man.'

'Someone or some*thing*?' Ross tested.

Delaney held him with his gaze. The person inside him

held him with his gaze, too. And the person inside that. 'A higher intelligence, Mr Hunter. Maybe it's true, maybe it's an urban legend, but in 1899, the Commissioner of the US Patent Office recommended to Congress that the Patent Office be closed because, he informed them, everything that could be invented had now been invented and there would be no new discoveries. Think about it. That was before an aeroplane had ever flown, before computers, before the internet, before almost everything modern there is in the world.'

'A genuine man of vision, if it's true,' Ross said with a grin. 'But you have to admit the Church doesn't have a great record of being helpful to scientists. In 1633 Galileo was found guilty of heresy by the Inquisition for saying the world went round the sun. Has religion tried to be too protectionist and anti-science?'

'Maybe.' Delaney sipped his whiskey. 'Maybe Christianity tried to hold on to old beliefs too long and instead of embracing science, turned it away. And the irony is that science is asking questions that only religion can answer, but to accept those answers would mean admitting defeat for the scientists.'

'What questions, specifically, do you think?' Ross asked.

'Do you know about quantum entanglement theory?'

'No.'

'Very simplified, if you split a subatomic particle into two, put one half in a lab in London and the other in a lab on the far side of the world – say Sydney – then you flip the one in London over, instantly the one in Sydney will flip too. Einstein was fascinated by this and he came up with his own name for it: *Spooky Action at a Distance*.'

Ross smiled again and sipped his beer. He still could not believe this conversation was really happening. He felt drawn deeper and deeper into the myriad eyes inside eyes.

'Another thing no one can explain, Mr Hunter, is magnetism. No one can actually tell you what causes it. Scientists know what it does, but that's all. Are you really going to explain how that happens, and how for example Quantum Entanglement Theory happens, through nothing more than evolution from the primal swamp? I don't think so. Of course evolution exists. But evolution is a part of existence. It is a *consequence* of life, not a primary cause.'

Delaney drank some more of his whiskey, and looked levelly at Ross. 'You're not sure about me, are you?'

'Honestly? If you really are who I think you are, I don't understand why you haven't made your presence known before. Why have you waited over two thousand years?'

Delaney was silent for some moments. Then very quietly, so quietly Ross could barely hear him above the music and ambient noise, he said, 'So tell me, who do you think I am?'

'You have a DNA match to a tooth believed to have been one of Jesus Christ's and to DNA recovered from what I think may be the Holy Grail.'

'You think that is accidental, Ross?'

He smiled at the man's use of his first name, as if they were becoming more intimate now. 'No.'

Delaney smiled back and the two men's eyes locked. Ross felt a current of electricity between them. An understanding. A bond.

'You need to understand I'm not the Son of God,' Delaney said, his voice still very quiet. 'Yes, I have the same DNA. I'm the forerunner, sent here to blend in and report. To see if humankind is ready for the Second Coming.'

'The Nicene Creed,' Ross replied. 'Jesus Christ ascended into Heaven and is seated at the right hand of the Father.

He will come again in glory to judge the living and the dead and His kingdom will have no end.'

'Word perfect!'

'And?'

'They are not ready.'

'Who do you mean by *they*?' Ross asked.

'Everyone with his or her own vested interests. Nothing has changed in over two millennia. Vanity, greed and fear are the drivers the world over. Always have been. Jesus was killed for all those reasons. People were afraid of what they might lose because of him. The Jewish religious leaders felt if He truly was the Messiah, He would be a threat to their authority. The Romans accused Him of claiming to be a king, which was a direct challenge to their emperor. Pontius Pilate genuinely believed He might be the Son of God, but he was a self-serving politician and a weak appeaser. So he washed his hands of responsibility, letting the mob decide – when he could have saved Jesus.'

Ross stared at him, wondering again. *Are you real? Can you possibly be real?*

As if reading his mind, Delaney said, 'You're doubting, aren't you? You are asking yourself, could this shabby old guy possibly be real? I've tried to live an ordinary life – well, as ordinary as possible. I know I'm different, but I'm clear what my role is.'

Ross felt his skin tingling, as if charged with static. It was weird, not unpleasant, energizing him as if he were standing in a hot shower. Delaney was grinning at him, knowingly.

As abruptly as it started, the tingling stopped.

'Maybe the world needs a wake-up call, that's what I'm thinking, before the Second Coming can happen,' Delaney said. 'Something no one can mistake. That no scientist can explain away. Something that defies the laws of physics of the universe.'

Ross frowned, remembering where he had heard just these words before. The Bishop of Monmouth, Benedict Carmichael. He had said the same thing.

'You mean a miracle? Like parting the Red Sea?' Ross said.

'A miracle the whole world will see and can't deny.'

Ross could see a steely determination in Delaney's eyes. A force. An immense cauldron of power behind the darkness of his pupils within pupils, within pupils. It both awed and scared him. 'What – what do you have in mind?'

'You'll know when it happens. The whole world will know. It is foretold in the Bible, in Genesis 9, when God said, "Here is the sign of the Covenant I make between myself and you and every living creature with you for all generations."'

'But how will you communicate its significance to a largely sceptical and hostile world?'

Delaney raised his hands. 'That's where I need your help, you see. This is where you come in, why you were chosen.' He nodded at Ross's phone on the table. 'The recording you're making on that phone gadget – the gadget that the head of the US Patent Office never figured would be invented – you're gonna need it one day soon. On that day, you'll be able to play it to all the Doubting Thomases.'

Ross felt a flush of embarrassment that he hadn't asked Delaney's permission to record him. How had he known it was recording? Had he seen him switch it on as he'd approached?

Delaney went on. 'It's written also in Matthew 24: "The sun will be darkened, the moon will lose its brightness, the stars will fall from the sky and the powers of heaven will be shaken. And then the Sign of the Son of Man will appear in heaven."'

Delaney fell silent and sat nodding for some moments before he spoke again, with a faraway gaze in his eyes. 'Soon, after I'm recalled, that will happen. You have the ear of the media. You've got the recording, Mr Hunter. You'll have absolute proof.' He drained his glass and stood up. 'Guess I gotta get to work. And keep you safe for as long as is needed.'

Ross stared at him. He was still struggling to get his head round any of this. 'Where – where will this sign appear?' There were a million questions he still had to ask him.

'Everywhere, at exactly the same moment, in every country in every time zone. There is not a soul in the world, not a single living creature, who will not have the ability to see it.'

Ross picked up his phone. 'Can I get a picture of you?'

Delaney looked hesitant. 'OK.'

He posed for a couple of shots.

Then Ross asked, 'How can I contact you? Do you have a card? Email?'

'I'm sorry, I don't have cards. I don't have email, not any more. I'm here most evenings, pretty much every day except Sundays. You can reach me here for as long as I'm around. But that won't be for much longer.'

As Delaney turned away, Ross surreptitiously pulled out his handkerchief, picked up the whiskey tumbler with it and slipped it into his pocket. When he was back in England, the lab might be able to get Delaney's DNA off it, he thought. Then he stopped the recording and checked it. At the next table along he heard Delaney's voice.

'Take a card, sir, any card. That's right, don't let me see it, though. Now write your name on the back with this pen.'

Ross sat for several minutes, finishing his beer which he had barely touched during the encounter, deeply shaken and reflecting. Trying to figure out what had just happened. Was Delaney like Harry Cook; were they a crazy double act?

There was laughter at the next table. Delaney was holding a small hammer and brought it down hard on an ice cube.

The forerunner to the Second Coming?

He watched Delaney pull a folded playing card from out of the remains of the ice cube. He unfolded the card and held it up. Ross could see writing on the back.

'This your card, sir? This your writing?'

Ross heard a shout of amazement.

129

Monday, 20 March

A few minutes later, Ross paid the tab, left a tip and walked in a daze towards the door. As he opened it, with difficultly, he felt a blast of wind. It was blowing a hooley, almost a full-scale gale, which had risen whilst he was in the bar.

It was dark outside now, with spots of rain, and the street was busy with traffic. He took a moment to get his bearings. There was a mini-mart directly opposite him, and a cafe next to it. He needed to cross the four-lane road, make a left, then a right two blocks north of Melrose, which would take him to where his car was parked. He pulled his phone from his pocket, impatient to tell Sally what had just happened, waiting for the lights to change. He began to text her, telling her he was on the way as he stepped out into the road.

Then, when he was halfway across, still focused on his phone screen, he heard the roar of an engine. Saw the bright, blazing headlights of a massive SUV bearing down at high speed.

Coming straight at him.

Not going to stop at the crossing.

He froze.

Closing on him.

The lights getting bigger. Brighter.

Time suddenly seemed to slow right down.

What should he do? Run across? Run back? He looked over his shoulder. And saw Mike Delaney standing on the sidewalk outside the Fairfax Lounge door.

A split second later, Delaney was racing towards him, his arms reaching out, his feet barely seeming to touch the ground, almost as if he were on a zip wire.

The roar of the SUV was deafening. The lights blinding him.

He heard a woman scream.

Then, before Delaney's hands touched him, from nowhere he felt a massive force hurtling him sideways. Propelling him across the street like he was riding a cushion of air. Slamming him against the wall of the mini-mart, with a jolt that winded him, that felt like he had broken every bone in his body.

All the while, as if in slow motion, he saw the SUV strike Delaney full-on. The old man was catapulted through the air and landed in a crumpled heap, twenty yards along the street.

The vehicle carried on, still accelerating, and within seconds all that was visible were its tail lights.

More screams.

People ran towards the old man. Ross, as if in a dream, stumbled towards him, too. A pool of dark blood was spreading out on the surface of the road from his head. He lay still.

'Did you see that?' a man said.

'He didn't stop!' said another.

'Call an ambulance!' someone else yelled.

Ross just stood still. In a total, horrified daze.

130

Monday, 20 March

'What's with this ridiculous traffic?' Ainsley Bloor peered angrily out through the darkened glass of the limousine's rear window. They hadn't moved for several minutes. He could see a Mobil gas station opposite, surrounded by lurid hoardings. The limousine crept forward. He stared at the bright signs. PLANET HOLLYWOOD. AMOEBA RECORDS. STARBUCKS. WHISKEY A GO GO.

'Can't we get off this bloody road?' he said to the driver.

The man at the wheel, who had no neck and looked like he was hewn from a block of granite, flicked his wrist over and the face of his gold watch glinted under the neon glare of a store sign. 'Eight o'clock, Monday. Don't know the problem, something going on for sure, but this is LA, you can't ever predict the traffic. Sunset's normally a good route this hour.'

'Yep, well it's not such a good route now, is it? How much further?'

'Without this traffic, five, maybe ten minutes.'

'Can't we get off this road?'

'Thought you folk wanted to see the sights.'

'What?' Bloor turned to Julius Helmsley, seated beside him in the rear of the vehicle, who was engrossed in his emails on his phone. 'Did you tell him we wanted to see the sights, Julius?'

Helmsley shook his head.

Bloor addressed the driver. 'Look, we are not here to see the bloody sights, OK? We want the fastest route you can do to the Fairfax Lounge.'

'Wasn't the message I got,' the driver said. 'Message came through from my office that you guys wanted a little tour on the way.'

'Well it's not what we want.' Bloor looked at his own watch. 'It's been forty minutes since we left the hotel – actually forty-five. Just get us there as fast as you can.'

'It's really a dump that place, the Fairfax Lounge. You sure you wanna go there?'

'Yes.'

'Trust me, smart folk like you, staying in a fancy hotel, you don't want to be in a rat-hole like that. There's a lot of better bars to visit. I can take you—'

'Just take us to the goddam Fairfax Lounge, and step on it!' Bloor said, his voice rising in pitch.

Seconds later the limousine made a hard right into a side street, the driver accelerating furiously, squealing the tyres and throwing Bloor against his door. Helmsley's phone flew out of his hands and he had to grope around on the floor to retrieve it. The next moment he was slammed against his door as the car made an equally violent left turn.

'Were you a getaway driver or something in a former life?' Bloor said, attempting humour.

'Uh-huh,' came the deadpan reply.

Minutes later they made a more sedate right at a stop light, into a four-lane street lined on both sides with stores, cheap restaurants and takeaway places. Cursing, the driver braked hard as all the traffic in front of them slowed, approaching another junction. 'Doesn't look like it's our lucky day.'

Bloor and Helmsley peered ahead at the blaze of strobing blue and red lights. A police cruiser was parked sideways across the entrance to the next section of the road, roof lights blazing. Yellow and black DO NOT CROSS tape behind it, sealing off the road, was flapping in the wind. Two cops on scene-guard duty stood in front of it. A short distance behind them sat a big, square ambulance, emergency lights also blazing, along with several more official vehicles. They heard the wail of an approaching siren.

'Where's the Fairfax Lounge?' Bloor demanded.

'Dead ahead, half a block on the left,' the driver said.

'What's going on?'

'We ain't getting any closer, tell you that.'

'I'll go and find out.' Bloor opened the door and hurried, almost bent double against the wind, over to one of the cops.

'Officer,' he said. 'I need to get to the Fairfax Lounge.'

'The where?'

Bloor could see its illuminated sign, just fifty yards or so along. Almost in front of the bar was a white sedan with the word CORONER written on the door, and next to the car was a white van with a bar of flashing lights on the roof. On the front door were the markings LOS ANGELES COUNTY CORONER and the legend LAW AND SCIENCE SERVING THE COMMUNITY.

He started to have a very bad feeling he could not explain. 'The Fairfax Lounge, officer – sir – it's just there,' he said. 'Can I go through?'

The cop looked at him and simply shook his head.

'How – how long – do you think – how long before I can get through?'

'Sir, there's been a fatality. I don't know more than that. I don't know how long.'

At that moment another cop, this one stocky and muscular, came out of the Fairfax Lounge's door and strode up to them with a swagger, like he owned the sidewalk. He and the scene guard were clearly buddies.

'Gonna be here a while,' he said, quietly, to him.

'What's the update?' asked the scene guard.

'Hit and run. Lot of confusion, the usual. Assholes taking pictures on their phones. Got a couple of good witnesses say the old guy was trying to save a younger guy's life. Pushed him clear. Sounds like the SUV driver was drunk or high on some shit. He came barrelling down out of nowhere, didn't stop, just carried on. Hopefully we'll pick up his plates from CCTV outside one of these stores.'

'Any ID on the victim?'

'Seems like his name's Mike Delaney – one of the bartenders in the Fairfax Lounge came out, took a look at him. Works in there, some kind of resident magician.'

'Too bad his magic wasn't working tonight,' the scene guard said.

'Excuse me, did you say *Mike Delaney*?' Bloor interrupted.

'Uh-huh,' said the cop who'd delivered the news.

Bloor felt as if his whole insides were plunging down a lift shaft.

'Mike Delaney?' he said again.

Neither cop replied.

'I – I was on my way – to see him. I – I've got to see him.'

'You're not going to find him too talkative, sir,' said the one who carried the news.

'No – you don't understand – I – I have to see him – I just – could you let me through, just for a few minutes?' His voice was desperate.

'I don't think you heard me right, sir. He's dead. There's nothing here for you.'

'Where – where will – where will they take him?'

'Are you a relative of the deceased, sir?' the scene guard asked.

'Yes – well – yes – my – my cousin,' he lied, thinking on his feet. 'I've flown from the UK to meet with him. Family reunion. My long-lost cousin – we only recently got connected again. This has been a big emotional journey for me. Where will they take his body?'

'Downtown, Department of the Medical Examiner. Mortuary there. Not a great place for a family reunion.'

Bloor grimaced. 'There's only one mortuary he'd be taken to?'

Very sarcastically, the scene guard said, 'Look, pal, it's not like hotels, right? When you're dead you don't get to choose your overnight accommodation. OK?'

'You don't understand – like – like – just who he is – might be.'

'I understand fine,' the other cop said. 'I think it's best if you leave now, sir, we need to keep this road clear.'

'No – no – please, you don't know!'

'No one will know for sure until formal identification, sir.'

'Where will that happen? At the Department of the Medical Examiner?' Bloor checked. 'The mortuary there, right?'

Both cops looked at him. The scene guard gave a single nod.

'Do you have the address?'

'You'll find it in the *Good Hotels Guide*,' the scene guard said.

His colleague smirked.

Bloor stared at them. They did not understand. Did not get it. They had no idea who it was lying dead and broken, just yards behind their smug faces.

But as he walked back to the waiting limousine, it dawned on him this might not be a disaster at all. It could be a golden opportunity.

A plan began forming in his mind.

As he climbed back into the limousine he said to the driver, 'Change of location. Can you take us downtown, to the Department of the Medical Examiner?'

'North Mission Road.'

'That's where it is?'

'Uh-huh.'

'Could we go there, please.'

'Good choice. I'd spend an evening there over the Fairfax Lounge any day.'

131

Monday, 20 March

Shortly after 10 p.m., Ross and Sally were seated in the bar area of a cool Asian fusion restaurant she had been recommended. She was sipping a margarita; Ross had already downed a double Scotch and was now holding a large draught beer in his shaking hand. Music was playing. Billy Joel's 'Piano Man'.

An assortment of dim sum lay in front of them, although Ross had no appetite. His whole body ached and several of his ribs hurt, but he barely noticed. Part of him wanted to tell Sally everything, have her listen to the recording, word by word. But he was struggling to know where to begin and he was still guarded.

'Hello!' she said, waving a hand across his face. 'Hello, are you with me?'

He looked at her with a start. 'I'm sorry,' he said. 'I'm –'

Somewhere else, he knew. Spaced out. Trying to make some sense. Sense of Imogen being here in LA. Sense of the fact someone had just tried to kill him. Sense of who he could really trust.

'Tell me what happened tonight right from the start, Ross,' she said. 'Seriously, you look like you've seen a ghost.'

'Maybe I have.'

'The Holy Ghost?'

He smiled, thinly. 'I guess – I don't know – I'm trying to

remember the sequence. Of what happened. It was incredible, Sally. I – it was like – I can't describe it. Something – otherworldly. I know that everything I'm going to tell you will sound crazy.'

'Try me.'

She managed to grip a dumpling with her chopsticks and raised it a few inches, but it slipped free and dropped back into the basket.

'The Chinese mash them up first then scoop them into their mouths,' he said, helpfully.

'Very elegant,' she said. 'So?' She picked up the dumpling with her fingers, dropped it on her plate, then began mashing it up. 'Forgive me, I'm ravenous, but I'm dying to know. So what did actually happen – I mean, what do you *think* happened after you left the Fairfax Lounge?'

'I started crossing the road, focusing on texting you, to arrange to meet.'

'Not smart,' she said with a reproachful smile. 'Crossing the road and texting – you have a death wish?'

'I was on a crossing – the lights were in my favour.'

'Yep, well I'd rather you were a few minutes late here than early in the hereafter!'

He grinned. 'Very apposite.'

'I'm good at apposite.'

'Anyhow, I was part-way across then this SUV thing just appeared from nowhere, coming at me like a bat out of hell. I heard the roar of its engine, saw headlights. It was like someone was driving at me, deliberately. I froze, just rooted to the spot. I honestly thought I was a goner. I didn't have anywhere to go. Then something – I don't know how to describe it other than *mystical* – happened.'

'In what sense?'

'Delaney. I saw him standing outside the Fairfax. He

must have followed me out. In just a split second, as the SUV was on me, hurtling towards me. Maybe I'm in a bit of shock and my mind's playing tricks on me, but Delaney came at me way faster than a man could move – and even more so a man of his age. I felt him push me and I was literally propelled across the road – it felt like I was on a cushion of air. For an instant, I thought I was dead – you know – like those people who've described near-death experiences. That's what I was convinced I was having. Sort of like when Ricky died. Then I crashed into the wall of a shop and I was lying on the ground. I –'

He paused, trying to remember more. 'I saw the car, a big SUV thing, racing down the street, and Delaney tumbling through the air like a – like a huge rag doll.'

She reached across the table and tenderly laid her hand on his.

'It was as if time just stopped for a split second.'

'Doesn't some strange thing happen to time when people have near-death experiences? You told me that extraordinary thing about your brother – when he was dying.'

'This was different. More like a . . .'

'Miracle?' she prompted

'It was a miracle. But why did he die? It should have been me.'

'You think he saved you?'

'Maybe.'

'Like – sacrificed his life for yours?'

'I don't know. Possibly. But why?'

She stared at him hard, her eyes lit up as if she totally understood. 'Because you have a mission to fulfil?'

'I don't know,' Ross answered. He drank some more of his beer. 'I got the sense he knew his death was imminent

– he implied it in the bar. Almost the last thing he said to me was: "Soon, after I'm recalled, that will happen. You have the ear of the media. You've got the recording, Mr Hunter. You'll have absolute proof."'

'How was it, seeing him in the bar?' Sally asked. 'Talking to him?'

'It was – I don't even know how to begin to describe it.' He thought for a moment. 'Very strange. Incredible. I kept feeling this energy coming off him, like static electricity or something. Like something supernatural.' He shrugged. 'Maybe it was my imagination.'

'Maybe it wasn't.' She leaned forward, studying his face intently. 'You said that he talked about a sign?'

'He quoted it from Genesis – I have it all recorded.'

'Can I hear it?'

'Sure.'

'Maybe after dinner?'

He nodded. 'He also referred to Matthew, chapter 24, I think it was. About the sun and the moon going dark, the stars falling out of the sky, and then there being a sign from God. This sign would be everywhere, at exactly the same moment, in every country in every time zone.'

'What about the people who are asleep or blind?'

'He covered that by saying there wouldn't be a soul in the world, not a single living creature, who would not have the ability to experience it.'

She stared at him in silence. 'If this is real – I mean, if *he* is real – that's –'

'Quite interesting?'

She grinned. 'Yeah, *quite interesting*. Is that the understatement of the year or of the past two thousand years?'

Ross patted his jacket pocket and there was a tinkle of broken glass – the tumbler Delaney had drunk from, which had smashed when he'd hit the wall. 'The glass he drank from. I may be able to verify it from this.'

'Smart!' she said. 'But I wouldn't have put you down for a kleptomaniac.'

'I'll return one day and pay for the glass.' He smiled.

'So, what was the very last thing he said to you?' Sally asked.

'Delaney finished his drink, stood up and said, "Guess I gotta get to work. And keep you safe for as long as is needed." I asked him when and where the sign would appear. He said it would be soon after he was called back – I guess to Heaven. He also said I could reach him there for as long as he was around, but it wouldn't be for much longer. Then he went off to the next table along and started doing card tricks. I paid and left.'

'And the next time you saw him he was outside, and then hit by the SUV?'

'Yes.'

'You think it was deliberate – the driver? Trying to kill you or Delaney?'

'Well, a while later I was sat in the back of a police car and gave them a statement. A cop told me he'd spoken to one of the bartenders. The guy said that a few nights earlier Delaney had been doing his magic tricks on one of their customers. Apparently, he has a whole pickpocket routine. He'd lifted this customer's wallet, then when he handed it back to him the guy accused him of taking fifty bucks from it. Things got ugly and the cops were called. They took Delaney into a back room and searched him, but he was clean, they didn't find any fifty-buck note on him. But the customer wasn't satisfied, he left saying he was going to come back and get even with Delaney. That's who they're focusing their enquiry on.' He fell silent for a moment, then added, 'But –'

'But?'

He was thinking about his journey so far, all that had happened, speculating who might have tried to kill him. With Wenceslas dead, he felt that made Kerr Kluge the prime suspects, for sure.

'Ross, your friend the Bishop of Monmouth, Benedict Carmichael, warned you that if someone claimed to have this evidence they'd risk being murdered. You had your experiences in Glastonbury, then Egypt, now possibly this. Maybe he was right,' Sally said.

'Maybe.'

'It's not going to stop you, is it, Ross?'

'No.'

'I'm glad. I don't want you to be harmed, but I admire your principles. So, you have some great material for your story. When are you going to write it?'

'I've started.'

'And your newspaper will take you seriously because of who you are?'

'I hope,' Ross said. 'But there's always a risk with every story you file that it comes out on a day of major breaking news, and your two-page spread gets shrunk into a few column inches.'

'Your story *is* that major breaking news. It's this story that will make everything else in the paper that day seem irrelevant.'

'I hope so, Sally, I really do. I've risked a lot for this. But I've also met some incredible people along the way.' He stared at her, meaningfully. Their eyes locked and she nodded.

He had a go at picking up a dim sum himself with his chopsticks, a shrimp dumpling. After a few failed attempts, he speared one and lifted it to his mouth. He chewed for some moments, unable to speak. As he finally swallowed, it brought home how badly low on energy he was, and he immediately ate another, thinking as he did.

'You really believe what Delaney said, Ross?'

'I don't know. I don't know what I believe. There's so much weird stuff going on. Stuff I haven't told you yet.'

'Such as?'

His mind went back to the Fairfax Lounge. It was like a dream. Had he just imagined that young man inside Delaney? That younger man still inside him. All the layers within layers?

'Hello!' she said. 'You've gone again!'

He looked at her, and hesitated, confused. What had they been talking about?

'You said there was stuff you hadn't told me.'

'Right.' He was focused again. 'Such as my wife being here in LA.'

'What?' She looked shaken. 'Imogen?'

He told her what had occurred.

'And you had no idea she would be here? She knows where you're staying and she hasn't tried to contact you? She hung up on your calls?'

'Yep.' He nodded. 'And money's tight. Go figure.'

'I'd figure she's having an affair.'

'That wouldn't be a first,' he said.

'Oh?'

'She's an intelligent woman, Sally. Put yourself in her shoes. Imagine you were married to me and you knew I'd come to LA. Would you seriously come here with your lover at the same time?'

'Only if I wanted to be caught. If I wanted out of the marriage.'

He stared at her in silence. 'I hadn't thought about it that way,' he said finally.

'Some human minds work in oblique ways, Ross,' she said.

'I don't think Imogen is devious – not that devious.'

She tilted her head towards him. 'You said she's a smart lady. Well, she must be to have married you!'

'Thank you, ma'am!'

'I've interviewed quite a few criminals over the years,' she said. 'Something I've learned from them is that the best hiding place is the one right under your nose.'

'It's a good theory. But I don't buy it in this situation.'

'You have a better one?'

'No, I don't. I'm feeling fresh out of theories. But I believe one thing and I'm going to cling to it, however much of a long shot it might be. Then we'll know for sure, one way or another.'

'The sign Delaney promised?'

'Yes.'

'And if it doesn't happen?'

'I've always loved that quote of Martin Luther – something like: "Even if I knew the world would end tomorrow, I would still plant my apple tree."' He looked at her. 'You know, that's how you make me feel. I apologize if I'm sounding cheesy. But you do.'

'It is pretty cheesy.' She grinned. 'But it's OK. I do cheesy.'

Van Morrison was singing now, 'Have I Told You Lately That I Love You?'.

Ross grinned back at her. 'What was it Noel Coward said about the potency of cheap music?'

She cocked her head. 'Tell me?'

132

'This the place,' the driver drawled as they arrived at the mortuary. 'I'm guessing we missed Happy Hour.'

It was nearly after 10 p.m. as he turned the limousine sedately in through the open gates, past a prominent sign: COUNTY OF LOS ANGELES, DEPARTMENT OF MEDICAL EXAMINER-CORONER.

In the beam of the headlights Bloor saw a row of linked, modern-looking two-storey buildings, each numbered. On the walls were several clear signs, in large blue script.

DEPARTMENT OF CORONER, FORENSIC LABORATORIES

DEPARTMENT OF CORONER, ADMINISTRATION OPERATIONS

A line of identical white sedans sat outside, each bearing the same emblem and the word CORONER on the front door.

As the driver pulled the limousine up at what looked like the main entrance he said, 'The party begins here.'

Ignoring him, Bloor got out, leaving Helmsley behind, still at work on his emails.

He walked up the steps, through howling wind, and over to the glass-panelled double doors, conscious of a CCTV camera pointing at him. A sign on the glass said NO PUBLIC ACCESS. Peering through, he could see a small waiting area with a couple of functional-looking sofas, a hand-sanitizing machine and a floor-standing display cabinet full of framed certificates.

A man appeared round the corner. He was middle-aged, with a greying Beatles-style haircut and a moustache, wearing a purple open-neck shirt and clutching a bunch of photographs.

Bloor rapped on the glass. The man glanced round, shook his head, gave a cut-throat sign and pointed past him. Bloor looked around, puzzled. The man pointed again and Bloor gave him a shrug. Finally the man walked over and unlocked the door. As it swung open, Bloor was struck by a strong smell of detergent.

'Help you, sir?' He had a friendly, efficient air. A phone was jammed in his breast pocket and an ID tag hung from a lanyard round his neck. It read, 'Mark Johnson, Head, Forensic Photographic & Support Services, Los Angeles County Department of Medical Examiner-Coroner'.

'Yes, I hope so,' Bloor said politely, trying hard to look mournful. 'You see, I'm over from England for a family visit with a cousin. But tragically he was killed earlier this evening by a hit-and-run driver up in West Hollywood. I thought it might be helpful if I formally identified him for you.'

'I'm sorry for your loss, but you need to go to that building behind you, talk to the reception, sir.'

Bloor glanced round at a much older, elegant brick building.

'But we don't do formal identifications from family any more,' he added.

'No?'

'Pretty much all done by DNA and fingerprints these days.'

'I see.'

'Sorry you've had a wasted journey.'

Bloor thought on his feet. 'Well, the thing is, I've come all the way from England – we were going to have a big family reunion. Would it be possible to see Mike? To pay my last respects?'

'I'm afraid we don't do viewings here any more, too many insurance risks. You'd have to do that at the mortuary where he is taken after here.'

'I thought this was the mortuary?'

'I guess in England you'd call the place a funeral home.'

'OK – where can I find out which one he'll go to?'

'What is the deceased's name?'

'Mike Delaney.'

'Ah, OK, right. I'm afraid he's classified as part of a crime scene. Only after the coroner authorizes release of his body to a funeral home can viewing take place.'

'When will that be?'

'Well, we'll have to wait for the autopsy, and we're pretty backed up, with over five hundred waiting. Could be a few days, maybe a week or longer.'

'I see,' Bloor said, thinking hard. 'I don't suppose you could break the rules – as I've come all this way and I have to fly back in two days – and just give me a very quick look at him?'

'I'm afraid that's not possible, sir. The only way would be if you came back tomorrow and put your case to the coroner.' He looked pensive. 'Oh no, sorry, he and the deputy are both away at a conference, won't be back until Thursday. I'm real sorry.'

Bloor thanked him, clocking his name again, and walked back out. But instead of going to the car, he turned right and walked, in darkness, along the side of the build- ing, peering in through each of the darkened casement windows as he passed them. Then, as he went down some outside steps, he smelled a sweet whiff of cigarette smoke coming from the car park below.

He skipped down some steps, walked past a row of coroner's vans, turned the corner and saw a short man in blue scrubs, a theatre cap pushed up over his forehead, standing outside a door, smoking a cigarette.

Bloor strode confidently towards him. 'That smells good!' he said.

'Want one?' The man dug a hand beneath his gown and produced a pack of cigarettes.

'You sure?' Bloor asked. He hadn't smoked a cigarette since his early twenties.

'Us smokers got to stick together.'

'Absolutely!' He pulled out a cigarette from the proffered pack, then accepted the man's light.

'You sound like a Brit?'

'I am a Brit.'

'So, what brings you here?'

'Oh, I'm a forensic pathologist back at home. We don't really have many gunshot deaths, and because of the terrorist threat, I've been seconded here to learn about them, at Mark Johnson's invitation – I've just been with him this evening.' Bloor shot a surreptitious glance at the man's tag. *Dr Wayne Linch*. 'Tomorrow Mark said I would be meeting a Dr Linch here and hopefully spending some time with him.'

'Dr Linch? That's me!'

They shook hands. 'Good to meet you – Dr?'

'Porter – Richard Porter.'

'Well, Richard, you're in the right place. That's why I'm working late tonight. Four people shot dead in Orange County in what seems like a drugs deal gone wrong. Want to take a look?'

'Sure,' Bloor said. 'That would be helpful.'

They finished their cigarettes and went inside.

Bloor followed him into a locker room. The pathologist handed him a blue gown, cap and a paper mask, then pulled out a pair of white rubber boots from beneath a bench.

'You want to see what kind of a gunshot death?'

'Handgun. We get some shotgun deaths, but rarely from a handgun.'

The pathologist led him along a corridor, then opened a door and switched on the lights.

Inside, on a steel gurney, lay a naked Hispanic man on his back, beneath a large, circular scanner. He had a massive tattoo on his chest and there was a small puncture mark on either side of his left nipple.

'See those marks on his chest?'

'The ones by his nipple?' Bloor asked.

'Yep. Made by a small bore – a dum-dummed .22 handgun. Tiny entry wounds, but the bullets exploded inside him, after impact. If I rolled him over you'd see most of his back is blown away, along with his internal organs.' He pointed up at the scanner. 'That's an X-ray – we're looking for all the bullet fragments still inside him.'

Bloor looked at the tattoo on the dead man's chest. It read: I AM HERE.

Noticing his interest, the pathologist looked at it, also. Then, addressing the dead man's face, he said, 'Not any more, dude.'

As they left the room the pathologist switched off the lights and closed the door behind them. 'OK, guess I'd better get back to work. Nice meeting you, Richard.'

'Nice meeting you, too. See you tomorrow. What time will you be in?'

'Oh, I'm an early one. Seven a.m.'

'Seven a.m. it is.'

As the pathologist walked away, Bloor stood still, unable to believe his luck. Mike Delaney's body had already been brought here – where was it?

He felt a moment of anxiety as a young, overweight and bearded man, in a blue gown similar to his own, but with no head covering, strode along towards him.

'Have a good one,' he said in passing.

Bloor grunted a reply, then walked quickly along the corridor. He opened the first door he reached. Through it he could see a long, narrow room, with operating theatre lights and a row of steel gurneys, some with bodies lying beneath plastic sheeting. All of the bodies were dark-skinned. At the far end was a man, similarly gowned to the pathologist he had just shared a cigarette with, at work on a tiny cadaver. A child.

He shut the door and moved on, passing doors to toilets, a water dispenser, a yellow rubbish can on wheels and several noticeboards. He came to a lift, wondering where it went to. Then he saw another door ahead.

He opened it.

A blast of cold air greeted him, thick and heavy with the cloying reek of decaying flesh. The lights were on. It was a vast cold store with the feel of a warehouse. A grid of strip lights hung beneath a corrugated roof. Rows of corpses were laid on tiered metal shelves, five high, and stretching away into the distance. Dozens of steel gurneys, most of them also containing a body, stood seemingly randomly placed around the room. Each cadaver was wrapped in plastic sheeting, some clear see-through, others opaque white. Two tags hung from a toe of each cadaver, one orange, the other buff.

Over five hundred, he thought, remembering the words of Mark Johnson.

One of them was Mike Delaney.

The lights flickered. Almost instantly, he heard a crash of thunder. It echoed through the room, a deep metallic boom.

Closing the door behind him, he stepped forward quickly to a gurney a short distance in front of him, on which lay a figure wrapped in white plastic sheeting. He checked behind him, but the door was still closed. He looked at the toe tags, but all they had were file numbers, no name. He lifted the cover over the head and stared down at a black man with the top half of his skull blown away, his brains exposed.

Swallowing in revulsion, he replaced the sheet and moved on. He had to find Delaney. Grab some of his hair and get the man's DNA.

Had to!

The lights flickered again. There was another clap of thunder. Followed by a second. Then a third, even louder, shaking the ground, booming as if he was inside a massive drum.

He looked at several more cadavers beneath clear sheeting. An enormously fat white woman. A thin young man. A beautiful young blonde. Then he approached another figure wrapped in white sheeting. He raised it, to expose the head, and looked down at the open, startled eyes of a black girl with a blood-crusted hole in the centre of her forehead.

Where are you, Delaney? Where in this hellhole are you?

The lights flickered again, went out totally, and after a few seconds came back on. Then an explosion like a bomb, directly above him, shook the entire building.

Feeling increasingly uneasy, he passed several more bodies in clear wrapping, none of them looking like the image of Mike Delaney he had imprinted in his mind. Then another body in white wrapping. As he reached it, the lights flickered again. Then they went out.

There was a crash of thunder so loud and so close he could feel the entire building shake once more.

He pulled out his phone and switched on the torch app and checked the face of the cadaver.

Thunder crashed again.

He approached another body wrapped in white. Lifted the cover to look at the head. A Chinese woman.

Then an angry voice, right behind him, a voice he recognized – Mark Johnson – called out, 'Hey! Hey, you! Mister!'

He turned in blind panic.

'What the hell do you think you—'

At that moment, he heard a crackle of electricity. The whole room lit up in a blue haze. He saw jagged blue spikes of lightning dancing around the ceiling, then across the metal racks, like the peaks and troughs on an ECG display. He glimpsed the furious face of the man in the purple shirt behind him. Then he heard a massive explosion above him.

He looked up and the whole ceiling was ablaze.

He ran past the man, pushing him aside so hard he fell over backwards, reached the door, yanked it open and ran out along the corridor.

Above him he heard another crash of thunder.

Then realized he was running the wrong way.

The ceiling above him exploded into searing flames.

He turned and ran, blindly, desperately, in the opposite direction. Sprinklers were spraying water down on him. He reached the reception desk and turned towards the door. Pushed it. Pulled it. Nothing happened.

There was another crash of thunder.

Part of the burning ceiling fell in behind him.

He saw a green button beside the door. Pressed it. Nothing happened. He ran back over to the reception desk, picked up the swivel chair and hurled it with all his strength at the glass door. It shattered open. He climbed through, then sprinted across towards the limousine, yanked open the rear door and climbed in.

'You OK?' Helmsley said, anxiously.

'Get out of here!' he screamed at the driver.

'Lightning,' Helmsley said. 'The building got two direct hits in a row.'

As they drove back out through the open gates, Bloor turned and stared back at the mortuary. The entire building was engulfed in flames.

In the distance, he heard sirens and the brutal honking of approaching fire trucks.

133

After a restless night, kept awake by the thunder and his turbulent thoughts, at 5 a.m. Ross finally gave up trying to sleep. Sally had invited him back to her hotel for a nightcap, after dinner, but he had declined. He was drawn more and more to her each time he saw her. He felt something with her that he had never felt with Imogen. He could not put a finger on what that was. A connection at some very deep level.

Thoughts of Imogen went round and round in his mind. What was she doing here? What was her game? It didn't make sense that she was here. But at this moment, what did make sense?

He reached over, grabbed his phone and peered at the display, hopefully.

Hoping for a message from Imogen to explain what she was doing in LA.

But there was only one and it was from Sally, sent at 11.30 p.m. last night.

Sleep tight, you saver of the world, you! XX

He texted back.

It's spelled 'saviour'. XX

The reply came straight back. Presumably, like him, she'd been having a sleepless night.

Now, now, don't get too big-headed ☺ XX

He grinned, his dark mood momentarily lightened.

His eyes felt like they had been rubbed with sandpaper. He picked up the remote, switched on the television and channel-surfed. An old episode of *ER*. A documentary on the melting Arctic. Then a local news channel, showing a blazing building with a mass of fire engines and emergency vehicles in front of it. Hosepipes. Firefighters. A mediagenic newscaster clutching a radio mic.

'. . . working through the night on a blaze started by a lightning strike on the offices of the Los Angeles County Medical Examiner and Coroner. I have with me Mark Johnson, who has responsibility for the entire building. How is it looking?'

Johnson, a sombre-looking, moustached man in a purple shirt, said, 'It's looking pretty bad. The principal strike appears to have occurred directly above the room we call the Crypt. It's where over five hundred bodies awaiting autopsy were stored. It's too soon to assess the damage, but what I hear from the firefighters is that this whole part of the building has been pretty much destroyed.'

Ross sat up. For the next hour, he was glued to the television, surfing between stations for news updates. Then his phone rang.

It was Sally.

'Hey, have you seen the news?' she asked.

'I'm watching it now.'

'Weird?'

'You could say that.'

'It was good seeing you yesterday.'

'You too.'

'Even though you fell asleep on me at the dinner table.'

'I did? Oh shit, no, I'm sorry!'

'I'll forgive you – on one condition.'

'Which is?'

'We have dinner again tonight.'

He smiled. He still hadn't totally figured her out, but he felt increasingly sure that she could be trusted. 'I'll try to keep awake.'

'I'll take it personally if you don't!'

Moments after he ended the call, his phone rang again. It was Imogen.

134

'What are you doing in LA?' Ross asked his wife.

'I can't talk about it on the phone. Could you meet me at 10 a.m. in the foyer of the Serena Hotel on Sunset?'

Her voice had a steely tone. She sounded like a stranger.

'Yes. But tell me – what—?'

There was a click.

She had hung up.

He called her back. It went to voicemail.

He didn't leave a message. Instead he lay in bed, wondering just what was going on. What game she was playing. Then he switched his thoughts back to the events of last night. He opened the Voice Memos app and played the recording of his encounter with Mike Delaney. Listening to the nuances in his voice. The sincerity.

'It's written also in Matthew 24: "The sun will be darkened, the moon will lose its brightness, the stars will fall from the sky and the powers of heaven will be shaken. And then the Sign of the Son of Man will appear in heaven."'

Wishing he'd thought to pack his trainers, so he could have used the hotel's gym, Ross got dressed in a T-shirt, jeans, boots and his leather jacket, and went out for a walk. The wind was even stronger than yesterday, and after the torrential rain that had come with the thunder, the air felt fresh. He made a random right turn into a quiet, tree-lined street and passed several swanky, secluded houses, then came across a small park. It was already busy with joggers and dog walkers at this hour and he did two brisk circuits.

Returning to his hotel, he ordered a room-service breakfast of a three-egg omelette, sourdough toast, a bowl of berries and coffee, showered and shaved, and ordered a taxi to take him to the Serena Hotel, fifteen minutes away, the concierge informed him, at 9.45 a.m.

135

It was coming up to 6 p.m. and Brother Pete cursed. He'd boarded the wrong train up from Sussex; he should have taken the Victoria train but instead, as a helpful passenger had told him, he was going to a different station, London Bridge. Unless he got off and changed.

Spats of rain slid down the carriage window and a cold draught blew on his face. They were travelling through a grey, urban landscape. Everything was confusing right at this moment. He was feeling a deep depression. A while ago his plan had seemed the right thing, but now he was experiencing doubts. His Bible sat on his lap, unopened during the journey.

He had intended not to return to Mount Athos. Not for a while, anyhow. He wanted to see some more of the world and test his faith. To see if his faith drew him back. He needed to understand something deep within his soul. Was it his faith that kept him at the monastery or just the way of life? A way of life which enabled him to be left alone by the world, which was all he had ever really wanted?

It was something his cousin, Brother Angus, had told him. Angus said it had taken him over forty years to understand his purpose in life, which was to serve the Lord alone, in solitude. Pete had helped carry his coffin earlier this afternoon into the peaceful, simple graveyard with the rows of plain wooden crosses.

He felt sad for the old man, but happy for him, too, because unlike so many people, Angus seemed to have found peace and contentment in his simple life. But now, as Pete sat on a seat in the train carriage, clutching the bag to his side, he was uncertain about what he should do. Inside the bag was the package the Prior had handed him for safekeeping. Items that Angus was anxious should be kept safe for eternity. On Mount Athos, they would be safe.

Inside his heart he was riddled with doubts.

If he returned to Athos, he might never be allowed to leave again. There was no way off the peninsula other than by boat, and only the Abbot could give you a ticket for it.

A drained-looking woman sat opposite him with a bawling baby, snot running from its nose. A little scrap of humanity. Next to him was a hunched youth playing music through his headset, far too loud. Pete could hear the constant, irritating *tsh-tsh-tsh-tsh-tsh* as the gormless-looking creature nodded his head to the beat. An elderly couple sat across the aisle in the facing seats. Both stared ahead, not out of the window, not at anything. The man held a walking stick in his bony hand, the woman was plump, with overlapping chins.

'I'm bored,' the man complained.

'I'm bored, too,' the woman replied.

'How much longer?' he asked.

'Dunno,' she replied.

The train was pulling into a station. Brother Pete saw a sign saying EAST CROYDON. The station where he could change trains to Victoria.

He stood up as the train halted and stepped out through the doors, relieved to be away from the claustrophobic environment. Back at Mount Athos he had space. He didn't have to look at babies with runny noses or endure someone else's ghastly music. He was missing the solitude, he realized, for the first time since he had left.

Navigating his way around the maze of platforms, through pelting rain, he eventually found the correct one for Victoria. An electronic sign indicated the next train would be along in fourteen minutes. He sat on an empty bench, beneath a shelter, took his Bible back out of his bag and began to read.

Moments later, it seemed, he sensed a group of people around him, crowding in on him. He smelled alcohol and cigarette smoke. A jeering voice said, 'What you fucking reading then, that the Qur'an?'

He looked up. There were four youths, all tattooed, two of them with shaven heads, one with a Mohican, one with nose and lip rings and spiky green hair. They were dressed in hoodies, tracksuit bottoms and trainers and were all holding beer cans. Three of them were smoking.

'It's the Bible,' he said, politely.

'Yeah?' said one.

He nodded.

The train was coming in. He put the book back in his bag and stood up. They were all looking at him with a kind of dumb hatred in their eyes.

Ignoring them, he walked across and entered the train, into an empty carriage. The youths, to his relief, got on further along, a different carriage. He settled into a seat, feeling shaken by the encounter. Why did there have to be such hostility in the world? Perhaps it was the way that God tested all of us, the way He'd put the anger into his own heart, Pete knew. Anger which sometimes flared up, uncontrollably.

Moments after the train pulled out, rain blew in through the open top of the window beside him. He was about to stand up and close it when he heard a door open and shut behind him. Smelled cigarette smoke again. Then a voice.

'You a fucking terrorist or what?'

He looked up and to his dismay the four yobs stood in the aisle. One held a cigarette between his finger and thumb and sucked on it.

'It's no smoking in here,' Brother Pete said before he could help himself, a flash of that uncontrollable anger rising again.

'It's no Muslims in here either, mate,' said the Mohican.

'I'm not a Muslim.'

'What are you then, with that face fungus and your black dressing gown?'

'I'm a Greek Orthodox monk,' he replied, and gave them a smile, hoping that might placate them.

'Yeah? How do we know you're not an effing terrorist then? You carrying a bomb inside that bag?'

'I'm a monk.'

'All right then, show us.' The one with the green hair lunged at the bag.

Pete swung his left arm, defensively, sending him flying. Then he grabbed the bag by the handles and swung it at them, screaming, 'Leave me alone! I'm a monk! I'm not a terrorist!' He swung it again, wildly, missing all of them and striking the window beside him.

The four of them looked at him.

'You're bloody mental,' the Mohican said.

The one with the green spiky hair punched him on the nose. His eyes watering with the pain, he saw, blurrily, the youth grab the bag and shove it through the open top part of the window.

'No!' Brother Pete screamed. 'No, no, no!'

'At least we're all fucking safe on this train now – we've chucked the bomb away!'

Roaring with laughter, they walked off down the aisle.

Pete stood, trying to look out of the window, wind and rain hammering his face, tears streaming from his eyes, as the train continued accelerating.

136

At a few minutes to ten, the taxi turned into the imposing driveway of the Serena Hotel. Of course, Ross thought, slightly angrily, wondering how much this was costing a night, Imogen wouldn't be staying in a cheap dump, would she?

One moment she was lecturing him on their need to conserve and save money for when she stopped working to have the baby and they would be reliant on his income alone. The next she was flying to Los Angeles and larging it in one of the city's swankiest hotels.

The taxi drove for several hundred yards up a curving, palm-lined driveway and arrived outside the columned front of the hotel, teeming with liveried staff and lined with top-of-the-range limousines, sports cars and SUVs.

Someone young, handsome and obsequiously friendly opened his door.

'Welcome to the Serena, sir!'

Ross paid and tipped the driver then headed towards the front entrance, passing bronze statues of past Hollywood icons. He recognized John Wayne, seated on a bench. Marilyn Monroe, cigarette in hand, laughing. Rock Hudson, leaning against a wall, gave him a wry smile.

The doors parted automatically and he entered a cavernous, white, scented atrium. Dominating it was a huge circular pond, with a fountain, sculpted out of three gold angels, rising from the middle. Groups of armchairs and sofas were dotted along the water's edge.

As he stood looking around, he saw Imogen walking towards him, dressed in a smart two-piece, as if for a business meeting.

She was flanked by two suited, middle-aged men, neither of them particularly good-looking. One was of medium height, with sleek silver hair, a trim figure and a hawk-like face bearing a smug smile. The other was tall and thin, with red-framed glasses that would have suited an art student, but just made him look a twat, Ross thought.

He recognized them now from their company website. If evil had a smell, these men would reek, he thought.

As if by an invisible military command, they stopped and Imogen continued, the last few paces towards him, alone.

The nearer she came, unsmiling, the more of a stranger she was to him.

'Hello, Ross,' she said, stopping well clear of his personal space.

His natural instinct was to step forward, embrace and kiss her. But her body language stopped him. It was like a barrier.

'What are you doing here, Imo? Not taking my calls? Do you want to tell me what's going on? I've been going out of my wits.'

'Oh, right, and I haven't? These past weeks? Since you decided to put us both at risk?'

'I'm doing my job.'

'People do jobs to earn *money*, Ross,' she retorted.

'Who are your flunkeys?' He nodded to the men behind her. 'You're getting very flash, flying to LA, staying here, hiring bodyguards.'

'They're not bodyguards, they're paying for everything. And they're offering us a lot of money, far more than the newspaper will ever pay you for the article.'

Lowering his voice so only Imogen could hear, he said, 'Really? Are these the shitbags who tried to have me killed in Egypt?'

'No, you're mistaken – they didn't want to kill you, they wanted what you had. But they are now offering a very good deal – far better than the Vatican. Can we go somewhere quiet to talk?'

'It's quiet here.' He stared at her, wondering, *Do I know you any more?*

'Let's go and sit down, at least.'

Joined by the two men, she headed over to a couple of sofas and armchairs grouped around a coffee table, close to the water and far enough from the next seating area not to be overheard.

'Ross,' Imogen said, 'this is Ainsley Bloor and Julius Helmsley.'

He reluctantly shook hands with the hawk-faced man first, then with the one with stupid glasses, and they sat down.

'Very nice to meet you, Ross,' said Bloor. His voice sounded sharp, overly friendly and completely insincere. 'Can we get you some tea or coffee?'

'An Americano with hot milk.'

Bloor clicked his finger in the air and a server in a beige jacket hurried over.

'Would you like anything to eat?' Bloor asked. 'Have you had breakfast?'

'I'm fine.'

They gave their orders to the server. Then Ross said, 'Do you gentlemen have business cards, please?'

'Of course.' Bloor fished out a fancy silver holder and handed one to him.

'Kerr Kluge?'

'That's right.' Bloor gave him the kind of smile a teacher gives a small child.

'You're the Chief Executive?'

'I am. And Julius is our Chief Operating Officer.'

Ross said nothing. Imogen was looking at him, anxiously.

'Perhaps your wife has explained why we are all here?'

'No, I have no idea.'

'Ah, right,' Bloor continued in his patronizing tone. 'We understand you came here to Los Angeles to meet a gentleman called Mike Delaney, who according to records you've managed to obtain, might well be Jesus Christ back on earth – however improbable that sounds.'

'Understand from whom?'

'From your wife,' Bloor said, disarmingly.

'Yes, so we are pretty much up to speed, Mr Hunter,' Julius Helmsley chipped in.

Ross frowned at Imogen. Then at each of the two men. 'Is that right? You're aware that he was killed last night by a hit-and-run driver. Nothing to do with you?'

'Ross!' Imogen said, crossly.

'To do with us?' Bloor said, still humouring the small child. 'We came here in the hope of meeting Mr Delaney, not to kill him. Kerr Kluge is a very well-respected public company as I am sure you know. Killing people is not our thing.'

'Except for me in Egypt and poor people in Africa?' Ross quizzed.

'I beg your pardon?' Helmsley said, affronted.

'Your company has been criticized on several occasions

for selling out-of-date drugs to the African continent,' he said, ignoring his wife's glare.

'Mr Hunter,' Helmsley said, 'there is a wide safety margin on the date stamping of all our pharmaceutical products. They may be out of date for the retailers we supply within Europe and the United States, but they are all still sound products. If it helps poorer countries by selling them cheaply, that's got to be a good thing, surely?'

'You're making yourself sound like a saint, Mr Helmsley,' Ross said.

'Well, I do think people like to demonize the pharmaceutical industry.'

'Really? I can't think why.'

'Ross!' Imogen hissed.

'Look, Mr Hunter,' Bloor said, 'I won't beat about the bush. We would like what we believe you have and we are prepared to pay handsomely for it.'

'What you *believe* I have? You've bugged my house, haven't you? You *know* what I have.'

Bloor reddened slightly.

'Since you had your people graffiti it, right? Under the guise of religious fanatics. Very clever of you.'

Bloor said nothing.

'Did your people kill poor Harry Cook and his solicitor?'

'There are a lot of people after what you have, Ross, not just us.'

'Really?'

'I think you know that.'

'And as ruthless as you lot? People willing to shoot at me in Egypt? To try to drown me in a well?'

'High stakes have always carried high risks,' Bloor said, cynically. 'Sometimes, people have to pay the ultimate price. That's how the world rolls and always has done. You have something that could change the world. A vial of fluid that very probably contains Jesus Christ's original DNA, obtained from crushing a tooth. Imagine that in the wrong hands.'

Ross looked at Imogen, totally gobsmacked. 'You told these people about the vial? These slimeballs?'

'They're not *slimeballs*, Ross. These are good people, doing good research, doing good for the world.'

'Really?' He looked, seething, at both men as their drinks arrived, along with a plate of tiny biscuits.

As the server walked away he said, 'Can you tell me, gentlemen, why Jesus Christ's DNA is so important to you? I know you are major players in the genetics field – are you planning to start cloning Him? Or are you worried, Mr Bloor, that someone else might, and you'll have hordes of miracle workers wandering around, healing people and putting you out of business?'

'I'm an atheist, Ross.' Bloor smiled. 'It is very simple. We are, as you correctly say, a major player in genetics research. I don't believe in Jesus Christ being the Son of God or being a healer or any of that claptrap. But there are over two billion practising Christians in the world, many of whom buy my company's products. This is about marketing, pure and simple.'

'What?' Ross said. 'I don't follow.'

Bloor had his condescending expression again. 'Very simply, Mr Hunter. You are a consumer and you have a choice of products. If you were a Christian believer shopping for headache tablets or a cold remedy, which product are you going to choose – assuming the same price? The one manufactured by a company you know nothing about or the one that has Jesus Christ's DNA?'

Ross was silent for some moments, absorbing this. Finally, he shook his head. 'That is so unbelievably cynical.'

Bloor continued, smiling at him. 'It's called *business*, Mr Hunter.'

Ross turned to his wife. 'What did they offer to pay you, Judas – sorry – Imogen. Thirty pieces of silver?'

'Ross,' Imogen said. 'They are offering to pay off our mortgage, all our debts and more.'

'We are prepared to make you a very generous offer,' Helmsley said.

Ross looked at his wife. 'I don't believe this. I have a chance to do something for mankind, and you're prepared to sell me out? First Silvestri, and now you bring these scumbags all the way here?'

'Yes, Ross, OK – I'm not doing it for the rest of the world, I'm doing it for us.'

'You're meant to be a Christian believer, Imogen!'

'Yup, well maybe I put practical considerations above my faith, sometimes.'

Ross looked at the men. 'What kind of money are you talking?'

'Before we enter detailed negotiations, we need to be completely sure of the provenance, Mr Hunter,' Helmsley said.

Ross pulled his wallet out of his breast pocket and held it up. 'Provenance?'

Bloor and Helmsley's eyes lit up.

He dug into the lining and tore it open. Then he tugged out the tiny vial, with an ATGC Forensics label around it, and held it up. 'You're asking for provenance for this?'

He registered alarm in Imogen's eyes.

'That's correct, Mr Hunter,' Helmsley said. 'We would need to satisfy our board.'

'But surely your board are already aware of the provenance?'

'I don't understand,' Helmsley replied.

'Really? You're telling me they don't know of its provenance? You tried to have me killed when I went to Egypt to get it.'

'That's outrageous!' Bloor protested.

'You know it's the truth, gentlemen.' He stared at the vial. 'And you know something? This little thing here really does seem to be the cause of a lot of problems.'

'Ross!' Imogen cautioned.

Holding the tiny vial in his left hand, he twisted off the stopper with his right hand, stood up and strode to the water's edge.

'Nooooo!' shrieked Bloor, so loudly people were turning round.

'Mr Hunter!' Helmsley called out, imploringly.

'Ross! Don't!' Imogen commanded.

He threw the vial, as hard as he could, towards the fountain. As it flew through the air, droplets fell from it. A moment later the vial was gone from view, below the surface.

Then he turned to the shocked faces of the two pharmaceutical executives. 'Quick, gentlemen, grab a bucket each! I'm giving you a gift. Holy water, totally free!'

137

Tuesday, 21 March

'You OK?'

Sally, seated beside him on the plane, looked pale. She nodded. 'Yep, thanks. It's just this is the bit I don't like – the take-off – and the landing.'

'I prefer landing to the alternative.'

'Don't!'

They had taxied out onto the runway and were now in a queue. The strengthening gale was battering the plane and they could feel it shaking.

Ross glanced at his watch. It was 6.20 p.m. They were due into London Heathrow at lunchtime, UK time, tomorrow.

'How strong does the wind need to be before planes can't fly, Ross?' she asked.

'It would have to be pretty bad – these things have hooks in the sky!'

'That's too bad – I was sort of hoping the flight might be cancelled, you know – and we get deplaned. And have another evening in LA.'

He studied her expression for some moments as the engines roared and the plane shuddered even more. 'I'm going to ask you a question and I want you to answer me honestly, OK?'

She grinned. 'I'll try.'

'Did you actually need to make this trip out here or was that bullshit?'

'Am I that transparent or shallow?'

'Neither, but I have a sneaking suspicion you might just be a tad devious.'

'Mr Ross Hunter!' she said with feigned indignation. 'Is that something you should say to a lady?'

'I'm a reporter, it's my job to ask questions. Just like it's your job, too.'

'Well, OK, I'll come clean. This trip was on my own dollar. You intrigue me. This mission you're on fascinates me, I wanted to be here to see what you found – and hopefully to give you support.'

The plane began to move. As it did, she gripped his hand, hard, her nails digging in, and closed her eyes.

It accelerated down the runway, picking up more and more speed, the wheels bumping beneath them, the wind shaking them more and more. Still on the runway. Faster and faster. Bumping. Bumping. Ross began to feel anxious too. Shit, were they ever going to lift off?

Then, suddenly, they were in the air, and the bumping became worse. Her nails dug in even harder. They were climbing. Buffeted. Jolting. Yawing. A massive bang right behind startled them both. Then they calmed down. It was just stuff crashing around in the rear galley.

Through the window, Ross could see the lights of the city below them. Then wisps of cloud. Suddenly, the lights were gone. They were climbing steeply. Bumping. Bumping.

'You can open your eyes now.'

She looked at him, still deathly pale, and gave a faint smile of relief.

'Thank you,' he said.

'For what?'

'For being honest with me.'

'Always.'

138

Two hours after Ross and Sally's flight had taken off from LAX, the Gulfstream taking Ainsley Bloor and Julius Helmsley back to the UK taxied along the runway of Santa Monica Airport, a few miles to the north.

The small jet was shaking in the wind, which had continued strengthening throughout the evening.

Both men were in furious moods. The pilot had tried to dissuade them from flying tonight, because of the weather conditions, but Bloor was in no mood to be told what to do.

Strapped in his seat, he drained his second glass of champagne and for the third or fourth time asked, 'Just tell me, Julius, how did that little shit, Hunter, know it was us in Egypt?'

'I don't know. I've told you, Ainsley. I don't know.'

'Someone enabled him to make the connection. Someone must have bloody told him.'

'I've already asked the pilots.'

Both the pilot and co-pilot of the Gulfstream had been in the helicopter in Egypt, along with a local Luxor pilot to help navigate.

Bloor stared out of the window. He could barely see the runway lights. It looked like mist swirling past.

The senior pilot's voice crackled over the intercom. 'Sandstorm's coming in, gentlemen. It will be a very uncomfortable ride. My advice is to abort and we'll see how the weather's looking in the morning.'

Bloor grabbed the microphone in his armrest and switched it on. 'Just go, OK? Go now, beat the bloody storm. You said we could get ahead of it if we went now.'

'OK, you're the boss. It's gonna be bumpy.'

'It'll be even bumpier for you if we don't go.'

'Your dollar, your call.'

The engines roared and the plane accelerated rapidly.

'Are you sure about this, Ainsley?' Helmsley said, nervously.

'This guy's flown like one hundred and ten missions in Iraq. They have proper sandstorms there. He knows what to do. This is a cakewalk for him.'

Moments later, as the plane lifted off, it shook violently, sideways, then plummeted.

Helmsley screamed.

It gained height again.

Plummeted again.

Bloor blanched.

Then it was as if the two of them were inside a cocktail shaker. The plane rose almost vertically, then plunged just as vertically for several seconds before levelling out. It felt like it was being thrown sideways. Spinning.

'Jesus!' Bloor yelled.

Helmsley vomited.

139

The pilot's voice came through the intercom, waking Ross from his light, uncomfortable sleep in his cramped seat. Sally was still asleep, her face inches from his, pressed against a small pillow. He could hear the clattering of a trolley and could smell hot food.

'Well, I'm sorry you've had such a bumpy night, everyone, but the good news is the tailwind has given us a useful push and we are going to be arriving at Heathrow almost an hour ahead of schedule. The weather in London is a mild fourteen degrees centigrade and it's a sunny day. I'll give you a further update in a while.'

Sally opened her eyes and smiled at him.

'Did you get some sleep?' he asked.

'Yep, you know, the kind you might get lying on a busy trampoline.'

He smiled, and before he realized what he was doing, kissed her lightly on the forehead.

She fixed her eyes on his. Clear, deep blue, trusting eyes. Smiling eyes. She yawned. 'So, see you again sometime?'

'Soon I hope.'

'Me, too,' she said. 'Make it very soon!'

* * *

Later, as Ross drove out of the long-term car park at Heathrow, he was thinking through everything that had happened in the past two days.

And already missing Sally's company.

She was under his skin.

He needed to put her out of his mind, focus on finishing his piece for the *Sunday Times* and somehow find a way forward with Imogen. Anger rose inside him. What a bitch. He didn't understand it. Didn't understand where she was coming from. She'd talked about the danger they were in, distressed, petrified, then suddenly it had become all about the money.

Fair dues. She had a point. Maybe she had been right and he was the one who was being stupid. Stubborn. Unrealistic.

Was it unrealistic to try to do something towards pulling the world back from the brink?

Or was he massively deluded? Had he thrown away the chance to make some serious money out of this whole thing? It was still an option. Brother Angus had the backup, both the chalice and the vial of DNA. He could recover the situation if he so decided.

The news came on the radio.

Freak storms were battering the West Coast of the USA, with Southern California being the worst hit. Los Angeles LAX Airport had been closed. They were lucky to have got out in time.

Maybe, he thought, the gods were angry at Mike Delaney's death.

Or rather, God?

His phone pinged with an incoming text. A few minutes later it pinged again. He ignored it. Imogen was always chiding him for looking at texts whilst driving, and a couple of months ago he'd written a piece about fatal road accidents caused by drivers doing just that. A Sussex Police traffic officer had told him about two recent separate fatals he had attended in which the drivers, one a female, the other a male, had veered, inexplicably, across the road into the path of oncoming lorries. It was later that the Collision Investigation experts had discovered texts, from each of the deceased's phones, had been sent at the corresponding time of impact.

Finally, shortly after 2.30 p.m., tired and hungry, and very badly in need of coffee, he turned into his empty driveway. He switched off the engine and looked at his messages.

The first was from Sally.

> Hey you, I'm sorry if I come across a bit stalkerish. I do really like you, but I totally get you're a married man, and I wouldn't want to do anything to compromise you. Been there, done that, still wearing the scars. So, bestest friends? Good luck with the article, tell me when it will be pubbed, and cannot wait to read! XXX

He smiled, wistfully. Then tapped out a reply.

> Safe home, my new bestest friend. XXX

Then he looked at the next text. It was from Imogen, and it was long.

> Ross, I'm not sure where you are. I don't know if you heard but Bloor and Helmsley were killed last night. Their jet went down – it's all over the

news here. I'm staying in America for a few days, going to visit an old girlfriend. I couldn't tell you when I saw you yesterday, sadly I've lost the baby. This is not easy to write, but I'm afraid I've also lost you, or rather, we've lost each other. I just don't know who you are any more. You love your work more than you will ever love me. I think it's better if we separate – I'm sure this won't be a surprise to you. I'm sorry and I hope this bland text isn't too hurtful. I did love you for a long time, I really did, and I know you loved me too. X

As he sat reading it through again, his emotions were in turmoil and he was fighting back tears. He'd lost his baby and his wife. Was it this story that had driven them apart or was it just the final nail in a crumbling relationship? He was convinced she'd been having an affair. Had the baby even been his?

He texted back.

Is there someone else?

A reply came back almost instantly.

Does it matter?

Life sure was full of surprises, he reflected, cynically.

His phone rang, interrupting his thoughts. He answered it, blinking back tears, and heard a Brummy accent.

'Mr Hunter?'

'Speaking.'

'It's DCI Starr, from Birmingham Major Crime Unit.'

'Yes, hello.'

'Is this a convenient time to speak?'

Hesitantly, he said, 'Yes, sure.'

'Well, just a couple of things to report, sir. The coroner has released Dr Cook's body and the funeral is scheduled for this coming Friday. I was wondering if you might be attending?'

'I've just, literally, flown in from the US, I'll have a look at my diary. But I think I'm free.'

'I was wondering, sir, if you do plan to attend, whether I might get a more formal statement from you, while you are up in the area?'

'Of course. I'll check my diary and get back to you.'

Starr gave him the best number to contact him on and thanked him.

Ross climbed out of the car, grabbed his suitcase and laptop bag from the boot, then walked to the house. He was too tired to look around to see if he was being watched. And beyond caring.

140

Ross drove round Spaghetti Junction, finding it hard to believe it was only ten days ago that he had last been here on this same nightmare of a road.

And somehow it didn't seem appropriate for a funeral that it should be such a fine, sunny day.

As if echoing his thoughts, Sally, seated beside him in the Audi, said, 'I thought the weather was meant to be horrible for funerals. All the ones I've been to, it's been drizzling and windy.'

'Me too.'

'What time's your appointment with the detective tomorrow?'

'Eleven thirty.'

'Good,' she said approvingly.

'I deliberately didn't make it too early.'

She cocked her head at him. 'Now why might that be?'

'Well, it's a lovely country house hotel. I thought we might want to use the facilities.'

'Maybe!' She continued looking at him, smiling. Turning her focus back to the navigation app on her phone, she read out directions through a tricky series of junctions. When she was confident they were on the right road she said, 'You know, I've been thinking about what you did, throwing the contents of the vial into the fountain. There's something . . .' Her voice tailed off.

'Something?' he prompted.

'I can't explain it, well at the moment, anyway. But I think you did the right thing.'

'Maybe.' He nodded. 'I know where the backup is, if I ever change my mind.'

He reflected for a moment, feeling a deep twinge of sadness that he had not known about Angus's death until his return from Los Angeles. He would have liked to have attended his funeral – if he would have been permitted.

'Personally, I hope you don't change your mind. Just my gut feeling that that – there's something very dangerous about it,' she said.

'Falling into the wrong hands?'

'As it would have done with Kerr Kluge.'

She put her hand on his arm and gave a gentle squeeze. 'How are you feeling?'

He thought before answering. Since getting Imogen's text he had been through a whole gamut of emotions. It had been a shock. And yet, he couldn't explain why, but ever since she'd told him she was pregnant he'd harboured doubts that he was the father. He should have felt sad – perhaps even devastated – that she had lost the baby, but he didn't. All he really felt now – however wrong that might be – was a sense of relief.

In truth, he was feeling more comfortable than he could remember. Sally looked even more lovely all in black. It felt as if she had always sat in the seat beside him, that she belonged there. He knew he should be feeling guilt about Imogen, but he felt none. Zero. He was feeling strangely liberated, in a way he could not rationalize.

'It's just great you came with me,' he said.

'I kind of like travelling with you, Mr Hunter. Not many people can turn going to a funeral into an adventure. I never met him but I feel as if I know Harry Cook quite well.'

'I guess I owe him a lot.'

'And maybe not only you? The whole world?'

'We'll find out on Sunday.'

'They're definitely running it then?'

'My editor loves it. She originally asked me to cut the story down to fit a two-page spread, then she said her boss liked it so much he wanted to extend it to three, maybe four pages!'

Brimming with delight, she said, 'That's amazing – and what you deserve!'

'Yep, but I'm not getting too excited, in case a bigger news story comes along. I've been there before.'

'Like, *what* could be bigger?'

'A major air disaster. The president of the US getting assassinated. A member of the Royal Family dying.'

'What happens then?'

'Well, if I'm lucky the story gets bumped for a week. If I'm unlucky, as I told you before, it gets cut to a few column inches. And if I'm really unlucky, it gets spiked.'

'Meaning?'

'It's history.'

'That cannot happen, Ross!'

'Welcome to the wonderful world of journalism.'

'You're going to cause a global sensation with this story, I know it. I believe in you.' She leaned over and kissed him on the cheek.

141

Forty minutes later they arrived at the attractive Norman village church. Just a few miles from where Ross had come a month ago to see Harry Cook – and found him dead.

There were a few cars outside, and Ross parked behind them. He pulled his black tie from his pocket and, with the help of his courtesy mirror, at the third attempt finally got the knot in the right position.

It was 11.40 a.m.

They climbed out of the Audi into the unseasonably warm day. The sun beat down hard as they headed towards the church, Ross feeling awkward in his navy suit. He was always much more comfortable in casual clothes.

They took the order of service sheets handed to them as they entered, walked a short distance down the aisle, then sat behind the small group of mostly elderly people in the church. A middle-aged couple with two teenage children, a boy and a girl, sat in the front row.

He looked at the service sheet and saw on the front a photograph of a much, much younger Harry Cook than he had met. He was in his early twenties, if that, in RAF uniform, with a bristling moustache and a very proud smile.

The service was officiated by a robed vicar with a white Santa Claus beard, who had clearly known Cook well. He described him as a dedicated family man, devastated by the death of his son who was killed in action in Afghanistan, and who had struggled to come to terms with the recent death of his beloved wife, Doreen. He doted on his niece, Angela, and her two children, Alice and Robert. A much-respected university professor, he displayed endless patience in conveying his love and passion for the history of art to his students over many years.

'All of you who knew Harry,' the vicar said, 'will have experienced both his sincerity and his humour. Some years ago, he was asked by a newspaper what he had learned about the evolution of human nature as studied through the eyes of an art historian. He told me how he had responded. "Don," he said to me, "let me tell you the one thing I've learned. Buy shares in food and ammunition. People are always going to have to eat, and they're always going to kill each other."'

There was a nervous titter of laughter.

'I told him that as vicar I didn't have the spare cash for gambling on the stock market, but that I would remember his advice. He was analytical and he was passionate about the things he believed in. Most of all he cared about this world of ours. His passing robs us of a fine man, but now he will be reunited in Heaven with his beloved Doreen and his son.'

There was a Bible reading from his nephew, and his niece read a poem. Finally, they filed outside into the cloudless sky. Ross and Sally, feeling almost intruders, followed the group across the graveyard, keeping well to the rear.

It was an idyllic setting, Ross thought. Beyond the walled graveyard were gentle hills, dotted with sheep. They could hear the chorus of bleating.

The vicar began the Committal: 'I am the Resurrection and the Life, says the Lord.'

Suddenly it felt as if the sun had clouded over.

Ross looked up.

There were no clouds. Just endless blue sky.

'Those who believe in Me, even though they die, will live, and everyone who lives and believes in Me will never die,' intoned the vicar.

The sky was darkening. In the space of a few seconds, its colour went from brilliant cobalt blue to navy. Ross looked up again, frowning.

'I am convinced that neither death, nor life, nor angels, nor rulers, nor things present, nor things to come, nor powers, nor height, nor depth, nor anything else in all creation, will be able to separate us from the love of God in Christ Jesus our Lord.'

It was as if night was falling.

Several people were now looking upwards, puzzled.

The sky was growing darker still.

A flock of starlings flew down, descending on the church roof to roost.

Ross and Sally looked at each other, puzzled.

It felt like a total eclipse of the sun was happening.

Ross had only ever seen one total eclipse, watching in fascination, through protective lenses, as the moon had slid in front of the sun. But he could see the dim disc of the moon now, a long way from the increasingly faint glow that was the sun.

'What's happening?' Sally whispered. 'Is there an eclipse today?'

The vicar's voice was faltering, and he kept looking upwards, distractedly. 'Since we believe that Jesus died and rose again, even so, through Jesus, God will bring with Him those who have died. So we will be with the Lord for ever. Therefore encourage one another with these words.'

It was now almost pitch dark.

'For as much as it hath pleased Almighty God of his great mercy to call unto himself the soul of our dear brother Harry here departed, we therefore commit his body –'

Then, as if a huge switch had been pulled in the sky, a brilliant, iridescent rainbow appeared above them in the stark blackness.

But something was different about it, Ross thought.

The vicar fell silent. There was a complete hush. Everyone was staring upwards. At the rainbow.

It spanned the entire void above them, each end touching a shimmering, far and ghostly horizon.

And as Ross looked, he remembered the rhyme he had learned at school, for getting all the colours of the rainbow in their correct order – the only possible order, the order in which the colours of every rainbow since time began had appeared. *Richard Of York Gave Battle In Vain.*

Red, Orange, Yellow, Green, Blue, Indigo, Violet.

The colours of this rainbow were the wrong way round. They were inverted.

Violet, Indigo, Blue, Green, Yellow, Orange, Red.

Mike Delaney's words in the bar in Los Angeles came back to him.

The sun will be darkened, the moon will lose its brightness, the stars will fall from the sky and the powers of heaven will be shaken. And then the Sign of the Son of Man will appear in heaven.

Was this the sign?

142

Friday, 24 March

Big Tony sat back in his yellow-cushioned window seat, smoking a cigar, drinking whisky and soaking up the sunlight pouring in through the window behind him. He'd been drinking more than usual this week, since arriving back from Los Angeles.

Big fuck-up Los Angeles.

Big fuck-up Tony.

He was feeling a little drunk. Never normally touched the stuff until 6 p.m. Never had – except perhaps that day he was finally released from jail. He went a bit crazy that day. Anyone would after that long in the Big House.

Outside it felt like the sun had clouded over, but he barely noticed. He was thinking about last Monday, trying to fathom it out.

Either he was losing the plot or –

Or?

The crazy old guy on the sidewalk had moved too fast, faster than any athlete could have sprinted. And he never pushed Ross Hunter, he never got that close to him, he was still yards away when Hunter catapulted sideways.

Then the old man had been right in front of him. Lit up bright by the headlights.

No chance to avoid him.

He could still see the white of the man's eyes now. His

whole face. He showed no fear. He was smiling. Like someone crazy, like someone who wanted to die, was ready to die.

Sacrificing himself.

It spooked the hell out of Tony. He had kept going for twenty blocks before he parked up, changed the plates and changed vehicles, into the one waiting. He then drove four hours to Vegas to catch up with the pal who had arranged the vehicles, and played in a poker game with him through the night. He'd lost heavily, too distracted to concentrate.

Dusk was falling. The room was growing dark. *What?* He looked at his watch. 1.25 p.m. Had the thing stopped? He shook it, then looked at the clock on his DVD player. 13.25.

He looked out of the window. Winking lights of a helicopter descending, passing his window level now. It was pitch dark. Dark as night. He looked up. 'What the –?'

He jumped to his feet, went over to the French windows, opened them and stepped out onto the balcony.

And could not believe his eyes. How much had he drunk?

He stared at the rainbow spanning the ink-black sky.

And something was odd about the rainbow. It took a moment to figure it out – the colours were the wrong way round – back to front. Violet, indigo, blue, green, yellow, orange, red.

He continued staring, half in awe, half in dark, undefined terror. What the heck was going on? Was this an alien invasion? The start of the end of the world?

He picked up his cell phone and went down to the concierge, asking him if he knew what was happening.

The Frenchman didn't. He was equally mystified.

Big Tony took the elevator back up to his apartment. He entered and hurried across, through the opened French windows, back out onto the balcony. Above him and below him he could see other people out on their balconies, too, watching and photographing this phenomenon.

143

Friday, 24 March

The door of Hassam Udin's office, on the first floor of his house, flew open.

'Hassam!'

It was his wife, Amira, and her voice sounded urgent and alarmed.

He was seated at his desk, with his usual cup of coffee, and cigarette smouldering in the ashtray. All morning he had been exchanging emails with a lady called Hilary Patel. It was a laborious process, his machine reading out each email one word at a time to him.

Hilary was the Team Leader for Faith Engagement, for the Government Department for Communities and Local Government. He wasn't actually sure what her title meant, but she was a delightful and hugely helpful lady. She was putting him in touch with a number of key faith leaders, helping him with a book he was writing, identifying the similarities between many of the world's religions and faiths.

'Hassam! Oh my God, I wish you could see this!' Amira said.

'Yes, my love, tell me?'

'Outside it has gone dark, completely dark. But it is not even half past twelve. Like it is a total eclipse of the sun! People are all out in the street, watching. Every car has stopped, all the drivers are out, watching. People are taking photographs with their phones, cameras, tablets!'

Udin tapped the phone he wore on his wrist, which spoke the time to him.

'Twelve twenty-seven,' it announced.

'Up in the sky, Hassam,' she said. 'There is a rainbow shining across the entire sky!'

Very quietly, he replied. 'I'm seeing it too, my love. Inside my head. But tell me, am I right, that the colours are all wrong?'

144

Brother Pete's return to Mount Athos had not been easy. God had tested him, he knew. Tested his faith.

For two days, he had frantically searched the railway line north of East Croydon, looking for his bag. He finally found it, nestling sodden among weeds in a ditch. Sodden and empty.

It had contained everything – his meagre savings, which he had brought with him as part of his plan to start a new life in England, and his passport. And the precious items he had been entrusted with, by Angus.

All gone.

He had fallen to his knees in despair, and did the only thing he knew, which was to pray for help.

Then, as he had grown increasingly desperate, hitch-hiking at the roadside, God had answered his prayers. Wet, cold, thirsty and hungry, he had found a saviour who had driven him to the Greek Embassy in London.

Now, finally, at 2.25 p.m., he was on the ferry from Thessaloniki back to Athos. Moments earlier it had been a fine, sunny day. But now the sky was darkening strangely, ominously.

Could it be an eclipse?

Within minutes it was like night-time.

A rainbow, its colours inverted, appeared in the sky

above him. Radiating light. Radiating warmth. Radiating love.

A sign.

Like all the other monks and the pilgrims around him on the open deck, he fell to his knees.

145

Ainsley's bloody monkeys! Cilla Bloor thought.

Shortly after 1 p.m., as the strangely coloured arc faded in the returning sunlight and lightening sky, it sounded like there was bedlam in the cages.

Grief-stricken, and still in shock following the phone call from Los Angeles, informing her that her husband's jet had crashed shortly after take-off, she had barely left the house all week. Both their children had come home, their nineteen-year-old daughter, Lucy, who had been backpacking in Europe in her gap year, and their son, Jake, who was reading biology at Oxford. The two of them had gone out earlier today to the American Embassy to discuss the return of the remains of their father, once his body had been released by the Los Angeles Coroner.

Cilla had been too distraught to go. Had Lucy and Jake both seen it, she wondered? The extraordinary, unpredicted eclipse, or whatever phenomenon it was, and that incredible coloured arc in the sky? She had not yet phoned them.

The screeching became louder.

Shut up, monkeys, for Heaven's sake!

It sounded like they were killing each other. The most terrible sounds. Where was Frank, their head gardener? Why wasn't he dealing with them?

She still had not bathed or dressed yet today. She left

the house, aware she looked a mess, and beyond caring, and walked in her velvet slippers and housecoat across the damp grass towards the orangery.

The screeching was even louder as she neared it.

Just as soon as the funeral was over, she had decided, she would get rid of the lot of them. Send them to a zoo or to some monkey sanctuary or whatever organization would be happy to have six noisy monkeys with poor typing skills.

She opened the door of the pretty Victorian red-brick orangery and stepped inside, trying to breathe in as little as possible of the smell. The screeching was piercing her ears.

She passed the first five cages. To her surprise, each occupant was subdued. One, Jefferson, cupped a peanut in his little hands and eyed her, disinterestedly. The next, Gwendolyn – where had her husband got these ridiculous names from? – was sitting on a perch high up, looking slightly traumatized, her laptop almost buried in excrement.

It was Boris, at the far end, who was making all the noise. He was leaping around his cage, almost dementedly, from perch to floor, to the desk on which his computer lay, to the cage bars, shaking them, screeching, screeching, screeching.

When he saw her, he opened his tiny jaws, baring his teeth, screeched again, then leaped a seemingly impossibly high jump up to the perch ten foot in the air.

'What is it, Boris?' she said.

He screeched again, jumped down on the desk, bounded onto the keypad, then leaped back up onto the high perch.

He was trying to show her something, she understood.

Then she noticed that a sheet of the perpetual paper feed that was sticking out of the printer had typing on it.

She entered the cage, warily, and walked over to it.

Stared at it.

Looked up at Boris then back at the single sheet of paper.

She had to look again, twice, to make sure her eyes were not deceiving her. She peered up at the monkey, and could have sworn he was grinning at her.

On the sheet of A4 paper, in large letters, was typed, in bold, one word, with an exclamation mark at the end:

RAINBOW!

146

Sunday, 26 March

The media had been full of little else for the past two days. Astronomers and meteorologists were all pontificating. Some newspaper headlines were predicting Armageddon. Just what was it that had occurred at 12.25 p.m. Greenwich Mean Time and, simultaneously, in every time zone of the world?

How could a rainbow occur in a sky in which there had been no rain? How could it occur in a pitch-dark night sky?

And the colours inverted?

Social media was agog with theories and speculations. Every channel on television carried interviews with eyewitnesses. Ross had seen two young backpackers standing outside Sydney Opera House, talking almost breathlessly about the extraordinary shimmering rainbow, with its colours the wrong way round, in the night sky. Something quite mystical about it, they were saying.

He'd seen a shepherd on a remote plain of the Andes trying to describe what he had seen. An oilman at an Arctic drilling station confirming the phenomenon. A Japanese whaler crew. A soldier outside the Kremlin. People lying prostrate in St Peter's Square in front of the Vatican. Market traders in Iraq. An imam in Baghdad. A meteorologist in Hawaii, saying that what he and his colleagues had witnessed was just not possible. Some kind of interference from an unpredicted galactic electrical storm was the best he could come up with.

What was equally extraordinary was that not a single photograph or video image of the rainbow, out of all the millions taken around the world, appeared to have survived. In every instance, the image had either simply failed to record or had somehow, subsequently, been erased.

It seemed that every scientist in the world, in China, Russia, the USA, Africa, Australia, New Zealand, Japan, Europe, Scandinavia, India and elsewhere, was stumped.

The world's faith leaders had put forward their own views. The Pope had declared it a miracle, a sign from God. The Archbishop of Canterbury was more circumspect. He had issued a press statement saying that something defying all our scientific knowledge had occurred. He called on scientists around the globe to come together to provide an explanation that was better than his own view, that it was divine intervention in our physical world.

On Saturday, Ross had driven to Monmouth to tell his friend, Benedict Carmichael, the background he had to the phenomenon. And to remind Benedict of his earlier words, about proof of God requiring something that defied the laws of physics of the universe.

'Let's see what the scientists come up with,' Carmichael had replied, tactfully, and a little too evasively for Ross's comfort.

Lying in the spare room in Sally's comfortable flat, Ross barely slept all Saturday night in the hard, single bed. He watched the clock ticking away the hours. 3 a.m. 4 a.m. 5 a.m. 6 a.m. 6.15 a.m.

Newsagents opened early. How early? 6.30 a.m.?

Then, when he next looked, it was 7.20 a.m.

He slipped out of bed, narrowly missing stepping on

Monty, who was asleep on the floor beside him, enjoying the white rug on the polished wood floor.

Ross threw some water on his face, brushed his teeth, then dressed in a T-shirt and tracksuit, pulled on his trainers and zipped his wallet into his pocket.

The dog jumped up and whined.

'Ssssshhhh!'

He heard Sally call out from her room.

Opening her door a crack, he said, 'Just going to get the papers.'

'Hurry back!' she murmured.

'Go back to sleep, I won't be long.'

He was anxious to get a copy of the *Sunday Times*, to see his story. He always looked forward to seeing his work in print, but never more so than today. He could not wait to see how much space they had given him. The four pages his editor's boss had indicated? That would be amazing!

Three flights of stairs down, he clipped on Monty's lead, checked he had a poop bag in his pocket, and the keys, opened the front door and stepped out into the fresh, morning air of the elegant Georgian crescent in Bristol. It was nearly full light.

He broke into a run, Monty loping happily beside him for a short distance. Then the dog stopped, yanking hard on the lead, wanting to sniff a lamp post.

'No!' Ross said, sternly. 'Later.'

They ran on, down a hill, and came to a parade of shops. One, to his joy, was an open newsagent. Securing Monty to a hoop outside the shop, he went in and bought a copy of all the national Sunday papers that they had.

The front-page splash of the *Sunday Times* was of course the story of Friday's mysterious worldwide total eclipse and freak rainbow.

PETER JAMES

THE WORLD PLUNGED INTO DARKNESS

For added emphasis, the entire front page was black, with an artist's depiction of the rainbow across it.

To the dog's dismay, Ross hurried straight back to Sally's flat.

'Don't worry, boy, we'll go for a longer walk later, I promise.'

Monty gave him a look that, if he could have translated doggy language, would have said, *Yeah, right, whatever.*

When he arrived back, Sally was awake, with the television in her bedroom switched on to Sky News, the sound muted.

'Hi, gorgeous!' she said. 'Is it in?'

'Just about to check.'

'Great! Let's watch the *Andrew Marr Show* at nine – let's see what he or his guests have to say. It's bound to be his big topic.'

Dumping all the papers on the round table in the dining area adjoining Sally's kitchen, he began to leaf through the pages of the *Sunday Times*. Page after page was full of the story of the darkness that engulfed the world on Friday. The shimmering, iridescent, shining, mysterious inverted rainbow.

Theories from scientists around the globe.

From bewildered politicians.

It wasn't until twenty-three pages in that he found his own story.

It had been cut to just one short column.

He stared at it, barely able to believe his eyes.

According to our reporter, Ross Hunter, Mike Delaney, an elderly, former magician and stage illusionist, predicted that God would give the world a sign as evidence of the Second Coming of Christ.

Delaney, who claimed to be a messenger from Christ, hosted a prime-time show on ABC Television during the 1990s, *Mickey Magic – Man of Mystery*.

In 2014 Delaney was convicted of DUI. He was killed last week when he stepped in front of a vehicle in West Hollywood.

Fuming, barely able to contain his anger – and hurt – Ross carried the paper into the bedroom and showed Sally.

'What?' she said, after she had read it. 'What are they playing at? You have the greatest story – maybe of the last two thousand years – and they print this? They can't do this to you!'

'They have. I told you,' he said, feeling totally gutted as the reality sank in. 'Bloody newspapers.'

Then he had a thought. Had that man from MI5, Stuart Ivens, who had accosted him in the motorway cafe two weeks ago, had something to do with this? He'd never got back to him on his request to see his article before publication.

He grabbed his phone and dialled his editor's number. She answered almost immediately. He hit the hands-free button so Sally could hear, too.

'Ross, hello?'

'Sorry to call so early, Natalie.'

'No, I'm up.'

'What the hell's happened to my piece?'

'What do you mean?'

'You said I was getting four pages, and probably the splash!'

'That's right – that's how I left it – everyone was really

excited about it. We're down in the country at the moment and the papers haven't arrived yet.'

'Did you or your editor get any interference from MI5?'

'MI5?'

'A man called Stuart Ivens.'

'I've never heard of him, Ross.'

'Are you certain?'

'Absolutely. Why, is there a problem?'

'A problem? Actually, yes.'

A couple of minutes later he hung up, leaving Natalie McCourt as mystified as he was. Turning to Sally, he said, 'Something very, very strange is going on.'

'Maybe I know what it is,' she replied.

'You do?'

'All the stuff that's happened to you. That dire warning you had from your bishop friend. That if someone had actual proof of God's existence they would probably be murdered. Maybe Delaney intervened – to protect you.'

He gave her a strange look.

'I mean it, Ross. What's happened has now happened. It's out there. So you don't get the credit for it. But at least you're safe. Isn't that a pretty good trade-off?'

He stared vacantly ahead, trying to take this in. 'I guess at least I still have the DNA safe with the monk from Mount Athos,' he said. 'Maybe, not now but at some point, when –'

She touched him gently, interrupting him, nodding at the screen. The *Andrew Marr Show* was starting. Grabbing the remote, she turned the sound up.

The renowned television interrogator, with neat short hair, a dark-grey suit and salmon-pink tie, sat against a curved backdrop of the Thames, the London Eye and the Houses of Parliament.

In front of him, splayed out on a table, were all the national Sunday newspapers.

'And the big story this week,' Marr said, 'is the extraordinary global eclipse of the sun on Friday, March 24th – if indeed that's what it was. At 12.25 p.m. Greenwich Mean Time, in every time zone of the world where it was light, it went dark and an inverted rainbow appeared. In those time zones where it was already dark, at the same moment the same rainbow appeared. Millions – billions – of people were outside in the streets witnessing the phenomenon. It has left astronomers – as well as meteorologists – totally caught on the hop and dumbfounded. What the world witnessed was not just an unpredicted total eclipse of the sun, but an impossible rainbow – at least impossible within the laws of physics as we currently know and understand them! I'll be joined in the studio by Dr Susan Meyer, Professor of Meteorology from the University of Leeds, Professor Sir Quentin Ferlinger, Astronomer Royal, and Colonel Jeff Hawke from the United States National Aeronautics and Space Administration.'

He went on to outline further guests on the show, including a folk band.

Then the news came up.

His mind in turmoil, Ross settled on the bed, beside Sally, leafing through other sections of the *Sunday Times*, just in case more of his story had been printed in a supplement. But he could find nothing.

After the news, Andrew Marr reappeared, seated on an apricot-coloured swivel chair, opposite two men and a woman on a matching sofa. One man was in his late sixties, in a grey suit, with long, straggly grey hair, the other a decade younger, with a military bearing. He had a crew cut and wore a shapeless beige jacket over a shirt and tie. The woman, in her late forties, was smartly dressed, with short, red hair, small round glasses and a rather fierce expression.

'So, welcome Dr Susan Meyer, Professor of Meteorology at Leeds University, Professor Sir Quentin Ferlinger, Astronomer Royal, and Colonel Jeff Hawke, Director of Space Research at NASA. The first question I would like to put to the three of you, regarding the events of this past Friday, is simply this: You and countless other experts are all rushing to find a scientific theory for what happened. We've heard about the possibility of freak meteorological conditions. Perhaps some unforeseen astronomical occurrence. A meteor shower. Or some extra-terrestrial attempt to communicate with us. Isn't there, possibly, a much simpler explanation for what – or *who* – could be responsible – that no one wants to accept?'

'Such as?' said Susan Meyer.

'God?'

Epilogue

Sunday, 26 March

Later that afternoon, Ross and Sally watched the *Andrew Marr Show* again. As the debate on the television programme became increasingly animated, Ross punched the sofa with his fist, raging with frustration. 'I could have told them!' he said. 'I should have been on the show, I could have –'

His phone rang, the number withheld. He looked at Sally.

She grabbed the remote and pressed the pause button. 'Answer it,' she urged.

'Ross Hunter,' he said.

A persuasive north-Atlantic accent replied, 'Mr Hunter, this is Jim Owen of Owen Media, do you have a moment?'

He frowned. Owen was the most powerful publicity agent in the media world, specializing in high-profile stories.

'Yes, OK,' Ross said, hesitantly, wondering what was coming.

'Your story in the *Sunday Times* today – I have information that there is a lot more you have on this incredible topic, and relating to the extraordinary supernatural occurrence across the globe. Am I correct?'

'Yes, you are.'

'I already have a bidding war starting, with newspapers

around the world. At the moment, one newspaper here is prepared to pay £3.5 million, but I think I can get you a lot more. Would you be interested in me taking you on as a client?'

Ross replied, 'Is the Pope Catholic?'

ACKNOWLEDGEMENTS

This novel began with a random phone call out of the blue, back in 1989, from an elderly sounding gentleman asking if I was Peter James, the author. He claimed to have been given absolute proof of God's existence, and stated that he had been told there was an author of my name who would help him to get taken seriously.

That phone call was the start of a twenty-nine-year journey of exploration into what indeed might be considered *absolute proof* – and just what the consequences might be. During this time, I've talked to people across many faiths, stayed in a Greek monastic commune in an attempt to discover the true belief a monk must have, as well as having many valuable discussions with scientists, academics, theologians and clerics at all levels.

Over the past four years, my wife, Lara, and I have met and spoken with numerous people, among them many eminent scientists and theologians, asking all of them the same two questions: What would they consider to be absolute proof of God's existence and what might be the consequence of such proof? We have put exactly the same questions to hard-core atheists, asking them what could change their minds, or at least, dent their certainty, just as hard-core Antony Flew famously had his mind changed back in 2004.

I have so many of you to acknowledge for your kindness

in both giving me the time and entering into the debate. Above all, three people really did help to make this book happen. The first is Dominic Walker, OGS, former Bishop of Reading and of Monmouth, who, inadvertently, sparked the idea of writing this book, and the second is my friend Ken Owen who has helped me in so many ways I simply cannot list them all. And thirdly, David Gaylor, whose tireless work and eye for detail has been utterly invaluable.

Thank you so much, also, for theological help to:

Dr Denis Alexander, the Faraday Institute for Science and Religion
His Grace Bishop Angealos
Qari Muhammad Asim MBE, Chief Imam, Makkah Masjid
The Abbot and monks of Mount Athos
Professor Andrew Briggs
Andrew Gosler FLS, FRSB
Venerable Paul Hackwood
Professor Rumy Hasan
Roger Homan
Professor Sir Colin Humphreys
Father Raphael, St Hugh's Charterhouse Monastery
Rt Rev. Richard Jackson, Bishop of Lewes
Father John O'Leary
Rabbi Natan Levy
Professor Simon Conway Morris FRS
Professor John Lennox
Professor Ard Louis
Alister McGrath FRSA
Professor Abid Nasir, Emirates University
Amy Orr-Ewing, Zacharias Trust
Nitin Palan MBE, Trustee, Swaminarayan Neasden Temple

Jack Palmer-White, Social & Public Affairs Adviser to the Archbishop of Canterbury

Hilary Patel, Team Leader, Faith Engagement. Dept for Communities and Local Government

The Reverend Dr John Polkinghorne KBE, FRS

Michael Ramsden, International Director, Ravi Zacharias International Ministries & Joint Director of the Oxford Centre for Christian Apologetics

David Ryall

Jasvir Sing, City Sikhs

Rev. Ish and Rev. Irene Smale

Rio Summers

Professor Lionel Tarassenko

Rev. Mark Townsend

Chloe Trotman

Rt Rev. Dr Martin Warner MA, PhD, Bishop of Chichester

The Most Rev. Justin Welby, Archbishop of Canterbury

Professor Bob White

And for invaluable general research and proofing help to:

Susan Ansell

Maria O'Brien

Tiffany Britt Darling

Mark and Debbie Brown

Danielle Brown

Linda Buckley

Rob Cohen

Jane Diplock

Martin Diplock

Jason Edge

Peter Faulding

Larry Finlay

Annabel Galsworthy
David Gaylor
Jack Gaylor
Jane Greenbank
Anna-Lisa Hancock
Christopher and Gill Hayes
James Hodge
Tom Homewood
Mark Johnson
Peter Johnson, LGC Forensics
Rachel Kenchington
Richard Kerbajr
Patrick Lahaise
Kitty Logan
Nick Lom
Sarah Middle
The late Sir Patrick Moore
Susan Opie
Ray Packham
Julian Quigley, LGC Forensics
Andrew Reeds
Ross Bartlett
Daniel Salter
Susan Sandon
Helen Shenston
James Simpson
James Stather
Guy Swayland
Jolene Thomas, LGC Forensics
Matt Wainwright
Martin Walsh
Arnie Wilson

ABSOLUTE PROOF

To my brilliant agents and my publishers:

Emanuela Anehcoum
Isobel Dixon
Julian Friedmann
Hattie Grunewald
James Pusey
Conrad Williams
Sarah Arratoon
Jonathan Atkins
Anna Bond
Wayne Brookes
Geoff Duffield
Stuart Dwyer
Claire Evans
Anthony Forbes Watson
Lucy Hines
Katie James
Daniel Jenkins
Sara Lloyd
Natalie McCourt
Alex Saunders
Jeremy Trevathan
Charlotte Williams

Above all, my wife, Lara, who believed in this book from the very start. She has been a constant source of wisdom, and has driven me on with her endless enthusiasm for this project. It has been undoubtedly the hardest book I've ever written, from the sheer scale of the subject matter, but also the one I have learned the most from. I'm immensely grateful to her and to every name I've listed – and please forgive any omissions.

My sources of reference include the following books:

In God We Doubt – John Humphrys
The Blind Watchmaker – Richard Dawkins
The God Delusion – Richard Dawkins
Who Made God? – Ravi Zacharias & Norman L. Geisler
Who Made God? – Edgar Andrews
God's Undertaker – John C. Lennox
God & Stephen Hawking – John C. Lennox
There Is a God – Antony Flew
Why God Won't Go Away – Alister McGrath
Inventing the Universe – Alister McGrath
Darwin & God – Nick Spencer
The Holy Bible
The God Particle – Leon Lederman & Dick Teresi
Does God Exist? – Hans Küng & E. Quinn
The Book Your Church Doesn't Want You to Read – Tim
    Leedom
Unapologetic – Francis Spufford
The Mystery of the Last Supper – Colin Humphreys

COMING OCTOBER 2019

THE SECRET OF COLD HILL

Turn the page for an exclusive extract from
the sequel to Peter James' bestselling ghost story
The House on Cold Hill . . .

1

Saturday, 16 September 2017

'There are of course no skeletons in this attic!' the estate agent said with a wink as she threw open the door with a flourish and ushered her clients into the loft space.

'Wow!' said Mike Diamond.

'Wow!' his wife, Julie, echoed.

'It sure has the *wow* factor, wouldn't you say, Mr and Mrs Diamond?'

'It sure has,' Mike replied.

And it sure did.

The young couple stared around in wonder as they entered the high-ceilinged room, painted all in white, that covered almost the entire floor area of the brand-new house and was flooded with light from gable windows in each of the four walls. The view to the north ran across the long, newly turfed garden ending at the lake, the fields and the hill that rose beyond, and to the south, across the partially completed housing estate and down to the village of Cold Hill half a mile below them. There was a rich smell of fresh paint and timber.

'I can tell you, this is a far superior property to the show house, which was sold in the first hour it was on sale. Far superior.' The agent pointed out the four Sonos speakers, the voice-activated electric blinds, then showed them the equally teched-up en-suite bathroom. 'This would make a great master bedroom, or an office,' she enthused. 'It's rare to find a room so well equipped like this in a modern home, you'd have to agree.'

Mike and Julie looked at each other. He pulled a face and his wife grinned at the signal. This estate agent was already irritating them, and they'd only been in the house for a few minutes. An elegant woman in her thirties, with short, dark hair, dressed in a black power-suit, white blouse and court shoes, she marched in front of them, brandishing the particulars as if she was about to present them with a certificate. *Future Owners Extraordinaire of Lake House, No. 47 Lakeview Drive!*

They followed her back down the spiral staircase to the first floor and along a short landing, where she opened another door with equal flourish to the last into a small bedroom. 'This will make a great room for your baby,' she said.

Again, the couple shot another secret glance at each other. Mike frowning and Julie frowning back a *what?* Her pregnancy had only been confirmed yesterday by their doctor, and there was no possible way it could be showing yet.

They followed the agent into a further two small bedrooms – perfect spare rooms for guests, she enthused, or maybe one of them a den? Then they moved into the master bedroom. 'You'd have to admit, this is pretty much a *wow* room, too!' She strode confidently across to the unlocked French windows and opened them onto a wide Juliet balcony.

'Can you imagine, on a fine day like today, Mrs Diamond? The two of you sitting out here, having an early morning coffee, looking across the lake?'

'It's north-facing,' Mike said. 'So no morning sunlight.'

'Who wants morning sunlight in a bedroom?' the agent

said. 'Not me! But of course, if that's a concern, then you could make your bedroom upstairs.' She gave them a con-spiratorial look. 'I tell you, if it was me – and I could afford a house this beautiful – I'd make that loft my master bed-room. It would make anyone feel like they were masters of the universe, just like you two truly are – I can tell!' She glanced at her watch. 'I'm so sorry, we'll have to hurry, I have viewings of this place every twenty minutes today. It won't be staying on the market for long, that's for sure. Not with the shortage of quality new-build stock there is today, believe you me.'

She hurried them through the downstairs; the open-plan kitchen–family room stacked with smart-gadgets such as the memory fridge; the dining room; the small office; the spacious hall; and then the pièce de résistance, the large, luxuriously carpeted living–dining room running the entire width of the house, with a photochromic-glass conserva-tory at the end. Beyond was the wide lawn running down to the lake. 'Of course, it would be easy to fence off the lawn part-way down, to make it safe for your baby.'

Again, the Diamonds looked at each other. *How did she know about the baby?*

Then, profusely apologetic, she ushered them to the front door. Her next clients were due any moment. If they wished to make an offer, she most strongly advised them to do it sooner rather than later. This was the first day of view-ings and this property, priced to sell, would not be hanging around on the market for long.

As she opened the door she said, 'Mr and Mrs Diamond, I can so see you living here – in your forever home! And your baby son – what a wonderful environment for him to grow up in. But please, I urge you, don't think about it for too long.'

As they stepped out into the bright, mid-morning sun-light, and the front door closed behind them, Mike and Julie Diamond stood on the path, with the newly turfed lawn on either side, as a car came along the road. They looked at each other. The same look.

What the fuck?

Son?

A Mini with the logo *Richwards Estate Agents* pulled up in front of them, behind their Mercedes. A tubby, smiling man in his forties, in a flamboyant suit, clambered out and hurried across to them, holding a bunch of keys like a gaoler.

'Mr and Mrs Diamond?'

'Yes,' Mike said hesitantly.

'Paul Jordan, I do apologize for being late – I had a view-ing of another property that ran over.' He shook hands with each of them, once again apologizing profusely. 'You are going to love this house, I promise you. It is really quite special. On the whole of the Cold Hill Park development, this is my very favourite, by a country mile.'

As he rummaged through his keys, Julie Diamond said, 'Yes, it is very lovely.'

'Wait until you view the inside! And let me show you the technology – wow!'

'We have actually just seen it,' Mike Diamond said.

Jordan looked at both of them, puzzled. 'Seen it?'

'Your colleague just showed us around.'

'Colleague?'

'Yes.'

The agent frowned. 'I'm sorry – we are the sole agents for this development, and none of my associates are here today.' He looked hesitant. 'Someone showed you around?'

'Yes,' the woman replied. 'A lady, she said she had viewings back to back all day and could only allocate twenty minutes to us.'

'It isn't possible,' he said. 'I – I don't understand. What was her name?'

The couple looked at each other, then the man shrugged. 'Well, she didn't give us her name. To be honest, she was a bit odd.'

'Can you excuse me?' Jordan asked. 'Please, just a couple of minutes?'

Reluctantly, the couple nodded.

He let himself into the house, walked through the hallway and called out, 'Hello! Hello! It's Paul Jordan – hello!'

He went into each of the downstairs rooms, then up to the first floor, checking each of the rooms there. Then up to the loft and looked around the bathroom.

There was no one.

Frowning, he hurried back downstairs and out through the front door. And caught a glimpse of the Diamond's Mercedes, already several hundred yards away.

2

Saturday, 28 October 2017

'I love it!'

'You do?'

'Don't you?'

'No!' he said with a big grin. 'I don't *love* it – I FUCKING love it!'

Standing in the huge loft, with autumn sunlight streaming in through the south-facing window, Jason put his arm around his wife and hugged her. 'I abso-fucking-lutely love it!'

'You'll have to excuse my husband's language!' Emily said to the estate agent.

'Oh, please, Mrs Danes,' Paul Jordan beamed. 'Artistic licence with language is permitted, for such a famous *artist* as your husband!'

'I'm hardly famous, but thank you,' Jason Danes replied.

'Oh, I would question your modesty, Mr Danes. I took the liberty of looking you up on Wikipedia, and imagine my excitement when I realized I have one of your oil paintings hanging in our living room – a wonderful picture of an old man in an armchair with a spaniel at his feet. So full of charm. My wife bought it for me for Christmas a couple of years ago, from a gallery in Lewes. In the Jordan household, you are indeed famous! And I'm quite certain that should you decide to buy this beautiful, unique home, one day there will be a blue plaque with your name on the wall out-side.'

'Not too soon, I hope,' Jason Danes replied. 'You have to be dead for that to happen.'

Jordan grinned. 'Well, don't they say that death is always a good career move for an artist?'

As if given a cue, the sun was covered by a cloud. The room darkened, and the expressions on the faces of his two clients darkened with it. Their enthusiasm for the property suddenly seemed to be draining away.

'Only joking!' Jordan said quickly, trying to recover the situation.

'Of course,' the painter replied. 'I'm only thirty-nine – I hope to have a few more years yet.'

His wife, five years his junior, gave the agent an awk-ward smile.

Neither of them, looking out at the views on all four sides in turn, noticed the nervous glance the agent sud-denly shot at the doorway.

Jason stared out through the rear gable at the huge lake, the sloping field, and the soft round contour of the hill rising up steeply beyond. He watched ducks – mallards and Indian runners – on the water. It was so tranquil. 'I could work here, I know I could – it's just, wow, so inspiring! Well, this view to the north is, anyway. It is north I'm looking at?'

'Yes indeed, Mr Danes, and that is part of the South Downs National Park, so it can never be built on.'

'Unlike the other three directions?'

He looked down at the brand-new houses directly opposite, and the rows of houses beyond, most of which were just shells still under construction. To the west was a vast, muddy site, on which there were bulldozers, diggers, men in yellow hard hats with theodolites, and marked-out plots. To the east was a huge empty and overgrown field.

'I'll show you the plan of the whole development,' the estate agent said, kneeling and unfolding a large map on the bare oak floor.

It was headed, COLD HILL PARK DEVELOPMENT – PHASE 1, PHASE 2, PHASE 3.

'The site comprises just over twenty-five acres, Mr and Mrs Danes. Now this, where we are, is Phase 1; frankly, the most exclusive area with the largest homes, the very best of which – and of which this house is the *very* best – have the lake and rural views. The position is superlative – you see, Phase 1 is built on the curtilage of the original mansion that was here, Cold Hill House. Whatever your views on aristocracy and gentry, you have to admit they all knew a thing or two about position and views. And all the infrastructure is already in place: the roads, drains, utilities, and of course, the all-important super-fast fibre broadband. The area to the west, which you can see through the window, is Phase 2, this will be smaller buildings, town houses, a few two-storey apartment buildings and some social housing.'

'You mean council houses?' Emily quizzed.

Jordan looked a little awkward. 'Well, in all but name, yes. But you'll never even know they're there, with their separate road network. And then to the east, that field, that will also be detached homes, very stylish ones.'

'How many residences in total will there be here?' Jason Danes asked.

'When Phase 3 is completed, it will be one hundred and thirty altogether.'

'So, this place will be a building site for the next two years?'

'Yes, Mr and Mrs Danes, but honestly you'll scarcely notice. There's very little construction in Phase 1 left, and of course the price of this house reflects the temporary inconvenience.'

Jordan noticed the flicker of doubt between the couple and went on, hastily. 'Let me show you a feature that is very rare in modern houses.' He strode over to one window, unlocked it and pulled it up. 'Genuine sash windows, in every room! A true Georgian feature. You see, this house has been designed almost as a miniature model of the original mansion that once stood here. I tell you, no expense was spared by the builders on this beautiful home.' He smiled. 'For your catering business, Mrs Danes, I don't think you'll find a more magnificent kitchen on the market anywhere in Sussex.'

'Let's take another look at it,' she said.

'Please follow me,' Jordan said, checking his watch, mindful that the Danes had already overrun their allotted thirty minutes and another couple would be arriving for a viewing shortly. But hell, they could wait. He had a good feeling about Mr and Mrs Danes. He could get them over the line.

He knelt, rolled up the plan, tucked it under his arm, and led the way down the glass spiral staircase to the first-floor landing. 'Note how wonderfully bright the house feels everywhere, from the clever use of mirrors on the walls, and even some on the ceilings.'

Jason and Emily looked around, and he was right. Mirrors lining the landing walls, and down in the hall, created both light and the illusion of even greater space. Entering the expansive kitchen, Jordan said, 'It's almost as if the architect designed this house with you two in mind. The kitchen is perfect for your catering business, the attic a truly divine artist's studio!'

'It *is* perfect,' Emily said, regaining her former enthusiasm as she strolled around. 'So much storage, and how rare to have a walk-in pantry!'

'Not to mention the technology,' Paul Jordan added. 'All the houses on this development have this feature.' He pointed at a small, square white box on the kitchen unit with a glowing, square green button on the top. 'All the switches and controls and taps throughout the house are voice activated from that one Command Centre – and its satellites around the house. You each have to programme your voices in. Then anything you want – heating turning up or down, appliances switched on or off, curtains and blinds opened or closed, can be done by simply saying, for instance, "Command! Kitchen blinds down!"'

There was a whirr. The kitchen darkened as blinds lowered over each window.

Again, unnoticed by the couple, Jordan shot another wary glance around, before saying, 'Command! Kitchen blinds up!'

Immediately they rose, and light returned.

'You can even open the fridge and freezer doors by voice command! So hygienic, never needing germ-infected hands to touch any switch or control.'

'Presumably there's a manual override?' Emily asked.

'Absolutely.' He walked over and pressed the green button. It turned red. 'Now everything is operated manually or by remote controls.'

'No one realizes quite how many germs are spread by hands,' Jason Danes said, solemnly. 'The average bowl of peanuts sitting on a pub counter contains twelve different traces of urine and five of human faeces.'

Jordan blanched slightly. 'Ah.' Then with an awkward grin he said, 'I think I've just developed a peanut allergy!' Then, rapidly changing the subject, 'And of course you can set up your phones to operate anything in this house remotely – just a simple app – from wherever you are in the country, or indeed the world! You can be lying on a beach in Greece and even check the contents of your fridge if you like!'

Emily opened the integral door to the double garage and went in, followed by her husband and the agent. The lights flickered on automatically. 'I could make this into my catering kitchen, it would work, don't you think, darling?'

He nodded. 'It could.'

'It *really* could!' she insisted. 'I could get all the fridges, freezers and ovens I need into here.'

'Of course,' Jordan said, 'some people – especially an artist of your calibre, Mr Danes – might prefer something old and quaint, or historic or rustic perhaps? If you would rather view an Edwardian property, or Victorian or even Georgian, I do have some very attractive houses within your price range I could show you. But of course, along with their beauty, old and historic properties come with a raft of maintenance issues. Here, with a totally new build, you get the builder's ten-year guarantee. Ten years maintenance free! You don't have to worry about draughts, or leaks, or doors sticking. When you buy new, you are buying worry-free.'

'And germ-free,' Jason Danes added.

'Absolutely, quite right! Germ free. Ah, yes indeed, germs are of course not included in the purchase price – they are extra!' he chuckled, but his clients stared blankly at him.

'It's an important consideration,' Emily Danes said. 'Germs.'

'Of course. In the catering business, you cannot be too careful, I'm sure. Old buildings can be full of bugs and all

kinds of things. Yech! All of them lying beneath the floorboards and in crevices for years, decades, centuries even,
waiting to pounce! Here, in addition to hygienic switch
activation, we have the very latest in state-of-the-art insu-
lation. I tell you what, if I found a cockroach in here, I'd
name it Houdini.' Behind him, he heard the sound of running water.

'It's actually more for my husband,' she said. 'He doesn't
do germs, bugs, dirt.'

'Quite right, who does, eh?' Jordan turned to see Jason
running his hands under a tap in one of the twin sinks, and
washing them with liquid soap from an electronic dispenser. 'Germs, eh, Mr Danes. Nasty little buggers.'

Absorbed in the ritual of cleaning his hands, Jason did
not appear to notice the comment.

Jordan frowned. There was something odd about the
man, something that was pushing him, just a little, out of
his comfort zone. But at the same time, he genuinely did
love that painting of the old man with the dog. Every time
he looked at it, he wondered what the man was thinking,
what his life was – and had been. Clearly Mr Danes was a
genius, and weren't all geniuses just a bit eccentric? But
would an artistic genius really want to live in a sterile, new-
build house?

'The houses on either side of this, Mr Jordan – are they
sold?' Emily asked.

'No, not yet, although I believe a couple – a very nice
couple, with two children – are going to buy number 55 – if
the sale of their house goes through. That's the house to the
east.' He pointed to the right.

'Children?' Jason said, dubiously. 'What age?'

'Oh – about ten and twelve.' The agent smiled. 'I know
what you are thinking, what a nightmare when you are

trying to paint, to have screaming children next door? I don't think you need to worry. And there's a quite elderly couple, retired, who are very interested in number 49. They're moving down from Yorkshire to be closer to their daughter who lives just outside Lewes.'

'How many other people are living on the estate at present?' Emily asked.

'Well –' he hesitated, smiling uncomfortably. 'At this moment, there's just the very nice couple diagonal, they've been here a month or so now, and directly opposite you, in number 34, there's a family due to move in soon. Elsewhere, no one at the moment. But the properties are selling like hot-cakes; such a fine development, so near to Brighton and to Lewes, close to rail links to London – just fifty minutes on the Brighton line. And surrounded by beautiful countryside. This is a very special position – quite unique.'

He glanced at his watch again. 'Look, I'm very sorry, but I have another couple arriving for a viewing. If you'd like to have a think about it and come back to me, we can always book a further appointment. But I do have to warn you, we have so much interest in this property – indeed in the whole estate. We've already sold over half the properties off-plan, and this one, which is the real jewel in the crown, is not going to be on the market for long, I can tell you. And of course, I can help you with a mortgage should you require. But I really would advise you, if you are interested, to move quickly. The couple I'm waiting for now are coming for their second viewing, and I'm told they don't have any property to sell – they are cash buyers.'

'We'll take it,' Jason said, decisively, rinsing his hands then soaping them once again. 'We'll pay the full asking price.' He looked at his wife, who nodded.

Jordan beamed. 'Well! What can I say? I don't think it is

a decision you could ever possibly regret. This is the finest house in the best property development I've ever been privileged to handle – and I've handled many, I can tell you. The location, the sheer build quality. The views. You could not have a better investment!'

'So, what do you need from us to take it off the market right now this minute?' Jason Danes asked. 'We're cash buyers, too. We sold our previous home and we're currently renting, and we don't need a mortgage.'

'Good, excellent.' The agent was pensive for a moment. 'It's Saturday, nothing can happen until Monday and solicitors are back at work. If you would like to go to my office and put down a ten-thousand-pound deposit – entirely refundable – as a show of good faith, I'll tell the couple who are coming that the house is under offer. I'd be prepared to give you a two-week window to exchange contracts. How does that sound?'

The Danes looked at each other. 'We might be able to move in before Christmas!' Emily said.

Rinsing then soaping his hands again, Jason Danes nodded enthusiastically and said, 'Very fair.'

'I'll even throw in some containers of soap!'

Neither of them smiled.

After an awkward moment, Jordan beamed again. 'In which case, Mr and Mrs Danes, I look forward to handing you the keys and to formally welcoming you to your new home in the next month or so. You won't regret this, I can assure you. This is a very special house. You are going to find it very creative, very creative indeed.'

3

Friday, 15 December 2017

Maurice and Claudette Penze-Weedell peered out through the slats of the Venetian blinds of Arden Lodge, 36 Lakeview Drive, watching the activity going on across the street at number 47, happy that after over a month, they would no longer be the only people living in the Cold Hill Park development. And very keen to catch a glimpse of their new neighbours.

'Not too wide, dear,' Maurice said. 'They'll notice, we don't want to seem like peeping Toms.' Maurice had originally suggested net curtains like the ones they'd had in their previous home in Purley, which prevented passers-by from seeing in, while still enabling them to see out. But, Mrs PW – as he referred to his wife – had put her foot down, saying net curtains were far too common. As owners of the grand *show house* – and the first residents of Cold Hill Park – she insisted they had to set standards. Venetian blinds it had to be, and vertical ones, in her view, were so much more elegant than horizontal ones.

Maurice agreed with Mrs PW. He always agreed with her. It was, he had learned over the years of his marriage – the very *many* years – the route to a happy one. 'Happy wife, happy life,' he had already told all the regulars several times at his new local, The Crown, down in the village. Well, perhaps more accurately, he reflected, a *tolerable* life. Although

his joke at their housewarming party – which, coinciden-
tally and economically, had doubled as their thirtieth
wedding anniversary celebration – that he would have got
less than thirty years for murder, had fallen somewhat flat.

'It's a rather *grand* design for a not very grand-sized
house don't you think, Maurice?'

'I think it's quite attractive.'

'Quite attractive? It's like a sort of bonsai stately home.
Gables in the attic, stone balls on the roof and that ludi-
crous chimney, like the house is wearing a top hat – it's just
so, soooo pretentious. And with the lake behind it and all.
Honestly!'

Unlike its rather uninspired neighbours on both sides,
which were quite squat, red-brick houses, with pantile
roofs, like a million others on new-build estates, number 47
stood proud and aloof. It was a Georgian-style house of
three storeys, the top being the attic in which were large,
gabled dormers. The exterior walls were fawn-coloured and
the door, framed by a handsome porch, was navy blue. The
front garden was a short lawn behind black railings, with a
car port and attached double garage to one side.

'I think the estate agent said the house was a homage to
the original ruined mansion that was here – that the architect had taken his inspiration from it.'

'So, which grand house did the architect take his inspiration from for ours?'

'I don't know, my love.'

A removals van the size of an ocean liner had pulled up
outside the house some ten minutes earlier and the removals men were milling around, two of them smoking, one on
his phone. Moments later a silver BMW drove onto the car
port and pulled up in front of the garage. The driver
remained in it, seemingly talking on his phone.

'That car's just like ours!' Claudette Penze-Weedell said with relief in her voice. 'Identical!'

'I'm afraid not,' her husband said, gloomily. 'Ours is a 520, that one is a 540i.'

'Is that more expensive?'

'Much.'

She stared at it, venomously. 'It's probably time to upgrade, isn't it, Maurice?'

Only weeks after moving in, Maurice Penze-Weedell had been made redundant by the insurance company in Brighton which had employed him for twenty-eight years. He had risen from the post-room to become its Chief Operating Officer. Although given a substantial pay-off, a new car for either of them at this moment was out of the question.

He hadn't yet told his wife just how serious their financial situation was and that – Heaven forbid – she might actually have to get up off her backside, which seemed to widen every day like the flow of volcanic lava, and get a job. They only had sufficient reserve funds to cover the mortgage for another twelve months, and he had been finding out to his dismay that the jobs market for a fifty-one-year-old in Brexit Britain was pretty shitty. 'My dearest, our BMW is only eleven months old, it's fine, we don't need to upgrade it for a few years.'

'In that case we should upgrade my car. I think the Lady of the Manor should have a dignified motor car and not a child's toy. Really, I feel like Noddy every time I get in it.' She was referring to her little Japanese car, currently in their garage, plugged into the charger. It was a regular bone of contention between them.

'I hardly think we're the Lord and Lady of the Manor, dear. We've bought the very nice show house on a very nice estate, but I don't think the other residents are going to be queuing at our front door to pay their annual tithes of chickens, bushels of corn and God knows what else.' He hesitated and smiled. 'Although I suppose, of course, *droit du seigneur* might be rather nice.'

'Droit de what?'

He smiled again. 'The ancient rite of the Lord of the Manor – to deflower any local virgin.'

'Dream on, you wouldn't know what to do with a virgin.' She tried to stop herself mid-sentence, but it was too late, it came out.

'Quite right, I never had that experience, my dear.' He delivered the trump-card smile she could not defend. She'd lost her virginity to his original best-man three weeks before their wedding. Maurice had caught them himself, *in flagrante*. It was a subsequent hold over her that had served him well for three decades.

'Anyhow,' he added, defensively. 'You hate parking and your Leaf has self-park. You said you liked that feature.'

'Only because I can do it when I'm outside the car, so no one can see me in it.'

Across the road a tall, gangly man in his mid thirties climbed out of the BMW and tossed his head, shaking his mop of fair hair from his eyes. Dressed in a leather jacket over a black polo-neck jumper, skinny jeans and boots, and arty glasses, he stood looking approvingly up at the front of his house, which was bathed in winter sunlight, then around and across the street. He clocked the twitch of the Venetian blinds in the large, rather ugly house, diagonally opposite, with the flashing blue and green Christmas lights adorning the porch and the hideous Santa's grotto that covered most of the garden.

'That must be him,' Mrs PW said. 'The painter!'

'Could come in handy when we need to redecorate.'

'Ha ha,' she said. 'Jason Danes is famous. He's all the talk at the village shop.' She smiled, coquettishly, at her husband. 'Just a thought – why don't you commission him to do a portrait of me for my birthday?'

'Why would I want that? I've got plenty of photographs of you.'

'That's not the same. God, you used to be so romantic, Maurice! Don't you think a portrait would be a romantic gesture?'

He looked at her. She'd put on a good five stone, if not more, since they'd first met. She had a stomach that she blamed on their two children, which made her look like she was expecting another, and her flabby face with its double-chin was a visual testament to the existence of gravity.

'Hmmmn,' he grunted. 'I imagine he charges a fortune.'

'And I'm not worth it?' She peered through the blinds again, very cautiously this time. Then she gasped. 'Please tell me that belongs to the removals company and not to these – these people?'

A small, bright pink refrigerated van, emblazoned with the legend *Taste Sensations – Emily's Pantry*, the words separated by a floral logo, pulled up onto the car port alongside the BMW. An attractive, red-headed woman in her early thirties got out, wearing a baggy, crimson parka over black tights and calf-length boots.

'Taste Sensations – Emily's – Pantry,' Maurice said. 'What does she have in there, then, Danish pastries?'

'Huh?' his wife said blankly.

'The Danes. Danish pastries. Geddit?'

'You're full of humour today – you been on the sauce or something?'

The Penze-Weedells watched as the couple kissed, then

hugged, then kissed again before heading towards the front door. Then she turned to her husband.

'Maurice,' she said, sternly. 'You are not going to permit them to leave that van parked on their driveway, are you?'

'What do you mean?'

'You know *exactly* what I mean. We're not going to sit here and allow the value of our house to be diminished by a hideous van parked outside a neighbour's.'

'I really don't see what business it is of ours. It's advertising her business, surely?'

'Yes, well, there's an awful lot of "you don't seem to see" moments these days. Perhaps you should go to Specsavers and check you don't have cataracts.'

'Don't be absurd, my love. My vision is perfectly good – 6/6 at my recent check-up.'

Releasing the blinds again she said, 'Don't you remember when we bought this house, the restrictive covenants? One of them said that no commercial vehicles were permitted to be parked on the estate overnight?' She pointed across the road. 'That is a commercial vehicle.'

'It's only a small van.'

'*Small?* It's hideous.'

'I'm getting a little bit confused.' He stroked his threadbare dome with his right hand. 'Do you want me to ask him to paint you, or to put his wife's van inside their garage.'

'Both!' she said emphatically.

'I think we need to be a little diplomatic. I'm not even sure that covenant applies to vehicles owned by residents.'

'Don't be ridiculous, of course it does. Let me tell you, I do not intend to spend the rest of my life staring out of my drawing-room window at a pink van. If you're not man enough to tell them, I certainly will. I'll go over tomorrow and tell them, very politely of course.'

'Perhaps give them a few days,' he suggested.

'A few days?'

He turned and pointed at their Christmas tree. Gaily wrapped presents lay around the base, and fairy lights twinkled in the branches of plastic pine needles. 'Isn't this meant to be the season of good will?'

She again parted the blinds, peering at the removals men who were starting to carry furniture towards the front door of the Danes's house. 'Yes, Maurice, *good will*. Which means respecting what this estate is all about. *Aspirational homes*. There are pikeys moving in at the end of our road next week, and now we have a pink van opposite. This is all just ghastly. I don't care if he is bloody Rembrandt reincarnated, they are not leaving a pink van on their driveway.' She paused. 'Oh look, a piano, well that's something, I suppose.'

'The people at the end of the road are not *pikeys*,' he said.

'No?' she rounded on him. 'They came in a Volkswagen camper with a yellow roundel in the rear window saying, *Nuclear Power – Nein Danke!* They're not pikeys?'

'No, they're New Age people. Probably lovely and very gentle. You have to remember, my love, that this whole estate got planning permission on the condition that a certain percentage was given over to affordable housing.'

'Yes, well, I'm beginning to think we've made a terrible mistake moving here.'

A woman stood right behind them watching them. She was wearing a long blue dress, with yellow shoes, and had an angry, shrivelled face.

Parvenus.

She did not like them, nor their ridiculous name.

Penze-Weedell.

All the warmth drained from the room. Maurice and Mrs PW shivered, suddenly. Inexplicably.

Each of them, as if drawn by a magnet, turned their heads.

All they saw was the flashing Christmas tree, and the cards on the mantelpiece above the electric dancing flames of the simulated coal fire in the fake grate.

'Has the heating gone off?' she said, giving her husband a sharp look. 'Are you economizing again?'

He shivered again. 'No, it's set for all day.' He hurried through into the kitchen and then into the utility room. The boiler was blazing away.